PENGUIN BOOKS

Sheer Cupidity

Raven Kennedy is a California girl born and raised, whose love for books pushed her into creating her own worlds. The Plated Prisoner Series, a dark fantasy romance, has already sold in over a dozen countries and is a #1 international bestseller with over 1 million copies sold to date. It was inspired by the myth of King Midas and a woman's journey with finding her own strength. Her debut series was a romcom fantasy about a cupid looking for love of her own. She has since gone on to write in a range of genres. Whether she makes you laugh or cry, or whether the series is about a cupid or a gold-touched woman living in King Midas's gilded castle, she hopes to create characters that readers can root for. The Plated Prisoner series is being adapted for series by Peter Guber's Mandalay Television.

SHEER CUPIDITY

A HEART HASSLE NOVEL

RAVEN KENNEDY

PENGUIN BOOKS

PENGUIN BOOKS

UK | USA | Canada | Ireland | Australia
India | New Zealand | South Africa

Penguin Books is part of the Penguin Random House group of companies
whose addresses can be found at global.penguinrandomhouse.com

First published in the United States of America by Raven Kennedy 2022
First published in Great Britain by Penguin Books 2023
001

Copyright © Raven Kennedy, 2022

The moral right of the author has been asserted

Edited by Polished Perfection
Printed and bound in Great Britain by Clays Ltd, Elcograf S.p.A.

The authorized representative in the EEA is Penguin Random House Ireland,
Morrison Chambers, 32 Nassau Street, Dublin D02 YH68

A CIP catalogue record for this book is available from the British Library

ISBN: 978–1–405–96074–8

www.greenpenguin.co.uk

INTRODUCTION

This book is a spin-off from the original Heart Hassle series. It is a stand-alone m/f romance, but has some continuing story arcs and familiar characters from the first 4 Cupidity books. There is explicit language and romance, and is intended for ages 18+.

For anyone who has ever been ghosted.

CHAPTER 1

BELREN

I'm a master thief. Notorious for my ability to find anything anywhere.

I'm a collector of treasures and secrets, and in all the realm, fae know who the Horned Hook is, even if they've never seen my face without the horned mask.

So how the hell did I end up here, stuck in a cell during the middle of a fucking battle?

It's not ideal.

Battles are not my specialty. I don't go charging horns-first into violence. I'm much more of a stealthy, behind-the-curtains kind of male. I prefer stealing over stabbing.

"Hurry up," the black-haired genfin, Evert, growls as I use my telekinetic powers to break the chains off him and the other one—Sylred.

I cock a brow as the last of the iron chains fall away from their arms and legs, clunking against the splintery wooden walls. "A simple thank you would suffice."

"Thank you," Sylred quickly says, but he's the polite one, so it's expected.

He and Evert get up from the filthy dirt floor and stalk toward the entrance of this shitty makeshift cell we're in. Honestly, I'm insulted that the prince actually thought this partially underground hole could hold me. Although, it's better when people underestimate me. It's why I largely keep my telekinesis power under wraps. The pompous prince didn't have a clue.

The twat.

As soon as I think of Prince Elphar, I see red. I've been searching all over the realm for my sister, and then there Benicia was, under his control, completely at his mercy.

My sister has worked her entire life for the rebellion. She's wanted to make life better for the other fae since she could say the word *injustice*. But the prince found her and made her into a pawn. Somehow, he found out the connection between Benicia and his wife, Princess Soora.

Bile rises up my throat. Soora betrayed us. Betrayed me. She must've let something slip, and the prince used Benicia to blackmail Soora into her betrayal.

Rage simmers in my gut so hot that my skin feels as if it could blister.

I'm not sure who I hate more: the prince for what he's done or the princess for lying to me about my sister.

I could have helped Soora, thought of a way to get Benicia out, *and* still supported the rebellion. If only she had told me what was going on. Instead, she chose to betray us all.

"Are you fucking pulling on your dick over there? Let's go," Evert hisses, making my attention flick to him. Sylred doesn't chastise him. I know they're a bit uptight about their cupid mate possibly being in danger, but I have half a mind to snap my fingers and put the chains back around him. At the very least, a gag would be nice.

"Fuck off."

They both crouch against the wood-slatted wall, trying to peer through slivers of light at the boarded ceiling. They're probably counting the number of guards that are outside. Amateurs.

With a roll of my eyes, I break the iron lock from the door and make it go careening out, using the force of it to smack into one of the guards. The other two are quickly overpowered by Sylred and Evert, knocked unconscious, and all three tossed into the room we just escaped from.

I slam the door shut with a twist of my wrist, and then the lock floats back up and clicks into place.

"There, was that quick enough for you?" I challenge before making the last of Evert's broken chains still stuck around his ankles fall away.

Before he can answer, a cupid suddenly pops into existence in front of us mid-run, holding a bow and arrow.

Lex.

My eyes are immediately riveted to her as she hurries toward us. "I've been looking everywhere for you," she says to the genfins.

Evert and Sylred startle at her appearance, but quickly tense up again when they realize it's not *their* cupid. "Where's Emelle?" Evert asks.

Lex points in the direction she came from. "She's over there. She sent me to look for you, and—"

A huge boom sounds, making all of us drop to our haunches as the ground vibrates with the force.

"What the fuck was that?" Evert calls, looking around

the island, though our view is blocked with another shoddy building just in front of us.

My ears are ringing, and magic practically spits in the air, making me grit my teeth. Whatever the fuck that was, it was strong.

"We have angels and demons fighting with us now," Lex says, delicate hand clenching her bow, and the sight makes my heart race with nerves. If I'm not suited for battles, then she *definitely* isn't. Especially with her ridiculous human clothes. I'm not even sure how she runs in that skirt or how the buttons on her blouse still look so shiny.

"You shouldn't be here," I growl as I get to my feet and grip her arm to help her stand back up.

"I had to find Madame Cupid's mates," she tells me, and I can't help noticing how good she smells. Like sugar and...paper? Weird combination, but alright. "And I'm perfectly safe in the Veil."

"Yes, but you're not *in* the Veil right now," I point out.

"Well, of course I'm not, or you wouldn't be able to see me," she snips back, sounding annoyed. For some reason, her tone makes my eyes latch onto her pretty pink lips, and I have the rushing urge to lean down and nibble them.

Well, I do enjoy beautiful, unique things, so it's really no surprise that I seem to be infatuated with her. I knew I was intrigued by cupids when Emelle stumbled into my life, but the second I laid eyes on Lex, I was entranced.

She's so deliciously *proper.* I want to peel back that high-necked blouse and see how *improper* I can make her.

"Cover my back," Evert says to Sylred. "I'm going to

check the building in front of us, and then we're getting to our mate."

Sylred nods, and we watch as Evert rushes to the slip-shod building and skirts around the edge, disappearing from sight just as another loud noise blares out. I glance up to see a burst of flames shooting through the sky.

I quickly pull Lex against the side of the building where we have somewhat more cover. "Go back into the Veil where it's safe. This is no place for a cupid."

She shoves a stray piece of hair behind her ear. "I'll have you know that I once made twelve Love Matches during a human war."

My eyes widen. "Don't you dare try to make Love Matches right now, Sixty-Nine."

"My name is Lex," she says primly, trying to cover up the Roman numeral cupid mark on the inside of her wrist. "And I will make a Match whenever the opportunity arises."

A growl of frustration rumbles through my chest. "*Pinky.* Get out of here."

Is she *trying* to get herself hurt? She's got pink nails for gods' sake. She shouldn't be here, vulnerable like this. What was Emelle thinking?

I decide right then and there that Lex needs someone looking out for her, and when this is over, I'm going to woo the shit out of her to assure her that *I'm* that someone.

One of our first discussions needs to be about the importance of reading a room. Or in this case, a literal *battlefield*.

Just as she opens her mouth no doubt to argue about the importance of spreading love even during dangerous times or some shit, her cupid mark glows. She shoots me a look, and then disappears in a cloud of pink.

I finally let out the breath that was tightening my chest.

When the smoke clears, I see Sylred smirking. "I know that look."

Yep. Should've gagged them. "Shut it."

Just then, Evert rushes back over with a few more droplets of blood on him than he had before. I don't think it's his. "The building is clear. Let's go."

Together, the three of us sprint from our hidden spot between the buildings, and step out into absolute fucking mayhem.

High fae and genfins are fighting on the ground and in the sky, power being wielded just as much as swords. We dodge it as much as we can, because Evert and Sylred's sole focus is getting back to their mate.

Mine is finding my sister.

The battle is a fucking mess.

Lex wasn't kidding, either. There are some males and females battling for us that are definitely *not* fae. If the black- or white-feathered wings didn't give them away, it's the sheer power that they emanate. I guess the cupids have a lot of pull to get actual demons and angels to come here and help us win this fight. And considering the fire spurts and blasts of light, I'm very glad we have them on our side.

The further the three of us run into the fray, the more fighting we have to dodge or block. Evert and Sylred don't have weapons, but *I'm* a weapon, which means the majority of it is up to me.

They should be very glad they have *me* on their side.

Left and right, above us and in front, I use my powers to knock fae out of the way and give us a clear path without myself or the genfins getting hurt. Emelle would probably shoot a Love Arrow through my balls if I let anything happen to them.

I do sort of owe her for saving my life.

Plus, I like her and her mates. Not that I would ever admit such a thing out loud.

But the battle, even if I'm just actively making it avoid us, is taking its toll on me. The more fae or weapons I have to send flying away, the weaker I become. Sweat is dripping down my back, it's hard to take a full breath, and my vision is going a little tunnelled. It's draining, having my senses on a swivel, trying to make sure no one sneaks up on us from any angle.

All the while, I'm searching for any glimpse of my sister or Soora, but they're not here in the fray.

I need to find Benicia...

I feel myself growing weaker, but I can't afford to hold back. I keep using my magic, not letting a single bastard catch us unawares. And plenty of the high fae come for us. With glazed, almost unseeing eyes, they try to hack at us with their swords anytime we come into their path. Knowing they're in full mind-control mode, I try my best to send them careening away or to yank the weapons from their grips instead of wounding them fatally.

With this much fighting going on, running across the field takes so much longer than it should. I don't catch every attack. Evert gets a fist of a high fae to the back of his head, and Sylred gets laid out by a wayward burst of ice power.

But I get us across the damn field, and that's what

matters. Unfortunately, I'm about ready to drop from exhaustion by the time we do, and still, no Benicia.

Where is she?

"It's winding down!" Evert shouts, and just as he says it, I'm able to shake my head and really take in the entire scene around us, instead of just the possible nearby threats. I didn't even notice that there aren't as many swords clashing or screams sounding until just now. The battle is definitely slowing.

With the angels and demons giving us aid, the genfins have gained the upper hand. I watch as a huge group of high fae are knocked unconscious with bouts of bright power coming from the angels, and another group is rounded up in a giant ring of fire by the demons.

There are still far too many fae dead littering the ground, but at least some of the high fae can be spared. It's not their fault we have a fucked-up monarchy.

"You okay?" Sylred asks me, hand on my shoulder.

I didn't even realize I was swaying.

"Fine," I say, shrugging him off.

He's frowning at me, but then his eyes shift to somewhere behind me. "There she is!"

Evert and I both turn our gazes, latching onto Emelle's pink hair.

"Fucking finally," Evert grits out, and I hear the stark relief in his tone.

But me? I'm not relieved. Because there is a *second* pink-haired female standing right there with her. Lex is standing beside Emelle, clearly *not* in the Veil, looking out of place and deliciously rumpled.

This just solidifies my previous thought. She *definitely* needs my protection. Or maybe I should put her over my lap and punish her for putting herself in danger *again* after I explicitly told her to stay in the Veil.

Evert and Sylred hurry over to reunite with Emelle and their two other covey members, Ronak and Okot, who are already with her.

Gods, she has a lot of mates.

My eyes stay latched onto Lex as I stalk over. As if she can feel me looking, her head turns and she locks onto me. She doesn't even have the forethought to pretend to look contrite.

Little minx.

She looks away, pretending to be aloof, but I smirk when I see the blush that stains her cheeks.

Oh, Pinky. Just you wait 'til I get you alone.

I'll have her blushing from head to toe, and show her exactly why she shouldn't put herself in danger. She might try to play this detached, innocent cupid, but I know better. There's something under that exterior that calls to me.

When she steals another quick glance my way, my lips curve. With that one look, something inside me just solidified.

I'm going to make her mine.

I don't know where the thought comes from, but as soon as it forms in my head, it's done, decided. I *will* do this.

Not as a conquest, either. Sure, there will be a chase and a catch, but I'm going to keep her. Perhaps Emelle came into my life not only to save it, but to lead me to Lex. The fates like to play funny games like that.

This new vow rushes through my veins and holds steady in my chest, like it's simply been waiting for me to acknowledge it. I can feel it with all-consuming determination as I watch the red-winged beauty who's now wringing her hands in front of her. Does she know I'm about to go on the hunt? Can she feel it? I have more adrenaline and excitement pumping in me than I've had in a long time. It's the old familiar rush that comes when I go for something truly momentous as a master thief.

I've stolen a lot of things in my life. Treasures. People. Secrets.

But now? I'm going for the most precious thing of all.

I'm going to steal this cupid's heart.

The distraction of this groundbreaking revelation costs me a precious second as I rip my gaze away from her in order to see that several feet away, Prince Elphar himself is being restrained by a couple of massive angels.

The fucker.

My fists curl, and I consider walking over there to punch him in the face for what he did to Benicia. It would feel good to get out a bit of this aggression the old-fashioned way, especially since I don't think I could do anything with my magic right now while I'm so depleted.

But I don't get the chance at any kind of revenge.

In less time than it takes to blink, the prince shoves out a massive blast of power, knocking down everyone nearby with the wrath of his magic.

The breath gets sucked out of me as I land flat on my back, my skull rattled and my back barking with pain. For a moment, I can't move, but then I finally manage to roll onto my stomach and push myself up. Before I can get to my feet though, I hear his bone-chilling shout that makes every hair on the back of my neck lift up.

"CUPID!"

He's furious. Enraged. Emelle has not only cost him this battle, but the entire war against the monarchy. He can never come back from this, and he knows it. All of that is relayed in this single shout he roars. He wants to make her pay.

My neck snaps up, and I see that Emelle is still down from the blast of power, her body smashed against the dirt, but Lex is up and trying to help her up. Lex's back is to the prince, pink hair loose and red wings on full display.

Horror washes over me when I realize that the prince's attention has latched onto the wrong cupid.

Lex.

Terror bursts in my chest when I see wicked light gather in his palm, and then he *throws it*.

I don't have time to think or breathe or blink. I don't even have the time to try to scrape together the last of my own magic and shove him away, because he's already released the power, and it's not something physical that I can control. So I'm forced to watch in horrifying slow-motion as it hurtles straight at *my* cupid.

No.

My body is up and moving before I even feel the pump of my legs. I jump in front of her without hesitation.

I'm not sure what happens first—my feet landing on the ground or the power hitting me square in the chest. It's hard to say, because all I feel in the next instant is blinding, insurmountable agony.

It hits me so quickly that I don't have the luxury of seeing my life pass before my eyes. And what does a thief really have to be proud of anyway in his last moments?

But the prince's magic crashes into me instead of Lex, and that's what matters.

The last thing I see as I'm thrown down on my back, as the power shatters my bones and explodes my insides, is her blurry form.

Pink hair, red wings.

And all I can think is, I wish I'd had more time.

But I guess even a master thief can't steal that.

CHAPTER 2

BELREN

There's nothing.

There is a grimy whiteness all around that is neither light nor shadow, cool nor warm. There is no land or water or air. I have no body. No sense of touch. No recollection of what came before or if anything is coming after.

But there is one thing in the nothing.

One single, solitary thing that I remember.

Her.

Red wings, serious face, pink hair pulled back tight.

I have no idea who she was. But I remember her in this nothingness.

I don't know how long I'm stuck in this strange existence. Maybe seconds. Maybe decades. Maybe I'm not here at all, and this is all a dream. But then suddenly, the nothingness shifts. And then I feel a *pull*.

I'm yanked out of this ether of nothing, and the next thing I know, I blink into being.

Confused and shaking, I look down, realizing that I

can look, and see a body. *My* body. I raise my silver hands in front of my face, and then carefully touch my cheeks. Except I don't feel a thing.

My fingers go through me, and I pull them back to study them again, and realize that they're slightly see-through.

"What…"

My voice sounds hoarse and loud, and not familiar at all.

Who am I?

Where am I?

"Next!"

My head jerks up, and I blink at the sight before me. I'm in a large room, and there are lots of other…translucent bodies around me.

All shapes, sizes, colors, sexes, and I can't be sure if I recognize any of them or not, because I don't even recognize myself.

"Next!" the voice calls out again, sounding irritated.

I look ahead again, only to realize that I'm actually standing in line. Based on the winged female sitting at the desk and glaring at me, I'd say that I'm next, and I'm wasting her time.

I step forward, but *this* translucent body doesn't actually step. It takes some finagling, but I manage to float forward until I'm standing before her.

"You're here to be processed."

I blanch. "What? What does that mean?"

She points to the brochures that are presented on her desk. One of them has an angel on it with the slogan "Were you good in life? Well, now you can be great!"

My eyes dart to the next brochure over, and I see a

picture of a black-winged demon with the words "Like it sizzling hot? Come down under for a good time!" When I lean in closer, I read the fine print that says "*Some torturing may apply" underneath.

I frown and look back up at the female. "What is this?"

Sighing, she gives me a look that says she's been asked to explain this far too many times for her liking. And judging by the length of the line behind me, I suppose she has.

"Welcome to the afterlife," she drawls. "Time to pick your new job."

CHAPTER 3

BELREN

I blink. At least, I think I do, but I can't feel my eyes, so it's hard to tell.

Wait, why can't I feel my eyes? That's probably concerning. I should be concerned. But instead, I feel a bit...floaty?

The winged female glances up at me expectantly. A roaring sounds in my ears, and I shake my head, something like panic clenching my stomach. "What...what is happening? What is this place?"

My voice jolts me again, as if I've forgotten what I sound like. Unfeeling eyes and unfamiliar voice. Call me pessimistic, but I don't think those are good signs. Besides, what kind of fucked up voice is this? Was it always this...raspy? Maybe I need to cough.

I try to do just that, but coughing without *feeling* the cough in my throat is really strange. Worse than the eyes, to be honest.

The female sighs, her white wings twitching with something like agitation as she tosses her gleaming gold hair over her shoulders. She opens a drawer in front of her and pulls out a pamphlet and starts reading it off in a stale monotone. "Welcome, newly arrived soul. You have perished, and your mortal life is now behind you. But you need not worry, because the afterlife is where all your dreams may come true, starting with deciding your new purpose. We have many options to choose from. So relax, enjoy your new start, and pick the path you believe is right for you. I can also have a recruiter come speak with you if you'd like more information."

She flops the paper back in her drawer with a flourish and slams it closed before looking up at me with an arched brow. "Haven't had to read that for a while. Most souls that get to me are already quite ready to move on."

All I can do is stare at her for a moment. "I'm...truly dead?"

"Yes."

Okay. So that explains the general numbness to my entire body.

"Are you...an angel?" I ask, gaze flicking to her white wings. They seem to glisten a bit more, as if light is shining through them.

"Of course I'm an angel."

I huff out a breath. "Right."

Attention swiveling, I look around, taking in the space all over again. There are countless translucent bodies behind me in a winding line. I can't even see the end of it. This place just keeps going, right along with the...souls. The person directly behind me is standing off a few feet, staring straight ahead, his body just as see-through as all the rest.

I look down at my own hands, frowning at the transparency.

I'm dead.

Dead.

My mind reels, trying to remember what happened, but it comes up blank. I know basic things, like which way is up and the fact that her hair looks like the color of gilded wheat fields, but I know nothing about *myself*. I lift my gaze back up to the angel behind the desk. "What's my name?"

She shakes her head. "There are no names here. Who and what you were in your past life has no bearing here in the afterlife. You may get a different designation when you pick your new job."

Irritation surges through me, and I find myself taking a step forward. Or...I suppose I just glide a bit closer, I don't fucking know. "I don't care about the afterlife," I snap. "I want to know everything about who I am. How did I die?"

"Who you *were*," she corrects. "And look behind you. See all of those souls? There are thousands more every second, from many different realms—and that's just in *my* line. You think I know all their names and how they died? We couldn't possibly keep track of something like that," she says with a shake of her head. "Besides, your death is irrelevant to us. All that matters is that you're here, and it's now time for you to be processed to take your rightful place in the Veil."

Denial, heavy and quick, surges up in me. Then I get a flash of that single memory again—pink hair, red wings. This just feels so *wrong*.

"I don't want to be *processed*. Send me back. I can't be dead."

All of the pity from her face leaves, irritation taking over as she narrows her eyes on me. "You *are* dead, and if you don't choose a job, the Veil will choose it for you. So I suggest you lose that tone and face facts, because I have *a lot* of souls to process, and you're holding up my line."

Behind me, the souls continue to just stand around morosely, appearing too out of it to even care that I'm holding up the line. Between their taciturn mood and the strange grayish-white lighting in the massive room that seems to have clouds for a ceiling, this entire place feels dour and humdrum.

It gives me the fucking creeps.

Frustration makes me want to scream, but I know that won't do me any good, so I decide to change tactics. Releasing the tension in my demeanor, I lean forward and paste a charming smile on my face. Maybe it's not the best plan to try to flirt with an angel, but I have a feeling life-me would've done the same thing. "I think we got off on the wrong foot, angel," I croon. "I apologize for holding up your line. You must work very hard."

She's quick to nod in agreement. "I do, as a matter of fact. The paperwork is absolutely abysmal."

I let out a tsk. "Someone as beautiful as you shouldn't have to spend hours slogging away on paperwork."

It seems that even angels like to be called beautiful, because her wings shine brighter, and a small smile comes over her face. "I keep saying that we need to make things electronic, but my supervisor insists that new souls need an angelic touch," she tells me with a slight roll of her eyes. "The archangels have a much more exciting job."

I have no idea what electronic means or what kinds of things an archangel does, but I nod anyway. "They should listen to your suggestions. I'm sure you have lots of great ideas."

"So many," she replies with an exaggerated nod.

"I can tell that about you. You're a forward-thinker, and you don't get caught up in the dredges of tradition or the constraints of rules. That's a rare trait, and it should be celebrated. Actively sought after, even. I for one am honored that I even get to talk to you."

A melodic giggle leaves her lips. "Oh, stop it."

My grin widens as I shoot her what I hope is a flirtatious smile. "I'm serious, angel. Simply being in your presence is a consolation for being dead. I bet if you could look it up, you'd see I died and went to heaven because my heart stopped when I saw you."

Another laugh escapes, her cheeks filling with a pretty blush as she looks me up and down. "You're a real charmer, aren't you?"

No idea. I'm winging this.

"Perhaps I was," I say smoothly. "Being the forward-thinker that you are, is there any way you can find out? I bet it would help break up the monotony of the day if you take a peep and see who I was, or better yet, send me back?"

Her entire demeanor suddenly shifts. The smile on her face drops, eyes hardening, even her wings dim. "Nice try."

Damn.

Dropping all flirtatious pretenses, my voice goes hard. "I need you to send me back."

"Impossible. Now be a good soul and pick a job so I can process you to the next available representative."

My eyes dart down to the desk where the array of afterlife brochures are stacked haphazardly. "You expect people to hear that they've died and to just...pick a damn job?"

"What, did you expect to relax in the afterlife?"

My brows pull down in a thoughtful frown. "Well...yeah, actually."

She rolls her eyes. "Do you think I *want* to process an endless line of souls? Do you think I want to be here right now, having this conversation I've already had with other difficult spirits a million times, when I could instead be lounging somewhere on a speckled beach sunning my glorious wings?"

Her wings are pretty glorious, even I can admit that.

"Erm...no?"

"Correct. So pick a job like everybody else, and then you can move forward to test your compatibility."

"You're very snippety for an angel."

"You're very chatty for a pre-processed soul."

She's right, considering the translucents behind me are rather quiet. I don't know why I'm different, why I seem more aware, but I'm not like most of the dazed-out spirits in line. Thank fuck.

She taps a testy fingernail on the pile of brochures. "Tick tock. Pick a job."

Turning back around, I try to cross my arms, but they go through each other and generally look ridiculous, so I drop them back to my sides. Levelling her with a glare, I shake my head. "I refuse."

The angel doesn't look impressed with my answer. "You *refuse?*"

"Yes. I refuse to pick an afterlife job."

Her teeth grit together so hard I can hear she's a bit more...solid than me. Must be nice. "You are *dead*. Just accept it. It's time for you to move on."

"See, you say that, but I can fucking feel it all the way down to my see-through shoes that something is wrong. I was supposed to do...something. Or...there was someone." Uncertainty swirls inside me in a whirl of red and pink, but I don't know how to explain it. "There was something important I was a part of and..." The thought trails off with my words, my mind unable to grasp any solid memory. "Look, I can't just be dead. I need to go back."

"What's the holdup here?"

The angel and I both whip our heads to the left, finding a male striding up to us. He has green-tinged skin and two large eyes, his shoulders nothing more than a ledge for a mop of golden hair to grow out of. Based on the matching white wings, I can tell that he's another angel.

"He's a difficult soul, sir. Having trouble accepting his place in the afterlife," the female tells him as he comes to a stop in front of her desk. He casts a look at the line behind me, as if he's tallying how much I've affected it.

But I don't care that I'm being a *difficult soul*. There's something nagging me at the back of my mind, roiling in the pit of my stomach. I feel like I was supposed to be somewhere, except I went and died instead. It's like walking into a room but forgetting why you went there, though you know it's because you needed something.

"Alright," the green-skinned angel turns to me. He has

a stern yet patronizing look on his face, as if I'm a wayward adolescent he's about to discipline. "We have a lot of souls to process. You need to choose some job options so that we can move you along."

"Is that all you two care about?" My voice cuts through the hollow din of the endless room.

"Yes. We are processing angels. That's our *job*. Just like *you* need to pick a job. You know, that thing we've been asking you to pick multiple times now," he says curtly.

I shake my head in irritation, but even that feels wrong —to be in motion without *feeling* it. No neck muscles to bunch, no skin to stretch. It's like my nerves have gone paralyzed though I'm still able to move.

I don't want to just choose a job. I shouldn't be here, but...I'm not sure where I should be.

It's as if someone cut into my head and then swiped my mind with a feather duster. Everything that was once written and known about myself and my life has been wiped away, leaving nothing behind but chalky dust. The pieces of sediment settled in the bottom of my skull are the only remnants of who I was.

"You're the supervisor, right? Do an angelic trick and send my spirit back."

He looks at me with both pity and annoyance. "That's not an option," he says, gesturing to the desk. "Now, if you could just look through your options here—"

I hold up a pair of silvery, see-through hands to ward him off. "No, you're not hearing me. I have to go back. There was something that I was doing or...not doing. Or something that I needed, or...something," I end feebly.

The two angels share a look. "See what I mean?" the female whispers.

The male murmurs something back, but I'm caught up in my own frustration, so I ignore them. I whirl around, as if the other dead souls in the curving, endless line behind me can give me some answers. But all of them are unfamiliar, and instead of jarring any kind of memory, they just leave me with more confusion.

How the hell did I die?

That seems like a really stupid thing to do.

When I turn back around, the male steps forward. "Listen, some souls have a difficult time acclimating at first, but it will get easier. There's nothing you need to do anymore. You can let go of those worries."

I know he's trying to be reassuring, but it's just pissing me off. I don't want his placating comfort.

He gives me a long look. "Your past life is just that—your *past*. It's time to focus on the afterlife now."

I try to ball my hands into fists to push out some of my inner frustration, but my fingers go through my palms. I have this useless, incorporeal body, no memories, and an unsettling feeling like I need to hurry up and get back...somewhere.

The female blows some golden hair out of her face and snatches up the pamphlets with impatience. "Just pick a—"

I surge forward, not stopping until my lower half is completely inside her desk and I'm looming over her. "Stop with the godsdamned brochures!" I yell at her, my frustration erupting. "I need to go ba—"

My words abruptly cut off when my eyes inadvertently snag onto one of the brochures she has clutched in her hand. One I hadn't noticed before.

An echo of a heartbeat pounds in my ears. My mouth falls open, and I'm unable to look away. "What's that?"

She looks down at the papers fanned in her hand. "Which one?"

"That one," I say, pointing at the peek of red I can see.

She drops the pamphlets on her desk and as soon as she spreads them out, I lean down, locking onto the picture of a beautiful female with pink hair and red wings.

Almost subconsciously, my fingers come down to graze against the paper, my fingertips passing right through it.

Pink hair. Red wings.

Pink hair.

Red wings.

Pink—

Memory suddenly surges through me like a lightning bolt coming down from the clouds to strike right into my skull, and I stumble back, away from the desk.

It hurts.

I didn't think anything could hurt in death, but I was very wrong.

My back arcs and my head is thrown back, mouth gaping open in a soundless scream while something surges through me like red-hot lava.

Memories rush through me like a swarm of wasps stinging me all at once, until I'm unable to pinpoint them all individually. My life plays out from start to finish, reeling like pictures behind my eyes. When I get all the way to the end, my mouth is gasping for breath I don't need, but I'm somehow suffocating anyway.

I'm Belren. Cernu fae. Master thief. The rebel and brother. I stepped in front of Prince Elphar, the high fae prick, and took the raw attack of power before it could hit *her*—Lex. I saw what he was going to do, and I launched into action.

It was simply instinctual. I couldn't stand the thought of her getting hurt. In my gut, I knew that if it hit her when she wasn't in the Veil, it would be fatal. She would cease to exist—even more than the way I now have. If his power hit her, her afterlife was going to be extinguished. So I stepped in front of her. I took the strike instead.

Remembering my life and subsequent death gives me whiplash.

My body jerks forward as I look around wildly, knowledge sitting heavy in my eyes. "I remember."

As soon as the words pass my lips, the angels look horrified.

"Oh *no*," the female says with a gasp before looking over at the green-skinned male. He has a grim look on his face. "You're not supposed to remember. You need to forget so you can be processed," she hisses adamantly, as if it's a matter of life and death. But I've already died, so what's the worst that could happen?

"Listen," Green begins, his eyes darting around. "Just stay calm, alright?"

Calm? How the fuck can I be calm when I can practically *feel* the surge of power that hit my body, killing me before I even hit the ground? How can I be calm when all of my memories have rushed back in like a flood, making me stagger on my insubstantial feet?

"That fucking prince killed me," I growl.

"Shh," the female says, shooing her hands at me as she gets to her feet. "You don't want to draw attention to yourself. You need to settle down, or you'll get—"

"Wait. This is the Veil," I say, the realization just dawning on me. "Where's Lex?"

"Who?"

I lean forward, my face twisted up in pissed off urgency. "Summon Emelle, the Head of Cupidity. The cupid boss. Whatever she calls herself. I need to speak to her."

Her eyes widen. "How do you..."

"Just do it!" I shout, my voice echoing throughout the massive room.

"Don't shout at her." Green steps forward with a scowl on his face, trying to block her from view. "Settle down."

"*Settle down?*" I snarl. I can remember everything, and they expect me to just...settle down?

The two of them share a look, silently communicating something with uneasy glances.

"Call the cupid boss. Right. Now."

Green shakes his head. "We can't do that. You shouldn't even know about cupids yet."

"Call. Her." My tone is lethal, my fists want to punch something, and I'm brimming with furious worry. I don't know what happened to Lex or Emelle or any of the others. Hell, I don't even know if the war is still going on, or if we won or lost. I need to go back. I need to get out of this damn afterlife and have my body again.

I need to go kill that fucking prince and find my sister and then make sure Lex is safe. What if Prince Elphar killed them all? What if my death was for nothing? Angry tension makes my shoulders go stiff.

"You need to accept that you've died," Green tells me with his hands held up in front of him, like he's trying to placate a child. "Trust me when I say that you need to let go of those memories. You shouldn't have them. You should've stayed wiped clean."

"Wiped clean?" I ask with derision. "Is that what you call it?" Not remembering who or what I am or how I died didn't feel *clean*. It felt desolate. Aching. Like there was a giant, gaping hole inside of me.

"The living have no place with the dead. Not even in your thoughts."

But that's not true at all. I may be dead, but I'm still *me*. They can wipe me clean, but those people are integral to my very soul.

I'm shaking my head before he finishes his spiel, and I start to walk away. If they won't help me, then I'll find someone who will. My steps go through the gleaming white floor, but I don't pay attention to it as I spin around in the vast room that seems to be lit up by some obscure sunlight.

"Cupid! Is there a cupid in here? *I need a fucking cupid!*" My shout echoes like my voice has been tossed into the abyss of a never-ending cave.

The winding line of spirits watch me, confusion seeping into their porous silhouettes.

"Hello?" I call out again, but I get nothing.

My desperation rises when I catch a glimpse of two more angels appearing out of the corner of my eye. Both of them are male and burly, with scowls on their faces as they head right for me. "Emelle! Get your ass over here and help get me the hell out of here!" I yell into the mild light.

Unfortunately, some of the other souls in line start to mouth my words, and then several start to mimic me. Pretty soon, there's a cacophony of voices screaming into the bright unknown, all of them shouting for Emelle.

Maybe it will help.

"Stop that! Be quiet!" Green and the female are frantically walking down the line, trying to get everyone to cease their shouts, but the souls seem to be too confused to really comprehend, so they just keep repeating it over and over. I've made the sulking, obedient dead spirits start to wander out of line, yelling incoherently, walking in circles and shouting for Emelle to help them as the angels desperately try to reinstate the peaceful, patient lines. But it's a no-go. I've riled up everyone too much.

Good.

I whirl back around, energized at the mayhem I've created since it means the two burly angels are now dealing with the other souls instead of me. I take the momentary distraction and turn and run. Well, glide. My feet go right through the shiny floor.

I've only run for a few steps when a surge of white light suddenly erupts in front of me with the sound of trumpets that cuts through the soul-shouting going on. I jolt to a stop, a grimace tugging at my features as the noise digs into my eardrums with a deafening melody.

When the light fades, I blink to find a single male angel standing in front of me, clad in some sort of white drapery. I can immediately tell that this one is different from the other two I've been dealing with. He's completely solid and gleaming. Aside from that, I can feel power emanating from him, something cool and pure, like rippling water in a crystal-clear lake.

I'm silent as I stand before him, but he casts his golden eyes behind me. "What is the meaning of this?" he demands, his tone lilting even as his face is set into a hard mask.

Green rushes over to him and bends at the waist. "Apologies, Archangel," he says with a quick deferential bow. "We just had a little bit of a mishap, but we're getting everyone back into order."

Arch's golden eyebrow arches. "Is that so? Then why aren't these souls in line like they're supposed to be?"

Green blanches, and I see some sweat beading on his brow. "Uh..."

The archangel looks at the wayward spirits. "Everyone back in line immediately."

That rippling power of his seems to shoot out like a calming breeze, and immediately, all of the souls practically jump back into position like naughty children who were caught sneaking around. Within moments, the line is once again quiet and orderly. Even I can't help but be impressed.

His heavy glare rests on me. "*You.* Why didn't you get back in line like the others?" He looks at me as if he's not seeing through me, but seeing *into* me. I don't fucking like it one bit. I falter for a moment under his intense scrutiny and open my mouth to say something, but the words get caught in my throat and won't come out.

"You may not lie to me," Arch adds, as if he knew that's exactly what I was going to do.

Clearing my throat, I regard him warily as my mouth opens and the truth comes spilling out, whether I want it to or not. "I remember," I say, my tone choked. "And I want to go back."

He cocks his head. The two of us stay locked in this awkward stare-off, and I'm unable to say anything else. I was glad for the angels who came to help us battle, but I have to say, I'm not so fond of the ones here.

"Hmm." That's all he says. Just a loaded, heavy hum that I have no way of interpreting.

Sweeping his eyes away from me, he settles his gaze on Green. "You know what needs to happen," he says ominously.

Green shoots me an almost apologetic look. "Yes, Archangel. I just thought that we could get him to settle—"

"That is not your job," Arch cuts him off. "Your job is to keep the processing moving smoothly. You cannot waste time with a soul who refuses to let go. You know the rules."

"Wait a minute, what rules?" I cut in. When neither of them answer, I ask, "Can someone send me back?"

Arch levels me with a look. "Yes."

For a moment, I think I've misheard him, but when he doesn't say anything else, my eyes widen. "Truly? You'll send me back?" I don't bother to hide the hope that's filled my tone. If I can get back, I can make sure Lex is okay. I can ensure that we fight against the prince until he's well and truly snuffed out. Then I can track down my sister, because I'm the Horned Hook. I can track down anything or anyone. It's what I do.

"Do it now," Arch orders the green male.

I can't keep the grin off my face as Green comes over. He looks like he just swallowed a bug.

I step forward, more than ready. "I'll go back into my body, right? Will I be healed, or will I wake up injured?"

Green shoots a look at the angel before shaking his head at me. "You don't understand what's about to happen at all, do you?" Behind him, the female is looking at me with pity.

The smile slips off my face like sand through fingers, a feeling of dread planted in the middle of my gut, waiting to take root. "What do you mean?"

"Get on with it," Arch orders brusquely. "Then get back to processing. This line is clogged up, and we can't allow this kind of delay."

"Yes, Archangel," Green says with a sigh.

I barely notice the sound of the trumpets or the bright light as he departs again. For some reason, I feel like I've made a horrible mistake.

"I hate doing this," Green mumbles as he stands in front of me with a sigh. "Why couldn't you have just settled and chosen a job?" he asks, though it sounds like he's talking more to himself than to me.

"I tried to tell him," the female pipes in as she once more takes a seat at her desk before shouting, "Next!"

"Wait, what's happening?" I take a nervous step back from Green. "I thought I was being sent back?"

"You are," he assures me, leaving me even more confused. Then his hand comes up to my chest, right over where my heart used to beat.

"What are you—" My words immediately die off when light starts to shine from beneath his palm.

His eyes are full of sympathy. "This is what happens when souls can't let go. You shouldn't have remembered," he mutters. "We tried to warn you, but you just wouldn't listen."

I try to jerk away from his hand, but it's like I'm frozen in place.

"It's not supposed to be this way," Green tells me. "Souls are supposed to move on. If you can't…"

"If I can't…?" I'm looking down at where his hand is on my chest, noting how the light is seeping into my translucent form.

"If you can't, then you get put back where you died…as a ghost. You'll remember nothing. You'll slowly go mad, desperate for answers until your waning spirit disappears completely. You'll have no true afterlife. No job. No purpose. You'll just…fade away when the Veil finally breaks you down into nothing."

For the first time since I woke up dead, I feel fear. Real, soul-chilling fear.

"Wait. No…"

He shakes his head somberly. "It's too late. I'm sorry."

For what it's worth, I think he means it.

With a bright flash, the light suddenly swallows me whole, taking over my every sense and making everything else disappear. The light surrounds me. Consumes me. Sinks into everything that I am. My incorporeal body is infected with it, my mind jellied. It's as if the light wants to burn up every memory, every sheer inch of me.

I open my mouth to shout or to beg, only to realize that the light has taken my voice too.

Then, I'm being sucked away, like a hook in my chest that's yanking me from the afterlife and spinning me through time itself.

I probably should've just picked a godsdamned job.

CHAPTER 4

BELREN

*I*n the span of a second, or perhaps a century, I don't exist. I don't have any sense of where anything is. There's just the light, the tug, and this feeling of being nowhere and yet everywhere all at once.

It's fucking weird.

I'm falling past time and air, through light and shadow. I go further and further, just particles of existence haphazardly skimming by worlds and then blowing past them all like a dry, tepid rain.

And then, there's a wind that somehow rushes all around me and acts like a vacuum to my spirit. I can do nothing as I'm sucked in and spat out like rotten air.

Just like that, my body re-forms in a desolate gust.

Gasping for air I can't breathe, I blink up at a crystal blue sky and a familiar sun that seems to be slowly inching away.

I'm back.

Sitting up, I look around me at the empty fields of overgrown grass. I trace my gaze across the entirety of the island as it floats in the sky, and a gloom settles over my mood.

It's not until I stand and look down that I see the scorched patch of earth beneath my feet. The ground is sunken slightly, the sand discolored. I don't know how I know, but innately, I understand that this is where I died.

"That's a bit dramatic," I grumble.

Kneeling down, I try to press my hand against the spot as if I can leach some life back into me, but my palm passes right through the earth, sinking into it like mist.

Great. I'm even hollower and more translucent than I was before.

When I was in line with the other souls, I was see-through, sure, but I'm different now. My skin has always been grayish silver, my hair white, but now I look lackluster and pallid. Like a damn sheet that's been left out in the sun too long.

I really am a ghost.

They sent me back, just not the way I wanted.

"Fucking archangels."

Standing up again, it takes me a moment to get my bearings as I hover slightly over the ground. After a few tentative steps, I start to explore the island, and realization quickly settles in.

The fields that King Beluar used to grow his mind-controlling plants are non-existent. Now, there's nothing but burned earth, as if they eradicated every bit of it. The wooden buildings that the king's army used are also gone, perhaps burned down alongside the fields.

But the most notable difference is the simple stacked-stone wall, barely as high as my knees, and inside are hundreds of headstones made of rock and worn wood.

How long was I gone?

The graveyard is located just past the only field that isn't burned. Instead of growing straight up, the over-grown grass lays down, the green pillowy tufts looking more like unmoving waves of water. It's actually a picturesque place. You know, if it weren't for all the dead people.

The graveyard is completely inundated with ghosts. They're meandering around, floating back and forth, some of them clumsily stumbling around and muttering.

My new neighbors, I suppose. They don't seem like a lively bunch.

I stop just outside the wall, my eyes taking in all the death. So many fae died, all because of a greedy king and a prick of a prince. It could've been a lot more, but even still, the amount sickens me.

"You're new."

The sudden voice that speaks directly into my left ear would've given me a heart attack if my heart could still attack. My hovering form flinches in the air before I whip my head around and spot the ghost standing entirely too close to me.

"What the fuck?" I demand, backing up a few steps until I'm nearly passing through the stone wall behind me.

The ghost is male, with stag antlers popping up from his head. Despite his muted ghostly form, I can see hints of faded blue coloring in his skin and hair. Yet my eyes drop down to the armor he's wearing, sporting the royal crest. For a moment, my lips curl into a sneer.

He was fighting against me and the other rebels. For all I know, he could've been responsible for hurting or killing someone I care about. Although, I have to remember that the king was controlling most of them. This male might not have been acting of his own free will, which makes him more of a victim than an enemy.

"You're new," he says, inching forward once again.

"I am," I reply with a nod. "Have you been here long?"

Instead of answering, he cocks his antlered head. "You're new."

My brows pull together in a frown. "Yes, we've been over this."

"You're new."

"Erm..."

"You're new."

Alright. This is going well. "Is that all you say?"

He just stares at me.

"I suppose you're one of these ghosts that isn't all there?"

He frowns and then opens his mouth again. "You're—"

"New. Yes, let's move on from that."

Walking past the wall, I approach another ghost. A female who has her eyes trained to the ground, her form gliding instead of walking. "Hey there, what's your—"

She keeps gliding. And godsdamn, it's a fast glide. I actually have to ghost-jog to keep up. "Miss, I was wondering—"

She disappears before I can finish. Just pops right out of existence, as if she'd rather disappear than listen to me.

"That was rude," I mutter before turning around to check out some other prospects. Surely, one of these other ghosts has to have some of their memory like I do.

One flies right past me, but I'm fairly certain she's speaking a language that doesn't exist. It's a lot of babbling.

I'll just...try another ghost.

Except every single one I pass by doesn't answer me. They're either mute, mumbling incoherently, or there's even one who just—

"AHHHHHH!"

Screams.

It's quite loud.

"You're new."

I turn to glare at Stag. "And that's getting old."

Standing in the middle of the graveyard with all of these incoherent ghosts makes a dire feeling come over me. How could it not? They're all looking so forlorn or flummoxed. It's worse than the souls from the processing line. Faded and lost, these ghosts seem unable to form a single response, as if they've forgotten how. As if they've forgotten everything.

Is that what's going to happen to me?

As soon as the thought pops in my head, I immediately steel against it.

No. I refuse. I don't care what Green said or how much pity the other angel wore on her face. They're wrong. They said I wouldn't let go? Well, they're fucking *right*. I'm going to prove that I can hold onto myself.

For as long as I can.

～

I think I've been here for a few days now, but I can't be positive because time passes strangely when you're dead. It feels like every second takes ages, and yet, I think perhaps hours are flying by without me noticing.

I don't want to think about why that may be.

Like a ritual, I constantly recall my memories, repeating them to myself until they become background noise. I don't want to think about why I do that either.

"Stag, you think my side won the battle, or yours?" I ask, walking across a patch of blackened soil.

"There was fighting."

I've found that my good friend Stag does indeed say other things other than *you're new*. The problem is, he usually latches on to one or two comments at a time and just repeats that for gods know how long. I tried to get him to say funny shit, but for some reason "I can't feel my balls" just wouldn't stick.

"I bet our side kicked your side's ass," I tell him.

His stag head swivels around. "There was fighting."

"You want to talk about fighting? I was once hired by a jilted wife to steal a husband's side lover for herself. Now *that* was a fight."

When Stag blinks at me, I nod.

"Yep. She thought the best revenge was not to leave him, but to take his side of sugar for herself and have a little dipping session. It was a nice bit of thievery that paid off well for her." I tilt my head in thought. "The priceless crystal obelisk probably wasn't bad either. But gods, the look on his face when he walked in on her with his other lover, the floor covered in shattered remnants of his crystal...spectacular. I used that bit of gossip to be paid for seven other jobs."

"There was fighting," Stag says.

"Indeed there was," I say with a smirk.

We pass by the graveyard, where the other ghosts are milling around, looking as dull as ever. What I wouldn't give to be able to use my powers or have my wings out, but those parts of me are gone, right along with being able to feel anything at all.

Just because I'm the only one here who can hold a conversation, doesn't mean I'm superior. I can't even leave. Every time I try to venture toward the edge of the island, I get this horrible sensation that pins me down. I'm haunting this place right alongside the others.

None of these ghosts are anyone I know, either. That fact is both a relief and a bitter disappointment. I'm enough of an asshole to admit it. Not that I want any of my friends to be dead, but it would've been a sort of comfort to see a familiar face. Oh, who am I kidding? I'd definitely prefer one damn acquaintance here with me. Couldn't at least one of them have died with me? Seems selfish that I'm the only one.

Grimacing at myself, I look up at the sky, noting that it's midday. You can trace the hour easily by watching the realm's sun as it slingshots closer or further away in the sky, and right now, it's as big as my fist.

I meander around, listening to the other ghosts for a moment. Yet when I look up again, the sun is now much smaller, barely the size of an eyeball. Confused, I look around, only to realize I'm no longer hovering around the burnt field, but hovering over my deathplace instead.

Again.

Fuck.

With nervousness bordering on fear, I start muttering to myself, keeping my eyes locked on the sun, as if my attention will stop me from losing time again. "My name is Belren. I'm a Cernu fae. I'm the fucking Horned Hook, the best godsdamned thief in the realm. I can find and steal anything. I will *not* forget who and where I am. I know about angels and demons and cupids, and I fucking hate that prig of a prince who shot me with his magic."

When I'm done, I feel minutely better.

It's not just the fact that I have to clench a proverbial fist around my mind all the time, either. This place is fucking with me.

Right at my deathplace, over that scorched bit of earth, something feels...perplexing.

Every time I find myself right back there near that piece of ground, I get the sense that I'm supposed to do something. Or see something that I'm not seeing. There's an unending draw I have to it, and yet, it's so maddening that every time I hover there, I grow more and more agitated.

In fact, it's happening right now. An incessant urging, like someone tapping you on the shoulder again and again to get your attention, except when you turn around, nobody's there.

"What the fuck do you want from me?" I growl as I spin in place. There's nothing here but an empty field and dust, and yet this coaxing, goading insistence won't go away. I'm spinning around in place, talking to the fucking air for gods' sakes.

Being a ghost is shitty.

"There was fighting."

Jerking my head to the left, I see Stag sprawled out next to my deathplace, looking like he's trying to sunbathe despite wearing full armor and boots. *And* missing a physical body. Can't forget that part.

"Well, I'm sure going to be fighting this," I say, because I'm determined not to end up like him.

41

Like I'm proving it to myself, I once more start murmuring random memories. More often than not, my mind strays to the day I died. Strays to *her*.

But she's not here. None of them are. Not Lex or my sister or Emelle and her gaggle of mates. Wait… *What were their names again?* Panic curls down my back.

I'm not forgetting. I'm *not*.

I walk to the end of the floating island, going through the heavy mist that clings to the edges. It makes it look like the land is sitting in a pillow of clouds, obscuring the open sky around us. I stop right at the end, my hollow boots stepping on the earth's rim between solid ground and air. I stare into the mist as if I can see through it to the other floating islands that speckle the sky.

I've been hoping to glean some information while I've been here, but not a single ghost is any help in answering my questions. I have no idea how long I've been dead. I have no idea who won the battle, if Prince Elphar is still in power. No idea if my friends and sister survived.

To be honest, I've been afraid to find out. This place feels like it's been forgotten and abandoned. Just like the ghosts.

I'm mentally jolted when Stag suddenly floats through my whole damn body. "Stag, how many times do I have to tell you? Don't float through me."

The antlered male turns and looks at me, bringing a hand up over the breastplate he's wearing like he's trying to feel the metal beneath his palm. "There was fighting."

"There's going to be *more* fighting if you keep fucking flying through me like that." I shiver. "It gives me the creeps."

My threat doesn't do a damn thing, because he's not

even paying attention to me anymore. Instead, he's slapping his hand around at the curling mist, like he's trying to beat it back.

With a shake of my head, I turn and float away before he sees and can follow. Having company is great, until it's fucking annoying.

I was the same way in life. I'd throw parties full of wonderful debauchery, and I'd be the life of it too, basking in the center of it all, but it would get old. I'd kick everyone out and then spend days alone afterward. It left me feeling like I was a liar as well as a thief. Pretentious and pretending. Filling the time and emptying myself in the process.

But left too long with only myself for company made me become agitated and antsy. I'd then need the company of others to drown out the silence. Perhaps it's because I always surrounded myself with surface acquaintances. I didn't want anything too deep. I wanted easy, to keep everyone at arm's length.

Maybe that's why I was so drawn to Lex. She didn't feel surface. She felt…important.

"How you doing today, Rocky?" I ask as I pass by a ghost who has a particular interest in a certain boulder. Unlike armor worn by most of the others, she wears a tattered dress made from a patchwork of furs, and a bonnet on her head. I can't tell what kind of fae she is, but the look in her eyes is hollower than her body. Day after day, all she does is float around this one huge rock just outside of the graveyard.

She startles at my voice before her phantom body dives into the boulder and disappears.

"Nice day, then?" I quip.

The rock shakes.

"That's good to hear." I walk around the rock, eyeing it carefully. "Care to tell me how you do this particular trick?"

Some sand that's gathered on the top of the boulder shakes off and goes through my boots, and I frown down at it. "I suppose that's a no."

Rocky's head pops out, but when she sees I'm still standing here, she disappears again. She's not much of a talker.

"Alright. See you later, love."

I turn and walk away, since I don't want to spook her too much. A ghost trying not to spook another ghost. Go figure. Rocky doesn't seem to have a lot of wherewithal, but she's the only ghost here that is able to go into an object and move it. She's gotten to some superior ghost skill, and quite frankly, I'm jealous.

Looking around, I spot a smaller boulder further away, and I try to mimic her. While I can certainly walk through it, I can't *imbed* myself into the damn thing like Rocky does, and I sure as hell can't move it with my old powers either.

After my three hundredth or so try, I give up, trying to kick the side of it for not cooperating. Kicking things isn't at all rewarding when your foot just goes through it.

"Stupid fucking rock."

Of course, Stag chooses that moment to find me and fly through my body again.

"*Stag,*" I grit out in frustration. "There are *boundaries.* You've got to stop floating through me. I don't care that we can't feel it. Stop. Doing. It." I've had it up to my ethereal neck with his incessant flybys.

It probably shouldn't bother me so much since it doesn't actually physically affect me, but it's happened so often now in a short amount of time that my temper gets hotter and hotter every time it happens.

"Oh," he says, looking around like he forgot he was even here next to me. "There was fighting," he blurts, his expression dazed and confused as he runs his hand around his armor again.

My irritation blows out with my sigh, because we've already had this conversation. "Yes, Stag. There was fighting."

The other more cognizant ghosts do this too. They keep repeating the tiny snippets. I don't like to think that in a way, I'm doing the same thing when I mumble my memories. Maybe they were like me at first. They remembered it all, spoke of it all. But day by day, they lost a little bit more, talked a little bit less. Until all they had was one fragment to repeat, until so much time passed that even that became meaningless.

I try to pretend that I'm not like them. That I'm better than these other ghosts who float around aimlessly day after day, too confused to carry on a conversation. But the truth is, I'm more like them than I care to admit.

We are ghosts, haunting this place, but our memories are haunting us.

"I think there was fighting…" Stag trails off, his feet sinking into the ground as he stares listlessly around, like he's trying to see a battle that isn't here. But others are far worse. Those ghosts can't even form sentences anymore. They simply groan or wail, confusion and suffering chilling their vocal chords that now only emit one haunting tone.

That's my fate.

The thought makes me feel even hollower than I already am.

I'm going to go mad. I'm going to lose the rest of the wits I have left. How long does it take to become one of those groaning and wailing beings? They don't even know *why* they moan and cry, and isn't that fucking cruel? My greatest fear is being here forever, wailing wordlessly for all eternity. If I stay, I'll become nothing but another mindless apparition.

I can't let that happen. I would rather cease to exist than slowly lose myself. The archangel wouldn't help me. He sent me to this fate. But fuck this fate. I'm the Horned Hook, and I don't give up that easily. Fuck angels, too, because they certainly didn't save my soul. Instead, they practically banished it.

No, what I need is a cupid.

It's time to try to get the hell off this island and find Emelle, no matter what it takes.

CHAPTER 5

BELREN

*W*ith my objective clear, I look around at all the hovering ghosts. "None of you want to tell me if there's a trick to leave our deathplace by chance, do you?"

Not a single one of them looks at me.

"Right," I say with a frustrated sigh. "Well, I'll just do it without any help then. I'm going to leave this gods-damned island," I say with determination filling my...well, not my veins. Maybe my vapor? Who the fuck knows. "Try not to miss me too much. Oh, and Screamer? Maybe stop screaming all the godsdamned time."

She replies with another echoing screech.

Won't miss that.

"Okay then. Have fun...haunting," I say to everyone, nodding as they continue to float around morosely. "Yep. Just like that. You're all doing great." *But I'm not going to end up like you.*

I turn around and walk away, passing Rocky as I go.

She's still in her boulder, a hollow knocking noise coming from inside.

"I'm going to learn that trick," I tell her as I pass by.

The boulder trembles for a moment before going still once again.

"Show off."

I walk past my deathplace, and of course, that tingling, nagging sensation hooks into me, but I refuse to give it any attention. I've come to the conclusion that it's just giving me a trick lure. Beseeching me, feeding me a false sense of intuition to keep me here. Perhaps that's why the other ghosts stick around—they can't get past it.

But I'm going to.

So, I keep going, right to the end of the island. I haven't actually successfully stepped off it before. Every time I got to the edge, that incessant sensation always made me turn right back around. But I'm determined not to give in this time.

The urgency to go back, to look around my deathplace and stay here comes back full force. It's almost something I can physically *feel*. I'd grit my teeth if I could, but instead, my feet try to sink into the ground a little more, like the damn island is trying to suck me back in.

"I'm not staying," I snarl.

I jerk my feet out one at a time, glaring at the ground. The toes of my boots balance on the end of the island, mist swirling around the soles, closing in on me like a bad omen.

As if my deathplace knows I'm trying to escape, its proverbial fist grips me in a restraining draw. I look over my shoulder, troubled. *I need to go back. There's something there I have to do. Something I'm missing... I'm supposed to—*

No.

"Fuck you," I spit. I'm the godsdamned Horned Hook. I can go anywhere I want to go, and right now, I am leaving this forsaken Ghost Island.

With as much stubborn fortitude as I can muster, I face forward and then force my foot to take that first step right off the edge.

My boot hovers on nothing but empty space, and a small, buoyed victory helps me to step off with the other foot, too. Then I'm standing on thin air, off of the island for the first time.

I look down at my feet, sucking in a false breath at the sensation of seeing nothing beneath me. Who wouldn't? I just walked right off the godsdamned ground. But I'm a ghost, so apparently, I can hover in the air. Small perks, I guess.

As soon as I test the air to make sure I'm not suddenly going to start plunging down, I take another step. Then another. Another. Through mist and empty nothingness, my transparent feet walk through the sky.

Since I died with my wings tucked away securely, I don't have them in my ghost form, and it feels inherently wrong to be in the air without them. I suppose it's the instinct of mortality that I keep expecting to start free-falling, but it never happens. Instead, I walk on the clouds.

Glancing behind me, I watch the mist swallow the island in a swirling shroud. My deathplace beckons to me like a shrill sound so high-pitched it can only be felt with cringing vibrations. That little voice is urging me to go back, but I won't. This is the farthest I've been able to get away from it, and I'm not giving in. So I keep going, putting one foot in front of the other.

When I get a little further out, the clouds part, and a view of floating islands greets me, speckling the sky in every direction. Up, down, north, south, far, and near, the islands are everywhere.

Some of them are tiny and uninhabited, while others are so large that they're home to sprawling cities. Being who I am with the profession I used to have in life, it's providential that I've visited most of them, because that means I know exactly where to go. It's a fortunate consequence of being the renowned Horned Hook. Fae from far and wide would hire me to find something for them, to steal some priceless heirloom, or locate a fae on the run, and I was able to travel all over, visiting all sorts of islands while I worked.

I always found my mark. Except for one, single, solitary time.

Benicia.

As I get further out, the imploring sense to turn around and return to my deathplace comes back full force, and I jolt mid-air, my entire body jerking to an ungraceful stop. The urge to go back is *strong*, like it knows it's losing, but I'll be damned if I let it win.

I just need to get to Emelle. She's the damn boss of all the cupids for gods' sakes. She can help me, and then I can find my sister. I can find Lex.

The pull gets more intense the further I go, and my face pulls into a grimace from the strain. "You're not winning this."

To distract myself, I mutter memories. Of Benicia and me. When Lex first appeared in my hideaway grotto. My first paid thieving. The time I left home to strike out on my own. When I had my Horned Hook mask made to keep my identity secret.

The further I go, the heavier I feel. Seems unfair, considering I'm incorporeal.

Despite the fact that my body feels stretched and weighed-down, everything screaming at me to turn back and return, I don't. I press on, going as fast as my ghostly limbs can take me. I even join a group of pixies for a while, their high-pitched chattering wonderfully distracting as I fly beside them.

Although, *fly* probably isn't the best word to describe what I'm doing. It's more of a lean that I do while walking on air. And as if that's not embarrassing enough, I also keep catching myself with my arm thrusted straight out in front me like it's a rudder on a damn ship, steering the way. As much as I hate being a ghost, I'm glad that I'm invisible right now. Those pixies would laugh their asses off if they saw me.

Aside from a few clouds dotted around, the skies are mostly clear, giving me a good view of the speckling islands floating leisurely in the sky. I used to fly around just for the fun of it, visiting places I hadn't been to before, getting a feel for the land and chatting up locals. After all, I didn't just get hired to steal *things*. One of the most lucrative avenues of my business was secrets. I love a good secret.

So does Benicia. She loves secrets so much that when she hid away, even I couldn't find her. I knew she'd had a love affair with Princess Soora, of course. Soora wasn't the princess back then, though. Yet high fae can be fickle and fluid lovers. When Soora's family worked to match her up with Prince Elphar, it was her best advantage of becoming royal and strengthening her political power. But she broke my sister's heart in the process. Cast her off, just like that, claiming it was for the good of the rebellion, to get an insider into the palace.

But an ugly part of me wondered if she just wanted the crown.

Part of me understands Soora's justification for betraying us all in order to make a deal with the prince— to end her role in the rebellion and take my sister to safety. But the other part of me doesn't forgive the treachery. She broke my sister's heart by marrying that prick, and then she threw the rest of us to the wolves.

I crick my neck, rolling my shoulders back as I once again make myself put my arm down. *I need to go back. I'm too far away. I need—*

"No," I snap, cutting off the deathplace drawl before it can drown out my thoughts.

Gods, what I would give to have a little wine right about now. Or my smoking pipe. It would've taken the edge off wonderfully. Instead, I have a flock of pixies, an incredibly awkward looking fly-pose, and bitterness.

With that lovely combination, I spend the rest of the daylight passing by islands like some crazed specter, fighting against my ghostly instinct every step of the way. When the sky goes from blue to a darkening gray, the already strained pull on me becomes much, much stronger.

I double down, leaving the pixies in my dust because stubbornness can only take me so far. I don't know how much longer I can last before I'm forced to turn around.

When darkness sets in, the strain becomes almost unbearable. My body starts to shake all over, and fear grips me by the balls.

My body shakes, the pull to my deathplace becoming a tangible, furious thing. Like talons trying to close in around me, take me in its grip and fling me right back.

I can't let that happen—not when I'm so close. I have to get to Emelle.

Grimacing, I push on, body propelling forward in an awkward, shaken zigzag through the sky.

And then, the genfin island finally comes into view.

Domed wooden buildings and thick forests appear from below, fairy lights making the island visible amidst its soft, welcoming glow.

The tension around me and the lapse of relief that I've gotten here makes me drop from the sky like a dead bird. I fall through branches and leaves, landing in a graceless heap on a grassy knoll. Half of my body sinks well below the ground, and it takes more than a few tries to heave myself up.

I lie on my back for a moment, panting heavily, though it's certainly not for the oxygen. This physical struggle bombards me, the pull so strong that it feels like it could break me in half. Somehow, I force myself to stand and manage to get to my feet. My head swims, dark blots spreading through my vision like droplets of black ink.

The problem is, those drops of ink aren't just affecting my sight. They're affecting my mind too. I feel each obsidian drip like a physical, ominous thing. Dizziness sets in, but then I realize my *memories* that are being blotted out.

Fuck.

Every bead lands inside my consciousness and creates a smudged mess. I try to grasp onto my memories, but they slip away, stained beyond recognition, fading into black nothingness.

"No..." I gasp, hands fumbling uselessly at the outline of my forehead as if I can try to keep the contents of my head inside. But I can't. My stubbornness to leave my deathplace is costing me. Dearly.

Please let me find Emelle...before I forget why I'm looking for her in the first place.

I dig down deep into my crumbling willpower, not allowing myself to give up, but even I know I've pushed it too much. I'm too far away from my deathplace. Like a bet on a hand of cards, I've gone all in, and if I lose, I can't afford to play again.

"Don't...black...out..." My voice is labored with breath I can't take, unsteady with a heart that won't beat.

Every fragment of my phantom body is cringing, shutting down, and still, there's that incessant, repulsive *pulling*, like the hands of a demon come to drag me back to hell.

It feels like it takes ages to reach the top of the hill, but perhaps that's just because I feel like I'm dying. Which is complete and utter shit, considering I'm already dead.

I crest the incline and trudge back down the other side, while more ink spots stain my gaze, blotting out another memory, each step slower and shakier than the last. An insidious thought creeps up my insubstantial spine.

I'm not going to make it.

Despair, deep and dark, tries to overtake me, but I shove it away.

"My name is Belren," I gasp out, voice sounding hoarse and pissed off. "I'm the Horned Hook. Master thief. Cernu fae."

I don't want to forget anything. This knowledge, it *makes* me. It *is* me. After all, are we not just a collection of our experiences? Of our choices? Fuck if I'm going to just let it all leave.

I take one step. Two. Each is labored and heavy, as if the soles of my shoes are burdened with stones, trying to weigh me down and keep me from going further.

But I must. It's all I can do—walk and repeat.

"My name is Belren. I'm a...fae. A prick of a prince killed me. I saved a cupid—Lex, with her smooth pink hair and pretty red wings. I just need to get to Emelle. She can fix this. Then I can find Lex. Find my sister. Steal something. Keep all my memories."

A walk that should've been quick takes me ages. Since becoming a ghost, there hasn't been a single physical need. No hunger or thirst, no drive to sleep or rest. Yet right now, I'm utterly exhausted, as if it's not just my memories being drained, but *I'm* being drained. Like I'm going to fade away into nothing.

It's not a very comforting feeling.

Just when I think I'm about to keel over, I spot it— Emelle's dome. I'd have a sense of relief if I wasn't so incredibly fucked up.

My vision tilts, more ink drops staining my eyes and tainting my mind, but I narrow my eyes, speckled gaze staring intently at that one dome I need to get to. It's nestled in the hill, a garden wrapped around it like a grassy cloak.

It's a godsdamned struggle.

Every. Single. Step.

Confusion and emptiness whirl in my head where certainty and fullness used to be. The pull has become a pain that's soul-deep, something that far surpasses anything physical. This is an attack against my very soul.

What used to be dripping blots of ink is now a rushing, sweeping tide of black waves in a violent sea, ready to wash everything away.

"Prince Prick...k-killed me. I protected...pink hair. Red wings. I have to get t-to Emelle. Have to...keep...going..." I grit out the last word and nearly go right through a door.

It's hard to focus on what's around me when what's inside me is slipping away. I try to follow the memories, to grab onto them and hold tight, but no matter what I do, they're being washed away.

Blearily, I glance up, seeing the house in front of me. I'm actually here. All I need to do is find Emelle. She can help me. She *has* to.

"My...name is..."

Something cleaves. Breaks. Frothy water black as onyx churns.

"I'm..." Lost. That's what I am. I'm fucking *lost*.

Panic is a noose around my godsdamned neck as I try to scrabble for my memories, but they're disappearing right through my hands, like grains of sand falling between fingers. *Why does everything hurt? Why do I feel like I'm supposed to be somewhere else?*

"Cupid. Pink hair. Red wings," I grit out, latching onto

that one thing that seems to be all I can see through the inky black waves sloshing in my head.

Just get to her.

So. Close.

I start forward, but the pull snaps at me just then like the sharp teeth of a fish. It's presence is circling, ready to tug me away and let this onyx sea drown the last of me.

Gasping, I press ineffective hands into my phantom stomach, unable to stop my mortal instincts. Dark spots speckle my vision, making me pitch forward, right through the wooden door. I practically trip down a set of stairs, barely able to stop before I go through another wall.

Everything spins.

My vision, the world, the pull trying to reel me in like I've been caught on its line. Confusion blares through me.

I look around, fear pounding like a pulse, and take in the dark living space I'm standing in. There are bookshelves on the far wall, though they're filled haphazardly with more children's toys than books. A seating area is sprawled out over a fur rug, and to the right, there appears to be a kitchen area through an open archway.

I frown in confusion.

Wait. Why am I here? How did I get here? And...where the fuck is here?

Closing my eyes, I will myself to wake up, because surely this is a dream. That's why I'm so disoriented. That's why I feel so lost. I fell asleep and none of this is real.

I can wake up and... I frown. Wait, why can't I picture where I fell asleep? Why can't I picture anything at all? The more I search my mind, the less I dredge up.

Panicked, I try to search for who the hell I am, but there's nothing. Absolutely *nothing*. There's a niggling maggot squirming in the mental soil of my dusted memories, telling me that what I lost was vital.

What was my name? I just had it—I know I did.

Swish, swish, swish goes the mind wipe. Dusted and then rinsed away with night's ocean. I need to wake the fuck up, but when I try to pinch myself, my fingers go uselessly through my arm. Staring down in shock, I look at this ghost of a body, eyes wide with horror.

What the hell is happening?

With the amount of fear coursing through me, my heart should be pounding, my body slick with terrified sweat, and my teeth gnashing in defiance.

But I'm nothing more than that chalky dust that I picture in my mind, fragments blowing around uselessly, unable to coalesce together, until everything is gone except for this single grain of powder.

I'm bereaved...until I even forget *that*. I can't hold onto being heartsick, because I don't remember why I'm feeling that in the first damn place.

The roiling, storming emotions slump down, stilling into calm, murky waters. I sway on feet that just sink into the wooden floor, and I know I'm well and truly fucked.

Spots in my vision start to take over. I'm either going to black out or wake up, and I desperately hope it's the latter. But before I can, something moves in my periphery.

I jerk my head up, letting out a gasp that's mirrored by the figure who jolts to a stop in front of me.

A small girl stands in the threshold between the kitchen and the living space, a little cup clenched in one hand, and an arrow in the other. She watches me with wide eyes, toes peeking through the bottom of her long nightgown, hair mussed from sleep, though it's too dark for me to see the color.

I'm frozen as I stare at her, that niggling worm in my head writhing around. Does she know me? Do I know her?

We continue to eye each other for a moment until she rubs her eyes sleepily, like she wants to make sure she's really seeing me. After she's tried that and I'm still frozen in front of her, she frowns. "Who...are you?" the girl asks, her voice lilting with childhood innocence, even if she is clutching an arrow like it's her favorite stuffie.

I open my mouth, but no answer comes out, because I have no idea who I am.

She steps forward into a shaft of moonlight coming from the window, and my gaze hooks to the pink of her hair. The feather duster that brushed through my mind does another sweep, but I claw forward and snatch up a solitary fragment, one dusty piece of a memory, right before it can take that too.

I clutch that grain in my figurative fist.

Pink hair, red wings, pink hair, red wings. *Pink hair.*

I stare at the little girl's hair, but my mind's eye is trying to picture another face, trying to come up with a name. I was supposed to do something...looking for someone...

A pull, its force stronger than a seismic wave, lurches me clear off my feet.

My eyes widen, a choked sound coming out of me, and the little girl gasps and reaches out, but it's no use.

Something rips me away with the strength of a terrorized sea.

The final wave of darkness claims me, taking me far, far away, erasing me until l have nothing…

Except a single piece of dust still clutched in my fist.

Pink hair.

Red wings.

CHAPTER 6

LEX

"*C*an we...ahh, take a break?" the cupid standing at my side asks. He's got pink hair that sits rigidly straight combed back on his head, and his red wings are held far too loosely. The end feathers are even dragging a little on the ground. Terrible habit.

My gaze cuts over to him. "A break? Already?"

"It's nearly nighttime."

My hold on my bow drops, the string loosening as I lower the arrow instead of shooting it through the hindquarters of the bear several paces away.

"Nighttime is no time to stop," I insist. "If anything, love and lust are only magnified under the cover of darkness, especially with the moon as full as it is here in the shifter realm. Their mating instincts will already be in overdrive."

"Yes, but tonight is the cupid potluck."

Surprise and then dread swims over my features. "Oh. That."

He gives me a once-over. "Let me guess, you're not a fan of parties?"

Well, that sounded judgmental. "What makes you say that?"

His blood-red eyes cast over my outfit—a knee-length red pencil skirt and pink blouse tucked in, my black blazer buttoned over it. When he keeps staring, I glance down to see if I have a wrinkle somewhere. Finding none, I wonder if a piece of hair has come loose from my bun, but since I don't have a corporeal body right now, I can't run my hand over it to check.

"You just...don't seem like the partying type," he finally finishes.

I sniff and tip my chin up. "I'll have you know that I've planned the last four cupid annual parties. Everybody raved about my themes."

One was "We make matches *mint* to be." My encourage-*mint* wall was a real hit.

"Okay, but that's planning. Did you actually *go* to the party?" he asks.

I frown. "Well...no. But that's beside the point."

His stodgy look argues that it's not. "I suppose for someone who can leave the Veil and become physical whenever they want, the parties aren't as exciting for you," he tells me with a little bit of bitterness. He won't outright insult me for it, not when I technically outrank him, but he sure lets it be known that he's green with envy. Well, not actually green. His wings are as red as mine.

I don't know what he sees in my expression, but he lets out a sigh and comes closer, the full moon enhancing his pale skin. He was a vampire in his past life, though I'm glad he's traded in his bloodlust for just plain lust. "Let's go back to headquarters. I'll bring you into the party so you can see for yourself. It'll be fun."

Fun.

As if I deserve to have any fun.

I don't say that out loud though, and instead give him a smile. "Sure. It would be uncouth of me to make you miss the potluck, Mac."

His actual cupid number designation is MMMC-MXCIX plus CVI. He has to have *two* rows of cupid numbers on the inside of his wrist, since there's been an influx of cupids in the last few years, and Cupidville ran out of Roman numerals. But since his numbered designation is way too much of a mouthful, he simply uses the first letter of each line to make a name: M and C, thus, Mac.

Roman numerals aren't really the most efficient way to tally us when we become cupids, but there was a Roman who was Head of Cupidity back in the day, and the practice has stuck. Then, Emelle became the boss and made a name for herself—literally. So making a name out of our cupid numbers caught on fast.

I can't say the name "Mac" exactly fits his ex-vampire-turned-cupid personality with his black suit and blood drops on his shirt collar, but who am I to judge? After all, my cupid number is LXIX. Sixty-nine. If only I had a Love Match for every time someone made a joke about it.

"Great, let's go," he beams, showing off the fangs lodged in his gums.

I stuff my Love Arrow into the quiver at my back and sling my bow onto its holder. We've been working the shifter realm for a few weeks now, and I've been waiting for tonight's full moon so I can succeed in my personal challenge: three hundred shifter mate matches, all instigated by my Lust Breath and carefully aimed Love Arrows. But the moon has only been in the sky for an hour, maybe two, and I've only been able to mate match twenty shifters.

Abysmal numbers.

Casting one disappointed look into the knotty woods of the forest that's currently crawling with shifters running around trying to mate, I let out a sigh and then turn away. "Alright, let's go to Cupidville," I say, unable to keep the grimace from my expression as I let my eyes scan the landscape, wishing I could stay here instead.

"You really like your job, don't you?" Mac asks.

Not anymore.

Now, it's just penance.

But to Mac, I say, "Of course I do. And I aim to be the best."

"You're always Cupid of the Month, so that makes sense."

"Not always," I mutter as I wait for him to put his bow away.

He casts me a curious glance, but I don't divulge further. I went through some dark years after... Well. I'm lucky that Emelle gave me space. But I had to stop sulking, so I got back to work. The fact that Emelle let me keep my higher-up status despite how low I was speaks volumes about her character. She really is the best Madame Cupid we've ever had.

And that's not just my opinion. I've handed out cupidity questionnaires and spoken with Cupidity

Resources, and she receives mostly five-star ratings on likability.

Now, a lot of the old cupid supervisors? They give her some poor feedback, but everyone knows it's because they don't appreciate her changes to all of cupidity—like giving us chances to become corporeal and have potluck parties. But myself and the rest of the cupids who are actually in the field know better. Emelle has made being a cupid so much more enjoyable. It's not a lonely, dead existence anymore. It's a true after*life*.

"Shifters are tough," Mac says, pulling me out of my thoughts as he tucks away his arrow. "I think I only got two matches."

He got one. And it wasn't even that good. Respectfully.

"Actually, shifters are one of the easiest pairs to make since their pheromones do half the work," I tell him.

He's not listening to my reply though. He's too excited about leaving and is practically bouncing on his heels. It's the most enthusiasm I've ever seen from him. Granted, he's only been my partner for a few weeks, but still.

"Ready?" he asks.

No. "Yes, of course."

We both let our fingers pass through our cupid marks, and within moments, they glow pink, and then we're yanked from this realm, through time and space, and pulled back into Cupidville.

Yay.

Landing in headquarters has changed too. We're no longer incorporeal or subjected to reprimands and an anxiety-inducing waiting room. Nowadays, when cupids get yanked, it's usually straight to parties or award ceremonies, and we always get our physical bodies upon landing. It's just one of the cupid perks Emelle has enacted over the years.

I'd be as excited as the rest of them if I didn't completely dread these get-togethers. Mac was right. I'm not a party sort of cupid. Maybe it's my workaholic attitude...or maybe it's the unrelenting guilt I feel every single day.

Because I still exist.

Me. A mild, goal-oriented, naïve cupid still exists, all because a male I barely knew jumped in front of a killing blow and saved me.

It's hard to party when you're riddled with guilt.

Mac and I land in an empty room, smack dab in front of a pink archway that seems to serve no purpose, considering it's not holding up any walls, and there's nothing on the other side. But cupids are bottlenecking through it in a constant stream, disappearing as soon as they go through it.

All around us, more cupids are appearing, materializing from whatever realm they were working in. All of them give some sort of cursory touch to their bodies—scraping hands through hair, fingers grazing over their cheeks and running up and down their arms as they readjust to having physical forms.

Beside me, Mac grins, his fangs on full display as he too gets used to having a body that can feel and touch again.

I quirk my head at him. "Can you still..."

He catches me eyeing his teeth. "Drink blood?" he asks, chucking his tongue to the side, the tip running over the sharp end of his fang.

I jerk my eyes back to his face. "Yeah, that."

"Tried it," he says with a shrug. "But cupids taste like cupcakes. Gives me a stomach ache."

"Ah."

Mac's attention lands on a pair of female cupids that pop into existence beside us, both of them winking at him in tandem. His grin returns. "Have fun," he tosses over his shoulder at me, already striding away.

I blow out a breath as I'm left behind. "Yeah. Fun."

Slinging his arms around the pair of cupids, he goes through the archway and disappears with all the rest. Cupids bump into me from behind, trying to get through the archway too, so rather than be trampled, I follow the red-winged herd.

As soon as I pass through, some magic snags me and then I'm thrust into the party. Instantly, I'm assaulted with a blast of music, shiny smoke, and obnoxious flashing lights. I shuffle off to the side before I get shoved by the throng of cupids joining the dance floor, and I find a wall to plant myself on.

"This is a potluck?" I say dubiously, because it looks more like a rave. My eyes skim the massive space, but it's hard to see with how dark it is, considering the only light sources are the spotlights and pink glow sticks hanging around some of the cupids' necks. "Hmm. I don't see a single casserole dish."

"Not that kind of fooking potluck, luv."

I turn at the accented voice to find Sev standing next to me, looking happy as a clam. Well. If a clam was a very beautiful cupid, wearing seven neon glow sticks and incredibly tight leather pants.

"What kind of potluck is it then?" I ask him.

He points ahead where there's a stage lit up with red

and pink spotlights, shining on a group of lady lucks who are dancing in very provocative bustiers while tossing out lucky pennies to the cupid crowd dancing below.

Oh. Luck.

"And the pot?" I ask.

Sev jerks his chin to the right, and I follow his gaze to the large lounge area filled with cupids passing around pipes and bongs. That explains the copious amount of smoke in here.

"I'm guessing that's marijuana?"

Sev smiles broadly. "A new strain made just for this party. Cupid Kush. It's pink and the smoke *glitters*."

He looks very proud of himself.

"You planned this potluck, didn't you?" I hazard to guess.

Sev grins, making his whole face even more beautiful. "What gave it away?"

"All of it, honestly."

Now he looks even prouder. Puffs his chest out and everything.

A server walks by—another lady luck—and he swipes two red cocktails from her tray, shooting her a wink before she trots off. He starts to pass one to me, but I shake my head. "No, thank you."

Sev just shrugs and then tosses the whole drink back before chucking the cup in a garbage can a few feet away. Taking more time with the second drink, his thick lips close around the striped straw. He takes sips while simultaneously stirring it with the heart lollipop sticking out to get the pink cotton candy to dissolve.

"Didn't expect you to come."

I don't want to say that I wouldn't have if it weren't for Mac. I don't want to hurt Sev's feelings.

"You look too tense, Lex," he tells me, frowning at the flats on my feet and the tight bun in my hair. "This is a party. Go on over to the pot part of this and maybe get lucky, yeah?" he says, wagging his brows.

I flinch at the horrifying thought.

"No, thank you. I'll just...watch."

An incredibly dramatic eye roll is what I get in reply.

"What?" I ask somewhat defensively.

Sev drinks the rest of his cocktail, dissolving cotton candy and all. "Listen, luv. The big boss and I are glad you're back to work. Doing your perfectionism shite."

"I'm not a perf—"

He slams his hand over my mouth, and I go perfectly frozen. "That's better," he says with a smirk. "Now, as I was saying. You're back to being Miss Perfect Cupid of the Month after your depressive episode."

I try to say that I didn't have a depressive episode, but all that comes out are muffled words trapped by his hand that smells like marijuana and cotton candy.

"You're committed to hitting these personal goals of yours, but you've gone through over twenty fooking cupid partners. All of them asking for a transfer. It's a problem, get it?"

I immediately start to defend myself but have to start over again when Sev deigns to lower his hand. With a smirk, I might add. "It's not my fault those other cupids aren't excited to spread love and desire," I tell him, my voice pitching louder so he can hear me over the music. "I just work better on my own."

Sev leans down so we're eye to eye. "Lex, luv, *no one* is as excited to spread love and desire as you."

Excited isn't quite the right word, but I don't want to tell him otherwise. He's already called me *depressive*. No need to make it worse. "Well...Mac has been with me for a bit now, and everything is fine," I say as I self-consciously adjust the strap where my bow and quiver hang on my back.

He arches a black brow. "Really? Cuz Mac told me he wanted to be partnered up with a different cupid."

Already?

My lips purse together like they've been done up with a button. What a rude ex-vampire.

Sev runs his hands through his thick pink hair and gives me a pitying look. "Don't worry about it, yeah? I'll get you someone new. Again."

"No," I say, shaking my head. "I'm going through cupids like hotcakes. No more partners."

Something perky and hopeful flashes through his expression. "You mean you're finally ready to take back your supervisory role, and I can step down?"

I shake my head. "No." The thought of not being on the field makes a cold sweat break out over my skin. "I need my goals. I need to be out there spreading love."

The way Sev's shoulders sag dejectedly nearly makes me smile. "Oh, don't pretend you hate it so much," I tell him. "We both know you enjoy all the perks you've had over the years."

He doesn't even try to deny it. "True. I have to admit, I like bossing these fooking wankers around. And the sex—I like that. Having a physical body all day every day is a big plus, get it?"

"Oh, I've got it." I've walked in on him more than once in some very compromised positions with a large number of participants. I don't think my eyes will ever recover.

A wistful yet wicked smile takes over his face, highlighted by the disco lights flashing from the dark ceiling. He looks like he's remembering every sexual escapade he's ever had since being promoted.

While he reminisces, I look around and shift on my feet, noting that a lot of cupids seem to be taking advantage of a back room. Based on the wafts of Lust Breath billowing from the doorway, it's quite clear what's going on in there. Actually, some of them aren't even bothering to go into the back room, and I feel a blush heat my face.

Sev follows my gaze before I can avert it, and laughs. "Luv, you're a *cupid*. You're not only a built-in voyeur, but you've caused people to get it on and shag their brains out, yet you're blushing at a little debauchery?"

"I wouldn't call that orgy *little*."

He shrugs, as if he's going to agree to disagree.

"Right then," Sev says, clearing his throat as the music takes on a faster beat and residual Lust mixes with the glitter smoke in the air. He levels me with a surprisingly soft look that he doesn't often show. "What are you gonna do? Because this…I don't think you're happy, luv. The boss and I, we just want you happy."

My throat goes dry and tight, and I have the sudden urge to cry, which is ridiculous. Cupids of the Month don't cry. But…he's right. I'm not happy, and all I'm doing is making up one goal after another. Not because I actually *like* the goals anymore, but because I need the distraction.

My eyes flick around nervously, feeling so out of place

in this loud, smoky place. "Maybe...maybe I should go back."

His eyes widen in shock, and then he leans in. "Are you sure about that?"

I nod slowly, even as dread collects in my stomach. "Yes. I should've gone back a long time ago."

"You sure you're ready for that?"

No.

"It needs to be done," I say, which isn't really an answer. "I need to go back to the fae realm and speak to Emelle face-to-face."

The declaration feels like a bucket of rocks being dumped in my stomach. I've been actively avoiding going back there because I haven't been able to face it. I have no idea how to come to terms with my survivor's guilt or my subsequent avoidance of Emelle. But I don't think I can avoid it any longer.

A look of pity flashes over his face, though I pretend not to see it. The next second, it's gone, replaced with a shrug. "Alright, luv. Whatever you wanna do. Not like you *need* a partner to make your quotas. Just...don't get all sad and shite, alright? And don't do anything I wouldn't do."

That last bit makes me laugh. "Sev, you do *everything*."

His teeth flash in a dazzling smile. "That's right, that. Speaking of..." He shoves his empty glass in my hands before licking his lips, eyes latched onto the dance floor. "It's time for me to go find someone to *do* at this glorious potluck. See you later, luv." With a pat on my shoulder, he starts walking off, but then he stops and says, "Oh, and for the love of all the hairy cupid arses, go enjoy yourself for once. Pot and luck. It's all you need for a good time!"

I watch him sidle himself onto the dance floor, a cupid

cheer rising up when all our red-winged peers see it's him. Sev is *very* popular. Unlike—

"Hey, could you...move?"

My head snaps toward the voice, noticing a group of cupids with mini bows and arrows in their hands. I frown, eyes flashing up to the male cupid and his friends as they all stare at me expectantly. "You're in the way of the dart board."

I whirl around to look over my shoulder on the wall I've perched on, and sure enough, there's a huge dart board in the shape of a heart.

"Oh, yes. Sorry."

Shuffling out of the way, still awkwardly holding Sev's empty cocktail glass, I make sure to move before I get shot with a fake Love Arrow. The group immediately claps when the big burly male who so kindly told me to move aims his tiny arrow and hits the heart on the top curve.

"I would've gotten a bullseye," I say to myself with a sniff.

If I were Sev, they'd have probably asked if I wanted to play with them. But I'm...me. Lex. Miss Goodie-Two-Wings. Obsessed with Love Matches and hitting quotas. Every cupid here thinks I'm nothing but a rule-following workaholic, and they're right.

I have no friends, no ability to *let loose*. I'm not the fun person anyone seeks out at a party. I'm a loner, and that's the way I prefer it. It makes me more efficient. At least, that's what I tell myself.

With a frown, I turn and stride for the archway to leave, setting down the glass on a passing server's tray as I go. If I hurry, I can probably make it back to the shifters in time to hit my mate match goal first. Just to give myself a confidence boost.

Yep, I'll go make some matches, and then I'll drag myself back to the fae realm, and I'll finally face Emelle.

It's far past overdue.

CHAPTER 7

LEX

*T*he fae realm.

Floating islands, glittering night skies, magic, and so many different types of fae that there's no shortage of new people and cultures to experience. There's also no shortage of opportunities to spread love.

But that's not why I'm here. Not this time, anyway.

Taking stock of the place I've popped onto—*Cupid of the Month perks really are handy*—I glance around the town square of the genfin island.

It's nighttime here, but it must not be too late, based on how lively the streets are. The last time I saw this place, it was still being rebuilt after the sneak attack ordered by the late King Beluar. Now, you'd never be able to tell that the domed buildings once lay in ruins or that genfin bodies once lined the streets.

I shove away the morbid memories and instead enjoy watching the townspeople. Their genfin tails remind me of lions, and the mated males have their fur wings out on display proudly. Their ears are pointed like every other fae, but the genfins move with a feline grace. Every single shop and inn has their doors wide open to the lantern-lit street, and the people are mingling about, going in and out, their voices loud with friendly merriment.

There are far more male than female genfins, but I smile softly at how the male coveys dote on their mates. They have to earn their mates, and it shows in the way they walk protectively around them, or make sure their females are carrying nothing, or feed them from their fingers inside the restaurants.

Yet my smile is tilted with sadness. It's a slant of emotion that always seems to be hanging along my edges lately. It seems unfair that a smile, the very gesture we make to show happiness on the outside, can instead expose the truth on the inside.

Turning away, I choose to stay invisible inside the Veil as I begin to make my way down the road. A cupid appearing in the middle of the square would only draw attention, and that's one thing I don't want.

I used to enjoy attention, or perhaps *recognition*. It was part of why I always worked so hard to be the very best cupid. I liked to excel at my job, to be heralded as a model cupid who exceeded expectations in every category. I liked winning Cupid of the Month and earning my pat on the back.

But now, I work hard because everything else in my afterlife is hardly working. I have nothing *except* for my work. Plus, if I'm always hyper-focused on my job, there's no room in my head to think about anything else.

At least, that's the feeble theory.

I soon walk out of the square, the sounds fading behind me as I choose a quiet grassy path that leads to the genfins' homes. Each one is made of smooth domed wood and usually nestled into the hillsides, and I see a few wooden toys scattered around the grass just inside the fence.

It isn't until I make it all the way to Emelle's front door that I realize I probably should've warned her I was coming. It's not very polite to just...show up.

Hesitating, I almost turn back until I hear muffled voices from the other side. I can't use the excuse that they might be sleeping, and I know that if I leave now, it'll probably take another year for me to muster up the courage to come back. I've avoided Emelle for long enough. And considering time is finicky between realms and the Veil, I don't even know how much of it has passed.

When I hear children laughing, I finally force myself to pop out of the Veil. I take in a deep breath, needing the fresh pull of oxygen in my lungs before I raise my hand and knock. My knuckles rap against the wood in three quick jabs, and then I quickly smooth my skirt and blazer before nervously running a hand over my pulled-tight hair.

The voices quiet for a moment, but then the door jerks open, and one of my boss's mates is there to greet me, brown eyes crinkled with friendliness.

I give a smile. "Good evening, Sylred."

The pink-haired genfin blinks at me in surprise. "Lex? Is that really you?"

I shift on my feet. "Yes, I know this is unexpected, and

I'm sorry to intrude, but I was wondering if I could speak with Emelle?"

He seems at a loss for words for a second before he quickly jerks the door all the way open. "Of course. Come on in. We were just finishing up dinner."

"Thank you."

Unable to help myself from wringing my hands, I walk down the steps of their home, and Sylred leads me straight into the dining and kitchen area. One sweep of my eyes shows me a busy, bursting-at-the-seams space.

The kitchen area is a bit messy from whatever meal they cooked. The tails of fresh veggies are left on the countertop, and flour is powdered along the sink, but whatever they ate smells delicious—like spiced meat and warm bread. The dining table is stuffed with nearly empty plates, while Emelle, her mates, and children all sit crammed together around it.

My gaze lands on Emelle immediately, but her back is to me as she wrestles with a little girl in a wooden high chair while she tries to clean the girl's face.

As soon as I step through the threshold, all three of Emelle's remaining mates immediately look over at me. Stopping, I blush beneath their attention, while they start to dart furtive looks at my boss.

Luckily, their attention gets diverted when a little boy in another wooden high chair decides it's a good time to chuck a fistful of green goop from his tray. It lands with a splat on Okot's shirt, making Evert and Ronak snicker. But the lamassu fae just smiles lovingly at the boy as he wipes himself off.

Dinnertime seems to be quite hectic here.

"Syl, who was at the door?" Emelle asks, jerking my attention back to her.

"Well..." Syl says from beside me.

His hesitancy makes Emelle turn, and when she does, her prism eyes widen and she goes still, rag forgotten in her hand. "*Lex?*"

I give her a silly wave. "Hello, Madame Cupid."

One second, she's sitting down at the table, and the next, she's launched herself at me, pulling me into a hug. "Oh my gods! I can't believe you're here!"

The strength of her embrace nearly chokes the air right out of me, but I manage to pat her on the back. "I'm here," I squawk.

"Oh, sorry," she says, releasing me from her chokehold to instead grip my arms and lean back to get a look at me. Her beautiful face lights up into a smile, and my eyes nearly go misty. "You look just the same. Sexy librarian schoolteacher kind of thing."

My blush comes back full force.

"We'll clean up dinner," Sylred offers as he walks over to the sink.

Emelle tosses him a smile. "You're earning lots of points right now."

"Suck up," Evert chimes in, just as all four of the males begin to scoop up the kids.

"Yeah," Sylred says, "Which means she sucks my—"

"Are you hungry?" Emelle blurts loudly, cutting him off. "Thirsty? Need a bathroom break?"

I shake my head. "I'm alright, thank you."

With a nod, Emelle takes my arm and pulls me into the living area. "Come in and relax. I want to hear everything. We have so much to catch up on."

Both of us have to step over a few wooden blocks and sewn dolls as we make our way to the couch. "Excuse the mess," she tells me. "I'd make up some excuse about it not normally looking like this, but...we have four kids. It would be a lie."

I sink down onto the cushions next to her and fold my hands into my lap, wings resting down.

Emelle is still smiling as she looks at me, and not an ounce of judgment or bitterness enters her expression. I don't know why. If I were her, I'd definitely be judging me.

As if she can sense this dip in self-confidence, she reaches over and squeezes my hand. "I want you to know that I'm super glad you're here. I've missed you."

Guilt fills my stomach, making it ache. "I'm sorry for neglecting my assistant duties for so long."

She waves me off. "Oh, I don't care about that. Sev and the others have been doing just fine in my stead."

"You still can't go into the Veil or Cupidville?"

"Nope. Ronak goes full feral if I do, like I've died or something," she tells me with a roll of her eyes. "So dramatic."

"I heard that," Ronak growls from the kitchen.

Emelle shoots me a wink and laughs under her breath. "But anyway, it's fine. Sev calls me if he needs something."

"Calls you?"

To demonstrate, she lifts up her arm where her cupid boss markings are just below her number. "I light up like a neon sign whenever he needs something, and then I know a visit is impending."

"I suppose it's good to have a warning before Sev comes."

She snorts. "Tell me about it. We have to hide him from the kids now because they think it's hilarious to say *fooking*."

In the other room, all three children start chanting, "Fooking! Fooking! Fooking!"

"Emelle!" Sylred groans.

She winces. "Whoopsie."

Just then, three kids come racing into the room. I say racing because they do just that—they race so competitively that one of the girls takes out the boy by purposely pushing him, while the other girl tries to kick a toy block at them. The boy retaliates by suddenly shifting into a tiny black bull with red wings sprouted from his back. Who would've thought a half-cupid half-bull fae would be so darn cute?

"Aww," I croon.

But I've *aww*ed too soon, because he suddenly drops his head, scratches his front hoof on the rug, and then starts charging at the girls as fast as his short legs can go. Both girls let out high-pitched squeals, part terror and part laughter as they turn and race for the hallway.

Before the little bull boy can collide horns-first into his retreating sisters, Emelle plucks him up and then holds his face in front of hers. "Arrow, it's not nice to shift and then charge at people, remember? We've talked about this."

The little bull slumps with a grunt and then nuzzles at her neck in what I'm guessing is his bull apology.

"Good boy," she says, peppering a kiss on his snout. "Now go play nice with Kalila and Ettie."

He clops away as soon as she sets him back on the floor, picking up a block in his mouth as he goes.

"Can he fly?" I ask curiously.

Emelle shakes her head. "Not yet—though it's not for a lack of trying. His wings are too underdeveloped for the size of his lamassu body, but Okot says that will change once he hits puberty."

"You're going to have a lot on your plate."

She lets out a laugh. "Tell me about it. Amorette can already fly. Her daddies have been teaching her for a couple of years now, and she gets better every day."

"Which one was she?"

"Oh, you haven't seen her yet. Amorette is sleeping over at my friend Mossie's house. She's been talking about having ghost nightmares here. But I'm pretty sure it's just so she can go to Mossie's, since she lets Amorette have entirely too much sugar," she tells me before waving her hand in the direction of the hallway. "You've just seen the triplets. Two lamassus and one genfin."

I blink in surprise. "Wait..."

"Yep," Emelle says, popping the *p*. "My super amazing genfin mates knocked me up *while I was already knocked up*. Isn't that freaking rude? I can't even begin to tell you what it did to my cherish channel, if you know what I mean."

I hear a chorus of male groans.

"I swear she calls it something different every time," Ronak grumbles.

"When are you going to forgive us for that, Scratch?" Evert calls out, just as he and the other three males saunter into the room.

She arches a brow at them. "Oh, I've forgiven you. I'm just not going to ever stop talking about it. Because you made me give birth *three times in a row*."

They have the good sense to wince.

Okot looks at me, his red mohawk nearly identical to his son's. "We left a plate of food for you in case you are hungry."

"Oh, thank you," I reply, surprised at their thoughtfulness. I always forget to eat when I'm in this physical form, especially when I've been staying in the Veil so often lately.

"We'll get the kids washed up and ready for bed," Sylred tells Emelle, and then all four of them turn and disappear down the hall, giving us privacy.

Emelle watches them go, tucking her long pink hair behind her ear before she turns back to me.

She opens her mouth to say something, but I cut in. "Tell me all about them," I urge. Yes, I'm stalling, but I'm also relishing in the love I can feel inside these walls. It's so prevalent that it makes my heart ache.

As if just the mere thought of her children fills her with unimaginable joy, Emelle smiles again before leaning back on the couch to get more comfortable. "Well, Amorette was our first, but she's five years old now."

My brows lift in surprise. "Five years?"

How long was I gone?

As if she can read my mind, Emelle gives me a knowing look before continuing. "It's been six years since the battle," she says gently, and I sit back breathlessly, reeling in the information. Sure, I checked in with Sev every time I went to Cupidville, and I was admittedly avoiding things, but *six years?* I am the *worst* Cupid of the Month.

"As for the triplets, they're three," Emelle goes on, like she's trying to soften the blow by distracting me. "Arrow is the only one who can shift into a bull like Okot. We aren't sure if Ettie ever will. So far, the only làmassu thing about her is her red-rimmed irises." She pauses at that. "Well, that, plus the fact that she's ridiculously stubborn and can act downright beastly when she's tired. Okot is great with her, though."

"And the genfin girl?"

"Kalila is a sweetheart. Hardly ever makes a fuss except when her sister yanks on her tail."

I let out a laugh, but then my previous guilt shoves its way forward again, making me shift in my seat. "You have a beautiful family."

She beams. "We're an odd, loud, crazy, very messy covey, but...they're the best thing that's ever happened to me."

Eyes dropping, I watch my fingers twist together in my lap. "I'm sorry."

The words tumble out of me all wrinkled and stretched, like clothes shoved aside and neglected for far too long. It's time I hang them out. "I'm sorry I ran away and avoided you. Especially since you've had your hands full here, and my absence probably made things harder when you've had so much on your plate as a mate and a mother. You should've been able to simply enjoy your family. I should've done my cupid duties and been around to help you."

My throat tries to close up, but I know I have to get the rest out now, or I'll jumble it all up and lose the pitiful courage I have. Emelle stays perfectly quiet and still, like she doesn't want to spook me, and I'm grateful for that, because to be honest, I'm feeling timider than a startled deer.

Taking a deep breath, I say, "The truth is, I ran away from it all because I couldn't face you. I couldn't face anyone who was there with us on that field that day. He..." This time, my throat really does tighten, strangling on that one word. *He.* The *he* that has consumed my guilty thoughts and tangled feelings since that fateful day. He told me to stay in the Veil, but I didn't. I didn't, and I got him killed.

Finally, I lift my eyes to hers. "He died for me. He took the blast that was meant for me, and I never understood why."

"No?" she asks, cocking her head.

Mine shakes in response. "No. I mean, why would he do that? Why jump in front of me like that? He *died* for goodness sake."

Her eyes flash with sadness, her lips tilting down. "I know."

"But why? Why me? We barely knew each other."

After all this time, I've finally let out the question that's been haunting me. Since I knelt over Belren's dead body and wept my eyes out. Why would he die for *me*?

It doesn't make any sense.

"I can't answer that," Emelle says, and I feel my shoulders slump. "But I can say that Belren never did anything he didn't want to."

That doesn't make me feel better. "I still shouldn't have avoided you or my responsibilities."

"I understand why you did," she replies softly. "You don't have to feel guilty, Lex. Things have been going just fine. And according to Sev, you've been crushing the quotas again."

"Yes," I say simply.

Once more, Emelle reaches over to squeeze my hand. "Never apologize for needing a break or for taking the time for yourself to heal."

How do I tell her that I haven't healed? That I'm still one giant injury that refuses to mend? How do I explain that even *that* makes me feel guilty, because who am I to complain? I'm alive because of him.

With a soft squeeze, she releases me before getting to her feet. "You look tired. Why don't you go eat the plate they left while I make up a bed for you? Ronak and Evert built another add-on downstairs to expand the house. We use it as a guest suite when any of the in-laws visit or when Mossie gets drunk off agave during the celebratory sowing season."

"Oh, no, you really don't have to go to any trouble. I was going to return to the Veil after I spoke to you."

She frowns. "No, you just got here. Stay the night at least."

"Well…" I waver. "If you're sure it's not too much trouble…"

"Of course not." Emelle jumps to her feet. "I'll go make the bed. You eat and then head downstairs and rest. Oh, and you might want to get an early bedtime."

"Why?" I ask curiously as she starts heading down the hall. Not that I'm a late sleeper.

She tosses a look at me over her shoulder. "You think these kids are cute tonight, but you won't when they're up before the sun and wake you when they start screaming like banshees for their oatmeal. Trust me. Try to go to bed early so you hate life a little bit less. Try as I may, I still haven't found their volume buttons."

I laugh as she disappears to the end of the hall, passing the bathroom where playful shrieks and splashing sounds are currently emanating. My stomach takes that moment to grumble, so I quietly head to the kitchen, finding the plate they left for me on the now clean and empty table.

After I finish eating, I wash up after myself and then search the hallway until I find a set of steps that lead downstairs, where I then find the guest bedroom. It's nice and simple, with a bed made up with cream linens and fluffy pillows, and a nightstand made of the same wood that's curving over the ceiling and polished on the floors.

A soft shard of moonlight is spilling in from the half-circle window high on the wall, and the reminder of night makes a yawn crack my jaw. I didn't realize until now how tired I am. I'm actually looking forward to sleep. It's one of the things I miss dearly when I'm in the Veil and have no need of it. Sleep—the restful oblivion of it—is a wonderful escape. One I have every intention of relishing tonight.

After closing the door behind me, I remove my bow and quiver from my back and lean them both against the wall. I take off my blazer, blouse and skirt next, carefully draping them over the small dresser next to me so they don't wrinkle.

In only my skirt slip and thin undershirt, I climb into bed and lie on my side, wings tucked in tight as I let out a sigh. I did it. I came back.

I finally faced Emelle, finally spoke about him. But… why don't I feel any better?

Tears prick my eyes, and I loosen the shroud of guilt that's been covering me, letting it peek out for just a moment. Maybe it wasn't enough to just come here. But I think a part of me knew it wouldn't be.

My entire afterlife changed the moment a thief stepped in front of me. It's time I figure out how to put him behind me.

CHAPTER 8

LEX

The sudden weight of something on top of me yanks me from sleep. Blearily, I open my eyes to the morning light and find that it isn't a pillow or blankets that have piled up on me. No, there's a small, aggressive person straddling my stomach and pointing an arrow at my face.

It's not the best wake-up call I've ever had.

Though, it's also not the worst...

The little person has pink ringlets hanging in tangled ropes around her shoulders, red wings flared on either side of her, and multi-colored eyes just like her mom. She's also older than the triplets I saw last night, which means...

"Umm...Amorette?"

The fierce looking girl narrows her eyes, and the Love Arrow she's clutching in her hand presses into my cheek. Not hard enough to hurt, but I wince anyway. "Are those my arrows?" I ask.

"Who are you?" she replies, looking very suspicious.

"I'm Lex. Your mom's friend."

The suspicion on her face only grows. "My mommy doesn't have any friends. Well...except Mossie. And I just came from her house, so you're not her."

"Well, I'm actually more of her assistant?"

"That's Sev."

That's...that's true. I feel like I'm losing here.

My gaze flicks to the side where the arrow is still perched against my face. "You really shouldn't play with weapons."

The girl makes a noise of disgust. "I'm not *playing*. And anyway, I bet I'm better with weapons than *you*. You sure you know how to shoot?" she asks, eyeing me dubiously.

My mouth drops open in offense. "Excuse me, young lady, but I'll have you know that I've won the short-range *and* long-range shooting competitions in all of cupidity multiple times."

Amorette snorts and says something under her breath. I can't be sure, but I think it might've been *yeah, right*. She jumps off the bed and lands nimbly on her feet, and I have to admit, she seems like she has a lot of muscles in her arms for a five-year-old.

Not wanting to miss my chance before she shoves another weapon into my face, I quickly yank back the covers and get up from bed. Amorette watches me with an arched brow as I pull on my clothes from last night, though I leave off the blazer. Slipping my feet into my flats, I take in her fitted trousers and long shirt that's tied at the back, allowing her wings plenty of room.

"Do you often point weapons threateningly at strangers?"

She looks at me like I'm an idiot. "Of course I do. Don't you?"

"Of course not!" I quickly say.

"Oh really?" she asks before she reaches behind her to *my* quiver and bow that's now strapped to *her* back. "You don't shoot these at strangers?"

My open mouth quickly clamps shut. "I do it to spread love," I argue.

She rolls her eyes. "Well, I do it to spread violence. My way is better."

I laugh, but when she doesn't join in on the joke, I realize she's serious. My laughter dies away *very* quickly.

Luckily, I'm saved by a knock at the door, and I practically pounce on it, yanking it open.

"Good morning!" Emelle chirps at me before her eyes land on her daughter. "Amorette? What are you doing in here?"

The girl points at me. "Did you know that this person came into our home with *weapons*?" she accuses, crossing her little arms in front of her. "You're lucky I came in here and took them."

Emelle lets out a sigh. "This *person* is Lex, and she's a cupid. Which you know, because she has the same pink hair and red wings as you. And those aren't weapons, they're just Love Arrows."

Amorette doesn't look placated. "Love Arrows are probably worse. If someone Love Arrowed a stupid boy and he tried to kiss me, I'd stab him for sure."

"Gods, it's too early for this," Emelle mumbles to herself before straightening up. "Right. Apologize to Lex for sneaking into her room and probably threatening to stab her."

I feel like this might have happened before.

"Sorry," Amorette mutters before she flicks her attention to her mom. "Can I go?"

"Yes. Go have breakfast. *After* you give Lex her stuff back."

Amorette's bottom lip puckers out in a pout, but she grudgingly hands me my bow and quiver back before she quickly turns and takes off down the hall.

"You've got your hands full," I say with a smile.

"*So* freaking full," Emelle replies. "Believe it or not, this scenario has happened a time or two before."

"You don't say," I reply dryly.

The two of us make our way up the stairs and down the hall, to where breakfast is in full swing. If I thought things were boisterous last night, it's nothing compared to now. Okot is plopping down what looks like pancakes on everyone's plates, while Evert is arguing with Arrow about eating his applesauce. Ronak has Amorette on his lap, and they're both cutting their ham with actual daggers, while Ettie wails about not having a bigger pancake than her sister Kalila.

Madness. It's madness. And quite loud.

"Here you go, Lex," Sylred says, plunking down a chair for me before pulling out another for his mate. "Good morning, mate."

She pecks a kiss on his lips. "Always the nice one."

"I was *very* nice last night," he replies, making her cheeks go pink as she shoots him a smile.

Looking away from their private moment, I'm glad for Okot's timing when he flips a pancake onto my empty plate. "Thank you."

For the duration of breakfast, I enjoy just watching

them all. There's absolutely nothing orderly about them, but they're endearing, and funny, and *real*. No pretenses, no awkwardness. There's nothing but resounding love in this house, and for an overachieving cupid, it makes me both incredibly happy and inconceivably sad.

I'll never have this.

That quiet thought tries to wriggle in like a worm and burrow down deep, but I sniff it away. Stay busy. I just need to stay busy.

"So, I was thinking, if it's alright with you, I'd like to fly to some of the neighboring islands and work."

Emelle looks over, fork poised in front of her mouth. "You want to work here?"

My brows draw together. "Of course," I say, confused by her hesitancy. "But if you'd rather me help out with some assistant work, I can do that instead."

"That's not what I meant. If you want to work, you *can*, but I thought you'd enjoy a break."

A break? Where I would do nothing? Where I'd be without any distraction or goals? That sounds awful.

"No," I answer quickly. Probably *too* quickly, based on the way her eyebrows lift. "I mean, I like staying busy."

She searches my face for a moment. "Okay. Whatever you want to do. Honestly, I meant what I said last night. Everything's been fine. You don't need to feel bad about doing your own thing for the last few years. It wouldn't matter to me if you never wanted to do any kind of assistant work or cupid work or anything ever again. It's your life, Lex." She pauses with a tilt of her head. "Well. Your *afterlife*. Cupid life? You know what I mean."

I smile. "I'm happiest when I'm working."

Happi*est*. Not *happy*. Key distinction.

"I understand," Emelle replies, and the way she looks at me makes me think that she truly does. "I mean, not from *personal* experience," she adds. "I got really tired of the whole cupid thing." She wrinkles her nose. "Probably not awesome, considering I'm in charge of the whole thing."

"But you've made things better for all cupids everywhere. So really, it's a good thing that you didn't particularly...excel when you worked on the front lines," I supply helpfully.

She pats me on the shoulder. "This is why you're my favorite."

~

*A*fter breakfast, I clean up in the bathroom, and even though Emelle offers to let me borrow her clothes, I decline. She's given me enough already.

"You sure you don't want to stay here a bit longer?" Emelle asks as she walks me outside.

Stepping into the front garden, I breathe in the fresh air and sunshine. "I'm sure. Besides, if I do, your daughter might stab me."

She bobs her head back and forth. "True. I'd better put you on the no-stab list."

My eyebrows jump up. "There's a list?"

A long-suffering sigh escapes her. "She *must* be Ronak's biological daughter. It's the only explanation."

I think of the glaring, hulking genfin and nod. "That...would make sense."

"So, what's your personal goal this time?" Emelle asks. "Shooting five hundred Love Arrows? Blowing enough Lust Breath to fuel an entire fae city's fertility festival?"

I fidget, not quite meeting her eyes. "Something like that."

Her eyes narrow, and for a second, I swear her wings flare with a bit of light. "Did you know that when I went in and out of the Veil before I was a boss, I got all messed up and accidentally took on some of the other entities' powers?"

"Yes…"

In a blink, her feathered wings pop out, but unlike every other cupid, they aren't solid red. Instead, some of the feathers fade into black and white. She taps at one of the white-edged ones. "That includes angel powers. Which means I know when someone's lying."

My heart pounds in my chest, but I keep my face impassive, even though I start to feel all sweaty. "Oh? That's probably handy with four kids."

"It really is. It's gonna be awesome when they're teenagers."

We stare at each other for a beat, but Emelle doesn't relent. "So are you gonna tell me why you're lying?"

My hands wring together. "Well, I hadn't planned on it."

It's not even something I've fully thought out yet, and I'm a planner. But last night while I was lying in bed, I knew that my journey here to the fae realm had to include more than just me facing Emelle again.

I have to face the thief who's haunting me.

But I'm not ready to tell her that, so I stay quiet.

"Fine," she says with a sigh. "Keep your secrets. But before you go, I just wanted to talk to you about something you said last night. About not knowing why Belren died for you."

Nervousness has me shuffling my feet. "Yes…"

Her gentle hand goes to my shoulder. "He jumped in front of you that day to protect you—it was as simple as that," she tells me, making me meet her eyes again. "Belren was…impulsive. But he also knew his own mind. He knew you were worth saving, Lex. And I hope you know that too."

Emotion gets stuck in my throat like a clogged drain, and I'm unable to swallow it down, unable to even reply.

As if she can sense my struggle, she squeezes my shoulder before dropping it.

Just as she opens her mouth to say something else, all four kids come tearing out of the house, giggling like mad. Arrow shifts into his bull form the second he hits the grass. Their squeals and shrieks are loud enough to hurt my ears as they dash away, with a discombobulated Evert following, though he trips on his way up the stairs that lead from his sunken front door.

"Hey! I said you have to brush your teeth first!"

"Keep running!" Amorette war cries to the other kids, leading the way. "Never surrender!"

"Wow," I say through a whistle. "They're really fast."

Emelle lets out a sigh as we watch them race past the garden gate toward the grassy hill beyond. "Yep."

"Little help?" Evert calls as he races after them.

She wrinkles her nose and makes no move to follow. "You know how I feel about running!"

He shoots her a look over his shoulder. "You have wings!"

"Oh. Right." She turns to look at me. "I'd better go help him, or he'll get all grumpy."

"I don't get fucking grumpy!" Evert shouts back, though he's already out of sight.

Emelle snickers before turning to look at me. "You'll be okay?"

I'd say there's a sixty-forty chance.

"Of course," I tell her brightly.

She comes close and yanks me into a quick hug. "Don't disappear for several years again, okay?"

I'm the worst Cupid of the Month ever.

"I won't," I promise before lifting my arm to show my cupid number. "Call me if you need me."

She presses a finger to her cupid boss mark, which makes my own number light up in a flare of red that matches my wings' feathers, letting me know I'm being summoned. "Oooh, red!" she exclaims. "I've never seen what it actually looks like on your end. Good to know it works—and it's bright. No wonder Sev can't ignore it even when he's hungover. These are super-efficient."

I laugh as I imagine a grumbling Sev being blinded by its red, peppy glare.

"See you soon," Emelle tells me, though it sounds a bit like an order too.

With a grin, I readjust the bow and quiver at my back. I'm *definitely* short a Love Arrow, and I have a sneaking suspicion I know which cupid-genfin has it. Not that I'm going to rat Amorette out. She's far too keen on violence.

As soon as I pop into the Veil, going invisible once again, Emelle turns in the direction of her kids and mate, and I take flight into the sky. I see Evert being tackled by

97

all four little ones, and a smile tips my cheeks before I turn and fly away.

Once I'm far above the island, all of the lightness and contagious love I felt being around Emelle and her family starts to fade. Loneliness doesn't take long to settle in. It's always creeping behind me just waiting for me to stop, and when I do, it's right back at my side again.

My expression goes grim as I set my sights on where I need to go, and even though all I want to do is turn back around and take Emelle up on her offer for me to stay, I won't. Not yet.

I need to go back to where it all happened—to visit the one place I never had the courage to go.

The place where Belren died for me.

CHAPTER 9

LEX

For all my skills, sense of direction isn't one of them.

I'm very good at blowing the perfect amount of Lust Breath. I have a ninety-eight percent accuracy when letting loose a Love Arrow. I can make people want to get married with a single Flirt Touch. I'm also incredibly adept at knowing who's most compatible together, and my organizational skills are unparalleled. I'm a fast reader, I have excellent penmanship, and I've never tested the theory, but I'm certain I could handle myself at a royal dinner, innately knowing which spoon to use.

But remembering directions? It's like a foreign language. Harder even, since I've studied foreign languages, and I've easily mastered how to speak some simple phrases in troll. My weakness is in knowing where to go. I can be so sure something is one way, but be completely wrong.

I know where the battle island is in relation to the genfin island, but apparently that isn't enough, because I end up seriously lost. I eventually have to go corporeal and touch down on some random place to ask for directions. Luckily, a haggard-looking tree fae manages to draw me a map in the dirt and set me back on track.

So it's a day later than when I left Emelle's, but when I finally spot the empty island, I almost wish I'd stayed lost.

I go corporeal, needing to take a steadying breath in order to face this. After stalling in the clouds for a minute, I make myself land, my eyes skimming over the dreary landscape. The entire island looks worn out and scarred, as if it too is still trying to recover from what happened here.

My shoes scrape against the dried-out ground, still charred in places from where it was set aflame after the battle. The buildings that were erected are gone, just like the king's fields, torn away by the fae who wanted to erase what a corrupt monarchy had done.

Fog clings against the edges of the island, making everything seem so much more closed-in and isolated. Like nothing else exists in the whole realm except for this one place.

It's eerie.

I shiver as I walk, my footsteps way too loud in the dense silence. I try to match up what I'm seeing now with what I saw then, but it's different now with being so quiet and empty. Without the hundreds of bodies fighting against one another, it's hard to blend the two as one, when all I really saw last time was fighting and death happening everywhere I looked.

Though as I walk further, I realize that death never left.

The graveyard I find isn't fancy, but it isn't decrepit

either. With its simply-made headstones and stacked rock perimeter, it looks like it was hastily yet conscientiously made. I wonder if Emelle and her mates were here when it was created. I wonder if they helped. Just another thing to feel guilty for since I wasn't here to lend a hand.

I force myself to walk through it, my eyes jumping from headstone to headstone, although I know Belren's name isn't on any of them. Emelle felt like he wouldn't have wanted to be buried here, alone and tied to this place. So instead, she tracked down the island where he grew up. She had him buried in the prettiest cemetery she could find, with lots of flowers and trees, right smack dab in the middle of a town. There was even a pub next door, which Emelle said he would've liked.

I have to admit that when Sev told me that, it bothered me that Emelle seemed to know what he'd want. It bothered me because...shouldn't *I* be the one to know things like that, when I was the reason he was dead? Shouldn't I have put in some effort to know where he would've wanted to be laid to rest, since I essentially was the one to put him in the ground?

This is the one place I never could face, and now that I'm here, it's no wonder. It's a tomb of pulsing, painful memories.

I never told anyone this, but I searched for Belren. For a year, maybe longer. I looked in the afterlife processing center—abusing my cupid perks to get there. I searched other realms, searched every new cupid, angel, and demon, and the Minor entities too, always hoping against hope that I would see his face.

But I never found him.

I knew it was a long shot, that time is fickle. There's no

telling how long time passes from a life to an afterlife. It's all fluid and different. Still, I searched.

Then, after an endless loop of frustrated defeat, I gave up. I couldn't bear the repeated disappointment. I moped around the different realms, avoided my responsibilities, while also avoiding Emelle and Sev. I didn't dare tell them that I'd been searching for him. I couldn't bear to see the pity on their faces. For all we knew, it could take centuries for his spirit to show up, and even then, it would be like trying to find a needle in a haystack.

So I went from searching to avoiding to then making half-hearted attempts to do my job. From there, I made a real effort to buck up and pull myself together and get back to the way things were. To do that, I needed to stay busy and push myself even harder than before. I knew I had to forget about the horned fae and move on.

Except, I didn't. I *haven't*.

I shake my head at my thoughts, just as a breeze comes sweeping past me to whistle through the headstones. Did I say it was eerie before? Well, now, it's downright creepy. A prickling sensation lifts the hairs on the back of my neck, making my eyes dart around.

In an instant, I pop back into the Veil, and I suck in a non-existent breath. There are ghosts *everywhere*. Of course there are. It's pretty much par for the course when you're in a graveyard. Some are genfins, some are high fae, all of them shadowed and see-through, eyes looking at nothing as they mutter and mope.

I can't watch them for too long. Ghosts give me the creeps—which I know is hypocritical since, for all intents and purposes, I'm pretty ghostlike when I'm in the Veil.

"AHH!!!!"

I flinch at the female who screams bloody murder—probably accurate—and then just keeps floating along expressionlessly as she passes me by.

See? Creepy.

I turn around and leave the graveyard behind, but the skin-prickling sensation doesn't relent. If anything, it just gets worse. I turn around to look, but the ghosts are still hanging around the graves, not paying me any mind.

I'm about to pop out of the Veil just so I don't have to look at them anymore, but when I turn back around, something catches my eye.

No, that's a lie. It's not really my *eye* that catches on anything. It's more of a sense. Something draws me, ghosts forgotten as I walk forward, almost trance-like.

This sixth sense has me stopping, and I look down at the ground, frowning in thought. And then, all at once, I just *know*.

It looks like any other spot on this island, except...this was where Belren's body landed. This was where my knees buckled as I knelt over him. This was where I understood that saying "like a knife through the heart," because as I looked at him, probably dead before he even hit the ground, that's what it felt like.

A frown pulls down my mouth, and the skin between my brows creases. "I shouldn't have come here," I say to myself, because this isn't any kind of closure at all. I'm not sure why I thought coming here would do anything to help or to let me move past the guilt, because this just makes me feel *worse*. "This is pointless."

My head lifts, looking around the bleak island, and a deep-down anger starts to kick up.

"I shouldn't be wandering around with a bunch of

ghosts," I tell the spot on the ground, as if Belren were still lying there and I could give him a piece of my mind. Maybe that's what's been behind the guilt—anger. Anger that he got himself killed and left me to live with it.

"I should be filing cupidity reports. Making Love Matches. Perfecting my short-range shot," I say, a tic in my jaw pulsing with irritation. "I was *fine* before you went and died for me. Perfectly happy and busy and satisfied with my place and purpose. You know what this is, Belren-the-Horned-Hook? This is *rude*. You can't just shove yourself in front of someone like that and mess up their whole afterlife!"

I pace around the ground, mouth pinched, heels digging into the wounded earth. "I was doing perfectly well before you shoved your life in front of mine, thank you very much. Maybe I didn't want you to do that for me, did you ever think of that?" My voice is stronger now, nearly yelling, and I *never* yell.

After years of being confused and guilt-ridden, the anger comes pouring out in sharp shards, chipping away at my poised veneer like it's chipped away at everything else.

"I just want to put all of this behind me for cupid's sake. I want my easy, planned, organized, goal-oriented, *empty* existence back." A sob chokes out of me, because even though I hadn't meant to say it, it's absolutely true. My life was empty before, but at least it didn't hurt.

I sniff, like I can suck back in the emotion that slipped out. "I want to stop feeling so guilty all the darn time, so what do I have to do, huh?" I look around with my hands up, gaze directed at the sky in case the gods are listening. "What do I have to do to put him behind me?"

My loud words demand an answer, and my mind whirls to fulfill it, because enough is enough. I can't keep going on like this. So what can I do to make this right...?

And just like that, an idea suddenly blares through me.

"*That's it,*" I whisper, hand over my mouth.

It was silly to come here, I see that now. It's not what I need to do at all.

I've always set personal challenges for myself to be the best, to work the hardest. But the new goal I have in mind has nothing to do with being a cupid and everything to do with a shot at true closure.

My lips press into a grim line. "I know what I have to do."

It'll be a personal goal that might be the hardest challenge I've ever set for myself, but maybe this is what I'm meant to do. Maybe the arrows hanging on my back are meant for more than just love.

There were reasons Belren was at that island in the first place, and one of them was to help Princess Soora and the rebellion. Princess Soora, who ended up betraying everyone, but with Belren, that deception was personal. If she hadn't betrayed him, he might not have been there the moment the prince threw his power, and he'd still be alive.

I shove my shoulders back, this time pacing around with newfound ambition. "I have to kill Princess Soora," I declare boldly. "She's the one who lied to him, to everyone. His memory needs to be avenged, and I have to be the one to do it since it was my life he traded for his own."

It settles inside me, solidifying into something scary but sure, like a gut feeling that I'm on the right track.

"I'll just...find her. Get Belren some justice for her part

in siding with the prince. Easy. One arrow through the heart should do it." My head bobs. "Yes. That seems efficient. Just a simple, quick murder."

Maybe Amorette's violent tendencies rubbed off...

I wince but quickly cover it up. Now that I have a new goal set, I turn around, ready to start my search, only to stop cold at the sight of the ghost watching me, perched on top of a boulder a few feet away.

My entire body goes still, and I blink my eyes. Over and over again.

Slack-jawed, I try to reconcile what I'm seeing, but I can't, because it's not real. It can't be. If I wasn't in the Veil, I think I might've fainted, because my ears are ringing, my vision tunnelling, my head dizzy.

A pair of molten gray eyes look me up and down, and a sound like a choked sob rips from my throat. I stand frozen, waiting for this fake apparition to disappear and completely devastate me.

But instead, the ghost smirks at me. It's his slow, flirtatious tilt of his lips that brings the blaring truth to my mind and nearly makes me fall to my knees in buckled shock. *He's really here.*

Belren.

CHAPTER 10

LEX

I admit, I'm not usually one for dramatics.

I'm a logical sort of girl. I much prefer stoic, polite, even-tempered kinds of responses. They're more responsible. Less messy. I don't enjoy getting into the nitty gritty of things. Keeping things surface-level is just so much easier.

But suddenly seeing the ghost of the male I've looked for, grieved for, been out-of-my-head confused over, and most recently declared that I will *kill* for is enough to make even the most level-headed girl lose her mind.

So my reaction is to scream.

Loudly. And it's...okay. It gets quite high-pitched.

Belren winces, though he doesn't move from his spot on the boulder. "Must you do that?" he asks through his grimace. "We already have a screamer on Ghost Island, though I think you can give her a run for her money."

My mouth clamps shut, but I have no idea what he's saying, can't even comprehend the words. I'm too busy staring at him in disbelief.

"This isn't happening," I whisper to myself, head shaking with denial. "I'm sleeping. Dreaming. Gone delusional. This is absolutely *not* happening."

He tilts his head curiously. "What's not happening?"

"You!" I shriek, exasperated. "There is no way you can just be *here* after all this time!"

His lips tip up, as if my mental break is amusing him. "You're yelling again."

Barely hearing him, I start wringing my hands and moving away. "Did I do this?" I say to myself as I look around the island, at a loss. "Did I somehow...bring him here? Because this is crazy. He can't be here. He just *can't*."

When he sees me backing up, he jumps down from the rock and makes his way toward me. "Did you see that trick?" he asks, hiking a thumb over his shoulder. "Finally learned how to sit on top of the boulder, though I can't get inside of it. Still, it's progress."

I blink. Goodness. We're both crazy.

"Anyway," he continues. "Why can't I be here?"

All of a sudden, I'm terrified of him getting nearer. Sure, I searched for him, all my thoughts have been consumed by him, but did I ever really think I'd come face-to-face with him again?

Apparently not.

"Stop coming closer!" I shout, making him stop in his tracks.

"Why?"

My nerves are frazzled, my emotions gone haywire. "Because, I just...I need to think for a second. Just...just stay there. I need a good seven-foot radius of clear thinking space."

He snorts. "So...you're incapable of thought when others are in your think-radius?"

"What? No. I mean, yes!" I finish with a blurt when he starts to move forward again. My voice is flustered, my mind even more so as I try to adapt to the fact that I'm actually speaking to him.

He's here.

Like a phantom, his silvery skin and white hair give him an uncanny masculine beauty. It's an innate radiance, even amidst the shallowness of his form. The thick gray horns that curl up from the top of his forehead and stop below his ears are the darkest part about him, apart from his tunic, pants, and boots. But his eyes, those tin-gray eyes, are so sharp that they almost don't look as translucent as the rest of him.

How is this possible?

But then my mind immediately zeroes in on my declaration. It can't be a coincidence that he showed up right when that lightbulb went off and I realized what I needed to do with Soora. That has to be it. Why else would he suddenly appear?

Which means...killing the ex-princess really *is* what I have to do.

Gods. I really should've thought this through.

My mouth opens and closes several times as I continue staring at him. "How are you here?" I ask him, hoping for some clarification.

Belren glances around the island, his white brows lowering. "How? Well, I'm dead, and this is my deathplace, so..." He shrugs and turns his attention back to me. "Awfully boring place, though, isn't it?"

"How did you find me?" I press.

"Find? You're hard to miss, seeing as you're the only one here alive." His gaze casts over me with interest. "Nice trick, by the way. You look like a ghost, sound like a ghost, but you're not a ghost. Care to enlighten me?"

I frown at him. For the first time, I pause enough in my shock to really study him. I see the curiosity in his gaze, the loose posture, the way he keeps glancing around, and something is...off. Something isn't registering.

Admittedly, I don't know Belren very well, but I tend to have obsessive qualities. Shocking, I know. So when I say I have picked apart every previous interaction with him in hopes of understanding why he did what he did, I mean it. He should be calling me Sixty-Nine. He should be cracking more jokes or talking to me about Emelle, or demanding answers.

A horrible sinking sensation drags down my hope, making me swallow thickly. "Are you... Do you know who I am?"

The question feels like the heaviest I've ever asked, burdening the very air between us. But it has nothing on the weight of his answer.

He tilts his head. "No... Should I?"

I can't help but stagger in place, can't help the tiny bitter laugh that crawls up my throat.

How incredibly stupid I am. I was so caught up in his sudden appearance that I forgot for a second how ghosts are. *Of course* he doesn't remember me. He couldn't. This is just some mean twist of the fates, of the Veil cruelly giving me what I asked for.

I finally found him—or rather, he found me—and he doesn't even remember who I am. How's that for luck?

My eyes close tight, blocking out the emotion that

tries to well up inside of me. I can't cry in front of him. I *can't*.

I'm not sure when he floated closer, but when I open my eyes again, he's right in front of me, studying my expression. "Do you know, there's something strange about you..."

I have no idea what that means, but I forget to ask when his hand tentatively comes up in front of my face. Even though we're both in this in-between place where we can't touch or feel, a gasp escapes my lips as the back of his fingers trail down my cheek. It's a single second, a solitary blink, but I swear I can almost *feel* him.

Then his hand drops, and I'm left bereft. Maybe that's why I let out a moment of weakness when I quietly say, "I wish you remembered."

He frowns. "Remembered?"

"Yes," I urge hesitantly. "Can you *try* to remember?"

He gets the strangest look on his face and quickly glances away as if my request made him go deep in thought.

"Belren?"

His body goes very still, and I see him murmur something under his breath.

"What did you say?"

He mumbles again, and then all of a sudden, his gaze lifts to mine, all previous confusion gone. "Pink hair, red wings!" he shouts, making me flinch in surprise. For a split second, something like recognition flashes over his expression. "I—"

His voice abruptly cuts off, a pained noise bursting from his lips just as his eyes widen in horror. Before I can so much as move toward him, his ghostly body lurches back, and then he seems to be sucked right out of the air. He disappears with an audible crack, and all I'm left to look at is empty space in front of me.

What just happened?

"Belren?" I whirl in place, looking around wildly, but he's gone. "Belren!" My shout echoes through the barren island, my call left on the oblivious ears of the other ghosts. I leave the Veil for a second and then go back in, thinking that maybe that will fix this. Kind of like turning a cell phone off and then back on. But when he still doesn't reappear, I really start to panic.

I shoot around the island, wings snapping in the Veiled air as I call to him over and over.

This is all my fault.

I pushed him. Tried to force him to remember, and something happened to him because of it.

Turning in place, I desperately seek him, knowing that I might've just messed up my one shot at fixing things, at seeing him. "Where are you?" The call tears out of me, carrying all my frustration and desperation with it. "I said I was going to kill Princess Soora!"

"What did I tell you about yelling? We already have a screamer on Ghost Island."

I yelp and accidentally pop out of the Veil, nearly tumbling to the ground when I forget to flap my wings. I land with embarrassing clumsiness, but the relief I feel is so encompassing that I take a shuddering breath. Tears well up in my eyes before I go back into the Veil again. Whirling, I find him forty feet away, lying down on the ground with his arms and legs splayed like he's getting ready to make a snow angel.

"You're back!"

"Nice trick, going from alive to ghostly again. How do you manage that?"

I fly over as he sits up, looking me up and down as I kneel beside him. "Are you okay?"

He arches a brow. "I'm dead."

"Right. Umm… What are you doing?" I ask, watching him carefully as he continues to lie there.

"What do you mean? I'm relaxing on my deathplace. I keep getting sucked back here for some reason. Wicked annoying."

My eyes drop down to the ground. This really is the spot.

"Nice ambience, isn't it?" he drawls.

I'm kneeling over him now, just like I was before on that awful day. That day when his body was splayed out and his heart had already stopped. When power still crackled over his silvery skin, scorching the earth beneath him. I still remember the way my tears steamed when they landed on the ground.

I get yanked out of the memory when he quickly leaps to his feet and pretends to dust himself off. "Well, that was jarring. Now, where were we? Oh, yes. I heard you talking about leaving to commit murder. Let's get on that, shall we?"

That's all the confirmation I need. He remembered that, and he appeared both times when I said it.

"Do you…remember anything else we talked about?" I ask carefully as I stand up beside him.

"Mmm, no. Don't remember anything much really. Should I?"

I quickly shake my head. "Nope, no, not at all. There's nothing else to remember."

He gives me a funny look, but the last thing I want is to set him off again. I should consider myself lucky that he remembers anything at all. For whatever reason, he seemed to reset back to his deathplace when I tried to get him to try.

"Does that...happen a lot? Getting sucked back to your deathplace?"

He looks at the ground with disdain. "A fair few times that I know of, but if it's more than that, I can't remember," he replies, mouth pinching in confused aggravation.

I can only imagine how frustrating this must be for him. Still...

"You're not like the other ghosts," I note, nodding in the direction of the graveyard. "You might not remember everything, but you're not like them. They can't even really talk."

He follows my gaze to watch the despondent ghosts before he shrugs. "It's probably only a matter of time before I'm as boring and tedious as that lot."

I frown, not liking that thought at all. Not remembering me is one thing, but to see him become like those other ghosts, mumbling incoherently, too far gone to even make eye contact? That would be devastating.

"Anyway, let's hear all the details."

My brows pull together. "Details?"

"Yes, you're the murderess, so you must have a plan. If you're going to pull this off, you need to have a good one."

I let out a huff. "I'm not a murderess."

"Come now, don't be shy. It was the most entertainment I've had in...well, I don't know how long, to be honest. But who are we killing?"

"*We*? You mean...you want to come?"

Both hands come up as he gestures around. "Of course. You've seen this place. You wouldn't be so cruel as to leave a despairing ghost out of a good revenge mission, would you? Screamer over there is giving me a headache."

"Ghosts can't get headaches."

"Well, an annoyance-ache, then."

"There's no such thing."

He gives out a long-suffering sigh. "Are you always this literal?"

"Yes."

When he starts to laugh, I shake my head. This is a strange conversation. "Listen, you can't go off gallivanting around the realm."

Belren cocks his head and walks closer to me, and it's hard not to back up because of the intensity of his attention. "That's the thing, I've tried walking off the edge of the island, but I get this feeling like I can't leave. But for some reason, I think I could leave with you."

My mouth opens and shuts. I have no idea what to say.

For a moment, he's quiet and deep in thought. "I know —it's because of that trick you have of going solid. Maybe I can latch onto you?"

"Latch onto me? Like a leech?"

He rolls his eyes. "Like a ghost."

"How in the world would you do that?"

Belren looks around for a moment in thought before his gaze stops on our feet. A grin overtakes his expression. "You'll take my deathplace with you."

"Take *what* with me?"

"My deathplace. It's the perfect loophole," he says, kneeling down to gesture to the dirt while excitement rushes through his words. "This spot keeps sucking me back, so you can simply take it with you! Do your little trick with going anti-ghostly, and scoop up some of my deathplace. You can stick it in your haversack."

My lips turn down, hand going to the strap around my shoulders. "This is a *quiver*. It holds my Love Arrows, thank you very much."

"*Love Arrows?*"

"Yes, I'm a cupid."

Belren pauses. "A cupid?" For a moment, he's quiet, and I worry this will trigger him again, but then he simply shakes his head and says, "You mean to tell me you're in charge of love and mating, that sort of thing?"

"Yes."

"Well, that's surprising."

"Why?"

He waves a hand up and down my body. "I'd have thought that someone with the job of seduction would be dressed a bit more...seductively."

My lips purse. Before Emelle allowed cupids to become corporeal, we were dressed in whatever clothes we died in. Mine was something very similar to what I'm wearing now, and I haven't seen the need to change it.

I run my hand over the silhouette of my jacket and blouse. "I'm dressed like a professional."

"Oh, don't take any offense, love. I happen to enjoy what you're wearing *immensely*," he says with a wink.

Nervous butterflies seem to erupt in my stomach, and I have no idea how to reply.

His gray eyes jump over my shoulder. "I suppose that explains the bow and arrows you're carrying. Can you shoot one at me?"

My eyes nearly bug out. "Excuse me?"

116

Belren spreads his arms and backs up a step. "Just try it."

"No. Absolutely not."

"Come on, Pinky."

I falter in place at the nickname but quickly realize that it wasn't from memory. He's just looking at my hair. I try to pretend that disappointment doesn't swim in my gut.

"Love Arrows are *not* toys," I tell him firmly. "In order to even earn their quiver, a cupid has to agree to never shoot an arrow without pure purpose."

His arms drop. "You're no fun."

Oh, if only I had a fulfilled quota for every time someone said that to me.

"Alright, since you're not going to toss your cupid stick at me, let's get back to the task on hand."

I grit my teeth at the term *cupid stick*. "What task?"

"Taking my deathplace with you so I can tag along. Let's see if it works. Now quick, scoop up some of my muck and fill your quiver."

My nose scrunches. "That sounds dirty." When he flashes me a wicked smile, I immediately get flustered again. "I didn't mean it like *that*."

Goodness.

"No need to blush, Pinky."

"My name is *Lex*, and I can't blush when I'm in the Veil."

"Or gather my muck."

My eyes narrow on him. "This isn't going to work."

He shrugs. "I think it might."

I can tell that he's not going to let this go, and I really do feel bad about setting him off, so I decide the least I can do is appease him in this. In the next second, I pop myself out of the Veil.

If anything, it helps to take a moment to try to center my spinning thoughts. Having Belren here is...confusing. I'm not quite sure what to do or think, and he makes me feel nervous and undone. Like a schoolgirl with a crush.

Ridiculous.

But even more, I'm scared that at any moment, he could be set off again. What if he gets pulled back to his deathplace again and then becomes one of those moaning and muddled ghosts? Or what if he doesn't come back at all? This is my new purpose. To help him avenge his death. I have to try.

With a deep breath, I look at my feet before I grumble and kneel down. Since the dirt is so hard, I have to use a Love Arrow to break it up a bit. When I get enough to scoop up, I hesitate before dumping it in my quiver, because it's just so...*dirty*. I take great care of my cupid tools. I even go so far as to polish my arrows most nights until they're gleaming.

Apparently, I take too long for Belren, because an unnatural chill suddenly goes up my back. The kind of chill that happens when ghosts are about.

I whip around with a scowl. "Excuse you!" I may not be able to see him when I'm not in the Veil, but I'd bet my bow that was him.

With a sigh, I turn back around and grip the strap of my quiver before spilling my handful inside. "This is going to make my Love Arrows absolutely filthy," I gripe. "Not to mention that I don't see how this could possibly work." Still, I grab another two handfuls just to be sure.

After all, I'm not the sort of girl who does anything halfway.

Popping back into the Veil, I find Belren standing entirely too close. "You felt that, huh?" he asks with a grin.

I take a step back, because being so near to him makes me all jittery. "As a Veil entity, we are more attuned to ghosts," I tell him matter-of-factly.

"Or...*you* are just more attuned to *me*."

I frown. "No, I've studied a bit about cupids and ghosts. I'm sure it's what I said."

He seems to find this funny, because a smile breaks out and a light chuckle escapes him. "Forget what I said before. You are fun."

The most confusing part about what he said is that he seems to be serious.

Once again jumbled, I clear my throat. "Anyway, your muck has now soiled my quiver."

He snickers.

"That's *not* what I meant."

"You know, for a cupid, you're very easy to rile up."

The most embarrassing part is, he's right.

As if he can read my thoughts, he gives me a winning grin. "Time to put our money where my muck is. Lead the way, Pinky."

CHAPTER 11

LEX

I stare at him. "You want to go *right now?*"

"You have my muck in your quiver, don't you?"

Gods.

"Please stop saying that."

A chuckle spins from his twisted lips.

Before his laugh can finish though, another ghost suddenly comes out of nowhere and flies right through him. I leap back in surprise and hear Belren snarl out a curse. "Godsdammit, Stag, *stop doing that!*"

Belren glares daggers at the ghost who just violated him, but the ghost—aptly named with the stag antlers coming out of his head—just turns around and looks at me blankly. "There was fighting here," he says morosely.

Is he coherent like Belren too?

"Um, yes," I answer.

Stag spins in a circle, looking around, and nearly slides through Belren again. "There was fighting here, I think," he says again.

Oh. I guess not.

I glance at Belren, and he gives a shrug. "He's like an echo. Repeats the same thing over and over again until you want to pull your ears off."

My lips turn down as I watch Stag. He's started to mutter beneath his breath as he does laps around Belren. "It's not his fault. He can't help it."

"Yes, I know," Belren replies with a sigh. "I have a feeling he's annoyed me for a lot longer, but I just can't remember. This is yet another reason I want to leave."

Shuffling on my feet, I adjust the strap over my shoulder. "I'm not sure this is such a good idea."

Belren's eyes narrow on me. "And why is that?"

"What if it doesn't work? What if it makes you *more* like him? It seems like a big risk to take," I tell him.

I don't like risks. I like plans, goals, challenges. But risks? That's right down there alongside failure. And disorganized filing cabinets. I really hate those.

Belren seems to sober at my unease, and he comes closer, leaving Stag to mill around behind him. "Listen, if this doesn't work, it's no skin off my see-through back. I'll simply be brought right back here where I started. Or...ended. You know what I mean."

"Yes, but—"

"No buts, Pinky," he interrupts, taking another step forward. My body stiffens as he enters my space, his head tilted down. His graphite eyes skim over my face as slowly as a stroke, and nearly make me shudder. "Do you know what I was thinking of before you suddenly arrived?" he asks me.

"No...?" *Why is my voice so breathy?*

"Nothing," he says, a hint of bitterness edging the

word. "I was thinking of absolutely *nothing*. Because every time I seem to have a thought, it gets plucked away from me. Or I wake up in my deathplace, remembering not a damn thing, but knowing I just appeared there, knowing I was trying to do...*something*. I'm losing my mind here, Pinky."

For the first time since we came face to face, I see the hidden sadness and fear carved into the marble of his phantom eyes. It makes my heart hurt.

"I need to get off this godsdamned island," Belren goes on, more quietly this time, like he's pleading with me. "I'm not a fool. I know it's only a matter of time before I end up like Stag."

My eyes flick behind him to watch the poor antlered ghost mumbling at the ground.

"But I also know that, for some reason, I feel better around *you*."

The confession takes me by surprise, and my eyes snap back to Belren's face. "Me? Why?"

"I don't know. You make me feel not so...tied down," he answers without pause. "I'm more focused than I have been in gods only know how long. For some reason, I feel as if I *need* to stay with you."

I suck in a useless breath. This must be because of Princess Soora. It definitely can't have anything to do with just *me*. Not that I can tell that to the flutters in my stomach.

Expression intent, he passes a phantom finger through mine. "I know you don't know me, don't owe me anything, but let me do this with you, since it will probably be the last thing I *can* do before I turn into Stag."

Don't owe him anything? I owe him my entire afterlife.

Dropping my eyes, I clear my throat, unable to face such honest imploring, unable to face the curious hope. "But what if we try to leave and the quiver plan doesn't work?" I ask nervously. "I mean, it seems unlikely, doesn't it? For whatever reason, you're stuck here, at your death-place. Me carrying around some of the dirt isn't going to be enough."

"Won't know until we try, love," he says, another easy smile on his face again, making me all jumbled up inside. "And like I said, what's the difference? If it doesn't work, I end up right back here and you can be free of me."

Little does he know, I'll never be free of him. I haven't been since he died for me.

I shake my head, eyes lifting. "It's not about me. If this doesn't work and you get sucked back to your deathplace, you could end up worse off. Who knows, maybe all of these ghosts have tried to leave before too. Maybe it makes you forget faster," I tell him, desperate to make him see reason. "The safe thing to do is simply stay here and try to preserve yourself."

His mouth pulls into a sneer of distaste. "I don't want to *preserve myself*, and I am not interested in playing it safe. I may not remember who the hell I was, but I know who I am right *now*, and I have no interest in staying here to rot."

I stare at him, torn. On the one hand, I understand. This island is bleak, even without the sight of the spirits stuck here for eternity, left to dwindle into nothing. But on the other hand, I'm scared. I've just found him, and I don't want to ruin his afterlife as much as I inexplicably ruined his life. I don't want to be the reason for his end. Again.

But the longer I look at him, the more I see that I can't deny his request. I yelled at the fates and declared that I'd get revenge for him, and he appeared. Now I have to follow through.

I let out a defeatist sigh. "We can try to just leave the island first if you're really sure..."

A grin splits his face, making him practically light up. He's so handsome it hurts to look at him. "I knew you'd come around."

I give a nervous laugh. "Let's just hope you don't *come back around*, right?"

He blinks at me in silence. "Was that...was that you trying to make a joke?"

The small smile I had on is whisked away for a frown. "Of course it was a joke. *Come back around*. Like getting pulled back to your deathplace?" Another stilt of silence. "It's funny!" I insist.

Now he laughs. "My gods, you are adorable, Pinky. The worst sense of humor, and somehow, it makes you even more endearing."

"I...I'm not sure what to say to that. Was that an insult or a compliment?"

"Let's not get into the trap of putting a label on it," he replies before he turns and starts walking away again. "Now come on, before Stag starts to follow."

I shoot the other ghost a repentant look, but he doesn't see it since he's now talking to a rock a few feet away.

Hurrying to catch up, I take my place beside Belren, my nerves taking flight. When we reach the edge of the island, I look down at the swirl of haze clinging to the sides. "Are you sure?"

"You know, you're starting to sound like Stag, asking the same thing over and over again."

"I just think it might be helpful to really go over a pros and cons list before we—"

Not even letting me finish, he looks contemplatively at the edge and then walks right off it, disappearing into the gloom.

"Gods darn it," I mutter.

"*Oooh*, how blasphemous of you!" I hear him shout, though I can't see him. "Come on, Pinky, the mist's fine!"

"This is actually fog!" I holler back. "It's much denser than mist!"

I think I hear a snort, but I'm not sure.

"Are you there?" I call.

When I don't hear a reply, I quickly flare my wings out and take flight with a jump over the side of the island. The second I do, I become immersed in the haze, unable to see so much as a foot in front of me. I spin around mid-air, squinting for a ghostly silhouette. "Where are you?"

Nothing.

"If you're hiding from me, this isn't funny!"

Still nothing. The silence is creepy.

I open my mouth to call his name, only to clamp it shut again since he doesn't remember it.

"Hello?"

The further I fly, the more I get turned around. The fog isn't letting up, even though it should since I must be further away from the island now. Unless I've accidentally flown closer to it?

The longer I'm stuck in the smothering vapor, unable to see, the more unease filters through me. What if he's already gotten sucked back? Maybe I should go check?

Except...I have no idea which way the island is. Gods, my sense of direction is abysmal.

Where the heck is Belren?

"Hello!" I call again, my voice sounding high-pitched, laced with panic that I don't want to give in to. I don't panic. I plan. Panic doesn't help any situation.

"Okay, Lex, just calm down. Let's fly upward. If we go up, then we can get out of the fog," I say out loud in a little pep talk.

"Do you always talk to yourself?"

A scream tears from my throat, and I nearly fly right through Belren, who's suddenly appeared in front of me.

"Oh my good gods! *Don't do that!*"

"You know, for a quiet one, your screams are shockingly loud."

I narrow my eyes, still trying to rid myself of the surge of fear I just experienced. "If I could, I'd hit you."

"Mmm, violent too?" he purrs, seeming nearly like a disembodied voice since his silhouette mostly blended in with the fog. "You are just full of surprises, aren't you, Pinky?"

"That's it, we're going back to the island," I huff.

Turning around, I start to fly away, muttering under my breath about what an absolute jerk a certain ghost is. I hear him laugh.

"Pinky? The island is the other way."

Stopping in my tracks, I spin around and start flying in that direction instead. Belren sidles up beside me to follow, and while I'm using my wings to fly, he's simply walking on air, his steps eating up the space like he's on a moving walkway.

"So, did you want to tell me why you were at Ghost Island in the first place?" Belren asks conversationally.

I shoot him a look. "Ghost Island?"

"Yes. Why were you there? Unless cupids often try to get ghosts to fall in love or fu—"

"No," I quickly blurt. "Our powers only work on the living."

"Disappointing, but unsurprising," he replies. "So? Why were you there?"

I divert my attention, staring straight ahead. "Umm...closure."

Belren makes a face. "That sounds boring."

Well, that's rude.

"My closure isn't boring," I reply hotly.

He clicks his tongue, watching my wings as he walks. "Someone is sensitive about it. Does that mean you didn't get your closure?"

I laugh humorlessly. "Definitely not. No closures in sight. In fact, I'd say the whole thing is wide open."

"What a shame."

He doesn't sound like he thinks it's a shame at all. How fitting, considering he's the reason for it.

"Is that where this whole killing someone plan comes into effect?"

"As a matter of fact, yes."

He snickers. "You're never going to be able to do it."

I stop. "Excuse me?"

"Oh come now, look at you," he says, drawing a hand up and down my figure. "You're not the killing type."

I'm not sure why I feel so offended, but I do. "I could kill if I wanted to—and I will," I say defiantly. Because I think I sort of accidentally made a vow to the fates.

"Whatever you say, Pinky."

With a huff, I flap my wings again, and then we're suddenly breaking out of the fog—finally—but instead of the island, we're in the wide expanse of sky. "I thought you said this was the way to the island?"

"I lied," Belren says cheerfully. "Do you know, I couldn't even step off the island before you? But I feel fine. The muck is really working," he says, rolling back on his heels mid-air. "Now, which way to go on your killing spree?"

"It's not a *spree*. One fae surely can't be considered a spree."

Right? I'm actually not sure; I'll need to research it later.

"Well?" he presses.

"Well, what?"

"Which way?"

"Oh, umm...I don't know where she is," I admit.

He gives me a look. "Alright, well, you're not off to a strong start, but you came to the right ghost."

My gaze latches onto him. "I did?"

"Of course," he says with an air of confidence that reminds me of his old self. "I'll help you find her."

It's on the tip of my tongue to ask him if he remembers being good at finding things, but I immediately swallow it down.

"Who is this fae?"

"Umm...her name is Soora," I answer, watching him carefully. But his expression stays perfectly blank yet curious. "And she used to be a princess of the realm. She was supposed to be backing a rebellion and helping over-throw the tyrant king, but when it mattered most, she betrayed our side. Got a lot of good fae killed." I swallow thickly, throat filled with the heavy emotion of my explanation as well as the fear that this will spark a detrimental recognition.

But his expression doesn't change.

"Well, this just gets better and better," he says with clear excitement. "Let's head to those islands there, and you can start asking around." He points to a cluster of four islands in the distance, a couple of them with dripping waterfalls cascading off the sides.

I shift in the air uneasily, hesitation gnawing at me. Just because we got this far doesn't mean we should tempt fate. "I think I changed my mind."

His attention flicks toward me. "What?"

"I'm in over my head here," I admit, suddenly feeling overwhelmed. "You need to go back to your island, and I'll try to go get some hel—"

"No," he says, cutting me off.

"*No?*" I steel my spine at being told no. "Well, listen up, mister, you're actually not in charge."

We proceed to glare at each other.

He leans in, inches away from my face. "You know, you're sexy when you try to get all mad like that."

I sputter. "Excuse me?"

"You're excused," he replies smoothly, straightening back up. "And as it were, I *am* actually in charge."

"Is that so?"

"Yep. Because I'm a ghost, and you've gone and disturbed my peace by showing up on my island and making me feel awake—especially with all of your killing talk. Now I'm invested. We have to go along with the plan or I'll never be able to rest."

Worry gnaws at me.

He plants his feet in the air and stares at me with an arched brow. "Look, if you don't take me willingly, then I'll just haunt you."

I blink at him. "Can...can you do that?"

His eyes dart away, but he quickly covers it up with a scoff. "I'm a ghost. Of course I can haunt."

"You aren't sure, are you?"

He seems very put out by this conclusion. "That would be quite stupid if I'm a ghost who can't even haunt," he grumbles. "Besides, I think I've already latched onto my muck."

This takes me aback. "What do you mean?"

Belren shrugs a shoulder. "I can tell where you are. Even when you were in the mist—"

"Fog," I quickly correct.

He shoots me an unappreciative look. "Right. When we were in the *fog*, I could sort of sense where you were. Because of my muck."

"That's...strange."

He shrugs. "Must be a ghost thing."

"I wouldn't know. I'm not the ghost."

Belren arches a brow. "You don't need to brag about it."

For goodness sake.

"Fine," I finally relent. "We can try for the nearest island. But when we get there, I'm calling for help. And we aren't going any further. Deal?"

His handsome face gives me another heart-stopping grin. "Deal."

This time, I walk beside him as we start heading toward the island far off on the horizon. From here, I can see nothing much except a green blob in the distance, with clouds speckling the sky. Behind us, fog still clings to the air, obscuring Ghost Island.

"By the way, what should I call you?" I ask him.

Ever the flirt, he flashes me a smirk and wags his brows. "You can call me whatever you like, so long as I get to hear you say it over and over again in my ear."

I roll my eyes, but I bet my cheeks would be bright pink if I weren't in the Veil. "You don't have any preference?"

"Nope," he answers jovially. "Just don't pick a bad one."

"How about...Hook?"

Belren makes a face. "I *just* mentioned bad names."

I gesture to his head. "Your horns are curved like hooks. I think it fits."

He gives me a salacious smirk. "Oh, it'll fit, Pinky."

"Good grief."

His chuckle wraps around me and sets butterflies loose in my stomach. "I think Hook will do just fine."

CHAPTER 12

LEX

*I*t takes a surprisingly long time to get to the other island.

Maybe I'm just a terrible judge of both direction *and* distance, but I swear it seems like it's floating further away from us no matter how long we head toward it.

It's not until after the sun has bloomed fully in the sky, like a flower opening its petals, that we finally reach it. Its landscape is all jungle, the greenery so thick that we can't even see the ground from our bird's eye view. Yet smack dab in the middle of all that lush plant life is a cluster of three volcanoes, one of which has continuous lava flowing out of it like a glowing river before casting off the side of the island in a fiery waterfall.

Belren and I touch down in the only visible city here— one with roads of tar and houses made of matte black rock. I've never been to this particular island before, so I'm not sure what to expect. "How are you feeling?" I ask the moment our incorporeal forms come into contact with the ground.

He rolls his eyes. "You've asked me that every minute since we left."

"Well, that's an exaggeration. I actually asked you once every *ten* minutes, which I think is a very reasonable time frame, since we're trying to make sure you don't get plucked like a stray eyebrow hair and get sent with memory loss back to Ghost Island," I say snappishly.

Belren chuckles. "You're adorable when you get worked up."

I sniff, trying to pretend like him calling me adorable doesn't affect me at all. "You didn't answer the question."

"I feel fine, Pinky. Promise." He tries to tap my quiver, but his hand goes through it. "Muck's working great."

I can't exactly let out a breath of relief, but I nod, accepting his answer, just as loud music coming straight from the city pulls my attention away. Looking around, I realize that we've arrived during some sort of festival where fire sprites are busy juggling flaming balls in the street while others dance to pipe music and drink straight from a pond of churning lava.

"Now there's a drink that's sure to burn going down," I quip.

"Hmm, that was better," Belren says, pinching his thumb and pointer finger together. "Just slightly, but still progress."

Indignation rises up. "That was a good joke."

"It was *better*, yes."

This male.

Rolling my eyes, I turn away from him and watch the fire sprites, getting caught up in whatever it is that they're celebrating. The thing about fae is, they'll come up with a holiday for anything because they simply love to party. I bet they'd appreciate a good theme.

The street is lined with black rock houses, but everyone seems to be out here on the street to participate in the revelry. Volcanic rock on the side of the road is being used as seats and tables, dancers are spinning right in the middle of the street, and musicians walk up and down it to liven up the crowd.

There must be at least two hundred sprites around, their collective voices mingling with the music and laughter while they spin their flames.

"Crazy fae," Belren mutters.

The two of us continue to walk around and simply take in all the sights, but despite where I keep my gaze, my attention is always on him. I continuously watch Belren from the corner of my eye, afraid that if I get distracted for even a second, he'll disappear.

"No ghosts."

My eyes scan the city. "You're right. I don't see any here."

"Thank gods for that. Ghosts are the worst."

"*You're* a ghost," I point out.

He gives me a look. "Yes, but I'm the exception."

I can't argue that.

"How are you feeling?" I ask him.

Before he can answer, two sprite children come barreling down the street, kicking a fireball between them. I squeak in alarm as they race right through me. It doesn't hurt—I don't feel a thing, actually, but it's still incredibly off-putting.

Belren gives me an amused look. "Now you see why I hate it when Stag does it."

"Are you going to answer my question?" I ask, though I make sure to move off the street, bringing us further away from the party, toward some larger buildings up ahead.

"I feel great," he says, striding along beside me.

"Really?" I can't help the concern that laces my question.

"Relax. I told you the muck was going to work, didn't I?"

"I have to admit, I'm surprised you were able to make it all the way to this island," I tell him. "But I want you to tell me if you start to feel the pull. Maybe if we can hurry straight back to your island, we can stop you from being affected, or at the very least we can—"

Belren cuts me off abruptly by placing his hand over my mouth.

Why do people keep doing that to me?

My words stutter, and though I can't feel any touch, it still startles me enough to make me forget what I was saying.

"Huh. I'm surprised that actually worked," he says before dropping his hand. "Good to know."

"Why did you do that?" I ask with bewilderment.

"Because. You need to learn to loosen up a bit and stop worrying so much, Pinky."

"It's Lex," I tell him again. "And I'm not worrying. I'm simply trying to talk about what might happen if this goes wrong."

"Right. *Worrying.*"

I let out a disgruntled noise. "Well, *someone* needs to worry between us, and it obviously isn't going to be you."

"You're right, it's not going to be me," he replies. "And do you know why?"

"I'm sure you're going to tell me."

"Because worrying sucks the life right out of you. Worrying about something that *might* happen means you're giving that scenario all of your time and energy and thought rather than simply enjoying the moment." He leans down so that we're face to face, his silver eyes so bright that they don't even look translucent. "We don't know how many moments we have, Pinky. For all we know, this could be the very last one. So enjoy it."

His eyes flick between mine as his words sink in, but I give a nervous laugh. "I'm sorry, but no."

He rears back in surprise. "No?"

I shake my head. "That's nice that you can simply *enjoy the moment*, but I don't operate that way."

"And how do you operate?"

I fling my hands up in frustration. "I worry. And those worries help me to plan. To prioritize. If I worry about the things that might occur, it helps me be prepared for every scenario."

He stares at me like I'm insane. "That's exhausting. You can't possibly enjoy yourself if you're constantly thinking like that."

I sniff. "I'll have you know that I take great enjoyment from planning worst case scenarios. It keeps me calm."

Belren snorts out a laugh. "Now I see why the gods brought me to you."

Caught off guard by his statement, I tilt my head. "Why?"

"Because you're strung tighter than that twisted bun on your head," he says, nodding toward my hair. "I take back what I said about you not being off to a great start with your murder spree. Someone as crazy as you is probably great at it with all of your extra scenario planning."

"Thank you," I say automatically, but then I falter, because I'm not sure that was a good thing. Based on the way he chuckles, I'd say probably not.

Sighing, I whip around and start stalking away.

"Where are you going?"

"To find a clothes shop."

He easily catches up to me. "Why?"

"Because I'll need to get a proper fae outfit for when I leave the Veil. These are human clothes, after all. I stand out too much."

He looks me up and down. "You do. Though I can't say it's the clothes' fault. You stand out all on your own."

I frown as we pass by a fire sprite with burning hair that flows down to her butt, sending sparks off as she walks. "Was that an insult?"

All amusement drains away from his face, and something soft in his eyes makes my throat go tight. "No, Pinky. It definitely wasn't."

"Oh." My voice is suddenly small, unsure, like a tiny step taken on unfamiliar terrain.

I need to stay practical and responsible, but the truth is, my mind is spinning. It has been since he first appeared.

"How are you feeling?" I ask, just to get us back on steady ground where things make sense.

Belren groans. "Pinky."

"Alright, alright," I say, just as my eyes latch onto some larger buildings ahead with wooden signs hanging in front, words burned into them to denote what it is.

"There's the shops."

"Mmm, yes, let's have you go try some things on."

I stop in my tracks. "Umm, no. You wait here."

He sighs dramatically. "Fine."

Even with the festival happening just down the street, there are still sprites going in and out of other shops, but I hesitate. "Will you be alright if I go inside for a minute?"

"We were further away than this on our way here. I'd say the muck has a decent orbit."

I nod, but I still don't go inside, hands itching to wring together. I don't want to say out loud that it makes me nervous to let him out of my sight.

He seems to read my mind, because his gaze softens. "I'll be right here when you get out."

I hesitate for a moment longer. "Alright. I'll be quick. Stay right here."

He salutes and makes a point to plant his feet.

With one last lingering glance to make sure he's not going to suddenly disappear on me, I pop out of the Veil and stride for the door of the shop and open it. A bell jingles above me just before the heavy door swings closed at my back.

Flickering light surrounds me the moment the sunlight is closed out, and I look around the space. Instead of windows, the shop has inlets in all the walls, and inside each small crevice are small orbs of fire. There are too many of them to count, but the glow they give off is soft and welcoming.

It's also *sweltering*.

I'm sweating before I even take three steps inside. "Oh, a visitorrrrr!" someone calls. I look up as an aged fire sprite comes from somewhere in the back, rounding a counter. She comes right up to me, back slightly stooped

138

and two matching wrinkled brackets on both of her cheeks.

The female looks me up and down, red hair practically smoldering from where it hangs over her shoulder. "Well. You're not a sprite."

She seems very disappointed by that realization as she eyes my red feathered wings. I've learned that when visiting the different islands in the fae realm, you have to be careful as some of them are incredibly wary of outsiders. I don't blame them, either. From the research I've done, there's been a violent history between the different kinds of fae, often ending in bloody battles for territory.

"I'm not, but I can't help but admire your work," I praise with a smile. "I would love to purchase something you've made."

I've also learned that most fae like to be flattered.

The fire sprite doesn't smile, but she does lose an inch of the wary hostility she'd taken on, and trades it for mild annoyance.

She glances over my clothing again. "I can see why. This outfit you wear is horribly ugly." Her mouth turns down in distaste. "Come." She turns on her heel and waves me forward. "I have one dress that will fit you."

My brows pull together as I follow her past rows of neatly hung shirts and pants, skirts and blouses. "Just one?" I ask, waving a hand in front of my overheated face.

She shoots me a look over her shoulder. "Yes. Just one. Is that a problem?"

"No," I quickly reply.

She huffs and keeps walking while I try to discreetly wipe some sweat off my temple.

We stop in front of a cabinet that she wrenches open, making some of the fire balls behind the door flicker from the rush of air. She grabs something from inside and then shoves it toward me. "There. Go put it on."

I have to pry it away from my face before I can get a good look at it. "Oh, it's..."

The fire sprite puts her fists on her hips. "It's what?"

It's *very* red. And sparkly. And has so many panels of the fabric that I'm not even sure which end is up.

I clear my throat. "It's just... Do you think I could trouble you for some trousers and a simple tunic instead?"

The female scowls. "No, those are all spoken for. Besides, no outsiders come here except for the festival, so you *must* be here for the festival, yes?"

I blink at her, feeling hotter and hotter by the second —by both the flames surrounding me and her fiery glare. "Oh, umm, yes. Of course."

She nods and points to the dress in my hands. "This is a fire festival dress. You wear this."

It's not a question.

"Okay."

Pasting on a smile, I walk into the curtained dressing room. I carefully set down my bow and quiver, along with my belt and pouch. Then I yank off my human clothes, my nose wrinkling at the rings of sweat that had already pooled beneath both arms of my blouse. Even my wings feel damp. If I stay in here much longer, I'm going to melt.

I quickly pull on the dress, thankful that it's at least a bit airier with its open back that fits my wings, but I can't help but feel incredibly self-conscious. Although, I know that the female isn't going to budge on letting me try on anything else, and I want to get back to Belren.

"Well?" the female barks from the other side of the curtain.

"Umm, is there a shawl?" I ask hopefully, fanning my face again, though it does absolutely nothing to cool me down.

I hear a harrumph, and that's all the warning I get before the curtain is wrenched open and she's standing there scowling at me. "No shawl." She comes in, invading my space, and spins me around, hands tight on my arms as she looks me over. I feel a few tugs as she adjusts some of the panels beneath my wings before spinning me back around. "There. Fits."

I glance down, noting the multiple panels of red silky fabric that hang down from the waist, rather than one solid skirt. I'll definitely have to be careful if a swift wind comes up.

I pick at the bodice, which thankfully, has a bit more structure than the bottom. And I *need* structure on my top half since I'm quite busty. I glance at myself in the small mirror in the dressing room, though the lighting isn't the best. Overall, the dress is far more revealing than what I'm used to, the cherry-red fabric swooping around my neck and leaving my arms bare and my cleavage right out in the open. At least my stomach and hips are covered.

The fire sprite holds out her hand. "Pay now. Three coins."

Her directness continues to take me off guard. "Yes, ma'am."

I bend down and put on my quiver and belt. Reaching into my pouch, I pay her, placing the coins in her waiting palm. As soon as I do, she lights them up in her hand, making me flinch back. After a few seconds, she closes her fist around them, and the flames choke out. "Real," she confirms with a grunt, as if she thought I was going to try to give her fake ones.

She bends down to my discarded clothes and drags her finger across them. "I burn these."

I try to reach for them. "No, wait—"

She doesn't wait.

In a blink, my old outfit goes up in flames, which not only ruins them beyond repair but also makes the temperature kick up another notch.

Within seconds, my clothes are nothing but a pile of ash on the floor.

The fire sprite nods with pride, as if she just did the gods' work. "You go now," she says dismissively, her hand steaming a little as she waves me away.

Without another word, she turns and walks to the back of the shop, disappearing behind a pile of fabric and a curtained-off doorway.

Well.

"Have a nice day," I call brightly.

It's always good to end things on a polite note. Especially because I think she would've set my hair on fire if I'd paid her in fake coins...and she seemed a bit disappointed that I didn't.

Wiping the sweat from my forehead, I make my way out of the stifling clothing shop, the bell jingling behind me as the door shuts. The second I step outside, I take in a huge breath, my body sagging in relief at the fresh air. "Thank goodness," I sigh, closing my eyes for a moment. Sweat begins to cool against my fevered skin, and I make a mental note to make future purchases *anywhere* else except in a fire sprite's shop.

"Well...damn. I know I've been calling you Pinky, but *fuck*, you do look good in red. Though if your goal was not to stand out, you severely failed."

My eyes pop open, finding Belren standing in front of me. And he's *close*. His spectral form carries a cool brush of air, like shade beneath a tree that prickles my skin with exhilarating chills, and all I want to do is sway closer.

I feel my throat tighten, heart kicking up a beat, because he's just so *handsome*. Maybe it has something to do with the fact that he always had silver skin, but his ghostly condition does nothing to take away from his beauty.

For a second, we just watch each other, and it's like the rest of the street fades away.

He frowns at my continued stare and opens his mouth to say something, but then he stops, eyes dropping down to my lips. My cheeks flush, my stomach flutters, and I have the craziest idea that he's thinking about kissing me.

But the moment abruptly snaps off like a dry branch when one side of his mouth kicks up and he says, "You're covered in sweat. Like...an excessive amount. Yet somehow, even that makes you more enticing. Very curious."

Mortified, I quickly reach up to wipe at my forehead again. "It was very hot in there, and I—" We both seem to freeze at the same moment.

"Oh my gods," I blurt, sudden realization slapping me in the face. "I can *see* you."

I'm not in the Veil, and I can see him.

CHAPTER 13

LEX

My mouth is open in shock. "I'm...not. The Veil. How am I... How are you..."

Belren frowns at my incoherent stuttering. "Do you need your seven-foot think-radius again? Is that why you're unable to speak a single thought?"

My heart pounds in my chest as I gape at him. "How the heck is this happening?" I demand, but someone nearly barrels right through Belren just then, reminding me that we're standing in the middle of a busy street in broad daylight. "Come on."

He follows me down the side of the nearest building and all the way around to the back. I look to make sure no one is around, but nothing is behind the buildings except for some stacked crates and the border of the jungle.

Turning to him, I ask, "What's going on?" Confusion billows up around me like a sheet shaken in the wind.

"I don't know, you tell me."

"Well, *I* certainly don't know," I counter.

Thoughtful silence drops between us.

This doesn't make any sense. I shouldn't be able to see him unless I'm in my incorporeal state, inside the in-between of the Veil with him. I rack my mind, trying to think of when this could have happened. But the truth is, I don't know. When he disappeared in front of me back on his island, it could have happened then. But why? And why am I the only one who can see him? No one else was gaping at the ghost on the road—just the scantily dressed cupid.

My hands twist in front of me as I study him. "Do you feel any differently?"

He looks down at his form. "Nope. Still dead."

An undignified snort escapes me before I can stop it. "Alright...so. I can see you. Even when I'm not in the Veil with you."

"Like I said, you're full of surprises."

"Me?" I counter. "This could be a *you* thing. What if something happened with me carrying around your..."

"My muck in your quiver. Go on. Say it," he challenges with a smirk.

A blush creeps up my neck, but I try to cover it up by straightening the panels of my dress. "Do you suppose it's because of that?"

Belren shrugs. "No idea. But obviously you're the only one who can see me, considering that a fire sprite just tried to walk straight through me," he points out.

I nibble on my bottom lip and nervously move the pouch along my belt. His eyes drop down to the sound of jingling coins. "Cupidity pay well?"

"What?" I distractedly glance down at the pouch. "Oh, no. We get paid in the reward of being the one who brought about love and happiness."

He doesn't look impressed. "So how do you have money?"

I glance away, fingers picking at my dress. "I found these coins."

His white brow arches up. "You *found* them?"

"Well, if I happened to see some money fall or get lost, say while I was on duty, I'd simply make a note of it. And then when the room was cleared, I'd leave the Veil and pick it up for safekeeping."

A grin starts to spread over his face.

"It wasn't stealing!" I quickly put in, because I know that's what he's thinking, I just know it.

"Sure, Pinky."

Trying to pretend like I'm not blushing from both embarrassment and guilt, I say, "Okay, back to the real issue at hand—"

"Your predisposition for thievery?"

My eyes narrow. "The fact that I can *see* you."

"Oh. That."

"Unfortunately, I have no idea why. I've never read about this happening before during any of my research."

He starts peering into the different crates stacked around us. "And you researched a lot about ghost and cupid interactions?"

"Well, just a bit of leisurely reading back at Cupidity headquarters. It's always good to better understand the entities that share the Veil with us," I inform him. "Though the entries about ghosts were rather sparse and usually all said the same thing."

"That we're a mumbling, senseless lot?" he guesses before leaping up and sitting on one of the crates, though

146

his legs do sink into it a bit. He still looks very smug that he's able to do it.

"Well...yes," I admit.

He shrugs. "Guess there are no answers then. Oh well."

I blink at him incredulously. "*Oh well?*"

"There's not always going to be an answer for everything, Pinky. We can just go with the flow."

Go with the flow? I laugh, because that's absurd. I've never gone with the flow in my entire afterlife, not even when I got stuck in a river's current once.

"No, no. Definitely not," I say adamantly. "I'll have to research it, or..." I trail off, because I can't go back to Cupidville and leave him behind.

What I need to do becomes abundantly clear. I should've done it as soon as we landed here. "I have someone who can help."

That puts a curious spark in his eye. "You do?"

"Yes. I'm going to call my boss."

"Cupids have bosses?"

What, does he think we're all out here in a love free-for-all? That would be chaos.

"Of course. Cupidity is a thriving enterprise."

"Well, aren't you productive."

I used to have the highest productivity in all of cupidity, but I keep that to myself.

Lifting my hand, I pass my fingers over the cupid markings on my arm, feeling a tingle disperse over my skin.

The number on my skin flares red for a moment as I murmur her name. When the red light goes out, I tug down my sleeve and let out a breath.

He watches it with fascination before asking, "Now what?"

I jump up onto a crate across from him. "Now we wait."

~

It's full dark, hours and hours since I called to Emelle, and still no sign of her.

I'm hoping she'll know why I can suddenly see Belren even when I'm corporeal, but mostly, I'm hoping she can figure out a way to fix him.

Being a ghost is basically like being a dwindling hourglass. I fear that he's going to lose more of himself with every minute that passes. If there's a chance that we can fix him, then it's worth a shot. We need to do *something* before his memory completely fades and he doesn't even remember how to talk. I wouldn't be able to bear that.

Still, we've been waiting so long that I worry the cupid mark didn't work. *What if she didn't sense the call?*

When she used to summon me, I could simply close my eyes and let my cupid mark pop me right over to her. However, Emelle can't go into the Veil because of her mate; I know she has to fly here or take a portal. That must be why it's taking her so long. Hopefully.

Whatever celebration the fae were having earlier is still in full swing now and probably even more rambunctious under the cover of night. That also might have something to do with the fact that I blew a near constant stream of Lust Breath as we passed by earlier. Fire sprites did not disappoint on the heat factor.

The sounds of the crowd are a constant hum of background noise, and I'm itching to pass out a little bit of Lust Breath, but I don't want to risk missing her, so I stay put. Belren and I travelled far enough away to be apart from the festival while still being able to hear it.

Together, we sit beside a small lava pond where no one else is, watching as it pops and gurgles. Just past it, the jungle looms, strange bugs thrumming out with a noise that reminds me of crickets, while other nighttime creatures caw and clack inside the thick branches. Yet despite all of that, plus the bubbling magma and the celebratory fire sprites, it's somehow...peaceful here.

"I have to say, I really do like the new outfit choice," Belren says, head turned toward me as he looks me up and down.

I sit up a bit and glance down at the dress, still feeling a bit self-conscious. I make sure all the panels are covering my legs where they're tucked underneath me. "You don't think it's too..."

"No," Belren cuts in before I can finish, his eyes glinting with something I'm not brave enough to name. "It looks good on you, Pinky," he says softly, the pond illuminating his essence with an ethereal glow.

My cupid senses tingle, and I practically jolt when I realize it's because I'm picking up on strong desire. Not from him—I can't sense anything from ghosts—but from...*me*. That's never happened before.

I turn away, pulling my hands into my lap as I twist them together, my nerves getting the better of me.

This is a risk. Getting close to him. Indulging. Because the fact of the matter is, there's no guarantee that Belren's ghostly status can be changed. There's no guarantee that his memory can be fixed. He could fade away right in front of me and then never come back. There's so much I don't know when it comes to ghosts, and to be honest, I never thought he'd end up as one.

He was supposed to be processed. It's why I spent a year looking for him in those endless lines. No wonder the demon and angel processors never remembered seeing a silver-skinned horned male. I wonder how long he's been a ghost, stuck on that forgetful island. For the most part, he *seems* mostly with it, but what if he's worse off than I realize?

The sensible thing to do would be to make sure I don't get too close. I shouldn't let my emotions get all muddied up in him. But without my consent, it seems my emotions went and started doing that anyway.

I'll have to be careful. After all, he died to save me. I need to put him first. My emotions and wants don't matter.

"Hmm. That's a funny-looking bird."

I follow Belren's gaze to look up at the night sky.

"That's not a bird." I jump to my feet, Belren getting up beside me as we watch two dark forms flying down toward us, and relief floods my chest.

When they get closer, the glow from the pond lights up Emelle's wings and hair, and Belren hums thoughtfully. "I take it that's your boss?"

"Yes," I reply, shooting him a glance from the corner of my eye to see if any form of recognition sparks, but there's nothing in his expression except for curiosity.

"I see red wings and pink hair is a theme with you cupids."

Now that Emelle is closer, I can see that Ronak is with her, their matching red wings cutting through the air.

Emelle's flying is a bit...choppy, whereas Ronak flies with a sort of feline grace, his tail helping to steady him.

"Hi!" Emelle calls down from the air, while I give a welcome wave in reply, watching them fly closer.

"Who's the male?"

"It's one of her mates," I answer Belren quietly.

"*One* of?" he questions with a snort. "What a schmuck. If I were a mate, I wouldn't share."

"He's not a schmuck," I retort, feeling defensive on Emelle's behalf. "He's handsome and strong and a good mate to her. They all are."

Belren turns his head toward me with a fierce scowl, and I blink at the intensity of his stare. "What?" I ask.

His jaw works, and then he shakes his head, lips pressing together. "Nothing."

Shrugging it off, I take a breath. "Now, I'm going to talk to her, and obviously, they won't be able to see you. But just...behave. Okay?"

A mischievous look comes over his face.

"No," I say firmly from the corner of my mouth. "Whatever you're thinking, don't do it."

"You mean, don't stand entirely too close to you while they can't see me?"

"No."

He eats up the space between us, and my breath hitches when he stops right at my back, so close that we're nearly going through each other. "So this...this would be too close?" he asks huskily against my ear. For a moment, I swear I can feel his breath against my skin.

"Yes," I answer, though my voice cracks.

"Hmm," he murmurs, hands coming up to trace over the outline of my arms before settling on my hips as I stand frozen. My eyes lock onto the movement, and I have the strangest urge to arch my back, which is ridiculous, seeing as how that would only encourage him, and we wouldn't be able to feel it anyway.

"And by *behave*, you mean you also wouldn't want me to say dirty things into your ear while they can't hear me and get you all flustered?"

Something warm pools right at my center. "No, no. Definitely don't do that."

"So I shouldn't say..." He leans in even closer, transparent lips kissing against my ear and making that spot of my skin shoot chills down my neck and arms. "Thank you for stuffing my muck in your quiver."

I whip around. "Oh my gods, *stop.*"

He laughs uproariously, his entire body shaking with mirth as I step away to glare at him.

"You're terrible."

"I'm fun," he corrects, still smiling.

Rolling my eyes, I attempt to regain some semblance of composure, turning around just as Emelle and Ronak land a few feet away.

The moment her feet touch the ground, Emelle bends at the waist, hands propped on her knees as she gulps in huge breaths of air. "Freaking fornicators, that was a really long flight," she pants.

"You're a bit out of shape, mate," Ronak tells her, not even appearing winded as he tucks in his red cupid wings against his back, brown trousers hugging his form, tail muscles bulging out of his shirt.

Emelle shoves her sweaty, tousled hair off her forehead and straightens up, yanking at her tangled pink skirts from between her legs. "And *I* clearly picked the *wrong* mate to come with me."

"I'm the only one with wings besides the bull," he points out.

"Yeah, well, Okot would've let me ride him," she grumbles.

Ronak arches a brow and looks at her pointedly. "He did. Before we left."

Emelle cocks her head. "That's...that's true."

"Anyway, we obviously need to get back to doing our drills together. Your flying skills weren't great," Ronak says.

She turns and glares at him. "I'm top heavy," she retorts, pressing on her chest and making Ronak's gaze drop down. "My boobs throw me off-balance. Besides, you said you were gonna help me fly."

"I did help."

Her eyes narrow. "Saying *keep up, little demon* every time I started to lag behind is *not* helping, Ronak."

His mouth twitches beneath his beard as he passes a hand over his wind-blown brown hair. "I disagree. Every time I said it, you flew faster."

If her glare could produce daggers, he would've been stabbed right then. "That's because I was trying to catch up so I could kick you in the happy sacks," she snaps.

Beside me, Belren says, "I like her."

Ronak grins at Emelle, as if he enjoys her violent confession. "You can try, little demon, but if you remember from our old training, you could never land a hit."

Fast as a flash, she elbows him in the stomach, making his laugh splutter out into a surprised grunt.

"*Oooh*, look who landed a hit," Emelle chirps, patting him on the shoulder as he sucks in a breath. "Guess you should practice your drills more, Ro-Ro. You need to work on your blocks."

This time when he smiles, he looks a bit feral, like he wants to eat her up. Judging by the way her cheeks go pink, I'm sure she sees it too—and likes it.

After a moment, they break their heated eye contact, and Emelle clears her throat. "Anyway, you rang?" she asks, looking at me, then her eyes widen. "Wow. Lex. You look beautiful in that dress. It's so…"

"Provocative? Tight? Obscene?"

"I was going to say flashy," she finishes.

I tug at the panelled skirt. "Anyway, thank you for coming." I pause, because even though I've been waiting for her to show up, now I have to figure out how I'm going to tell her. And…well. How do you tell your boss that you accidentally found the ghost of the male who died for you?

Maybe I should talk about the weather first?

"This is an interesting island, wouldn't you say?"

Emelle looks around, gaze landing on the popping lava. "Yeah. Super…fiery."

Ronak coughs. A long pause stretches between us.

"Aren't you going to say something?" Belren mutters from the side of his mouth.

"Shh, I'm thinking."

Emelle's brows lift in surprise. "Oh. Sure. Think all you like. Thinking's important."

"No, sorry, I wasn't saying that to you," I quickly tell her.

She and Ronak exchange a look. "*Okay…*"

Belren walks up to Ronak and looks him up and down. "He's not that handsome, by the way. Passable, at best. It's his muscles that are doing the work, really."

I shoot him an incredulous look before I focus on Emelle again. "I'm sorry for bringing you here. If I could've come back to your island, I would've. I know you're busy with your family."

"Are you kidding?" she says. "With four kids at home, this is like getting a mini-vacation."

"Plus, she obviously needed the flying practice," Ronak interjects.

Emelle rolls her eyes at him, but his tail slips down and wraps around her ankle, making her smile.

"These two practically reek of sexual tension, eh?" Belren asks.

As a matter of fact, they *do*, but their lust is a very pleasant scent. Like strawberries.

"He could do with a beard trim if you ask me. And his hair looks like it hasn't seen a comb in a decade," Belren grumbles.

I contain my sigh.

"So," Emelle begins. "I know whatever you called me here for must've been important. What's wrong?"

I wring my hands together, fingers pinching, and Emelle frowns at the nervous gesture. "I've never seen you like this. You're all...jittery."

She's right. I'm *always* put-together, especially in front of her. After all, I took my job as her assistant very seriously. Professionalism is my middle name. Or it could be Barbara. I feel like a Barbara. But right now, my nerves are getting the better of me.

Just as my pulse begins to race and I start to feel like a

complete idiot, Belren steps up close to my side. I feel a shiver go down my back, and I whip my head to the left to see Belren's phantom finger trail over my shoulder. My breath hitches, and all my worried thoughts instantly evaporate.

His finger trails from my shoulder and then all the way down my bare back. My entire body shivers in response, nearly feeling a kiss of cold air exhaled in the wake of his touch. I realize I'm staring at him when he winks at me, and then he leans in close to my ear. "Go on," he purrs. "Tell her about…my *muck*."

The spell is immediately broken, and I jerk my elbow back at him, though my arm goes uselessly through his torso. "*Shut up*," I hiss, horrified that he just got me so flustered in front of my boss.

Belren chuckles and steps back, his touch falling away with the movement. I won't give credence to the bereft reaction I have at the loss.

"Lex?" Emelle says, sounding wary. "Are you okay over there? I'm not gonna lie, things are getting weird."

I shake my head to clear it and face her again, determined to get this out. "I'm sorry," I tell her. "I'm just having a difficult time figuring out how to explain."

"Oh, don't worry. Ronak once invited his mother over for dinner and then *forgot to tell me*. Believe me, there's no worse news than that."

Ronak winces at the memory.

"Well…" I hesitate once more, half expecting Belren to try something again, but luckily he keeps his phantom hands to himself. "After I left your house, I didn't actually start working. I went to the island where the battle happened."

Surprise flashes over her face. "*The* battle?"

"Yes. I was hoping to find some closure," I admit.

"Oh. Did you find it?"

"Not exactly."

Part of my nervousness stems from the fact that I need to tell Emelle without triggering Belren. I choose my next words carefully. "I didn't find closure because instead, I found a certain horned *ghost*."

CHAPTER 14

LEX

*M*y admission is met with silence.

Emelle and Ronak stare at me, and then after a second, Emelle's multi-colored eyes widen. "*Oh my gods*. Are you saying what I think you're saying?"

I nod slowly. "And the ghost...well. He's here."

She glances around the empty spaces like she's trying to spot him. "He's *here*? Right now?"

Belren strides over to her and holds out his hand. "Hello, other Pinky."

Of course, she doesn't see him, so it's his bad luck that Emelle bursts forward in that instant, walking right through him to wrap me up in a hug. "I can't believe this!" she exclaims. "You found—"

"Hook," I blurt, cutting her off.

She starts to pull away in confusion, but I bring my arms up and squeeze her tight, pressing my lips against her ear to whisper. "Call him Hook. He doesn't remember who he is, and we can't trigger him with memories, or he might get sucked back to his deathplace and forget

158

everything," I rush to explain. "And...I can *see* him. Even when I'm not in the Veil."

Emelle goes stiff in my arms as she takes in what I've said. "Like...right now?"

I nod against her and then release her slowly, my eyes flicking over to where Belren is standing next to Ronak a couple feet away. "This bastard has a lot of muscles, doesn't he? And why's his tunic undone at the top like that? What's he trying to prove?" Belren grouses.

Gods.

Pulling away, Emelle searches my face. "I can't believe this," she says quietly, tears in her eyes. "I never thought he'd be a ghost."

Sadness spears through my stomach. "Me either."

"He should've moved on. Should've picked a job," she goes on, quickly wiping her eyes. "Is he...is he okay?"

"He's better than any ghost I've ever come across. He's coherent." *For now* is the unspoken end to that sentence, and we both know it.

Emelle's eyes immediately fill as a sob wrenches out of her. The second she does, Ronak is at her side in a second. "What's wrong?" he demands.

Instead of answering, she buries her head against his chest as another cry comes out, muffled this time. But with this sudden flood of emotion, Lust Breath starts puffing out of her lips, her tucked wings begin to glow a bit with heavenly light, and lucky pennies fall from the sleeves of her gray dress.

Ronak flinches and makes a pained grunt as he gets a face-full of Lust. "You're leaking."

"What?" Emelle pulls back, eyes widening at the pink cupid power she's exhaling. "Whoops. Sorry." She pins her lips together and shakes her hands to try to stop the lucky coins from falling. I watch as they tinkle to the ground in a nice, neat little pile until she can get it to stop.

Belren pops up next to me. "Your penchant for coin thievery is tingling, isn't it?"

"It's not thievery," I sigh.

Emelle seems to get a handle on herself, wings dimming down as the coins stop falling and the last of the Lust Breath diminishes. "Are you talking to Hook?"

I nod. "He's standing right here."

Her gaze moves to where I indicated, and her eyes shine again, but she manages to keep the tears in. Ronak tenses up. "Who the fuck is Hook? And why is he making you cry?"

Emelle shakes her head at him. "Ook-hay is elren-bay so don't alk-tay about it right now, okay?"

Ronak stares at her like she's insane. "*What?*"

She sighs and looks at me with a shake of her head. "Fae. Always thinking they're so superior, when they can't even speak pig Latin."

"What the fuck is pig Latin?" Ronak asks incredulously.

"Well, it's an argot," I quickly jump in. When he turns that blank stare at me, I go on. "A pseudo-language that humans used, probably starting sometime in their 1800s. Mostly by children, but adults as well. It was a very effective way to talk in simple code."

"See?" Emelle says to Ronak. "Lex gets me."

Ronak shakes his head. "Cupids," he mutters.

Emelle tugs on his beard lightly, making him bend down until her mouth is next to his ear to whisper. His eyes widen as she speaks, presumably catching him up.

He lets out a whistle. "Fuck."

She rolls back on her heels. "Mm-hmm."

"I have to say, this is a very strange boss-employee meeting," Belren tells me.

He's not wrong.

"I'm sorry I sprung this on you. It was a shock to me as well."

"Don't be sorry," Emelle tells me, giving one last swipe beneath her eye. "Ever since I had the triplets, I'll cry at just about anything."

"Parenting sounds very...disconcerting," I sympathize.

"It really is," she agrees with a sigh. "So, how can I help?"

"For starters, I don't know why I'm able to see him outside of the Veil."

Her brows pull together. "Yeah, that's weird. I've never heard of that happening before."

"Me either."

"I also thought ghosts stayed put for the most part," Emelle points out. "Didn't you say you found him on the other island?"

"I did. He said his deathplace was keeping him there, but he was able to come with me, because..."

Belren sidles up to me. "My muck's in your quiver. Say it," he chimes in, voice chock-full of amusement.

"I scooped up some of the dirt from his deathplace spot and took it with me," I say pointedly.

Belren blows out a breath in disappointment. "That was the boring way to say it."

This male is going to give me an eye twitch.

"And that actually worked?" Emelle asks, surprise written all over her face.

"So far."

"Huh." I can't tell if she looks more confused or impressed.

"Tell her it was my idea," Belren says with a wag of his brows, practically bouncing back on his feet.

I roll my eyes and then glance at Ronak. "I meant to tell you earlier, but your muscles are looking quite impressive."

Belren's gray eyes darken, and he bristles beside me, while Ronak tips his head, looking smug. "Bigger than the fucking lamassu, even."

"Very nice."

"Don't encourage him," Emelle says.

Just like I'd hoped, Belren is adequately distracted with sizing Ronak up again, so I use the opportunity to take Emelle by her arm and lead her several steps away toward the lava pond where I'm hoping the bubbling will help cover up our voices.

"I'll have Sev ask around. The angels might know if this has happened before," Emelle whispers.

"Thank you." I cast a look over my shoulder before I ask the real question that's been burning on the tip of my tongue. "Is there something we can do to fix him? Can you...de-ghost him?"

Emelle blows out a deep breath, the light of the pond making her pink hair shine like sherbet. "Honestly? I don't know."

My heart drops.

"The stubborn, difficult ass couldn't just pass on and pick a damn afterlife job like the rest of us?" Emelle growls out, kicking at the ground. "He had to go and be a freaking ghost?"

A sad smile tips my lips.

"Although, it's kind of funny that he stuck around on that island and that the first person to find him was *you*."

"What do you mean?"

Emelle digs up her sleeve, plucking a stray coin that was left behind from the earlier outpour and tosses it into the pond with a fiery plop. "You don't think you were the only one who looked for him, do you?"

When I don't answer, she gives me a wry smile. "Oh, come on, Lex. I knew you were looking for him—looking all over headquarters. I got a few complaints from some Veil supervisors," she tells me with a snort. "But Sev and I were looking for him too. We've been to that island more times than I can count. Maybe he was waiting for you to find him."

My heart stutters. "Me?"

As if she can sense the turbulence inside of me, she offers me a smile. "It wasn't me that he jumped in front of that day. I don't think it's a coincidence that you're the one who found him."

Emotion that I don't know how to digest wells up in my throat, and she watches me expectantly.

"Technically, he found me."

She rolls her eyes at that. "Of course he did. The Horned Hook always shows off when it comes to finding things. When he gets his memory back, he's going to brag about this for years."

My eyes widen at her use of *when*. "So you think we actually have a chance at helping him?"

For the first time, she wavers, her expression turning less confident. "I gotta be honest, and I know this is going to come as a total shock to you, but I actually have no idea what I'm doing for cupids most days, let alone any other Veil entity. I have no idea if a ghost can be de-ghosted."

My stomach ties in knots. "Of course." I was stupid to hope.

She reaches over and gives my hand a quick squeeze. "*But* I'm the cupid boss bitch," she says, all that confidence swinging right back into her. "That means I'm going to figure something out. I'm going to talk to Sev and see if he can do some digging. I'd ask you, since you're obviously the better researcher, but you'll need to stay with B— Hook, to make sure you keep him grounded."

"Well, that's another thing," I say, hands wringing. "He sort of appeared when I came up with a certain idea. Something I thought I could do to help avenge his death and maybe gain some closure from the fates."

"What idea?"

I glance over briefly to see Belren intently studying Ronak's wings like he's trying to find a feather out of place.

Heat flames my cheeks, and it has nothing to do with the lava bubbling in front of us. "Well, see, I just got this idea into my head about getting retribution for him. So he sort of overheard me say that I was going to avenge his death by tracking down Princess Soora."

I leave off the *and kill her* part because I certainly don't want to make Emelle into an accessory. I'm already solidly in premeditated murder territory.

"When I said it aloud, that's the moment he appeared. So I think he might've come back because of it."

Emelle's brows jump up in surprise. "Did he recognize the name?"

"No. But he is insistent on going with me."

She nibbles her lip in thought. "Maybe you're right. Maybe the best thing to do is to help him do this."

"You think?"

"Keeping him focused is the best thing you can do. You know how ghosts are. They're flighty. Forgetful," Emelle says. "*You* are his line, Lex. Keep him invested, and maybe he'll keep fighting to stay as much of himself as he can. Keep him busy. Keep him focused. If he was brought here because of Soora, then help him do what he needs to. In the meantime, I'll find out everything I can and see how we can de-ghost him."

A seed of hope buries itself in the pit of my stomach. "Thank you."

"Don't thank me. He's my friend, and he doesn't deserve to waste away like that. Oh!" she exclaims with a sudden snap of her fingers. "That reminds me. I actually heard a rumor that Soora is holed up on a fae island that her father used to own. It was called Havershore... Or maybe Hackenshire? Something like that. You could check it out."

I file the information away as Ronak walks over just then, with Belren trailing behind him. "Did you know that his wings are roughly fifteen feet across?" Belren scoffs. "He must be compensating for something, don't you think?"

My eyes nearly bug out of my head when he gestures to his groin. "Stop it," I hiss.

He shrugs.

"Everything okay?" Ronak asks, but there's no way that I'm going to tell him what Belren has been saying about his privates.

Luckily, Emelle answers. "Yep, all good. But I have

some serious work to do. We need to get back home to check on the kids, and then I can call on Sev plus a certain angel and demon to find out some ghostly answers."

"Is this going to be okay?" I ask her worriedly. "I know you can't go to Cupidville…"

Emelle sighs. "Nope. Or into the Veil to see Hook," she says, and I don't miss the longing in her voice. Neither does Belren, because he grins at the attention. "I wish I could, but my freaking mate here goes all crazy."

Ronak scowls at her. "It's not my fault that the alpha in me takes over when you go into the Veil. It feels like a severed mate bond, like you've *died*. My animal turns feral over it."

"Like I said, dramatic."

He flicks his tail up to whip at her butt, making her jump. "Hey!"

"Oops," he deadpans. "Ready to go?"

"Yeah. But you have to carry me home this time. My wings are sore."

She barely has the words out of her mouth before Ronak has scooped her up into his arms, making her squeal out a laugh.

"I'll give you a better ride than that bull would've," he practically growls in her ear. He's a terrible whisperer.

Emelle's cheeks go pink, but she smiles at him before looking back at me and tapping on her cupid mark. "Call me if you need me, but I'll come find you when I have news. It might take me a bit, so just hang in there?"

"I will. Thank you."

Belren and I watch Ronak lunge up, red wings stretched out as he effortlessly gets them airborne.

"*Fifteen feet*," Belren grumbles. "Gotta be compensating."

Within seconds, the darkness of night swallows the two of them up, and they disappear from view.

"Well, that was entertaining," Belren notes, coming to stand beside me. "Let's leave on a positive note, shall we? Time to go murder that person."

"Goodness, can you stop saying it so willy-nilly?"

He frowns. "Who's Willy?"

"Never mind."

"Good. Let's go," he says as he starts striding away.

As I watch him, I repeat Emelle's words in my head. *Keep him busy. Keep him focused.*

Luckily for him, those are two things I excel at. And if tracking down the ex-princess will achieve that, then that's what we'll do.

After all, how hard can it be to find one of the most notorious fae in all the realm?

CHAPTER 15

LEX

*U*pdate: Trying to find one of the most notorious fae in all the realm is very, very hard.

Belren and I spend the next five days traveling from place to place, searching for information. It's a bit like leapfrog. We hop over the islands one by one in a seemingly never-ending procession. But each island we've been to so far has gone the same way. We go to the biggest city, I stay corporeal while Belren trails me, and I ask around for information about the place that Emelle mentioned.

The problem is, nobody seems to have ever heard of Havershore *or* Hackenshire. I really wish I'd taken the time to ask her more about it, to see where she'd heard the rumor exactly. For all I know, it doesn't even exist.

Although, it very well could. Afterall, the fae realm is big. *Huge.* There are so many islands speckled around the skies that I'm not even sure where this realm ends or begins—I have no idea just how far it stretches. I'd love to research it. I myself have been to precisely two hundred and fourteen islands, and even I have never come close to visiting them all.

"This place looks promising," Belren says beside me, boots sinking through the sandy street as he looks around the city.

I don't reply, because we're on the beaches of some green-tinged shore that's teeming with fae of all types and sizes. I've learned to be careful in crowds, since it's not going to do me any favors if people think I'm talking to myself. The thick crowd makes it so I have to zigzag as I walk, sand filling my silk slippers as I go.

Clusters of booths are set up all along the beach, and intense haggling is getting tossed back and forth between merchants and buyers. Fae shout at me, trying to sell their wares or asking what kind of fae I am because of my feathered wings, but I just keep a polite yet distant smile on my face and keep walking.

"You hate this, don't you?" Belren muses.

I cut him a quick glance before looking forward again. I have no idea how he's picked up on my discomfort. I mentally check myself, but my smile is still in place. He's right, though, I *do* hate this. The only time I like being surrounded by this many people is when I'm in the Veil and they can't see me. People are loud and messy and rude and *emotional*. To be honest, it's all a bit overwhelming.

Belren on the other hand seems to enjoy it, head swivelling on a pin like he doesn't want to miss a thing. His eyes practically glint with rapt attention. Any time we're around so much liveliness, it's as if he wants to soak it up like a sponge. Not that I blame him. It's the curse of the living to take life for granted. It's the curse of the dead to grieve for it.

"How about that place?"

I follow the direction Belren is pointing, where the beach market ends and the city's buildings begin. Just ahead, there's a tavern smooshed between two shops, its telltale sign of two toasting cups hanging from its weathered eave.

Thank goodness.

Nodding, I veer slightly and make my way up the short incline. My feet escape the deep sand as I step onto the hard packed dirt road instead, lifting my skirt so I don't get it dirty. This one, at least, isn't red. Belren was right about the fire sprite outfit. It definitely didn't help me to blend in. Which was why I bought new clothes at the next island over, going for this simple cream dress with no revealing, skintight panels.

I let out a little breath, silently grateful to leave the boisterous market behind. Some of the tension leaves my shoulders as we approach the buildings made of driftwood, their roofs lined with pretty shells.

Once inside, my eyes adjust to the darker lighting as the scent of soggy wood and stale alcohol fills my nose. Several people watch me while I make my way toward the back of the room where I nab an empty table. We must have missed the lunch rush, because it's relatively quiet in here, though there's a fae male in the corner playing a tiny instrument that resembles a door harp, with small wooden balls that he lets tap against the chord strings as he sings in a language I don't recognize.

The moment I'm seated, an orange-skinned server bustles over, her apron cinched so tight it's like a second corset. She doesn't even blink at the bow and quiver strapped to my back, but my wings give her pause. It's why I'm careful to keep my non-pointed ears hidden. "Happy midday. You just missed our luncheon, but I can get ya a bowl of stew and a pint if that's amenable?" she asks, and I'm sure her smile is friendly, but the row of razor sharp teeth is a bit disconcerting.

"Yes please on the stew, and just some water."

She nods with another flash of her sharp teeth and then leaves to disappear through a door behind the bar.

"Still not loosening up, I see," Belren notes as he frowns down at the empty chair next to me.

I look around to make sure no one is watching me before I ask quietly, "What do you mean?"

"The pint you turned down—you always drink water. It's so—"

"Boring," I finish, rolling my eyes at the table. "Yes, I know. You've told me," I mutter.

"*You're* not boring, just some of your choices are," he corrects, as if that's any better. "Like drinking water instead of getting nice and sloshed."

Nice and sloshed? Well, that sounds horribly irresponsible. Irritated, I flick my gaze toward the chair with my brow cocked at him in silent challenge.

Getting the hint, he starts to lower himself tentatively, like he's getting ready to do some squats rather than just sit down. He grimaces when he goes straight through the seat, and I have to hold back my smile by pinning my lips together.

He starts swearing like a sailor when he still can't manage to sit, cursing not only the chair, but the wood from the tree it came from too. I'm lucky that the female fae comes back and plops my stew and water in front of me so I can pretend I'm not a second away from laughing outright at him.

"Having trouble?" I murmur into my spoon, trying to keep my mouth from twitching.

"Fucking ghost body," he grumbles.

Finally, after a few more tries, he manages to sit poised on the chair instead of falling through, and he grins in victory. "Ha. There we go."

His triumph is fully celebrated as he lounges back like a lion poised over its kill. But despite the fact that I'm trying to hide it, he must notice my lips are turned up, because he says, "Something funny, Pinky?"

I sip some broth before looking up at him and shake my head with innocence.

He doesn't buy it. "You know, it's not nice to laugh at a ghost's impairment. We can't help our immaterial status."

This time, I snort into my cup.

He lets out a huff and tries to cross his arms, but he hasn't practiced that enough to pull it off. "How's the stew?"

I swallow another spoonful. "Delicious."

Another huff. "I think I miss food."

He says this every time I eat.

With a discreet nod in understanding, I bring the spoon up and drink down more of the warm broth. I lick my lips, soaking up the saltiness with the tip of my tongue. I can empathize with him on the food part, at least. There was a long time as a cupid where I was really nothing more than a glorified ghost with Love Arrows. That's why I always relish every meal I get to eat, even something as simple as midday stew.

As I continue to eat, I realize that Belren has gone

quiet. I glance up to see that he's watching me with rapt interest, gaze locked on my lips. I pause before taking my next bite, and my eyes flick around the room before settling on him again.

Maybe some of it dripped down my chin?

"What?" I whisper just as I wipe at my face—nothing.

He blinks, like being snapped out of a trance. "Nothing," he quickly says.

I finish the rest of my stew in silence, listening to the musician's quiet song that drowns out most of the noise filtering in from the street. Though every time I take a bite, my senses prickle, and I know Belren is watching me.

He's been doing that lately. A lot.

Sometimes, I wonder if I'm piquing some part of his broken memory. Like I'm a hint of déjà vu and he's not quite sure how to place the feeling. If that's the case, I can't encourage it.

I'm honestly shocked that this plan of his has worked. Every time we travel to yet another island, getting further away from his deathplace, it's a miracle he doesn't get pulled away, no matter how careful I am with his muck.

"Are you going to go chat with the locals?"

I get pulled from my thoughts at his question, and I can't help the sigh that escapes. He catches it, even though I do it under my breath. "Problem?"

I shake my head and put down the spoon in my empty bowl and glance around. There are only three other occupied tables, plus one person sitting at the bar, nursing a cup.

"This island seems more worldly, don't you think?" Belren notes. "There are a lot of different types of fae here, which means they've traveled from elsewhere. Plus, this island is bigger—big enough to have its own sea. Surely someone knows something about this Soora you're searching for."

He's right. Out of all the islands we've visited so far, this one has the most potential for answers.

The problem is...I'm stalling.

I know that I need to keep Belren's attention, but I'm worried that if we somehow do find Soora, he'll have nothing else to ground him afterward. Nothing else to keep him focused. If Emelle hasn't figured out a solution before that...what will happen to him then?

I'm terrified to find out.

"How about them?" Belren asks, pointing toward the trio of females sitting together near the front window.

They seem very...talkative. And animated. No doubt they probably have the most gossip, but chatty females make me nervous. They seem like the type of people who could talk for hours. The kind that you run into at the supermarket and they catch you up on their life for forty-five minutes when all you want is to buy your ice cream and go home to eat it in peace.

Better steer clear.

I shake my head at Belren and instead choose the lone male sitting at the bar. "Him? Really?" Belren says behind me with a groan.

I get up and walk over, holding my wings tight against my back and making sure my pulled-back hair is still covering my ears until I awkwardly take a seat next to him. Since there are at least ten other open stools, he jerks his head in my direction—probably to tell me off for sitting so close—but stops himself when he sees me.

"Well, hello," he drawls, tipping his non-existent hat.

He has deep blue skin that looks a bit like fish scales on his knuckles, and thick hair roped down his back. But what's distracting is the third eye sitting just in the center of his forehead. It doesn't blink as often as the others. "Can I buy you a drink?"

Not at all anticipating the offer, and fully sidetracked with staring at the third eye, I get caught by surprise. "Oh. Well...I'd love a chamomile tea with honey."

A frown pulls a crooked line between his brows.

The female server who brought my stew looks up from behind the bar where she's busily wiping down the counter. "We don't have that."

A snort directly behind me makes my shoulders stiffen when I realize Belren is right at my back. "They don't have tea here, Pinky."

True to the nickname, I can feel my cheeks going as pink as my hair.

"Go on. Butter him up with some small talk," Belren coaches.

Clearing my throat, I turn back to the male and offer him a smile. *Small talk, small talk, small talk...*

"So...how is it having a third eye?"

The male blinks at me—all three lids.

Belren practically cackles with laughter, making my face go fiery.

"I mean...as far as ocular perception goes, it must be quite helpful."

Another triple blink.

Small talk is not one of my greatest skills. Blowing out a breath, I give up since it's clear I'm not buttering him up for anything other than the desire to get away.

"Have you ever heard of Havershore or Hackenshire by chance?"

He takes a couple beats to answer and then gives me a gruff, "No."

Then he slides off his stool and leaves without so much as a backward glance.

Belren half groans and half chuckles. "Gods, you're awful at this."

"I guess he was touchy about the eye thing."

The female server behind the bar snickers. "Ya think?"

"I didn't mean to offend him."

"Nah, offend some more blokes. It tickles me," she laughs, making me smile right along with her.

"You wouldn't happen to have heard of those islands, have you?"

She shakes her head. "Nope. Why you looking?"

I hesitate a moment, quickly glancing at Belren, who gives a shrug.

"Well..." I lean in closer. "I actually heard that someone was hiding out there."

I have her full attention now, and she leans in toward me from the other side of the bar, slapping away a strand of orange hair that fell out of her bonnet, cleavage nearly spilling out onto the bartop.

"Who?" she asks, citrus eyes gleaming with interest.

"Oooh, you've got her now," Belren says with a chuckle.

"Soora," I answer quietly. "The ex-princess."

The female rears back, first in surprise and then with disgust. She turns her head and spits on the floor. "That high fae traitor!" she hisses, sharp maw snapping. "I'd gut her with my teeth if I ever saw her, I would."

This is pretty much the same reaction I've gotten from everyone else. Sometimes it's them spitting, sometimes it's them cursing her name, but the sentiment is the same. Soora certainly won't be winning any realm-wide popularity contests anytime soon.

"She sided with that bloody king and prince in the end —those rotters thinkin' they're so much better than lesser fae. Turned her back on the rebellion, all so she could save her own skin." She spits again just for good measure.

"No one likes a turncoat."

She gives me a look, lips curling down. "What the blazes is you talkin' about coats for?"

"Nothing, never mind," I quickly say. "So you're sure you haven't heard of those islands?"

She shakes her head. "No."

Belren slumps in disappointment, but I can't say that I'm surprised about her answer. "Well, thank you for entertaining my curiosity," I tell her with a smile. I get up off the stool and pull out some coins from my pouch and set them on the bar in front of her. "And thank you again for the stew."

Just as I turn to leave, her hand shoots out and grabs hold of my arm. I jolt to a stop and turn back to her, Belren leaping to my side as if he can do something.

But the female just flashes me a smug, sharp smile. "Now, I said I've never heard about those islands. I *didn't* say that I don't know someone who can help you find that traitor bitch princess."

CHAPTER 16

LEX

The sky decided to collect little cotton balls of clouds earlier, and now those very same clouds have puffed up and decided to drip all over us.

Luckily, I'm not getting soaked since I'm hiding in the Veil with Belren while we stare across the dirt road. A road that's forlorn, empty of anything next to it except for a solitary driftwood fence that seems to stretch on for miles.

We followed the server's directions exactly, walking for at least an hour to get here. Yet now, I'm not sure if *here* is where I want to be.

"It looks unsafe, doesn't it?" I ask from my perch on the wooden fence. Belren gave up trying to sit on it with me when he went through the post for the tenth time.

Standing next to me, he stares past the path. It cuts away from the road, through a field of wheat so tall we would've missed the building right in the middle if it weren't for the fact that the house is seven stories high.

Seven.

And for every one of those levels, it tilts in a different direction and is made with a different material. It looks like it's one strong gust away from blowing over into a mismatched heap.

"I'm sure it's fine," Belren replies.

"That does not look fine," I retort. "That looks like a disaster waiting to happen. The roof is almost *sideways*."

He grimaces at that and tilts his head in the same direction that the top of the roof is leaning. "It just has character."

I shoot him an incredulous look.

"Oh, come on, Pinky," he says, moving to stand in front of me. "If it really does start to lose its battle with gravity, you can just flick back into the Veil before it crashes down on your pretty head."

I will *not* get butterflies in my stomach for the fact that he just called my head pretty. Logically, it's not even a very good compliment as far as compliments go.

This is what I tell myself as I stare at him, right up until my traitorous stomach flutters anyway.

Gods.

"Should we really go in there?"

"This is our only lead," Belren reminds me.

There is that.

"Fine." I begin to make my way across the road, heading straight for the small walking path that diverts through the field. It's still raining, so there are puddles on the ground that I'm thankful I'm not stepping in.

We walk quietly for a few moments, my eyes locked on the seven-story atrocity ahead. "This fae that we're going to visit...I should admit that I don't really believe this person is an actual fortune-teller who can give us information on the ex-princess."

"The barmaid didn't say fortune-teller. She said he's a seer."

"You know what I mean," I tell him as I sidestep a cluster of wheat stalks that have been snapped in the middle, bent in defeat. "I'm not sure I really believe that this person is actually a seer."

Belren cocks a white brow, the silver of his skin muted to the same drab gray of the rain clouds. "You're a cupid in the fae realm, walking with a ghost whose muck you're carrying in your quiver, and yet you're doubting the existence of a seer?"

I don't like his tone.

"I've been to a lot of different realms and seen a lot of different magic, but I've never seen someone who could actually see the future. Even angels can't do that."

"I suppose we're about to find out."

At that moment, we reach the end of the path and come to the house that now looms over us like a jagged shadow. The front of the home is just as ramshackle as the rest of it, with a crooked yellow door surrounded by crooked red bricks. Above the brick is wood paneling painted stark white, above that is cobbled stone, above that is some kind of plaster, above *that* is another kind of wood... On and on. It's a mess.

"This thing is breaking so many building and safety codes," I grumble.

"The flowers are a nice touch," Belren says, gesturing to the window boxes overflowing with plants—though I wouldn't call them flowers. They're more like weeds with some petals that have somehow managed to cling on.

Belren glances over at me. "Ready?"

With a disinclined nod, I start to walk to the front door, which for some reason, he finds hilarious. "Forgetting something?"

I look down. Oh. Right.

Grudgingly, I pop out of the Veil, blinking back into the physical world. I straighten my shoulders, adjusting to the sudden weight of my body, while rain splatters over me, saturating my feathers and making tendrils of my pink hair stick to the back of my neck. Raising my fist, I very lightly rap on the splintered wood, dropping my hand again as quickly as I can.

Belren looks from me to the door and back again. "*That* was your knock? You barely made a sound."

I shove water out of my eyes, getting more and more soaked by the second. "Well, excuse me, but I'm afraid to do it any harder!"

A devilish smirk lifts up his lips. "Oh, Pinky. Doing it harder is half the fun."

My brow furrows. "What? Of course it's not. One firm knock and this place will keel right over."

He chuckles and shakes his head. "Why is it that whenever I try to flirt with you, you either don't realize it or your face blushes so red that it nearly matches your wings?"

I blink at him. "When were you flirting with me?"

"You know, as a cupid, you should really be more adept at sexual innuendos. Especially when you're the one saying them."

I rewind my brain to remember what I said, and my cheeks flame. "I didn't...that's not what I meant."

His grin widens, and it does something warm and fluttery to my insides. "I know, Pinky."

See, he's saying, *I know, Pinky,* which in itself is innocent. But the *way* he says it is something else entirely. He soothes it out, like a caress. And not a platonic kind, either. It's a sensual one. I don't know how to logically explain that, but it's true. I even get a shiver when he says it. The male can speak sensual caress. It's not good.

I turn my attention away from him to stare at the door. I'm not walking into that conversation, because not only am I woefully unprepared, but I'm also confused. Was Belren a flirt to everyone while he was alive? Is this just the pieces of his preserved personality that he's using like muscle memory? ...Or is he actually flirting with *me*?

Unsure of what to do with myself, I tentatively knock again.

"That was even quieter than the first time," Belren says. He lifts his fist and tries to knock himself, but his hand goes right through the door.

"Godsdammit," he curses. "How the hell did Rocky manage it?"

Here we go.

"Still jealous?" I tease.

"Me? Jealous?" he scoffs. Then pauses. "Actually, yeah."

I let out a snort, and in the exact moment I make that impolite noise, the door suddenly wrenches open. My eyes widen and I instinctively take a step back in surprise. Of course, my foot lands right in a puddle, making mud splash up onto my pretty cream hem.

I lift my foot up, my shoe already soggy, my skirt ruined. "Oh, fudge."

The fae in front of me makes a grunt. "Well, I don't have fudge, but I've got some sugar cubes that I can dip in cocoa beans. It will cost you, though." He looks at me like he's trying to decide how much money he can get out of me for his offer.

The fae is short, only about three feet tall, wearing red button-up footie pajamas, complete with a nightcap on his stringy brown hair that hangs down from beneath it. I have no idea what kind of fae he is, but I know better than to ask. Considering he's in footies, I'd expect him to either be very young or very old, but in fact, he's actually somewhere right smack in the middle.

"Hello, I'm so sorry to bother you."

He grunts again, watching dispassionately as I continue to get rained on.

"I was told you might be able to help me find someone?"

He thinks about it for a moment, scratching at his prickly chin. "That'll cost you, along with the cocoa sugar cubes."

I pat the pouch on my belt. "I can pay."

Turning, he starts striding back through his house and waves for me to follow him. "Come on, then. But wipe your feet. I like to keep a tidy house."

I hesitate for a moment, looking up at the house to make sure it's not actually swaying before I head inside. I frown at the crinkling noise that happens as soon as I step onto the floor. Instead of a welcome mat or woven rug, there's a few layers of paper wrappings laid down.

"Well, go on—wipe your feet, Pinky," Belren laughs.

Wrinkling my nose, I hastily wipe as much mud off of my shoe as I can, though the paper keeps ripping. I finally give up and decide to take them off entirely and leave them beside the door as I close it behind me.

When I turn back around, I get a good look at the inside for the first time. Just like the outside, it's a crooked, disheveled, mismatched mess. His idea of a *tidy house* is very different from mine.

"Goodness," I whisper, cringing as I look around.

The ceiling is so warped some of the wood panels are bowing. The walls are caked-on slashes of different colored paint bright enough to give me a headache. The staircase just looks like a health and safety issue. None of the steps are even or straight, the banister is missing in some parts, and yet it curves on and on and on, high up enough in its spiral that I can't see the top.

This place is so disjointed that it's making me dizzy.

Belren stops by a spot on the wall that's covered with a portrait of the small fae, his visage smoking a two-pronged pipe. Of course, the painting is hung crookedly. "Fancy fella, eh?" he grins.

"I'm gonna be sick," I whisper-groan.

Belren glances around, noting the chartreuse paint splatters all over the crooked wood flooring. "Honestly, I don't think he'd notice."

"Oy! It's rude to linger in someone's house!" I look up in the direction of the fae, who's glowering at me from the spiral stairwell. "Now come on. I don't have all day."

My eyes widen. "You...want me to come up there?" I think my question might end in a terrified squeak, but my ears are ringing with too much adrenaline to know.

He doesn't deign to answer me and instead rolls his eyes and turns around to disappear into whatever offshoot his slanted staircase leads to.

"Come on, Pinky, I'll go first," Belren offers before making his way to the stairs. He travels up the first few steps before turning around with a flourish. "See? It's fine."

"It's not comforting when you don't actually have a physical body," I hiss under my breath, eyeing the structure once more.

"Aww, come on. Live a little."

That's rich coming from a literal *ghost*.

Both forlorn and fearful for my life, I follow. When my bare foot lands on the very first step, the wood groans under my weight, making me shoot Belren a dirty look. "If I die on this staircase and the whole disfigured house comes toppling down on me, I'm going to come back and haunt *you*," I threaten.

But the male just grins at me over his shoulder before he continues his way up. "There's that viciously vindictive side I love about you."

That shouldn't make my heart skip a beat.

It does anyway.

Each step I take either creaks, groans, or pops. I'm not sure which sound is the most concerning.

"I don't think this is a good idea," I whisper.

"I have a good feeling about this," he says at the same time.

A huff comes out as I grip the railing, though it's all different heights, sometimes way too tall for me to reach, and then way too short, and then it's just...gone.

Luckily, I only have to go up the first flight of stairs before Belren disappears through a doorway. I pause at the landing for a moment before joining him inside.

"Gods, it's just getting worse," I mumble.

The walls are covered in plates. Dinner plates, saucer plates, tin plates, glass plates, china plates, painted plates... They're everywhere, stuck to all four walls with gods know what to make them hang there. And they aren't hung in nice symmetrical patterns either, because why would they be? No, there's zero rhyme or reason to any of their placements.

"Nice, huh?" Belren says, rolling back on his heels with glee as he takes it all in.

I spot the fae across the room, sitting at a table, carpets folded haphazardly over the wooden floor. I feel like the Mad Hatter is about to offer me some tea. I don't care what that server told me, there is no way that this male is a real seer. Surely if he had that kind of magic, he'd be living...better.

"You have lovely plates," I say, because I think it's always good to lead with a compliment. "So many."

"Not nearly enough," he replies with a grumble. "I need more. Can't stay in this room longer than twenty-two minutes, or it'll start to bother me and I'll have to go straight down to the shops, and I don't want to walk to the shops while it's raining. And anyway, they probably won't have anything new. Do you know how hard it is to get good plates on this island?"

I take a wild guess. "Very?"

He nods so emphatically that his red sleeping cap tips forward over his eyes before he shoves it back up again. "Yup. I need so many more than those ignorant shop-keepers can supply me with."

Oh goodness. He's not just untidy. He's also a hoarder.

"Come. Sit, sit," he orders as he plops himself down at a small table.

Walking by the plethora of plates, my feet sink into the knotted rug on the floor as I cross the small room. There's a tilted window just behind him, with a view of the rain still coming down. The closer I get to him, the more the ceiling starts to drop, until I have to bend over almost in half by the time I reach the table. It's really only meant for one, since there's only a single chair, and the table itself is tiny. But the fae just glares up at me impatiently, scratching at the buttons on his pajamas.

Looking around, I spot something that resembles an oversized pincushion, so I drag that over to sit on. Even as low down as it puts me, my knees still hit the table. I finally curl my legs beneath me, slightly hunched and wings cramped as I look across the round table to the fae. He doesn't look happy.

"I said *sit*."

Taken aback, I look down at my lap and then back up at him. "Umm...I am?"

He rolls his eyes. "Not you."

The fae's attention snags over my shoulder, and my body goes rigid when his gaze lands on Belren.

Oh my good gods. This fae can see him.

CHAPTER 17

LEX

Stunned, I stare at the fae. "You can really *see* him?" I ask, shock coursing through my tone.

"I'm a *seer*," he scoffs. "'Course I can see him. Wouldn't be a very good seer if I couldn't, now would I?" He looks back at Belren and hooks a thumb in my direction. "This one isn't the quickest, is she?"

Belren strides up with an excited glint in his eye. "On the contrary, she's too smart for her own good."

Stopping at my side, he slowly lowers himself down on the open portion of my pincushion seat. But as soon as he manages to sit, a jolt goes through me as the outline of his thigh brushes up against mine.

What in the world was that?

An embarrassing squeal bursts out of me at the sensation, but I don't dare move. I can *feel* him. It's not quite the same as the sense of touch though, it's...softer than that. Quieter. Like the way a bead of dew forms on a blade of grass, cooled and condensing against my skin.

My eyes fasten to his face, but he's already looking at me with wide, metallic eyes. As if he felt something too. I open my mouth to ask him, but the seer interrupts me before I can.

"Now that you're finally both sitting, we can have a cordial conversation. I swear, your manners aren't the best."

Yanking my attention away from Belren, I feel righteous indignation well up in me because *excuse me*, I am the most well-mannered person I have ever met, thank you very much.

Belren must sense my need to defend my honor, because his hand drops to my thigh, like an automatic nudge to stave off my rebuttal. Except his hand should go *through* my leg.

It doesn't.

As one, both of our faces drop, gazes locked onto where his palm rests on my thigh as if it were solid. My heartbeat starts galloping, but Belren isn't even breathing. Oh, wait. Dead. Never mind.

"How are you doing that?"

He answers without letting go. "I don't know." His gaze lifts up to my face. "Can you feel it?"

I feel *something*.

Like an almost-touch. Like the way a soft sigh feels against the arc of a neck. Like I'm both hot and cold at the same time, a lick of sweat over pebbled skin.

So, yes. I feel it.

But my heart is beating wildly, and my breathing is choppy, and I'm feeling *way* too much and not even in the way he means. Which is why, instead of the truth, I hear myself saying, "No."

Something flickers in his sterling eyes. Disappointment. Or suspicion.

Guilt and panic make me look away from him, though my body is still as stiff as a board. I find the seer watching us.

I clear my throat, trying to rid the tense air. "So sorry. I forgot to ask for your name."

"Chuckrey."

"Pleasure to meet you, Mr. Chuckrey," I say pleasantly, relaxing a bit when Belren finally looks away from me. Though, when he drops his hand from my thigh, something in me aches. It takes everything in me to keep that silly smile glued to my lips—to keep my eyes staring straight ahead and act unaffected. "I have to admit. When we were told you were a seer, I thought they meant something else."

"What, like a future-seer?" He scoffs and rolls his eyes so far that I worry he's going to get cornea rugburn from his bushy eyebrows. "Have you ever met a future-seer? They're crazy," he tells me with a shudder. "They have weird obsessive and hoarding habits."

I laugh at his joke, but his scowl deepens and I immediately swallow it. Okay. I guess we're in denial about the plates.

"Lucky for you, I'm loads better than *them*."

"Of course," I quickly say. "So, umm, what exactly is it that you can do?"

He seems aggravated by the question. "Well, I can see anyone, can't I?"

Belren cocks his head. "Can you see people who aren't here?"

Now Chuckrey turns his scowl on him. "Course I can't

190

see people who aren't here, you idiot. I thought she was the slow one?"

I can see now why a true seer would live in a falling-down house like this. He's a jerk.

"We're looking for someone, and we were sent to you for help," Belren tells him.

"Who are you looking for?"

Belren opens his mouth to just blurt it out, but I intervene before he can. "We just need to know if you're *able* to find someone. If not, we'll go out the way we came in and be out of your hair."

Chuckrey sits back in his chair and watches me like he's sizing me up, while I try not to stare at a particularly nasty tangle in his hair that makes me really want to grab a comb.

Finally, he sighs, breaking the silence. "Fine. I can try. But I need payment first."

My hand immediately goes to my pouch, but Belren stops me. "Hold on a moment. We'll pay *half* now and half when you find the person."

Shrewd eyes flicker with aggravation. "Yes, yes, fine!" he grumbles. "But hurry up about it. I don't have all day, and it's nearly time for my night nap."

I blink. "Isn't that just...sleeping?"

The look he shoots me lets me know exactly what he thinks of me, and it's...well. It's not good.

Since I'm probably about a second away from getting us kicked out, I dig into the pouch and pull out a coin and place it carefully on the table right in front of me.

His eyes snap to it. "Another."

Digging out another coin, I stack it perfectly on top.

"Another."

A third coin gets placed with the others.

"Another."

I start to reach for a fourth, but Belren shakes his head. "That's plenty."

I've no idea if he actually remembers the value of money here or if he's just faking it, but either way, it works.

The fae gives a sly grin. "Know my worth, do you?" he cackles. "Fine. Give me a coin."

I've barely lifted my finger away from the stack before his hand darts out and pockets one of them.

"Alright," he says, patting the breast pocket in his pajamas. "Tell me who you want to see."

"The ex-princess Soora," Belren replies without hesitation.

The pair of Chuckrey's untamed brows shoot up his forehead right before he spits on the floor. "The exiled one? Why do you wanna see *her*?"

Belren tips his head in my direction and smirks. "This one wants to murder her."

Oh my gods.

My head snaps over, and I give him a wide-eyed look, but he just winks at me. I don't know if they have any sort of law enforcement on this island, but if they do, the seer would probably sell me out in a second.

But instead of jumping on a chance to put me in my place, Chuckrey nods. "Oh, that's alright then." All the earlier disgust is gone from his face, as if killing her is perfectly reasonable and makes him like me more. "That's one of the most interesting requests I've had, but unfortunately, I can't *see* her."

"What? Why not?" Belren and I say at the same exact time.

Chuckrey shrugs. "You think other seers haven't already tried to find the most reviled exile in the realm? There's a bounty on her head big enough to buy your own island. But magic won't work. She's got a blocker on her or something. No surprise there, she's got glamoured barrier magic."

Belren's shoulders slump at the news, though I don't know if this is a good thing or a bad thing for him. I need to keep him focused and stay on this track since the fates obviously want me to, but I'm not really sure if it's safe for him to find Soora.

"Well, then that doesn't help us at all, does it?" Belren says. "Give her the coin back."

Chuckrey's hand slaps over his pocket. "I think *not*. This was the agreement. Not my fault you asked to see the unseeable."

Something close to a growl crawls up Belren's throat. The noise is so jolting, so darn *cold* sounding, that even I get a little scared.

"A Cernu fae, hmm? Haven't heard a Cernu fae growl in a long time," Chuckrey muses as he scratches his buttoned belly, completely unfazed. "But no need to get your knickers twisted. Even though I can't *see* her with my magic, I know where you might be able to find her."

The residual growling instantly stops, and Belren's eyes flash. "Where?"

Chuckrey arches a brow and waits.

Sighing, I pass him another coin from the pile that he snatches up so fast it's just a golden blur. He pats his pocket lovingly.

"Well?" Belren presses. "Where can we find her?"

"The exiled princess is loathed by all high fae because they think she betrayed her own kind. But the lesser fae? They hate her even more. She made promises to them and then went and abandoned them all. But there's one kind of fae that still stayed loyal to her."

I sit forward, curiosity piquing my interest. "Which one?"

"The hob fae, of course," Chuckrey replies. "Commonly called brownies—for the brown cloaks they used to always wear. But they go by lots of different names. Hobs, silkies, uruisgs, kobolds. I personally prefer to call them hearth hobs. Yep, many names for them, but it's all the same. You find the hearth hobs, and you can bet that you'll find her."

Belren and I share a look, and this time, it's not full of any previous awkwardness, because this is our first truly solid lead.

"If this is true, why has no one else tried to find them to get to her?" Belren asks him.

"Well, no one wants to piss off a hob. They might be a bit on the short side, but they get powerful magic from cleaning, doing the odd job, or if you anger them, malicious tricks that give them an extra spring in their step. They're also deathly loyal to that wench for some reason," he says, somewhat perturbed. "Doesn't matter that others have searched. I bet they're helping her."

"Where can we find them?" I ask.

Chuckrey frowns and then digs out a pair of glasses that were stuffed beneath his pajamas and hanging on a string. He perches them on his nose, and then looks away, staring at the wall of plates for so long that I get worried.

"Chuckrey?"

"Shh!" he snaps. "I'm trying to *see*."

Oh. Right.

Seconds tick by. I try not to make a sound for fear of distracting him.

Yet the longer we sit in silence, the more aware I become of Belren's closeness again. He's moved his thigh, so it's not quite *touching* mine anymore, but there's barely an inch between us. If my arm wasn't pulled so close to my body, it would be brushing up against his. Even my wings are huddled painfully close, too nervous for even a feather to brush into him.

I want to know what he felt when he touched me. Did he feel the same things that I did? Was it more?

My traitorous eyes flick over to him, and once again, he's already looking at me. A slow, steady watchfulness. A curious heat.

"You're blushing, Pinky," he murmurs.

Three words and a look. That's all it takes for my heart to start pounding again, for my hands to start wringing. I don't know if I was blushing before, but I am now.

A slow smirk crawls over his face. "I like it when you're flustered." My mouth parts, and his eyes move to my lips. "So distressed..."

Goodness.

Our moment is severed when Chuckrey yanks off his glasses with a huff. "Well. I've seen enough hearth hobs to last a lifetime."

"What did you find out?" Belren asks.

Unsurprisingly, Chuckrey's eyes dart down to the last coin. As soon as I slide it over to him, he puts it with the others. "Saw a few different hob islands," he begins before hopping down from his chair and going behind us to a pile of plates on the ground. There's a clattering of glass and tin, and then he reappears, hopping into his seat with a piece of paper ripped from a book, and a quill in his other hand. He scribbles some island names down, along with some hurried directions.

"There," he says, pushing the paper over. "I bet your exiled princess is at one of these islands. But she'll probably be deep in hiding, and the hearth hobs are too loyal to give her up. It'll be a chore to find her."

"I'll find her." Belren's reply is said with so much confidence that I believe him. Maybe he's feeling the remnants of his mortal life and his ability to find things. I don't know if that's a good thing or a bad thing.

I glance at the paper for a moment before moving to grab it, but Chuckrey slams his hand down on the other end, making me jump.

When I look up, I see him watching Belren. "The ghosts I *see* aren't usually like you, you know."

Belren's posture has gone stiff, but he tries to play it off with an easygoing smile. "Yes, I know. I'm much better company."

"Doesn't matter though," Chuckrey goes on. "In the end, you're all here for the same reason. You've all got a hook dangling on the line. Unfinished business."

Now it's my shoulders that go stiff. "What?"

Chuckrey drags his eyes away from Belren long enough to answer me. "This one might seem more alive, but make no mistake. He's as dead as the rest of them," he tells me, making dread sink like rocks into the pit of my stomach. "And all the deads have only two fates."

"And what might those be?" Belren asks, and although

his tone seems light, I can somehow feel an undercurrent of anger in it.

"Usually, they slowly fade from their wallowing madness until they disintegrate into air and nothingness," Chuckrey says, and just the thought of that makes nausea churn through me. "*Or*...they finish their unfinished business and then lose what little hold they had on the mortal world and get sucked back into the ether, gone. Either way, ghosts aren't permanent, and neither are you."

The skin around Belren's eyes goes tight, and his smile goes feral and cold. My heart races, worry making my palms go slick, as the words *unfinished business* repeat in my mind.

After a second of tense silence, Belren seems to put on his blasé mask once again. "Is that so? Well, it sounds like you're doing a bit of fortune-telling after all. My fate sounds *very* exciting." When his gray eyes drop down to the paper that Chuckrey is still holding hostage, the seer takes the hint and lets go. I quickly slip the paper into my pouch and get to my feet, Belren right at my side.

The two of them glare at each other, and I clear my throat at the awkwardness that's descended on us. "Well, thank you very much, Chuckrey. You've helped us a great deal."

He helped...and got a little aggressive there at the end. And also at the beginning. Also, some parts in the middle. I don't think he gets out much, unless it's to buy more plates.

He waves a dismissive hand. "Yes, yes, of course I helped. Now get out. I don't want to miss my dusk doze before my night nap."

Of course. How silly of me.

Belren and I walk out, and luckily, the house doesn't topple down over my head. That, plus the fact that we actually have a more solid lead on Soora's whereabouts should make me feel accomplished. Instead, my emotions are in turmoil, all because of the male walking beside me. The male who's either going to disintegrate after slowly going crazy or snap out of existence if he finishes his unfinished business that he may have. Which may or may not be me tracking down Soora. Which we are *actively* trying to do, because I worry he'll slip away from me if he doesn't have a goal to focus on.

Great.

I wasn't supposed to let things get so muddled. I *also* wasn't supposed to let myself grow attached. But despite all my efforts...I have anyway, and now look at what I've done. I've put him on a track to disaster.

Unless Emelle finds a way to de-ghost him, we're stuck between a rock and a dead place, and completely out of options.

CHAPTER 18

LEX

"So, let's talk about this murder spree."

I bite back a groan, wishing I could bury my head in the pillow I'm resting on. Though, there's really nothing to *bury* into. It's the sorriest pillow I've ever seen. Just a straw-filled, flattened sack. But at least this inn room has a washbasin and curtains. It's been three days since we left the seer, and although I've mostly stayed in the Veil as we travelled, I opted to go corporeal tonight so I could have some food and sleep for a little reset.

Glancing down at Belren, I take in his silvery silhouette. He's glowing a bit like my own personal moonlit night-light, and despite the noises I can hear coming from the dining area downstairs, this little room feels removed, far away from anything or anyone else. "For the last time, it's not a *spree*."

I see him smirk where he's lying down on the wooden floor, body stretching across the whole length of the small room, from the points of his tucked elbows to the soles of his shoes.

"What about this ex-princess everyone detests so much? How did you know her? Seems personal, since you want to go off and kill her."

"I didn't really know her," I hedge. "But every fae I've met curses her name for going against the rebellion when she was supposed to be leading it."

"Yes, the rebellion. Sounds titillating."

I'm fairly certain he only used that word because the first three letters are *t-i-t*.

"Admittedly, I didn't do much research on the rebellion. I know it was mainly about the lesser fae rising up against the high fae for unfair treatment stemming from the laws set forth by the monarchy. But the ex-princess betrayed her loyalty to the lesser fae, and I don't think they'll ever forgive her for it."

He turns his head to look at me, and I worry my lip. It's a fine line to shepherd Belren's questions, because I worry that I'll say too much.

"Still, I don't get why *you* are the one who wants to end her. You're not a lesser fae—you're not a fae at all. Plus the fact that I'm still not convinced you're the killing type."

"You'd be surprised what people are capable of," I say smartly. "I've studied others during my time as a cupid, and I've seen ex-lovers go to great lengths to exact revenge on one another. They always seemed to get some satisfaction out of it."

"And that's what you want? The satisfaction of revenge?"

"Umm..."

I frown. How am I supposed to explain that the idea came to me simply because I was desperate to stop thinking about him? In theory, by avenging his death and taking down Soora, I thought I could earn some kind of closure. It seemed logical in the moment. And probably slightly unhinged.

"Revenge isn't really my cup of tea, to be honest."

"Exactly," he says, pointing at me. "Which is why I find it so fascinating."

"Glad I can be entertaining," I say with a twist of my lips.

Belren looks at me with a sober expression. "You are certainly captivating."

My breath hitches, and I'm caught in the silvery web of Belren's gaze. He keeps doing this, keeps saying little things that make my heart race and my mind swirl with warring emotions. "You shouldn't say things like that to me."

His brow arches. "Why not?"

"I'm just a cupid. I'm not captivating. Ask any of my previous cupid partners. They've all opted to be partnered up with somebody else."

"Their loss," he says with a shrug. "I prefer your company."

I squirm under his reply. I'm not used to being talked to like this. To being watched like he watches me. "Well." I sniff, trying to dislodge the butterflies in my stomach. "You're a ghost, so you don't have a lot of options for companions."

He laughs. "True. But even if I did, I'd still want you."

My eyes hook to his.

I'd still want you. Not "I'd still want to be around you."

The distinction of his chosen words makes those butterflies come right back.

I wonder what it was like for him before he found me. By saying what I did back at Ghost Island, I set him off, tied him to this mission, but what if I'd never gone there? I feel as if I nearly failed him, was the cause once again for his downfall, and I hate that feeling.

I don't deserve the attention he gives me.

"You're just drawn to me because of this murderous mission," I say, trying to wave him off. That truth hurts more than I want to admit. I set off his unfinished business trigger. That's all this is. That's why he feels drawn to me.

"Keep thinking that, Pinky." With a shake of his head, Belren settles back down. His body is sheer enough to view the floor beneath him, but solid enough that I can see every bend and crook of his body. I trail my gaze over him as he looks up at the ceiling, his hair not moving an inch, no matter how he lies. His pants are forever tucked into his boots, tunic sleeves taut against his arms. He really is a handsome fae, even as a dead one.

I can only hope that Emelle can de-ghost him, because if she can't...

No. I won't think about that.

The two of us lie in silence, and although I burn to know what he's thinking, I hold my questions back.

Tomorrow, we're heading to the next island over, which is going to take all day and night. But once we reach it, supposedly we will have a straight shot at one of the islands the seer mentioned, if he can be believed about where the hearth hobs live.

I settle in for sleep with a sigh, my wings tucked in

against my body and slightly turned, giving me more padding as I lie on my side. I'm just starting to fall asleep when Belren's voice rumbles out. "I think it's time we stop avoiding a certain subject, don't you?"

My eyes startle open to look at Belren's face, panic infusing in me. My mind whirls as I wonder how I slipped up. *Did he figure out that I knew him when he was alive?*

He turns his head to look at me. "We haven't spoken about the touch."

Oh. That. Now this topic...this one I've been actively ignoring.

When I say nothing, he sits up in one smooth motion, becoming eye level with me and reminding me exactly how small this room really is.

"At the seer's house, I placed my hand on your leg."

My heart begins to beat so hard that I can feel it in my throat. "You did."

Those bright silver eyes of his glow like a cat's as he watches me, the poignant moment deepening with every blink.

"We don't need to talk about it," I blurt.

"Oh, I think we do," he replies before dragging a knee up and draping his outstretched arm over it in a show of casual comfort, though I know it's taken him a lot of practice. "In fact, I don't just think we should talk about it, but I think we should try it again. You've been purposely avoiding me ever since."

I'm frozen on the bed, unable to even shift my head away from the straw poking through the pillow and stabbing into my cheek.

He tilts his head, looking entirely too wolfish. "Can I try to touch you again?"

I blanch. "You want to...to..."

"Touch you, yes."

Gods, why does it feel like there's a horse galloping in my chest? Why am I suddenly so hot that I want to throw off the blankets, even as I want to hide beneath them? I should say no. I should turn away and stop this right now. Nothing good can come of this dangerous exploration.

He's a ghost. I'm a cupid. He's dead, and I'm... Okay, I'm also technically dead since this is my afterlife, but I'm certainly *less* dead than he is. Surely that means this is a bad idea.

"I don't know..." I say with a shake of my head.

Undeterred, Belren inches closer to the bed, taking up all my ability to think logically when he stops right next to me, our faces level with each other.

"Pinky, something is happening here," he says quietly, his voice slipping around my skin like a cool breeze. "First, I find you at my deathplace. Then, you can see me even when you're not in the Veil. And now, for some reason, I was able to...*touch* you, in a way. It doesn't make sense, does it?"

That, at least, is an easy answer. "No, it doesn't." Not at all, and I abhor things that don't make sense.

His eyes flick down to my mouth for the briefest of moments. "We should try it again then, don't you think? Test it out?"

I blink, my mind much slower at processing words when he's this close. "Platonically, you mean? For science?"

Belren's lips curl up into the most amused smirk that makes my stomach flip. "Sure. We should touch for science."

Well, I can't argue with things in the name of science. That wouldn't be logical. And he's right. I should stop being a coward about it. It was barely even a touch, after all. We should know what he's capable of, simply for observation's sake.

I clear my throat. "Alright, then. It will be an experiment."

His smirk widens in victory before his eyes move down toward my neck. "If we're going to try this though, you're going to need to release the death-grip you've got on that blanket and stop wearing it like a noose."

I glance down and realize with some embarrassment that I am in fact holding the blankets for dear life like a woman worried her virtue is about to be stolen. With great effort, I uncurl my palms and sit up, letting the blanket fall to my lap. I'm dressed in my simple under-dress, and while it's perfectly respectable with sleeves and a long skirt, I feel almost naked.

"It's hot in here all of a sudden, isn't it?" I ask, fanning my face.

He gives me a wry look. "I wouldn't know."

Oh. Right.

Fidgeting, I cross my legs beneath me and settle my hands in my lap. "So, how do you want to do this?"

He hums beneath his breath and then gets to his feet until he's towering over me. I tip my head back, a hard swallow coiling down my throat. *Was he always this tall?*

"Where do you want me to touch you, Lex?" He practically purrs my name out. It's not just the rasping tone of his voice, but the way the words seem to vibrate through the air. Sensual caress.

"I don't know," I whisper, my entire focus on him, on

every single movement, every iridescent edge.

As if we weren't close enough already, Belren perches himself on the bed next to me. Now we're face-to-face, body-to-body, with only inches between us, and I instinctively scoot back.

He chuckles. "Why are you backing away?"

"Why are you scooting forward?" I retort, my shoulders hitting the wall and scratchy curtain as he eats up all the space that I created.

"Does my being close to you make you nervous?"

I let out a shaky laugh that's not at all convincing. "Of course not. I'm not nervous. Why would that make me nervous? Nothing to be nervous about."

Why did that sound so nervous?

His eyes soften. "Just relax."

A bubble of laughter bursts out of me. *Relax.* Sure. Like that's possible. I can't relax when it comes to this male.

Belren cocks his head, studying me. "Are you more nervous about finding out I can't touch you...or that I *can*?"

I can't admit that both options terrify me for completely different reasons.

Instead, I hold out my hand, palm up. "Just...make it quick," I tell him, unable to even meet his eye.

"You really *are* nervous," he says, as if the very notion bewilders him.

It probably is confusing to him, considering he lacks knowledge of his own history.

"I'd think a cupid wouldn't be so shy."

"I'm not shy, I'm just...disagreeable to attention."

He laughs. "Of course. My mistake."

After a pause, I jostle my hand, which is still held in

front of me. "Are you going to do it?"

Belren leans in. "Shh," he soothes, his mouth right next to my ear. A shiver travels down the curve of my neck, cooled with his proximity even as my cheeks blaze. "Close your eyes."

Of course, my eyes widen, head shifting to look at him. "Why do I need to close my eyes?"

"Because I can hear your heart racing, and if you don't settle down, you're going to join me from a heart attack."

I scoff, but he's not entirely wrong. My pulse really is flying. After a moment's hesitation, I relent, my lids fluttering shut.

"Breathe," he murmurs, making another chill scrape down the edge of my back.

"Now I'm taking breathing advice from a ghost," I mutter.

"Yes, you are," he lightly admonishes. "So be a good girl and follow directions."

Well.

My spine straightens. I have a feeling I was a star pupil in my previous life. Why else would I really like hearing him call me a *good girl*?

I find myself taking deep breaths just like he said, preening a little when he tells me well done.

"That's better," he says.

And then I suck in a breath, because I somehow know that he just shifted on the bed, even though there's no movement on the mattress, no stir in the air. Maybe I'm just so attuned to him I've picked up some sort of sixth sense.

There's a pause, and then his voice comes again, this time from directly in front of me. "Still breathing?"

An exhale puffs out of me. "Yep."

"Good girl."

Oh gods. Yep, I think I may have a praise kink.

A newfound blush is probably reddening my entire face, but I'm focused entirely on my hand. It feels so heavy, and I have to repress the urge to fidget.

"Here we go, Pinky."

All thoughts of breathing go out the window as I hold my breath in anticipation. My entire body is buzzing with it—with the need to feel him again. Even my thigh is tingling from where he touched me before, as if my skin has held an imprint of him ever since.

I wait, brow furrowed, concentrating on my shaky palm and stiff fingers.

But nothing happens.

"Hmm."

My eyes snap open to see Belren's hand going right through mine. His hand doesn't rest against my palm. His fingers don't skate over my skin.

"I don't feel anything." My words come out with blatant disappointment.

Belren's hand drops. "I suppose it was just a fluke then."

Never, not once, have I ever heard his voice sound like this. There's something like defeat in his tone. Like a bitter pill washed down, yet leaving an aftertaste to stain every word on his tongue.

My own hand folds in on itself before falling to my lap. "I suppose so."

I was terrified of feeling his touch again because of what it might mean for my muddled emotions. But this? This is worse.

"Maybe it had something to do with being at the seer's house," I offer.

"Perhaps." Belren gets to his feet. I may be imagining it, but I swear, some of the luster has gone from his eyes. "Have a good sleep," he says without looking at me as he heads for the door.

A frown pulls my brows together. "What do you mean? Where are you going?" The worry is evident in my voice, but I don't care. I don't like the slump of his shoulders or the look on his face.

"Just going to go for a walk while you sleep."

"Don't leave." The words blurt out of me before I can hold them in.

Belren stops and glances at me over his shoulder. I don't know what he sees on my face, but whatever it is makes him adopt a smile, though it's forced. "Don't worry, Pinky. I'll be here when you wake up."

My throat feels tight, my stomach in knots. "You promise?" I ask quietly.

He gives me a nod, eyes full of something I can't decipher. "Promise."

With that, he turns and walks through the door, away from my sight, and I'm left alone in the small space that suddenly seems far too big.

For a long time, I lie in bed, trying to tell myself that this is for the best. It's better this way, because it reminds me that even though we're together, we still exist on entirely different planes. Whatever happened before was just a fluke. And it's just as well. Touching would've been far too messy, and I prefer an orderly, tidy afterlife.

I remind myself of this over and over again.

The problem is, I've begun to crave the mess.

CHAPTER 19

BELREN

I couldn't touch her.

I was so sure that it would happen again—whatever *it* exactly is. When my hand touched her leg, it was like a memory. A manifestation of life. I was so close to becoming what I used to be, I could almost taste it. There's something about her that makes me feel alive. And for a damn ghost, that feeling is dangerously addictive.

What is it about her?

I may not taste life, but I can taste the bitter disappointment that I wasn't able to touch her again.

My hand went through hers. I felt absolutely nothing.

With a dark scowl, I stalk up the street, barely sparing a glance at the fae I pass by. This island is nothing special. Just another metropolis stuffed into a stone city. I walk off the road, past the storied homes and locked shops, drawn toward the outcropping of bedrock stacked above a grassy knoll.

The lined rock formation hitches up like a nature-made

fence, and when I get past it, I see exactly why I was drawn in this direction. A fae burial site lies just ahead, with a few empty pyres erected, making up three points of a triangle. In the center, a massive slab of gray rock stands as high as four fae, one on top of the other.

As I get closer, I see that names of the dead have been engraved into the rock, of all the fae who must've died and were burned and then buried here, their smoke released to the skies and their ashes sunk into the ground.

Of course I'm drawn to another deathplace, even if it's not mine. Even from here, I can feel exactly where my own deathplace is. I could return to it with my eyes closed, because it still calls to me.

I stop in front of the engraved stone, eyes skimming over the chiseled letters. With as many names as there are on that rock, there's surprisingly very few ghosts hovering around. As I walk past them, not one of them looks in my direction. "Nice night for haunting, isn't it?" I ask a male that floats by.

He doesn't answer, though I do notice that his form seems more faded than mine. Actually, now that I'm really paying attention, all of the ghosts are duller and dimmer than I am. I practically glow in comparison. I can't help but think that it has something to do with Lex.

Truly, I thought tonight I was going to be able to do more than simply touch her hand. Turns out, I couldn't even do that.

The way she sat on the bed, her white nightgown luminous in the night, made her look like an angel rather than a cupid. Her eyes were so wide with timid nervousness, the race of her pulse thrumming along her neck...yet she swayed toward me and not away. I don't even think she realized that she did it. Or that her gaze kept flicking down to my lips, as if that's where she truly wanted us to touch.

Little did she know, I would've done far more than just kiss her.

Glaring down at my hands, I'm filled with resentment. Useless fucking ghost body. With a sigh, I sit down next to the stone, staring at the empty pyres, at the ghosts who meander around.

Idly, I wonder if the rebellion that everyone talks about had anything to do with me. Maybe it did. Although, I'm not dressed in armor. So maybe I just had a heart attack over that island and dropped down to the ground like a tossed rock. I'll probably never know, but at least I was able to leave Ghost Island. I was fading there, in more ways than one.

Lex is my lifeline.

If I can't touch her, then I can at least help her on her mission. But I worry that even that is going to be denied to me. Every day, I've been feeling the pull of my death-place just a little bit more. The seer told us to search the islands where the hearth hobs live, and that's where we're going, but the distance has begun to strain.

I don't want to tell Lex. She's finally relaxed a little bit about the topic, and I don't want to put that worry back in her eyes. I know she'll insist that she bring me back, and that island is the last place I want to be. For the death of me, I can't imagine why she lets me hang around her, but the last thing I want to do is remind her of my predicament. There's a very real possibility that I'll get yanked back, but I'm trying my damnedest not to let that happen.

Lost in my thoughts, I stay at the burial site for much longer than I anticipated.

By the time I stop brooding, I realize the sun is sprouting from the sky's dark soil. Time to return. It doesn't take me long to walk back into the city, where the laborers and merchants are already waking up to start their day. The inn is still relatively quiet, so I don't even have to float through anyone, which is a win.

Yet when I make it to Lex's room, I walk right in, only to find that it's empty.

My head swivels around, but there's absolutely nowhere my cupid could be hiding out of sight. The room is too small, and I realize with a sinking dread that her bow and arrow is gone, and the bed is already made up.

I stand there in shock. *Did she leave?*

But why? She doesn't seem the type to just up and walk off without saying something.

Then again...maybe I wasn't reading her correctly earlier when I tried to touch her. I knew she'd been avoiding the topic ever since the seer's house, but I chalked it up to her innocent shyness. Yet maybe I had it all wrong. Perhaps I was seeing things as I was willfully misinterpreting them.

I scared her off.

A string of curses unravels from my mouth, just as dread and guilt fills me.

If I were a good ghost, I'd respect the fact that she left willfully. And I know without a doubt that she did, in fact, leave of her own accord, because she made the gods-damned bed. Who does that in an inn?

Her. Every time.

With a scowl, I turn on my heel and stalk out of the

room, anger darkening my vision. I don't care that she left. She's my neurotic cupid, and I'm not going to just let her walk away.

I snarl at the yawning people downstairs who stumble into me before I make it back outside. The sky is already changing from light gray to a soft blue, and my eyes squint in all directions as I try to catch sight of her, but there's nothing.

Yet just like I intuitively know where my deathplace is, I also get a certain pull toward her. Maybe it's just my muck, but I close my eyes, focusing past my taut worry, and feel for her.

There.

Like a tug in my gut, it hooks me on a line. As soon as I latch onto the direction I need to go, I stride down the street, letting instinct guide me. My steps are so determined that the soles of my boots don't even dare to go through the ground.

Down the road I go, cutting through the gathering crowd, swooping right past them like an irrational wind. And then, I see her.

Her wings are tucked tight against her back, and for once, her pink hair isn't pulled back tight, but loose around her shoulders, tangled with the feathered ends of her arrows strung against her back. From this angle, I have a delectable view of her ass. It's one of my favorite things when she wears trousers.

My long stride is quickly eating up the space between us as she continues to walk away from me. I'm half tempted to just stay behind her to see where she intends to go, but she suddenly stops dead in her tracks. As if she senses me too, she whips around, and her eyes go wide when they land on me.

I'm right up in front of her a moment later, a finger pointed at her gorgeous fucking face. "You brag about being Princess Polite, but then you try to just leave without saying goodbye?" I challenge, my scowl fastened into the grooves of my brow. "You left me behind awfully quick, though you sure as hell had time to make the damned bed, didn't you? Who does that, anyway? It's an inn!"

She rears back at the vehemence in my voice, mouth stuck open as she stares at me.

I lean down until we're eye level and get pissed off all over again that I can't feel that hitch in her breath against my skin, or smell her hair, or grip her chin to tilt her mouth up to mine. "We have unfinished business, and until that's done, you're stuck with me, Pinky," I tell her, making her brows shoot up. "I will haunt your ass to the end of the world, with or without my damn muck," I growl quietly. "So the next time you try to walk out on me, just remember that. You're mine."

The declaration slams down between us, but as soon as I say it, I know it's true. She *is* mine.

Silence drips between us like honey, thickened with unmistakable tension, and there's no doubting what kind. Her cheeks are flushed, her pupils slightly dilated, her nipples hardening to points through her tunic. And just seeing her like this, all breathless and a little dazed, makes me want to hook my fingers around her jaw and pull her in for a kiss.

Other fae walk around us, some of them shooting her curious glances, since I've no doubt she looks very peculiar, standing in the middle of the street, staring with her sex eyes at no one at all. But those eyes are for me, so if anyone so much as tries to approach her, I will figure out how to possess the fuckers and cut off their cocks.

The stilled moment shatters abruptly when Lex sucks in a breath and shakes her head. "Excuse me?" she asks, all the previous heat suddenly replaced with sharp irritation. "First of all, you can't threaten to haunt me when you don't even know that you're a proper ghost who can properly haunt!"

I open my mouth to defend the fact that I'm quite certain I can fucking haunt, thank you very much, but she's far too quick for me to get a word in edgewise.

"Secondly, I am a perfectly able-bodied person, and I'm not going to *not* make a bed that I sleep in! That's just rude!"

I roll my eyes, but then she's jamming a finger at my face, and fucking hell, her angry look is the sexiest thing I've ever seen.

"And thirdly, *you* promised me you'd be there when I woke up, and you weren't! I wasn't leaving you. I was *looking* for you! You big, sheer butthead!"

I blink at her.

Her words sink in, and all of my irritation at being left behind evaporates. I instantly start laughing my see-through ass off.

Bewildered, she watches me as I lose it, and then she seems to realize that while she's staring at me, everyone else on the street is staring at her, probably thinking that she's gone mad and is talking to thin air. Lex blushes so fiercely that it's a wonder her hair doesn't turn red.

Without another word, she spins around and starts hurrying off. "Wait up!"

"Go haunt a rock," she mumbles, which just makes me laugh harder.

"Tried that, couldn't stick it," I tease as I catch up and start walking beside her.

"You made me look like a crazy person."

I shrug, feeling a godsdamned pep in my step with the knowledge that she wasn't leaving me. "Don't worry, talking to yourself is one of the least crazy things the fae can do."

She doesn't argue with that. It's only been a handful of days, and we've seen some things.

"I can't believe you accused me of leaving you," she snips. "And you were the one who broke your promise!"

"Yeah, I'm sorry about that," I tell her genuinely. "I lost track of time. Won't happen again."

She rolls her eyes, but she stops stomping quite so aggressively.

"Anyway, we should talk about your bed-making obsession."

Lex stops at the end of the road and glares at me, with her hands on her hips and everything. "It's not an obsession, it's common courtesy!"

She's quite adorable.

"You also woke up at a very early hour."

Lex huffs. "I couldn't sleep well."

That admission brings a grin to my face. "Couldn't sleep without me, could you?"

She sighs but doesn't deny it. "You seem to be in better *spirits* this morning," she says, lips twitching.

"Maybe you should stick to making beds instead of jokes."

Lex turns to look at me, loose hair slinging around her face. "Oh, come on. Spirits! It's ghost humor."

See? Adorable. "Sure. Ready to head to the next island?"

That pull to my deathplace is tugging at me as if it knows I intend to travel even further away, but I ignore it, burying it deep.

"Yes," she says before she reaches up to gather her hair, ready to tie it up, but I stop her.

"Leave it."

She freezes, gaze flicking over to me. "What?"

"Your hair. Leave it down. It looks nice."

She looks torn. "But...I never leave my hair down."

I just watch her to see what she'll do. But nervousness wins out, and she pulls it up into a high ponytail, making me grin.

"That's fine, Pinky," I say, leaning in close to her ear just like I did last night, because even now, I'm craving her. "One of these days, I *will* touch you again, and the first thing I'll do is tug that hair down myself and wrap it around my fist as I claim your mouth. *That's a fucking promise.*"

And that's one I intend to keep.

CHAPTER 20

LEX

*W*e make it to one of the islands where the hearth hobs live. I can tell right away we're at the right place, because the place is *immaculate*. Even the terrain looks tidy, like the green hills in the distance don't dare to curve sloppily.

"Goodness, I think we could eat right off the street."

Belren nods as we walk together up the pathway. Honestly, there isn't a single speck of dirt on the entire thing. And I can see why, because about every twenty feet, a hob is sweeping the path or polishing the stones.

The buildings are a bit utilitarian looking, every single one matching perfectly, made with bricks painted in a gleaming cream color. Even the front gardens are identical. The hedges are snipped into the same boxy shape and height, with no twig or leaf out of place.

Nearly every fae in the city is definitely a hearth hob, like Chuckrey said. Most of them are on the shorter side, wearing the neat brown cloaks that gave them their brownie nickname, and every single one of them has tight ringlet hair. And I mean *all* hair—the hair on the top of their heads, their eyebrows, lashes, beards. The ones wearing short sleeves and exposed legs even show off ringlets on those parts. Hearth hobs of every age and hair color have that one physical attribute in common, plus they're all about a head shorter than me. I realize that I'm going to stick out like a failing grade. I don't have a single curly hair in sight, and my red wings are kind of a give-away, but for the time being, I'm still in the Veil with Belren.

Another thing the hearth hobs have in common, of course, is how tidy they are. It seems like they have a penchant for wearing fabrics that really show off their lack of stains and wrinkles too. Their brown cloaks are shiny and silken, or stitched in beautiful, neat fur. They also *walk* neatly, practically in lines, sticking to only one side of the path depending on which direction they're heading. It's all very organized.

I love it.

"Where should we go?" I ask Belren, careful to stick to the middle of the path where we aren't in danger of being walked through.

He scans our surroundings, head turning at a perpendicular split-off in the path. "I don't know. Let's try this way."

I absentmindedly run a palm over my cupid mark as I walk beside him. I'm getting antsy, worried about why Emelle hasn't tried to contact me yet. It's been days, and not one peep. What if there's no way to undo this? What if Belren is going to be stuck as a ghost forever? My heart hurts just thinking about it. I know that all entities, no matter what afterlife job they choose, don't remember their previous lives. But ghosts are the only ones in danger of forgetting the here and now.

"What are you thinking so hard about over there?" he asks, pulling me from my thoughts.

"Nothing," I say quickly.

He scoffs. "Come now. It's not polite to lie."

That's...that's actually true.

"I was thinking about you, actually," I say, doing my best not to sound embarrassed about that.

He shoots me a smirk. "Were they dirty thoughts?"

"No!" I look around, but then remember that no one can hear us. "It's just, well, what the seer said, about your unfinished business. Do you think your unfinished business has to do with the princess?"

When it's done, will you disappear entirely?

His expression turns contemplative. "I don't know," he admits before casting a look over my shoulder. "But don't worry, I wouldn't expect you to carry my muck with you for the rest of your afterlife." He plays his words off like a joke, but I can tell there's underlying worry in his tone.

It's there on the tip of my tongue to tell him that I'll carry his deathplace dirt forever, but something holds me back. Could I really watch him slowly fade?

"How are you feeling, by the way?" I ask, rerouting the conversation. "I haven't checked in a couple days."

"I'm fine, Pinky," he says dismissively.

I know he gets sick of me asking him, so I let the subject drop.

We crest a small hill, and I see the cleanest, most orderly town square I've ever seen. One freckled and red-haired hearth hob seems to be selling some fruit, but instead of having them in barrels, they're stacked in perfect pyramids. There's one corner made up entirely of cleaning supplies, too. The square itself is gleaming with four polished pillars and a matching stone ground that people are cleaning or standing around in very patient lines as they do their shopping.

Just seeing how civil and composed everyone is makes me a little worried. "I might be wrong...but these fae don't seem like the type to get tipsy and spill secrets about an ex-princess over their roast dinner."

Belren frowns. "You're right. They probably don't even eat roast. Too messy."

We stop in the center of the square, watching the fae as they go about their orderly business. Most of them are intent on their to-do, walking with purpose and getting right down to business about whatever they need to buy or sell. There's not much small talk happening, and half of them are cleaning things.

There's even a line of hobs waiting for the shallow water well like it's a line to get free ice cream. They're quite animated about washing things, only rude when it comes to getting their turn at the scrubbers and brooms. But I can see why. Each and every one of the hearth hobs practically sparkles with power as they clean. It must be because I'm in the Veil, but I can see a faint gleam to their silhouettes, as if energy is feeding into them.

"The hearth hobs really are powerful," I note.

Belren hums thoughtfully. "See, now *they* have an excuse to make up the bed in a rented room."

I groan. "Are you ever going to let that go?"

"I don't anticipate it."

With a shake of my head, I look around the square, but

I'm feeling less and less hopeful that we're going to glean any information from eavesdropping.

"These fae don't seem to be into gossiping, but we could still try to find some sort of tavern," I offer.

When Belren doesn't reply, I look over only to find that he's distracted, gaze set off unseeingly as he runs a hand over his translucent chest.

"Is something wrong?" He jerks at my question, as if I've startled him from his thoughts.

"What?" he asks absently.

Uneasiness starts to trickle in as I note the tension in his shoulders. "Are you okay?"

"Yes," he says slowly before clearing his throat, erasing whatever he was thinking of as he re-instills his easygoing demeanor. "Alright, let's find someplace to spy on these tidy fae, shall we?" Belren leads the way, walking off before I can question him more.

Troubled, I follow after him, but it's clear he doesn't want to say more, and I don't want to push him. We scope out a couple of taverns, but they're nothing like the others we've visited. What they lack in the scent of food and stained tables, they make up for in their gleaming silverware and fancy presentation.

For the next several hours, we wander around, trying to pick up any kind of chatter, but not a single fae talks about anything personal. In fact, the most interesting conversation we witness is a very heated argument between two hobs about which soap is better to use on windows. There was a lot of talk about streaks. I'm surprised they didn't come to blows.

"Well, this is going to be more difficult than I thought," Belren says when we're back outside. It's late now, but there's a perfect row of lanterns lit up along the path to light our way as we head back toward the square.

I nod in agreement. "We might be here for a while before we can find anything out." We've been moving from island to island so much lately, it will be kind of nice to stick around. "I don't know that the seer was right when he sent us here, but it's the only lead we've got. The information isn't going to fall in our laps. We're going to have to be patient, I think."

Belren looks around thoughtfully. "Agreed. Let's go exploring."

I arch a brow. "Exploring?"

"We can't expect them to just blurt out that they're harboring the traitor princess the first day we're here," Belren tells me with a shrug. "Like you said, we're going to have to be patient. So let's go explore for a bit. It's getting late anyway. All the hearth hobs are going to be tucked tidily into their beds soon."

After I nod, Belren and I do exactly that—explore.

We're able to see a lot of the city, and we get rewarded when we find a really nice garden just behind the main square that has the most impeccable rows of flowers that I've ever seen.

I pop out of the Veil so I can lean over and rub one of them between my fingers. "How do you think they get the leaves so shiny?" I ask curiously. They practically show our reflections.

Belren watches as I caress another leaf. "They probably spit-shine them."

I snap my hand back with a cringe. "Yuck."

He laughs, the throaty sound making me want to shiver. I turn to look at him, but something past him makes my eyes go wide, and I immediately go back into the Veil.

When he sees me reaching back and grabbing my bow and arrow, his brows lift up. "It was a joke. You don't need to shoot me."

"Shh," I say impatiently before I shoo him. "Move, please."

Looking bewildered, he steps out of the way, letting me breeze past him, though he quickly follows at my side. "Um, what are you doing?"

Instead of answering, I hurry toward the hedge maze up ahead and take the immediate left once inside it. Wisps of energy have been left behind like a glittery trail that lights my way. I follow it, taking each turn until I come to an abrupt stop where I find the two fae I'd spotted sneaking in here.

Belren snorts beside me. "I should've known."

A smile curls my lips as I look at the couple. It's two male hearth hobs, one of whom is sitting at the base of a small hedge tree, while the other is meticulously snipping a few of the leaves that have grown a centimeter too high. When the cutter finds a flower in it, he passes it to the other hob, making him blush.

My cupid heart swells at the shy flirtatiousness I can feel coming from both of them.

"What's it gonna be this time?" Belren asks. "Flirt Touches? Lust Breath?"

But I shake my head, my smile spreading. "Nope. They're ready for the next stage."

I lift the bow and arrow in my hand, relishing in the feel of the wood and string beneath my fingers. I nock the arrow and pull back my hand, my grip firm but not tense.

In a blink, I release the Love Arrow and it hits its mark, bursting into a cloud of hazy red, right at the heart of the fae clutching his scissors. I already have the next arrow flying before the haze disappears, and then it's joined with a burst of pink at the second fae.

"Right to the heart, both times," Belren comments. "Impressive."

I slip my bow behind me with a proud nod. "Thank you."

The two males are giving each other such lovey-dovey eyes that I don't even need my cupid power to see the love take effect. They're on each other in a second, scissors and flowers forgotten, and I turn back to Belren in victory. "My job here is done."

He's still watching the fae, head tilting. "You know, hobs might love cleanliness, but I think things are about to get *very* dirty."

"Yeah...we should probably give them their privacy."

Together, we walk back out of the maze, while I crackle with the offshoots of their newfound love.

Belren and I wander to a different part of the garden, where trimmed trees are lined along a winding path. My entire body is practically buzzing, and I can't help the smile that seems to be stuck on my face.

"You really get a kick out of your job, don't you?" he asks, side-eyeing me.

"Yes!" I say giddily, popping back into my corporeal body. I even skip a little down the path, that's how happy I am. The rush of it feels good, like it used to be when I first became a cupid.

"What would've happened to them if there hadn't been a cupid around?"

"Well, cupids can't *force* anything," I explain. "There are all sorts of rules, and our magic only works in specific situations. You have to look at cupids as...love encouragers."

Belren smirks. "Love encouragers?"

"Yes. It's like feeding wood into a fire. The sparks were already there, and we just coax it to life." I hook my thumb over my shoulder. "Those two would've gotten to that next stage with or without me. I just encouraged them along. Fed the fire."

"You're quite the love pyro."

I beam.

"Doesn't it ever get old?" he asks curiously. "You've been a cupid for a long time. I'd think you'd be a little sick of it by now."

"Of course not," I reply. Though, I can't tell him the whole truth—that I'd lost my love for it when he died and went missing. With him here, I have my old drive for it again, and it feels amazing. Like I'm myself again.

"But you're just doing the same thing over and over, for all these people who will never even know to thank you for it."

"I don't need any thanks, and it's not about *me*. Love is a gift that everyone deserves. It's the most important thing in existence. It brings joy and fulfillment, devotion and loyalty. For a cupid, it's the ultimate prize to see a true Love Match come to fruition. It's all I want for people—for them to love deeply and to be loved with the same fervor in return. It's...magic."

He stops walking suddenly, and we turn toward each other. For a moment, he just sweeps his silvery gaze over my face, and a loaded hush falls between us. "And what about you?" he asks quietly.

"What do you mean?"

"You give love to people, but what about you? Don't *you* want love?"

It feels like my heart goes tight. I look down at my feet, try to tamp down the rush of emotion that swells up. "It's a cupid's duty to spread love, not take it for her own."

I've said that so many times before. Believed it, too. For a long time, that's all there was—giving. I never dreamed that I could ever have it for myself, it just wasn't an option before.

"But your boss has love," he points out.

"Well, yes, but she's the exception."

Belren doesn't back down. "You're telling me that in all the time you've been a cupid, handing out love left and right, that you've never once wanted that for yourself?"

Defensiveness squirms down my back. "I've been entirely too focused and too goal-oriented to worry about something like that."

He levels me with a look. "I don't believe you."

"I don't need you to believe me," I snap. "Can we change the subject? You're ruining my love-high." I turn around to keep walking, but Belren blocks me.

"Why don't you want to talk about this?"

I huff, crossing my arms in front of me. "Because. That's not the purpose of a cupid. I'm not supposed to be selfish like that. I chose this path, and it's my honor to give love to those I can. End of story."

Sliding left, I try to sidestep him, but Belren just matches my move to continue to block me. "Sure, it's an honor," he says with a shrug. "I'm not dismissing your work or downplaying the importance of it. I'm simply asking for you to think about yourself for a second."

I shake my head. "No."

"Why not?" he counters, taking a step closer to me.

I back up, but he just takes another step. My chest feels tight, palms wringing in front of me as my emotions start to rise up. "Because."

"That's not an answer, Pinky."

"What do you care?"

Belren lifts his arm like he's trying to run a hand through his hair, only for his palm to go through it without any traction. He growls out a curse under his breath, arm dropping to his side again. "You're the cupid," he counters. "Why do you *think* I care?"

I blink at him, not understanding why he's so *frustrated* all of a sudden. "I don't know."

He shakes his head like he's disappointed in me. My lips purse.

"It's an easy question, Lex. You're a cupid who loves giving love. Are you going to stand there and try to act like it's never even crossed your mind?" he challenges. "Do you or do you not want love for yourself?"

A roaring fills my ears as I stare at him.

I can't reply. I'm too shell-shocked by the blunt question. Denial and arguments reel through my head, but it's like Belren can read my mind, because he swarms my space, invading it completely so that I don't voice a single one. He doesn't give me time to even turn away.

I thought he was close before, but now he's *right* in front of me, silver eyes blazing. "I'm drawn to you, dammit. And it's more than just because you can see me or because you came to my deathplace. It's not one-sided either. I know you're drawn to me too." His gaze sears into mine. "You're someone to me, aren't you?"

I go completely still, and all I can do is gape at him.

"Aren't you?" he demands.

"No," I blurt out, but even I can hear the lie.

"Who are you to me?"

How did this get so out of hand so fast? "N-no one."

Belren's glare is sharp enough that I feel the stab of it through my chest. "Liar." As mad as he is, he somehow purrs that word like a seductive accusation. I watch with wide, unblinking eyes as he raises a hand and whispers. "Such a gorgeous, infuriating liar."

And then, his knuckles skim against my cheek, and I *feel* it.

My breath sucks in, shock spinning down my tight throat. Belren freezes too, but just for a moment. Before I can even blink, his hand has turned to grip my jaw, and then his lips are slamming down against mine.

And here. Right *here*.

This is where I realize I really am a liar. But I wasn't lying to him. No, I was lying to myself.

Because I *have* always wanted love, though I'd never admit it. I'd never even let myself *think* about it, because it was an impossibility before.

After all, those who can't learn, teach. And those who can't love, cupid.

But it seems I went and broke the cupid's cardinal rule.

I got greedy and started to fall in love.

CHAPTER 21

LEX

I don't know how to tell time when Belren kisses me. There's no way to count the seconds. It's just the pressure of his lips against mine, the weight of his hand against my jaw, the depth of his tongue slipping into my mouth. There's no other measurement.

With my eyes closed, my vision isn't there to muddy up what I'm feeling. So the kiss is all I'm aware of—the only thing my mind and body are attuned to.

When my tongue slips against his in a tentative stroke, Belren groans into my mouth, and the sound zips straight down to my core, making me emboldened. He grips my face harder, not hurting me, but with a grasp that tells me he's terrified that he'll lose the ability to feel me at any moment.

His touch is more substantial this time, with more weight and *realness*. There's no warmth to his skin, but it doesn't feel strange. If anything, he's invigorating. Like taking a deep breath of fresh air.

Our tongues tease and our teeth nip, and this kiss feels exactly like falling in love.

It's exhilarating and soft, demanding and tentative. I've never kissed anyone, never wanted to in all my time in this afterlife. But now, with Belren's lips against mine, I realize just how much *more* this is.

Watching and encouraging it between others on the sidelines just isn't the same. Love, lust, yearning, it's all so much more consuming than I could ever comprehend as a bystander, no matter how qualified.

Finally, after I'm not sure how long, I pull away, only because I have to catch my breath. I'm panting so hard that I probably should feel embarrassed, but my thoughts are far too steeped in desire to care.

I just had my first kiss.

Momentous—that's how it feels. Like mountains shifting on the ground, changing the landscape completely.

Our eyes are locked together here beneath the shadowed trees, and I'm so thankful for the moonlight, because it makes him seem even more tangible—albeit glowy. Even though we aren't far from the hedge maze, this spot amongst the trimmed grass and rowed trees feels private, like its own separate island.

"You're so bright," I whisper through swollen lips, my voice dropped down and sounding like a demure secret.

He smirks, though his hand doesn't drop from my face. Instead, he brings a thumb over to rub across my bottom lip. "You're so beautiful."

A blush tinges my cheeks. It's my knee-jerk reaction to turn away and wave him off, but before I can, his hold shifts to my chin, and he tilts my head up. "You *are*," he tells me sternly, sterling eyes boring into me.

"How are you touching me?"

He shakes his head slowly, eyes still full of hunger. "I don't know. But I'm not going to stop now."

I suck in a breath as his mouth comes down to press softly against my neck. Shivers erupt on my skin as he skims kisses across the spot just below my ear where I'm most sensitive right now, hand tilting my head to give him better access. "I can even smell you," he murmurs. "Like a memory. Of roses dipped in spun sugar, pressed between my favorite pages of a book."

His other hand comes to rest on my shoulder, grazing over my skin with the lightest touch that somehow has the heaviest impact. An ache begins to pulse between my legs, steady and warm, as that hand dips down past my collarbone before fingering the hem of my shirt collar.

"What does it feel like to you?" I ask breathily.

"It feels like walking into the sun after being in the cold darkness for too long."

Unbidden, I feel a tear spill from my eye and trickle down my cheek. I don't even know why I'm crying. Probably because I'm overwhelmed with too many emotions, both sad and full of joy, excitement and fear.

Belren notices immediately but doesn't hesitate to press his lips against it, kissing it away. "You even taste sweet."

My heart feels so full, so euphoric, that I'm surprised it's not bursting from my chest. I'm not sure how he's broken down my barriers so thoroughly, but they're wiped from the planes of my personality completely. I'm more open than I've ever been, more vulnerable, and it scares the heck out of me.

My breathing picks up, and Belren pauses, fingers not straying below my collar. Pulling back, he looks me in the eye. "Tell me what you want, Pinky."

But I can't, because I don't know.

"I have no idea what I'm doing, just that I want to do it," I confess. This foreign, clumsy need is throbbing through me, winding me up as tightly as a coil about to snap. I know all about pleasures of the flesh, since I've been the catalyst to so much of it. Yet experiencing it firsthand is something I have absolutely no experience with.

Belren's eyes soften. "Come here."

As if he knows I need some kind of reassurance, he wraps me up in his arms. I carefully rest my cheek against his chest, in awe as my skin lands against the cooled press of his body. He's substantial, yet not quite completely solid. His silhouette feels like cool satin, rather than the true feel of the fabric of his tunic or the hardness of his masculine body.

I try to imagine what this embrace would've felt like when he was alive. Would I have felt heat coming from his body? If I breathed him in, would he have had a spicy scent or something wilder?

I'm acutely aware of his fingers playing with the waist-band of my pants, and I instinctively press myself even harder into him. He makes a gravelly noise deep in his throat, which only excites me more, though I'm not sure what to do about it.

"I've got you," he assures me.

And he does.

Suddenly, his thigh is between my legs, giving me the pressure my body is craving, *right* where I'm craving it.

A whimper comes out of me, which only seems to spur him on. "I know my cupid hasn't felt any love for herself...but what about lust?" he asks, the question purring through his body to mine.

As if he's summoned some just by bringing it up, a little bit of Lust Breath slips from between my lips like an exhale in a wintry night. The pink fog puffs between us, and I look up just as it rises up around his face.

Belren takes a deep breath, and his entire body goes still before his eyes flick down to me. "Was that..."

I nod slowly. "You felt my power?"

"I felt it," he replies, his voice rough and low. "Do it again."

A smile spreads over my face before I gently purse my lips, and then I slowly blow out a stream. Wisps of power permeate the air, condensing between us in a haze.

"*Fuck*," he growls out.

I don't know how I have the nerve to be so wanton, but his response spurs me on, and I find my feet widening so I can fit him better between my legs and start rocking against his thigh. His hands grip my waist, and then he's dragging me closer, leg lifting slightly to give myself the friction that my body is so desperately craving.

"I need more..." I whisper out, hands clasped tight to his shoulders, legs shaking like they're not going to keep holding me up.

"Where are those manners you're so proud of?" he teases.

"*Please*," I blurt out, because, first of all, he's right. Manners are very important. Secondly, he could ask me to say just about anything right now, and I'd do it; that's how desperate I am.

Belren's hand reaches behind me to grip my butt, making me jump. "You have no idea how much I like hearing that word in this context."

I think I have some idea, since something hard is pressing against my stomach.

Should I be curious about how it's even possible for a ghost to get hard? Probably. But do I care right now? Absolutely not.

"I asked nicely," I remind him.

"You did. Such good behavior means that I should reward you."

I nod emphatically. "Definitely."

With a grin, Belren somehow maneuvers us until we're sitting down together in the grass, his back against a smooth tree. He settles my body on his lap, my legs wrapped around his waist, my hands still balanced on his shoulders. He's never stopped touching me. Not once, as if he won't risk letting go and then losing the ability completely.

"Lie back," he instructs.

I hesitate, teeth capturing my bottom lip.

"Don't worry, Pinky," Belren tells me. "Just a reward, remember? Nothing but pleasure."

With a nod, I slowly lean back until my wings are resting on the grass, the cool blades pillowing my body. I start to pull my legs off of his waist, but he clamps a hand down on my thigh to keep them locked around him. "Stay," he orders.

I feel a little bit like I'm trying to do a yoga pose, but I do as he says because I *really* want that reward.

He leans forward slightly, his hand coming down to trail over my stomach. Even with my shirt acting as a layer between us, the touch makes me suck in a breath, my eyes going wide.

"B—Hook," I catch myself. "I..." What am I going to say? That I want it, but that I'm scared? That sounds silly, considering my profession. I shouldn't be frightened of intimacy. I celebrate it on a daily basis.

At the uncertainty in my tone, his hand goes still as he looks down at me. His gray horns are curled back, white hair mussed, and I wonder what it would feel like if I tried to run my hand through it.

"Do you want to stop?" he asks.

I shake my head, but I'm trembling.

"It's alright," Belren soothes. "Close your eyes, Lex."

I'm nervous at first, but as soon as my lids flutter shut, my worries go quiet. I'm able to focus on his touch and his touch alone, making me instantly more relaxed.

"Good girl."

My feathers ruffle from the praise.

"Now, just feel."

Slowly, his hand slips beneath my shirt, his cool touch grazing against my stomach. My skin jumps at the contact, but then he goes higher until he's dragging a finger against the underside of my breast.

I shut my lids tight so that they don't spring open as that teasing finger swoops over my curve, and then his entire palm is gripping my breast, squeezing it lightly. A gasp tears out of me when his bracing touch shifts, and he brings my shirt up to expose my chest. I can't help but look. I peek so I can watch his reaction through half-lidded eyes.

Belren has gone still, his gaze latched onto my body. The expression on his face captures one word perfectly.

Crave.

His attention flicks up, catching me, but I'm so glad I had my eyes open for this moment. He tsks at me like he's caught me being naughty, and I probably shouldn't find that exciting, but I do.

Watching me, he brings both hands to my bare waist and then yanks my hips against him, my groin grinding against his hard length. I let out an incomprehensible noise at the sudden friction that leaves me throbbing.

His hands hook into the waistband of my pants, loosening the ties until the fabric flares open. "Put your feet down on the ground, but make sure your thighs are still wrapped around me, understand?"

I nod, swallowing hard, before I do as he said. When my feet are planted on the ground behind him, he lifts my hips and starts to slowly tug down my pants as far as they'll go. With the fabric strapped around my thighs and his body positioning them open, my lower half feels pinned in place. And I like it.

Belren glances down at my underwear, which are simple and plain white. I have a snap-reaction to feel self-conscious, since they're probably not the most exciting undergarments he's seen, but then I remember...that *he* doesn't remember any of his previous escapades anyway. It's oddly reassuring.

I relax a bit...right up until his knuckle skims across the front of my underwear, dragging over the bundle of nerves that, up until now, have been wholly ignored in my afterlife.

My hips buck up on accident, from both surprise and

pleasure, but Belren's hand is there on my stomach, pinning my body securely down. When he rubs it again, my knees try to fuse together, but of course they can't.

Belren watches me steadily, like he's learning me. With my bottom half secured on his lap, upper body exposed and sprawled out on the grass, I feel entirely vulnerable. Shyness starts to overtake me, but it stops short when he says, "You are the most gorgeous thing I've ever beheld."

My heart flutters. He just gave me a compliment and used the word *beheld*. I'm a goner.

"Do you want me to give you pleasure now?"

I don't have the breath to tell him that I feel pleasure every single time he touches me, so I just reply, "Yes, please."

Belren's hand slips beneath the fabric of my underwear, dragging a cooled, silken finger across my seam. "Mmm. Such a good little cupid."

My knees tremble as he gathers my wetness, and when the pad of his thumb presses against the spot where I'm throbbing, I squeeze my eyes closed again.

Yes, right there.

Blinking, breathing, trembling—it all becomes secondary and background. It's as if everything has been narrowed down to this one single part of me.

"Where am I touching you, Lex?" he asks.

I bite my bottom lip hard, my hips jolting up again as he continues to rub that perfect spot. Yet when I don't answer, he stops, making a whine escape me.

"Don't stop."

"Then tell me where my hand is right now. Tell me what I'm doing to you. I want to hear those naughty words coming from your prim and proper mouth."

My cheeks flare. "I...can't."

When his hand moves, at first I think he's taking his touch away completely, and I begin to protest, but he simply tugs my panties down to my pants, making me swallow my words.

Panting up at him, my chest heaves, and Belren takes the opportunity to lean down, placing his mouth right over my pebbled nipple, and a staggered exhale escapes me.

His tongue moves over my peak, flicking it back and forth before he sucks, letting it fall out of his mouth with a dirty *pop*.

"Please," I plead, because now that he's exposed me *down there*, it feels like it's aching even more, the cool night air making me all too aware of how hot and throbbing I am.

Belren swirls his finger around my other breast. "Tell me where you want my touch."

I blink up at him, because I'm so desperate for him to resume, my body *so close* to that blessed release that I've caused but never experienced. He smirks at me, and then his finger comes back down, yet he avoids the spot where I need him most, and instead gathers my wetness and spreads it around.

"Come on, Pinky. Tell me that you want me to rub your clit until you explode. Tell me that you want my fingers inside your tight, wet pussy until I make you come."

My mouth falls open, and I probably look like a deer in headlights. "I...I can't say *that*."

"Course you can," he replies, his finger barely grazing me, and my eyes flare.

"Don't be mean."

"On the contrary," Belren counters. "I want nothing more than to be very, *very* nice to you. But if you need me to be nice, then I need you to be a little *naughty*."

My wings flare behind me at his words, and more Lust comes floating out of my mouth. He leans down again, this time to pepper kisses over my chest before licking a path up the curve of my neck that gives me full-body chills.

"Be naughty. Just this once, let go. There's no embarrassment between us," he murmurs against my heated skin.

Squirming, I clear my throat. "I would like you to please touch me."

"Touch you where, Lex? Use your words," he says, lifting his head to sit back up.

I glance around to make sure no one is around to hear me. I don't know why I'm more bothered about saying dirty words aloud. I mean, I'm lying here basically naked, doing *very* inappropriate things, but saying a naughty word seems so much more scandalous.

Still, I aim to succeed.

When I'm certain that we're still alone and under the cover of night, I turn my head back toward him, though I don't meet his eyes. I can't.

"I would like you to please touch my…"

"Pussy," he purrs. "Go on. Say it."

Feeling like I might combust from fiery embarrassment, I mumble it out as fast as I can under my breath. *"Please touch my pussy."*

He hums. "Despite the fact that what you said was barely audible, I'm going to give it to you, because hearing you say that was both adorable and arousing as hell."

I smile, because I really love when someone is proud of me.

But my smile slips right off when his hand slides back down. He wastes no time, one hand gripping my thigh, the other doing exactly as I asked.

If I thought his touch was pleasurable before, it's nothing compared to now. I'm slicker, too, because he uses the moisture there to run over my throbbing core as he starts to spin me up toward the dizzying heights of pleasure.

My hands clamp down on the lush grass beneath me, gripping the blades between fists because it feels like I might just float away otherwise. I have no idea how he knows just how to touch me, but he does. He rubs me in that perfect spot, and my eyes clamp shut as I let the sensation consume me.

When he slips a finger inside of me, we both groan.

"Gods, this pussy..." he growls out. I squeal, overcome, as he begins to thrust his cool finger in and out, while continuing his rough fondling that's bringing me higher and higher to an unknown peak. "You're hot and dripping, your body practically begging to be fucked."

Goodness.

He adds another finger, and then he curls them inside of me while putting pressure on my clit, and a garbled noise gets stuck in my throat. Does it always feel like this? I don't know. But his touch is a confliction of sensations. Soft yet substantial. Cool yet making me throb with heat. He's bringing me higher and higher, more moans spilling out of me, and I'm *almost*...

"There it is," he croons. "Let go and come for me."

And because I'm *excellent* at following instructions, I do.

That unsteady climb I've been on suddenly expands to a precipice, and then I'm plunging right off the edge, and what a delicious edge it is.

An orgasm racks through my entire body, heating from the soles of my feet to the apples of my cheeks. I quake all over, and he doesn't relent, just keeps touching me, making my pleasure go on and on.

When the fall finally slows, I come back down to the ground, tingling all over. My eyes are dazed and heavy as I open them, and I find Belren slipping his fingers out of me, only to bring them up to his mouth and lick them off.

He groans. "You're sweet everywhere. The best taste I could ever have on my tongue."

I'm too languid and glazed-over to even clutch any pearls over the fact that he just *licked* me off of him. As far as I'm concerned, he can do whatever dirty, inappropriate thing he wants, since he gave me my very first orgasm.

But his caring for me doesn't end with the pleasure-giving. Belren carefully grips one thigh and helps me bring my legs together. He pulls up my underwear and pants, even knots the ties before he straightens my shirt down over my breasts.

When I'm recouped enough to speak, I ask, "Don't you want me to..." My eyes dart down to his groin. "You know," I finish lamely as I shake out my wings and fix my ponytail.

"No," he says with a smile. "My little cupid needs to be eased into these things slowly, I think." He pulls me into his lap again, but this time sideways so my wings don't get in the way of me resting my head against his chest.

Just being held by him like this is its very own kind of pleasure. Not one where you fall off an edge, but something softer, slower. Like a wayward feather floating through the air.

Right now, I'm not embarrassed about what we did. I'm not thinking about how exposed or vulnerable I was. It's like we're in our own private bubble, and I don't want it to pop, though I know it will.

"What if you won't be able to touch me again?" I whisper, worry spreading through my quiet tone.

Belren's arms tighten around me like he shares the same fear. Like what we just shared was just as significant for him as it was for me. "Then I'll hold you now for as long as I can, and I'll enjoy every moment."

CHAPTER 22

LEX

*B*elren and I went to the other hearth hob islands on the seer's list, but found nothing. The second one was so small we could walk from one end of the island to the other in about a hundred steps, so it was clear no one was hiding there. The third had a close-knit collection of fae who probably only said a handful of words in the entire two days we were there, and there was a strict no visitors policy, so we struck out there too.

We doubled back to the first island again, and we've been searching all across it for several days, but not once have we heard even a whisper of anything about Princess Soora. Nothing even remotely political has been said, nor has Emelle tried to call me for an update. I'd be doubting Chuckrey's legitimacy if it weren't for the fact that he saw Belren. It's probably the only reason that keeps me hopeful and searching, no matter how fruitless it seems.

But this wild goose chase isn't what's truly frustrating me. Nope, my chagrin is entirely selfish. Since *that night*, Belren hasn't been able to touch me. Not once.

After he'd given me pleasure, I stayed locked in his lap for a long time until I started yawning and my stomach grumbled. Together, we held hands all the way back into the town where I found an inn to get cleaned up, eat, and sleep. But when I woke up the next morning and he tried to reach for me, his hand went right through me.

It's been like that ever since.

I wish I knew what it was that was making it possible for us to touch. But for the life of me, I can't figure it out. Even though it shouldn't be possible, I still worry that our lack of touch now means something bad. I also worry that this unfinished business has hit a lull, and that's what has him in a rut. *Will the fates take him away if I can't keep my end of the deal?*

He won't talk about it, but Belren is troubled. I don't know if it's only the touch thing that's bothering him or if there's something else, but sometimes, I catch him looking off into the distance. I might be bad with my sense of direction, but I have a gut feeling that he's always looking back toward his deathplace.

Right now, we're sitting outside on a polished stone fence, watching hearth hobs walk by on the clean cobbled street. There are a few other types of fae around too, but not very many. Considering their very strict rules on cleanliness here, I'm not that surprised. There are framed notices in *very* neat handwriting hung up on most public posts that say if you should soil or sully anything, you'll be imprisoned for an indeterminate amount of time.

I mean...I'm sure their jail is very well tended, but still.

"Should we try to fly around and see if there's another town on this island?" I offer, eyes idly following the people who pass us.

Belren is staring straight ahead, scowling. That scowl has evolved slowly over the past few days. First, when he couldn't touch me again, it started off as the tiniest pucker of his brow. Then it accompanied a slight downturn of his mouth. Now, it's a full blown glare, as if he's angry at the world.

"We tried that. We didn't see any."

"True, but maybe we should look harder?"

"No."

At his short answer, I look over at him from the corner of my eyes. "Alright..." I concede. "Do you want to try going through some of their houses? Maybe they're more likely to gossip in the privacy of their homes."

He snorts, still looking forward. "Doubt it."

Irritation niggles up my spine, and my wings flare a bit before snapping against my back. "Fine," I say, blowing out a breath as I try to keep my polite, positive tone. "Then what about—"

Belren cuts me off. "Don't you get it?" he demands, tone pissed off. "It's useless. Nothing is going to work."

"Don't snap at me," I admonish, my shoulders as prickly as my thinning patience. "I'm just trying to come up with ways that can help."

He finally moves his head to scowl in my direction instead of the air. "You ever think there is no help?" he retorts.

I know he has every reason to be frustrated, but that still doesn't give him the right to be rude to me. "No, I don't. Because unlike you, I'm not just going to give up and sit here all sullen and pouting. I said I'd find Princess Soora, so that's what I'm going to do." I jerk a finger toward his face. "And if you're just going to pout, then I'll do it without you!"

Belren jumps down off the fence and spins around to face me like an angry god. His silvery skin is darker, like a storm is brewing right there on his face. Even his eyes flash like impending lightning. He slaps his hands down on the wall on either side of me, leaning in until we're face to face, and I suck in a useless breath, frozen as he cages me in.

"You sure as hell won't be doing it without me," he snarls. "But I'll let you in on a secret—I don't even care about the damned traitor princess! What I really want to know is why the *fuck* can't we touch?"

There it is.

His fury is like a boom of thunder, rattling my emotions. "I don't know!" I yell back, thankful that I'm in the Veil and no one can hear me. "But regardless of that, we *are* finding Soora, because this is your unfinished business in the first place!"

Belren shakes his head. "We don't know that for sure."

"Yes, I do," I blurt out and then immediately slap a hand over my mouth, eyes going wide.

He goes still. "Excuse me?"

It takes a few blinks before I can drop my hand and shake my head. "Nothing." I try to look away, but he moves his head to stay in my line of sight.

"Don't even think about it, Pinky. Tell me what you meant. Now."

I'm frozen on the fence, inwardly kicking myself. Why did I have to go and open my mouth?

His jaw tenses. "I'm waiting."

When I realize he's not going to let this go, my shoulders slump. "Fine," I say with a huff. "But if this gets you yanked back to your deathplace, don't even think about blaming me."

"Just tell me what the hell you're talking about."

"You were right, okay? I *am* someone to you. Kind of," I amend.

An indiscernible expression crosses his face. "Explain."

My throat tightens, my eyes blurring with moisture. If this makes him disappear and forget...

"You died for me," I blurt out.

For a few long seconds, he says nothing. Just stares.

"I...died for you."

"Yes. That battle that everyone talks about? The one Soora was involved in right before she left, leaving the rebellion to fend for itself? That's when you died."

There's a long pause.

"How?"

I swallow hard. "The prince was trying to attack Emelle. I don't know if you've noticed or not...but we sort of look alike. He threw power at me instead, and you...you jumped in front of me." My words get slower and thicker, emotion clogging me up. I hate that this is how he's finding out. That an argument has led to this. All my guilt for that day is rising right alongside the sadness. "You told me to stay in the Veil, but I didn't because I wanted to help..." I have to choke off a sob, push out every cracked word. "You jumped in front of me, took the blast that was aimed for me, and you died in my place."

I wish I could read his mind, because his expression goes completely unreadable, which only makes me panic even more. I'm waiting for him to get pulled—to disappear right in front of my eyes, but he doesn't.

Finally, he says, "Right before I...reappeared, or whatever the fuck I did at Ghost Island, I thought you were calling something."

I let out a shaky breath. "Belren."

He mouths it silently, his brows pulling together as if he's frustrated that it doesn't feel familiar. "So we were..." He gestures between us. "You and I were *something*."

My chest constricts as I have to admit this part. "No," I reply. "We weren't anything. I don't know why you did it. Why you did it for *me*. You barely knew me."

He watches me steadily, unblinking, unmoving, and I'm just waiting for him to start yelling at me. Once it sinks in, he's going to be angry. I mean, who wouldn't be? I'm the reason he died. He's going to hate me, and he'll probably—

A giant laugh suddenly booms out of him, making me flinch in surprise. The laugh goes on and on, and I'm just left gaping at him with my mouth open like a fish.

This is even worse than him getting yanked. He's finally lost it. He's cracked. His ghostly deficiencies have claimed what was left of his mind, and now he's just going to be known as the laughing ghost of hob island, where he will forever haunt the pristine streets with his inappropriate cackling.

Goodness, I've really done it now.

"Alright, it's okay. I'll help you through this," I quickly say. He's bowing at the waist, hands on his knees, still laughing like a madman, not even stopping to take in air. "Just take a deep breath before you pass out."

At that, he looks over at me and just starts laughing harder.

Oh, right. Dead. It's strange how I keep forgetting.

Burying my head in my hands, I take a moment to lament. It seems like the right timing for it, seeing as how I've messed things up so colossally. "I've ruined your life and now your afterlife. I deserve for you to laugh-haunt me forever," I say into my palms.

I peek through my hands to get a handle on his mental state, but I'm also already wincing in preparation. But he's not looking dazed or daft. In fact, he's looking at me like *I'm* crazy, which is a bit insulting, to be honest.

"I find it hilarious that you think *we weren't anything*," he says, his laughter abating.

My hands drop and I stare at him in shock. "Are you...are you okay?"

"Of course I'm okay, why wouldn't I be?"

I sit up straighter, eyeing him warily because I don't quite believe him. *Is he dimmer than he was before?* I immediately pop out of the Veil, as if my corporeal senses can take him in better. He definitely looks a little dimmer, but he's not disappearing.

"The last time I tried to talk to you about the past, I made you get yanked twenty feet away to your deathplace."

Belren looks down at himself. "I'm still here."

I frown. "Hmm. Strange."

He leans into my ear. "Probably because you've been a very good cupid, keeping my muck on you all across the islands," he murmurs, his playful demeanor bouncing back, the low tone of voice making me nearly swallow my own tongue.

When he pulls away, he chuckles at the look on my face, which just makes me scowl and then lift my hands to his chest so I can shove him away.

It takes me a second to realize it worked.

Belren is even so shocked himself that he staggers back a few steps from my push and then stands there gaping at me.

I look down at my hands and then back up to him. "Huh."

He's back in front of me in the blink of an eye, lifting his hand to my arm. Tensing up, I watch the descent...

Only for his hand to go right through me.

Annnnd his scowl is back. Just peachy.

"What the fuck?" he grounds out. "Why can't I touch you back?"

I cross my arms in front of me, feeling a bit defensive, because I don't want him back in his bad mood again. "I don't know, maybe it's because you have a poor attitude," I say, glad that there aren't any fae walking by right now.

He shoots his gaze up to mine. "What?"

I cock a brow. "Maybe if you weren't pouting about it so much and being such a butthead about it, you'd be allowed to touch me again," I say primly.

He has the nerve to look offended. "I have not been a butthead."

"You definitely have," I counter. "Moping around with a frown on your face the whole time. Maybe you need to use your manners and the Veil will reward you."

Thundercloud eyes narrow on me. "You know what I think, Pinky?" he challenges. "I think *you* are the one doing it. I think you're unintentionally blocking me."

I scoff. "What? That makes no sense."

"Yes, it does. Every time I've touched you, it's been when you least expect it. It's been when you were...distracted." His glance drops down my body before coming back up. "But when you knew my touch was coming...you braced yourself. You tensed up, like you're nervous."

Have I been doing that? I don't know, but I certainly don't want to prove him right.

"Touch me," he challenges.

I roll my eyes before jumping down from the fence with a flip of my hair. "No, thank you," I reply breezily as I start to walk away.

He's in front of me again after just a handful of steps. "Touch me," he says again.

"Maybe I don't want to touch you," I snip.

His eyes grow half angry, half heated. I have to be honest, it's a very attractive look on him. "Don't lie, Pinky. It's not polite."

Darn it.

"You're making me want to push you again," I reply tersely.

He laughs. "If that's what it takes to get your hands on me again, go right ahead. I like it a little rough."

"Oh my goodness." I whirl around to start walking the other way.

Belren continues to laugh behind me. "Oh, come on, Pinky! You know you want to try to touch me!"

"You can just stay right there while I go try to find your unfinished business without you!" I toss back over my shoulder.

I find a shadowed spot between two buildings and start marching back down the road again, barely missing a beat.

Of course, he's already caught up with me, looking as cheerful as ever. "You're going to touch me sooner or later, and I'm going to prove my theory was right."

"Go haunt an outhouse," I grumble beneath my breath before smiling sweetly at some passing fae.

He chuckles and continues to walk beside me. "Look at that, anger makes your jokes better."

I swear to the heavens, I am going to touch him just so I can throttle him.

Pointedly ignoring him, I spot several hobs grouped together in front of a row of houses nearest to the square. I head right for them, deciding I'm just going to go up and introduce myself to see if I can get any of them talking. It'll be easier to ignore him that way.

But I stop short when they start arguing heatedly about whose roof is cleaner.

"My roof is the best on the whole street!" I hear one of them shout.

There's a bit of an uproar, with several of them jumping in to deny that claim.

"Oh, please. I cleaned mine so well that I'll have enough power for a week!"

"No, no, no. Everyone can tell that my roof is the cleanest. My shingles are gleaming, Perryl!" one of the hobs retorts, jabbing a finger in the direction of the houses.

Another hearth hob—presumably Perryl—snorts through his nose. "You call that gleaming? I got shinier shits than that!"

Half of them start laughing. The other half start arguing even louder.

"Well, they seem preoccupied," Belren chirps up.

Changing course, I walk into the town square, where I spot some sort of stall setup near the sparkling fountain. There's one hearth hob behind the stall who's selling her things, with an orderly line milling around it. As I get closer, I realize it's a soap stall, because *of course* it is.

When I stop in front to look at the wares, the hobs around me give me sidelong looks, gazes lingering on my wings. Luckily, they're too enamored with the different soaps to be bothered about staring at me for long. And honestly, the soap collection is quite impressive. There are multi-layered solid bars, bottled liquid, and even something called gem soap that sparkles like diamonds in little containers. Very fancy.

Belren props himself next to me. "You think they're hiding the princess behind the stall?" he jokes before leaning over to look.

Ignoring him, I smile at the stall owner. "Hello there."

The female just frowns at me before looking me up and down. "You need a good washing."

I rear back in surprise. "Oh. Umm..."

"Hey, that wasn't fucking nice," Belren growls.

Feeling flustered, I press a hand to my hair to make sure it's still in its smooth bun while my other hand straightens my tunic. Looking around, I notice all the hobs in line are staring at me again, as if they too are assessing my cleanliness. Judging by their expressions, it's not looking good.

"This is a new shirt, and I had it laundered, and I washed my hair..." I say, trailing off as I frown down at my boots. "My shoes could probably use a polish."

Everyone in line nods in agreement.

"That hair could do with a rinse."

"Her nails with a good soaking too."

"It's the feathers for me," another one says, wrinkling

his nose. "Those need constant care. How often do you groom them?"

I wring my hands together. "Umm..."

Another one starts to open his mouth, but the stall owner cuts across him. "What's that dirty thing hanging off your back?"

I glance over my shoulder at my strap before I gently swing it around for her to see. "Oh, this? It's just my quiver holding my arrows." When I notice a piece of dried mud that somehow ended up on the string of my bow, I quickly pick it off. "It's not that bad."

"You're right," she agrees. "It's worse."

Well, that's not polite at all.

She gestures an impatient hand at me. "Give it here."

My eyes widen. "What?"

The female leans her arms on the counter of the wooden stall and glares at me. "Did you know we can feel when something needs cleaning?"

"Well, no, I didn't, but—"

"I'll test my new batch of soaps and wash it for you," she tells me. "It'll be shining by the time I'm done with it."

"I think it's time to leave now, Pinky," Belren cautions.

I swing my bow and arrows behind my back again as I shake my head at her. "That's nice of you to offer, but no thank you. I'm going to go now."

I start to back up, but then someone from the line rips the quiver right off my back, making me stumble, shoving it toward the stall owner before I can do anything. "I want to see you use that new lavender gem soap!"

Lurching forward, I try to snatch it back, and I manage to snag hold of the strap, but when I tug, it jerks from both of our holds. My bow and arrows go flying, and then I watch in slow motion as my quiver careens end over top, dumping all of the mucky contents of Belren's deathplace out, right there in the middle of the square. It lands with an audible splat.

"Is that...*dirt?*"

There is a collective horrified gasp.

I swear, every hob in a fifty-foot radius makes that noise, all of them stunned with shock at seeing dirt in a messy pile on their polished stone street.

Then, the split second of stillness erupts. The herd of fae pounce on it, sweepers and rags and soap bottles appearing in their hands like cowboys whipping out pistols for a shoot-out, and I get thrown back from the crowd.

I go flying backward, but just when I'm about to land hard on my butt, a pair of sturdy arms catch me from behind.

Gasping, I look up at Belren towering over me, his hands firmly under my armpits, holding me steady. To everyone else who can't see him, my positioning probably looks very strange.

"Told you you'd want to touch me," he says cockily before his expression morphs into a scowl as he turns his attention at the cloying crowd in front of us. "Now which one of these assholes pushed you? Because I swear to the gods, I really will haunt them in an outhouse for laying their hands on you. I'll scare the shit out of them for the rest of their days if I have to."

As far as ghost promises go, that's quite romantic.

"I don't know, I couldn't—" I cut myself off, eyes widening in horror. "Oh my gods, your muck!"

I clumsily straighten up and then shove myself through the crowd of fighting hearth hobs.

When I manage to elbow my way through to the center, I'm too late. The hobs have finished, and they disperse, looking highly pleased with themselves now that they've defeated the evil dirt.

But my stomach bottoms out as I stare down in horror at my scattered arrows, my bow, and my shining quiver. My shining, *empty* quiver, right alongside the spot on the ground that's now completely wiped clean of any speck of dirt from Belren's deathplace.

For the first time in my afterlife, I say something that is really, really not polite.

"Well...fuck."

CHAPTER 23

LEX

*M*y ears are ringing in a solid, constant garble.

"They cleaned away my muck," Belren mutters beside me. "That's unfortunate."

For a moment, I can't move. I'm too stunned at what just happened—at how fast things went out of control. Carefully, I sling my bow over my shoulder and grab my arrows, picking up my quiver last. One glance down confirms that the muck is gone, the inside now gleaming. My arrows land inside of it with a hollow thud.

I like control. I don't like *this*. I also usually like cleanliness. But right now, I couldn't be more furious at it.

Snapping back into action, I shove the quiver onto my back and then whirl around at the hobs that have cleared out. "I want that dirt back!" I shout at their retreating backs. Not one of them stops or even turns around. "Hey! Come back here right this instant and give me back my pile of muck! That's stealing!"

Everyone just walks further and further away.

No.

"I need it!" I yell, my voice gone shrill and desperate. "You don't understand!" I feel tears start to spill out over my cheeks, and I can't do anything to stop them. The soap stall owner glowers at me, as if my tears are offending her. She's probably worried that they'll land on the ground and ruin the polish. "What are you looking at?" I snip at her, making her glower deepen. "Did you take my dirt? Huh? This whole thing was your fault."

"Alright," Belren says, suddenly sweeping in front of me with his hands up. "Calm down."

I can hardly believe my ears. "Calm down?" I repeat through clenched teeth. "How can I calm down? How can *you* be so calm? They just took off with your muck! You're going to get pulled back!"

"Oh great. Unkempt *and* crazy," I hear the hob mumble.

I can still see her through Belren's translucent body, and I stick my tongue out at her. I'll give her crazy. "Where are my arrows? I need an arrow!"

Belren waves a hand in front of my face. "Hey. Eyes up here."

My gaze flicks upward, where I find an amused expression and *not* an arrow.

"Don't laugh at me right now," I snap at him, wiping my cheeks.

Behind him, the hearth hob drawls, "Does it look like I'm laughing?"

I sidestep around Belren so fast that he can't even react before I'm right up at the stall and pointing at her face. "I'm not talking to you. And your soaps aren't even that clean looking!"

She gasps and tosses a hand over her heart, like that's the worst insult anyone could ever say to her. "Take that back!"

I shake my head and cross my arms. "No."

Looking positively steaming, she opens her mouth and starts yelling for the constable. "Rule breaker! Dirt maker!" She points with heated accusation.

"I didn't *make* the dirt, I just carried it around with me, thank you very much!" I retort haughtily.

Belren is at my side in a flash. "*Ooookay*, time to go." He instantly hooks an arm around my waist and starts pulling me away. I struggle, so it probably looks really strange to all the gaping hobs.

"Let go!" I hiss, trying to bat his hand away. For a ghost, he's surprisingly strong.

"Do you want to get arrested?" Belren asks me with exasperation. "Stop struggling."

I don't though, because I'm too wound up. He yanks me off the square and into a narrow alley between two buildings, taking us all the way to the back and away from the gawkers.

"What are you doing?" I demand. "I have to go back. I need to go track down the rest of the hobs before it's too late and try to see if we can salvage—"

"*Lex*," he barks, just as he spins me around and pushes me back against the building, making my eyes go wide, a whoosh of air escaping me from the impact.

"*What?*"

He shakes his head while I try not to think about the way his hips are pressing against mine. "My muck is long gone."

"No," I argue, shaking my head. "We can still—"

He cuts me off with a pinching grip on my chin. "No, Pinky. It's done. They got rid of every speck."

An embarrassing wave of tears fill up in my eyes again and start to spill right over.

His eyes soften right alongside his tone. "Don't cry," he says, but that just makes me cry harder. His cool, not-quite-solid fingers swipe them away. "Look at me."

I do, but my vision is so blurry I can't look properly, which just makes me more upset.

"*Lex*," he says, a light rebuke in his tone.

I quickly rub my eyes on the sleeves of my shirt. "What?" I snap.

"If I was truly anchored to that deathplace dirt, I would've been gone from you already."

I just blink at him as the words slowly process. "That's…" I frown dubiously. "Do you really think so?"

I'm too worried to believe him at first. I don't want him to disappear. But he barrels right through my doubtful anguish.

"Yes," he says without hesitation before leaning in closer until we're cheek to cheek and his low voice is right in my ear. "You see, Pinky, I don't think it was my muck after all. I think it's just...you." He pulls away again but only far enough so that he can look me in the eye. "I think *you're* keeping me from getting yanked back. I think *you're* making it so that I'm not losing my damn ghostly mind. I think I'm tied to *you* for this unfinished business with the princess. I had my suspicions, but it seemed even more possible once you confessed who you are to me."

My mind trips over that last part, and I immediately open my mouth to set him straight again, but before I can actually speak, he shakes his head at me and says, "Don't even *think* about trying to tell me that you're not anything to me. I heard that bullshit the other night, but I won't hear it again."

"It's true!"

Belren rolls his eyes. "Come on. Males don't go around *dying* for a female who means nothing to them."

"Well...maybe you were just altruistic."

At that, he snorts. "I doubt that."

My head tilts in thought. "Okay, you did steal things from people for a living, so maybe not."

"I was a thief?" Belren asks, and for a second, I'm worried this is going to upset him.

Silly me.

Nope, he gets a grin on his face, and his eyes practically *sparkle*. "Now that feels more like me."

I want to ask him how he can tell, but we're interrupted by a male hob stomping toward us. "You there!"

Looking over in surprise, I immediately note the sewn-on emblem on his jacket that says "Constable." Standing just behind him with her hands on her hips, is the soap stall owner. She flashes me a mean smile before turning on her heel and marching away.

"Tattletale," I mutter.

"Shit." Belren releases me, standing at my side as I straighten up.

"You," the constable says as he comes to a stop in front of me, his stature just coming up to my chin, though his fluffy tuft of gray spirals gives him an extra few inches. "I've had several eyewitnesses saying you purposely caused a mess in the town square."

"I did no such thing, Sir."

He doesn't seem convinced. "I'm going to have to take you in for questioning."

I blanch. "For a little pile of dirt? That's not even there anymore?"

His lips turn down, eyes going severe. "We take cleanliness very seriously here, miss. Our livelihood depends on it."

"Yes…" I agree. "But your livelihood *also* depends on the act of cleaning. So when my dirt mucked up your square, it then allowed the hearth hobs to clean it up. Which means that they got a power boost from it," I point out.

Belren chuckles. "Nicely done."

The constable obviously disagrees. "Think you're smart, do you? Well, you can spend the night in the jailhouse. That should make you think before you mouth off again."

"The fuck she will," Belren says, getting in the constable's face.

"It's alright."

"No, it's not alright," they both say at the same time.

"Let's go," the constable says.

Belren motions for me. "Let's run and lose this asshole so you can go back in the Veil. There's no way I'm letting him put you in jail."

I bite my lip. Of course, going into the Veil would solve the issue, but running from the law seems very uncivil.

Yet I don't have to make that decision because right then, a female hob comes walking up to us, her eyes assessing the situation. She's got a slightly hunched back, and some of her blonde hair is going silver, but her skin is relatively smooth, her eyes sharp. "Jarth, there you are," she says, making the constable turn toward her. "There's an issue down at the tea tavern."

He sighs, making his belly rise up surprisingly far. "Another fight break out over who washes the dishes?"

She nods solemnly. "Yep. They need you immediately."

He looks irritated by this, but he's a man of his duty, and apparently, I'm lower on the scale of importance than a fight about cleaning. With a pointed glower, he tells me, "You make even a speck of a mess anywhere else here, and I'll have your hide."

"Yes, sir," I reply with a respectful nod.

He lets his scowl linger for one more moment before he turns and walks away. Once he's out of sight, I turn toward the female with a smile. "I'm sure you didn't mean to, but that was very good timing for me, so thank you."

"Oh, I meant to," she replies, looking me up and down.

Surprise flashes through me. "You mean, you were helping me?"

Considering none of the hobs seem to even want to tell me the time, I'm shocked that she wanted to help me stay out of jail.

Belren circles around her like a vulture. "She probably wants something from you in return," he says. "Don't give her anything."

I stop myself from rolling my eyes, because not everyone is out to do a good deed solely for their own gain. He's far too pessimistic.

"I helped you because I want you to do something for me," she says.

Belren shoots me the cockiest *I was right* look that makes me want to shove him.

Instead, I clear my throat and keep my attention on the female. The last thing I want is to get into another tussle with a hob. I admit, I was not on my best behavior back at the square.

"What do you want?" I ask curiously. "Money?"

My hand goes to the coin pouch at my waist, but the female shakes her head with a scoff. "Of course I don't want your dirty money," she says, lips curled in disgust.

"Then what do you want?"

She looks around us as if to make sure we're still alone in this little alleyway before turning back. Her blue eyes lock onto me. "I know who you are. You're that cupid, Emelle."

I blink in surprise, though it's not as if other fae haven't mistaken me for Emelle before, because they have. After the war and the new monarchy took reign here, Emelle became a bit of a legend. After all, she's the only cupid living in this realm. But the intensity of her statement is what's caught me off guard. "Oh, well I—"

She doesn't give me an opportunity to explain that I'm not Emelle though, because she flings her hand out, fingers wrapping around my wrist. She pulls me a little closer to her. "I was told that if you ever came here, that you have to come with me."

"That's a no," Belren says.

I look at her uneasily, a little stooped so we're face to face. "Go with you where?"

Her eyes are filled with secret intensity, voice dropping low. "I'm to take you to the princess."

CHAPTER 24

LEX

It's a bit of a whirlwind, but soon, I find myself sitting at the hearth hob's dining room table in her immaculate house.

She's busy behind me pulling off the kettle and filling a couple of teacups while my eyes flick over the crisp linen of the tablecloth that's the exact same shade as the white of the walls and floors.

Yes. White *floors*. And there isn't a single scuff or stain on them. I cringed with every step I took from the front door to here, worrying that I was going to get something on it.

Belren is walking around through the front living room, and my eyes dart to the right when I see him pass by the doorway. "This place is a bit boring. Too organized," he calls out before he turns and disappears up a set of stairs. After a moment, I hear a muffled, "She hangs up her socks! What kind of psychopath hangs up their socks?"

I dart a look at the female, immensely thankful that

she's unaware of the ghost rifling through her house. I twist my fingers around in my lap. "So, I—"

"Here's the tea," she says before bustling over and placing the teacup in front of me. This is the third time I've tried to broach the subject of the bomb she dropped back in the alleyway. Yet each time, she's shut me down when I've asked her to elaborate. She said it wasn't something we could talk about in public.

Clearing my throat, I start talking awkwardly. "Umm, Miss Hearth Hob…or Madame Brownie?" I venture, glancing down at her brown cloak. "Or perhaps you like to be called a hobs?" There were a few other terms Chuckrey mentioned, but now they've escaped me.

She levels me with an unimpressed look. "My name is Miur."

"Right." My cheeks are shaking a little from how much I'm trying to smile. Maybe I'm smiling too much? Is there a level of too smiley in a somewhat awkward setting? I should look into it.

"Miur," I repeat as she takes a seat across from me at the small round table. "Thank you for inviting me into your home."

She straightens the sprig of pine she has poised in the glass vase in front of us before lifting her own teacup to her mouth for a sip. She looks up at me expectantly, her curly blonde brow arched. "You don't like tea?" The way she asks it makes it very clear that if I say no, her assessment of me will plummet.

"I love tea," I quickly say, my eyes flicking down to the cup in front of me that's been filled to the brim. I can't stop worrying that I'm going to accidentally slosh the liquid over and stain her tablecloth. Or worse yet, spill the whole thing and make a puddle on the floor. But Miur is still looking at me with judgment in her eyes, so I shoot her a tight smile before reaching for the cup.

It takes me ages to lift the thing to my lips, because I'm being extra careful with it. When I manage to take a sip and set it back down on the table without mishap, a small sigh of relief escapes me.

With a terse nod, she gets up again to search through some cupboards. "So, Miur," I try again. "You said something about the princess..."

She comes back, setting a tray of biscuits in front of me, and I swear my face must drain of all color, because I just *know* that these things are crumbly as all get out. My strained smile becomes just a little more tense. "These look...delicious."

They look like a test I'm going to fail, if I'm honest.

"Just made them this morning. Go on and have one."

My eyes widen. "Oh, I don't know—"

"Eat."

Alright then.

Reaching for it, I pick one up like it's a stick of dynamite. I know it's going to detonate at any moment, the crumbs of its shrapnel ready to take me out. She watches me as I take a tentative bite, my eyes widening as I feel crumbs stick to my lips and fingers. We both know this is a disaster in the making.

It's crumbling. I can feel it. The whole thing has split into little pieces, and if I move it away from my lips, it's going to cascade down into a disintegrated mess that I won't be able to come back from.

So there's really only one option. I shove the whole thing into my mouth. I can't close my lips around it, but

I'm committed now. I chew and churn and maneuver it around my tongue like a champ. A painful amount of slow seconds tick by, with me struggling to chew this dry thing while she awkwardly watches me.

When I finish, I lick my lips to make sure I've gotten every single morsel, and then I beam at her like the victorious cupid I am.

Miur lets out the tiniest grunt of annoyance. Her lips purse, eyes searching over the tabletop. When she isn't successful there, she leans sideways to take a look at the floor. It's like she's just itching to find a solitary crumb so she can blame me while simultaneously getting very excited about cleaning it up.

With my victorious smile still plastered on my face, I lift up my cup of tea with a mock salute. I start guzzling it to rinse away the dry-mouth I have going on when I hear, "Well, *that* was an interesting thing for me to witness. Who knew you could fit so much into your mouth at one time?"

Belren scares the beats right out of my heart, and I jump a half a foot off the chair, spilling tea all over myself. I sputter out a choked cough as droplets go flying everywhere, landing on the tablecloth, dripping down my chin, soaking into my shirt. And yes, some of it even spills onto the white floor.

The victory that my mouth had just battled for is now completely saturated in blotted defeat.

"Don't worry, Pinky. You look good when you choke, too."

I blink at him, chin still dripping, and the second I realize his meaning, my cheeks go so hot I'm surprised my whole face doesn't catch on fire.

I really want to shove him again.

Across from me, Miur's face spreads into an expression of pleased arrogance. "What a mess you've made," she tuts. "I'll need to clean that up straight away."

She gets right to work, humming happily as she starts to strip the tablecloth, ignoring me completely. Muttering out an apology, I quickly excuse myself to the washroom, not at all surprised when Belren follows me, walking right through the closed door.

I glare at him as I dry my chin off with a towel before trying to soak up the splatters that have plastered the shirt to my chest. "You did that on purpose."

"What, made you choke on it?" he asks with a smirk. "Like I said, you took it beautifully."

"I'm going to murder you."

"You said that about the princess too, and you still haven't offed her. I think I'm safe, especially since you kind of already did that," he teases.

I go still at his words, my mouth dropping open because...oh my gods, he's *right*. I may not have actually done the deed, but it was because of me that he was murdered. And now here I am, saying that so callously... A sudden surge of emotions slams into me.

So of course, I burst into tears.

Belren freezes, hands shooting up in front of him like he's warding off an attack. I'd say he looks pale as a ghost, but he always looks like that. "What's happening? What's wrong?" he asks, the pitch of his voice bordering on panic.

"I murdered you!" I stuff the towel into my face and cry, all the pent-up guilt I've had for so long feeling like it's suddenly wringing out of me. All this time, when I've slacked at my work or when I've doubled down on it, no matter what, this guilt has cornered and crowded me so much I couldn't even breathe. Couldn't even *think*.

I hear Belren curse under his breath, but when I look up, he's right at my side. His hand comes up to try to grab mine, but it goes right through me.

His silver eyes lift to mine. "Stop blocking me and let me touch you."

"I can't," I sniffle. "I'm not purposely blocking you."

"Well, then stop *unpurposely* blocking me," he says, trying to joke again to lighten the mood. But I'm in full rain cloud mode right now. There is no light.

When my chin wobbles, his face softens as he comes around to stand in front of me. "No crying, Pinky. I can't stand it."

"How can you stand to be around me now that you know I'm the reason you're like this?" I ask miserably. "You should hate me."

Belren cocks his head. "You don't get it yet, do you? I could never hate you."

You should, I think to myself.

More tears drip down my cheeks, and Belren lifts a hand to try to wipe them away. But when his fingers come up to my face, I don't feel a thing, his touch going right through me. Still, he doesn't drop his hand. "Come on, Pinky," he implores. "Let me touch you."

"Why do you assume it's *me* blocking *you*?" I retort. "Maybe it's the other way around."

He doesn't even hesitate before shaking his head. "Nope. That's not it."

I open my mouth to dispute that claim, but he shushes me. "As much as I love that sassy mouth of yours, I need you to hold back from arguing with me for the moment," he says. "Close your eyes."

Shooting him a dubious look, I then let out a shaky sigh before I relent.

"That's it," he praises. "Now, I want you to imagine that we're back at the gardens." His voice has dropped down to that timbre I've come to recognize as my favorite.

It takes me a few seconds, but I manage to clear my head enough to do as he said. But when I picture that night, it's just a collage of dirty snapshots and grass stains.

"I can see you're thinking about it," Belren says with a knowing chuckle. "Next, I want you to think about the way it felt when I touched you. How did it feel when I skimmed my mouth along your neck? Or when my hands gripped your hips?"

The low growl of his voice makes my core clench. Apparently, my body has zero issues remembering.

"Remember what it was like when I slipped my hand against your pussy? Remember the sound of your moans?" His voice comes closer, right at my ear, making chills scatter and my legs press together. My body seems to be as receptive as ever, even if he is sheerer than a sheet. "You want me to touch you again like that, don't you, Lex?"

Goodness gracious.

"Yes," I whisper.

"Then let me touch you." Cold lips press against my neck. My breath hitches, chills scattering over my entire body, and my eyes spring open in surprise.

Belren's head tilts back with smug victory that somehow makes him even more handsome. "*Good girl.*"

Yep. That praise obviously does something for me. Because in the next instant, I launch myself at him.

My hands are flung around his neck like I'm gripping a tree branch, my legs scrabbling to shimmy up his trunk of a body, and my lips slam against his. I kiss him like his mouth is the way to the promised land and I have to lick my way through.

It's not...look, I know what I'm doing right now doesn't have a lot of finesse. I can feel that without seeing it. But where my charm is lacking, I make up for with pure vigor.

I can tell Belren is caught off guard at first, purely from the way he freezes against me, but if there's one thing I've learned about him, it's that he's excellent at adapting.

Pause forgotten, his hands come to my hips, and then he's spinning me around and placing me on the pedestal of the washbasin. I land a bit crookedly, wings skewed, half my butt sinking into the basin, the other half perched awkwardly around the lip. But the logical solution to that is me wrapping my legs around Belren and grinding against him. Obviously.

I'm still doing my best impersonation of licking through an ice cream cone when Belren pulls away from me. I try to go right back to suction-mouth mode, but he chuckles, squishing my cheeks between his hands as he holds me in place.

His eyes skate over my face in something that looks like adoration. "You're *very* energetic today."

I shrug a shoulder, legs still wrapped around him, hands tangled around the nape of his neck. I get the best chance to play with the ends of his white hair too. It feels less like normal hair and more like the individual strands that make up a feather.

Getting curious, I move my hand up to one of his curling horns, placing the pad of my finger at the blunt tip. He jerks in surprise, eyes snapping to mine. "Do that again."

Bolder now, I run my finger up, following the ridged curve, and Belren's entire body shudders. "What does it feel like?" I ask quietly.

"If I had to guess?" he replies, voice sounding a bit strained. "A bit like it would if you'd stroke my cock, I believe."

My hand freezes for a moment, my eyes widening on his face. When he doesn't crack a smile, I realize he's serious. I also realize that he looks very, *very* turned on, almost to the point of pain.

Biting my lip, I shift my touch until I'm gripping both horns, one in each hand, and then I stroke upward in a firm grasp.

Belren lets out a groan that curls my toes. I mean...I'm not an expert on groans or anything—although, I probably should be—but I think the one he just made was the sexiest in the world. In the top ten, at the very least.

I continue to stroke, gently at first, before I start to grip a bit harder, stealing another one of his sexy sounds. I can't even fully fathom the power of the fact that I'm making him not just feel, but feel *good*.

Really good, if I were to judge based on the look on his face.

When I make another pass down the curve of his horn, he reaches up to grip one of my wrists. Wordlessly, he brings my hand down to his groin, where I find exactly how good he's doing.

Watching his face, I cup my hand around him and squeeze, making his hips buck forward. "Fucking gods. Do that again."

A thrill travels up my spine. "Say please."

His eyes flash. "Oh, Pinky. When I have my hands on your skin and your hand is on my cock, you don't give the orders."

I think...I think I just swooned a little.

Which is odd, considering I always thought swooning was just a poorly described fake flirtatious faint, or perhaps an excuse to get away from people. But I feel a real life swoon going on right now, all from his domineering words. A warm, lightheaded giddiness has taken over, like my secret crush just smiled at me.

"My innocent cupid always with a blush on her cheeks as bright as her hair," he says, tucking a flyaway behind my ear.

"Does that bother you?" I ask. "That I'm innocent?"

"Why would it?"

I glance away, embarrassed. "While you were alive... Well, what I mean is that I heard...umm." I trail off.

Mirth curves his lips up. "Are you implying—yet too polite to outright say—that I was a bit of a sleep-around in my mortal life?"

"Yep. Yes. Yes, you were."

He laughs. "Well, as far as I'm concerned, none of those...encounters happened, since I can't remember them anyway. I'm also dead, so I'm fairly sure that all of that experience I gained in my life means absolutely nothing now. Consider us both innocent."

I snort at the thought.

Belren's eyes narrow, though they're filled with a hungry spark. "Think that's funny, do you?" His hand comes down between my legs, and he cups me with a firm, possessive grip that steals my breath. "Let's see how long until I make you moan instead."

My eyes flare. On the one hand, my needy body is very aware of the pleasure he can give me, but on the other hand... "We can't," I tell him. "Miur is waiting for me."

"She'll be scrubbing that tablecloth bare, getting as much of a power boost out of it that she can. We have plenty of time for a little fun."

I drop my eyes down to his groin. "How little?"

His hand grinds against me, making me yelp as the heel of his palm presses hard against my throbbing clit. "You are quite sassy today, aren't you?"

"I thought it was a valid question," I pant, trying and failing to keep the smile off my face, even as I continue to cup him, feeling the evidence of his substantial size. Curiosity takes over. "Can you...you know. Do the deed?"

Belren grins. "Ready to find out, are we?"

"Considering where both of our hands are..."

He lets out a rumbling chuckle, his fingers circling. "Pinky, when I fuck you, it's not going to be in a strange hob's bathroom. I don't think even she would appreciate the cleanup."

My eyes widen as reality comes crashing down around me, and I jerk my hand away from him. "Oh gods, you're right." I look down between us, noting the way my legs are still wrapped around his waist, my hips tilted toward him obscenely. "I can't believe I did that," I say, hands coming down to his chest to push him away. He doesn't budge.

"I told you I wouldn't fuck you." He reaches around with his other hand to slip off the strap that secures the bow and quiver to my back, setting them both down on the floor. "But that doesn't mean I'd leave my cupid wanting."

I gulp. "That's generous of you."

"I'm benevolent."

"You used to be a thief," I remind him.

He shrugs before stepping away, forcing my legs to drop...and then he drops right along with them. I stare wide eyed as he kneels, and then he's tugging my pants down until both they and his mouth are skimming my calves.

"What are you—"

"Remember when I said I wanted to taste your sweetness everywhere?"

My shaky knees knock together like a drunk rapping on the wrong door. "You can't do *that* right now!"

Firm hands grip my bare knees, and he gently pries them apart again. "If you really don't want me to, I won't," he tells me seriously. "But if you're just nervous, don't be. I'll always make you feel good, and like I told you, there's no embarrassment between us."

My mouth feels about as dry as a desert. Which is funny, considering how wet I am between my legs.

"Okay," I say, swallowing hard as I try to relax my legs, but I can't. I'm frozen stiff, unsure of what to do. My hands are a tangle in my lap before I snap them down to grip the basin...and then put them right back in my lap again.

Belren takes note of my nervous fidgeting. "Lean back against the wall."

I'm so grateful for the direction that I lean with an overabundance of enthusiasm. I smack my head so hard into the wall that I see stars. I swear, if I get concussed from this, I'll never live it down.

Trying to play it off, I squint open my eyes, but I find Belren trying to repress a laugh from his spot between my legs. "You okay up there?"

"Yes," I reply quickly, rubbing the back of my head.

"Good. Now, lean back *carefully*."

I let my head rest against the wall gently this time. "How was that?"

"That was very good, Pinky."

My wings ruffle up. "Thanks."

"I'm going to start licking you now, if you're ready."

I laugh nervously. "Ready steady, Freddy."

Belren frowns. "Who the hell is Freddy?"

"Oh, um. I actually have no clue."

"Maybe...hold off on saying other male's names when my face is next to your cunt."

I blush at his words but nod sagely. "That's reasonable."

His hands stroke up my thighs in long, slow movements, as if he's acclimating me to the feel of him. It's nice. For a moment, that's all he does. Just caresses my skin with his light touch. Then, he leans in and places a kiss over my underwear, making me jolt. "Oh!"

Belren looks up at me. "Doing okay?"

All I can do is give him a sloppy nod.

As soon as I do, he drags my underwear down. *With his teeth.*

Goodness.

When I'm bare to him, he lets out a growl, taking me all in. I have to suppress the intense urge to cover myself. My hands flit around my thighs nervously. "Can you stop looking at it?"

Belren's eyes flick up to my face, and then his hand cups me again, making me shudder. "This pretty pussy is mine right now, so I'll look my fill. No need to be shy, because everything about you is perfect."

If I like being praised, I *really* like being called perfect. Not even just the word itself, really, but the fact that I can tell he really means it. He truly thinks I'm perfect, and that makes all the difference.

While I'm momentarily distracted, Belren leans in and *licks*.

It's a good thing he's gripping my thighs, because otherwise, I think I would've fallen right off the edge of the washbasin. "Oh gods, you're getting right in there."

I feel him chuckle against my inner thigh.

"I wasn't expecting this," I start to blabber, my nerves and curiosity dueling for supremacy. "It just feels like a normal tongue—at least, I think it does. Not that I have experience with feeling a tongue...down there," I say quickly, only for Belren to lick again, making my head loll against the wall. "Except it's not warm, probably because none of you is warm," I add, my voice strained as I try to keep my composure. "But are alive tongues *too warm*, do you think?" I frown at my own unanswered question. "I wonder what temperature they are on average. I'll have to see if I can look that up later. It would be interesting to compare."

A growl comes from between my legs, and I look

down as Belren meets my eye. "You are not *comparing* other tongues. Mine will be the only one that gets to taste you."

"Oh. Of course. Forget I said that, please. I'm just nervous."

He snorts. "I can tell. But if you're talking and over-thinking this much, that means I'm not doing my job right."

My brows pull together. "I'm sure that's not true," I say, hoping to boost his confidence. "I've witnessed a lot of cunnilingus as a cupid, and you're performing all the necessary steps."

My hands continue to flick around nervously, going from my lap to my thighs to the basin and then repeating all over again. "What should I do with my hands? I don't know what to do with them. Maybe I should just..." For some reason completely unknown to me, I think it's a good idea to thread my fingers together and prop them behind my head like I'm lying on a beach sunbathing. I'm self-aware enough to know that it's a weird position, but I'm just stuck, eyes wide with worry, no idea what to do. Surely, there's some sort of protocol for this.

Belren's gaze flicks from my awkward hands back to my face as he slowly arches a brow. "Hey, Pinky?"

"Yes?"

"I'm going to need you to do three things for me. Can you do that?"

I nod emphatically, because I am fully cognizant of the fact that I am spiralling, and I really need some direction. And so do my hands, apparently.

"You're too in your head to enjoy this," he goes on. "So

I need you to close your eyes, take a deep breath, and then grip my horns and don't let go."

My eyes widen. "You want me to—"

He cocks his head, tsking with disapproval. "Talking and worrying wasn't on that list I gave you, was it, love?"

I clamp my lips shut and shake my head no. I have to admit, my stomach is doing little flips because of his domineering tone and his choice of nickname. Maybe it's a cupid thing. Love really excites me.

Belren's eyes flash. "You want to be a good girl, don't you?"

My head nods so hard I get a crick in my neck. "Yes. Absolutely. Definitely, I do. The *best* girl, in fact."

He cracks a smile. "Good," he says, thumbs rubbing comforting circles on my thighs. It feels delightful, and manages to relax me a bit. "Go on then."

Mentally clamping onto his instructions, I slide my eyes closed and then take a deep breath. I force myself to count to seven for both inhaling and exhaling, just to make sure I'm overachieving. Then I lift shaky hands until my fingers wrap around his horns, my grip tightening when he groans.

"That's it. Now don't let go, or that'll count against you."

I feel my lips turn down involuntarily because I definitely don't want marks against me, and I'm a little offended that he thinks I'd even allow that to happen.

"Just like in the gardens, Pinky," he says in that low tone of his that makes me shiver, the sound even more intense when my eyes are closed. "It's just you and me, and all you need to do right now is to feel my tongue on you."

"I can do that," I say breathlessly. I can excel at it too. I'll make sure of it.

His cool fingers skate higher up, trailing over my hip bones before dipping down to the junction between. I tense up, but Belren doesn't chastise me for it. Instead, he takes away my ability to think completely.

His mouth descends onto me without hesitation, his tongue going up in one slow stroke that makes a little yelp escape me. Then his mouth is moving again, lips closing around my clit, and he *sucks.*

Literally, not figuratively, just to be clear. He's excellent at it.

"Oh gods..."

Belren's tongue flicks and laps, mouth suctioning between movements, until I've forgotten all about the *what do I do with my hands* conundrum, and I start directing his face by his horns. It's like a steering wheel and a fidget stick all in one. Very handy.

"Don't let go," he cautions, and I snort, because there's absolutely no danger of that happening now. In fact, he should really be more concerned with me never letting him go. I've boa-constrictored myself right onto him and am now considering the limit of greediness for how long I can keep his head stuffed between my legs.

The faintest feel of scratchy stubble scrapes against my thighs in the most sensual way, and just when I thought things couldn't get any better, he pushes a finger inside of me and curls it, hitting a spot that makes my wings flare out behind me, one of them knocking into the glass of the small window.

"A plus, A plus," I pant out in a jumble.

Lick. "Are you grading me, Pinky?" *Suck.*

"Exceeds Expectations," I blurt, feeling hot all over, tingling on the arches of my wings

"Happy to hear it."

He starts thrusting in and out, pads of his finger curling again and again to stroke the bolt of lightning that seems to stir to life there every time he does it.

Someone dead should not be so good at this, but here we are.

I'm getting eaten out by a ghost. Honestly, if more hauntings were like this, it would be so much better.

"Stroke my horns while I lick your pussy, Lex. Show me how you'd stroke my cock."

His rumbled order has my hands moving instantly, and even though I've never done it before, I fancy myself an expert at observation, so I stroke and squeeze perfectly. Belren lets out a sexy groan, making it travel directly from his lips...to mine.

"Good fucking girl."

Praise Kink Level 3: Unlocked.

He sucks again, making Lust slip out of me in ribbons of pink. My back arches, head knocking against the wall that is *definitely* not quiet, and I think I start chanting his name, but I can't be sure, because he starts thrusting his finger in and out while doing his sucky licky thing, and I'm done.

I'm done.

I yank on his head so hard that a grunt escapes him as I smash him closer to me. There's no way he can breathe with the way my thighs are clamped around his head, but he's a ghost. Breathing is unnecessary.

He's fine.

My orgasm hits me with a force of its own. It takes the

breath right out of my chest, and his name chant that I'm still not sure I was saying out loud turns into one I definitely know *is* said out loud, because I shout it.

I shout it to the rooftops, coming apart in a million pieces, and I don't even care about ever being put back together again.

CHAPTER 25

LEX

*I*t takes me several seconds to come down from the explosive bliss Belren just gave me. Little white dots pop behind my closed lids as I breathe out with the last shudders of pleasure.

"Yuw nt tol etgo ow?"

Belren's mumbled words yank my eyes open, and I look down at where I still have him plastered against my feminine junction.

"Sorry," I quickly say as he tilts his head up to look at me.

I think I see his cheeks crease with a smile when I don't move.

"Gonna let go?" he manages to say against my thigh.

Oh. Right.

Regretfully, I peel my fingers off his horns, releasing him. He sits back on his haunches, wiping his mouth with the back of his hand in a move that's erotic for some strange reason.

"You were quite loud," he says, grinning so hard I can tell it pleased him immensely.

"Why don't *you* try having someone's mouth latched onto you like a sucker fish and see how quiet you can be," I shoot back as I straighten my clothing so I can look like a presentable lady.

I'm not sure presentable ladies let their nether regions get sloppy kissed in a stranger's bathroom, but still.

Belren's grin grows wolfish as he stands up, hands balanced on the basin as he leans in. "Is that an invitation?"

My eyes widen, and now I'm picturing that it's *me* kneeling in front of him, his pants around his ankles while I lick and suck him until he comes. I've never ever done that, but I've considered the logistics many times and deduced that I'd be great at it.

Belren groans, making me blink away the scene. "Stop looking like that, or I'm going to put you on your knees right now."

I tilt my head, wondering if I could pull it off.

"No," he says, as if he can read my mind. "We don't have time."

"I bet you I could make you orgasm faster than you made me."

His eyes narrow. "Are you issuing a challenge, Pinky?"

My wings wiggle a little, because I *love* challenges. I especially love winning them. "Yes."

Belren's gray eyes practically glow, so I know he likes the idea, but he shakes his head. "As much as I'd love to take you up on that right now, we're going to have to take a rain check."

I smirk. "Because you'd lose?"

"I'm not sure there's really any *losing* in this scenario, but no." Belren leans in, tongue licking over my bottom lip before he nips it with a hard kiss. "Because when I get your mouth on me, I want it to be just you and me, no distractions, no interruptions," he says intently, eyes boring into me. "When I have you, I'm going to take my time, draw it out for as long as possible. There will be no rushing for your challenge—at least, not the first time."

The first time. As in, he wants us to do this more than once. "Who said I was going to do it twice?"

Gods, when he smirks at me, eyes pinning me in place, it makes my toes curl. "Don't lie to yourself, Pinky. You're much too logical for that."

My heartbeat flutters. I like it when he compliments my body, but I really like it when he compliments my mind.

"You're very good at this," I tell him.

"I'm very good with *you*."

That too.

I smooth my hands down my clothes, and maybe it was the high he just gave me, but for some reason, my mind starts slipping down into a low. All the pleasure and happiness has gone stale with the stark cold reality, and doubts and fears take over. The seer's previous warning filters into my mind, and although I've tried to ignore it, I must be too vulnerable right now, because I can't block it off.

"What the seer said..." I begin tentatively. "About the way ghosts...fade. Do you think he was right?"

I've clearly caught him off guard at my sudden subject change, because the happy, sexy look on Belren's face disappears. "Probably."

"Are you worried?"

"About what? Getting squished down by my own madness after years of ghosting?"

"No," I reply, trying to contain the fraction of frustration that starts to stir. "The other part. The unfinished business."

He shrugs. "I have no idea. Why are you worrying about this?"

Flabbergasted, I shake my head. "Why are you *not* worrying about this?"

"You know my thoughts on worrying."

"I think we should talk about it properly. We can't keep pretending like you aren't a ghost, just because you can touch me sometimes."

His lips curve up. "I do more than just touch."

"Belren, this is important," I persist, and even though his expression grows annoyed, I keep going. "What if Soora really *is* your unfinished business?"

"What about it?" he snaps, making my pulse kick up. "Are you so ready to be rid of me?"

"What? No, that's not—"

"You think I *want* to be like this? A useless fucking ghost who can go crazy or expire in the blink of an eye?" he challenges with a shake of his head. "No. I want to exist in the moment while I *can* still exist. So just let it go."

"No," I say, completely frustrated that he wants to continue to ignore this. "I know it's not fun to think about, and I've been trying not to worry out loud because I know that's what you want, but that isn't reality. We need to confront this."

He backs away from me to lean against the wall, and even though it's just a couple of feet, I feel the distance like a chasm. "And what's reality?" he lobs back, crossing his arms in front of him.

"Reality is that we might be on our way to finish your unfinished business, and we're in here, hiding in a bathroom and doing things we probably shouldn't be doing."

Belren's eyes grow molten with anger, deepening in color as he stares at me. "*Shouldn't be doing?* That's not what you were saying just a few minutes ago."

Flustered, my hands twist together, pinching the skin. "I know, and it was wonderful, but it's also distracting us. There's a very real chance that the seer was right."

"There's also a chance he was wrong," he counters. "Ghosts shouldn't be able to touch anyone, yet I can touch you. Maybe I don't play by the rules. Maybe things are different for me."

I open my mouth to reply, but he suddenly jolts, body going stiff all over, and his silhouette wavers, becoming slightly more transparent. My chest squeezes at the grimace contorting his face. "What's wrong?"

"Nothing," he grits out.

"This is *not* nothing," I say, eyes sweeping over the pained way he's holding himself. "What's happening? Talk to me."

"Fucking. Deathplace."

My eyes widen. "Oh my goodness, is it trying to pull you back?"

"I'm fine," he tells me, which is ridiculous, because he obviously isn't. "It happens sometimes."

Something like betrayal slashes through me. "This has been happening to you, and you never told me?"

After a second, he rolls his tense shoulders, and the

grimace leaves his face, like whatever it was has passed. "See? Like I said, it's fine."

Shaking my head, I pick up my bow and quiver from the floor before slinging them on my back. "I can't believe you kept this from me."

"Why would I willingly worry you?"

"You can't just use worrying as an excuse to keep things from me!"

His eyes move away from me, and he shakes his head, like I'm being the ridiculous one. I wish I could live in that denial that he's perfected, but I can't keep ignoring everything. I can't pretend like these things aren't happening.

"I asked Emelle to help you. To see if she could reverse your ghost status. But she hasn't contacted me—not once —so I'm losing hope. Which means we're probably on a course to complete your unfinished business, and yet you want to keep going on in blissful ignorance."

"And what would you rather do?" he counters. "Make a pros and cons list? Worry yourself into an early grave for me to haunt?"

"Don't joke about haunting right now, Belren. I'm serious."

"Oh, I know. You're *always* serious," he says under his breath.

Something sharp twists in my chest, but I try to ignore the jab. "Have you ever considered that this isn't fair to me?" I ask him quietly, but as soon as the words are out of my mouth, I want to take them back because of the way he visibly flinches.

"Care to elaborate?"

Not really, but I started this, so I suppose I may as well finish it, even though it hurts.

Shoring up, I brace myself enough to look him in the eye. "At the end of the day, you're a ghost. If Emelle can't figure out a solution, then I might have to slowly watch you go crazy for years and years, until you finally disappear."

Something slams shut in his gaze, his expression going flat. "Right. How selfish of me to drag you around for that long," he seethes. "I guess we'd better get back to finding the princess. Get it over with in hopes that it triggers my *unfinished business* so that I can disintegrate into nothingness a bit quicker for you, and we can go our separate ways. Or maybe next time, I'll just give in to the fucking pull on me and zap back to my deathplace and leave you in peace."

I rear back like I've just been slapped. The scathing tone of his voice and the anger in his face make tears prick my eyes. As soon as the first drop trickles out, Belren's face slackens, eyes rounding. "Pinky, I'm sorry. That's—fuck." He tries to run a hand over his horns, but it passes through, and he drops it again in frustration. "I was just pissed. I know that's not what you're saying, not what you want. But I fucking hate talking about this, alright?"

He hates talking about *anything* difficult or real, and that's what concerns me. You have to have someone by your side who can help you handle the rain, not just enjoy the sunshine.

But that's not him, that's not what he wants.

I quickly wipe at my cheek and blink down at my shoes to make the rest of the tears go away. "Alright."

In two strides, he's right in front of me again, and he reaches for me to either pull me against his chest or to hold me by the arms. I'm not sure which one he intended though, and I never will, because his hands go right through me.

He lets out a litany of curses. "Fuck, Lex. Let me touch you."

Even if he's right about me being the one to allow him to touch me, I'm not emotionally stable enough right now to figure out how to let down my guard. In fact, I'm relieved that he can't. Because when he touches me, all thoughts go right out the window.

Taking a deep breath, I let it out between tight lips as I consider the reality of my options. At first, I thought it was luck and some muck that kept him with me, but that's obviously not the case. I thought I needed to keep him focused on this mission to keep him sane, but I don't think that's true either. All I'm doing is driving us on a crash course toward his destruction.

"I'm going to go back out there and tell Miur that I can't go to the princess," I tell him, looking anywhere but his face. "If she really does have to do with your unfinished business...it's just not worth the risk. We'll go find Emelle and talk to her. Hopefully she knows something by now, and we can prolong this."

"Pinky."

I shake my head. "No, you're right. We don't need to talk. We'll just be in the moment." I lift my eyes to him and try to give him a smile, though considering how shaky it is, it's bound to be pathetic. "I promise to try to help you get as many of those moments as you can have, for as long as you can have them."

"Lex—"

I turn away, wrenching open the door and walking

out. Once again, I've made a mess of things. I'd be a terrible hearth hob.

But I meant what I said. I'm going to do whatever I can to keep him here, to keep him sane, for as long as possible. I just wish I could live in the moment too. Instead, I'll be feeling this cloud of dread hanging over my head every single second, until the end.

CHAPTER 26

BELREN

I wish that the blush staining Lex's cheeks had to do with the post-coital glow, but I know that's not it. No, that pink tinge is a good old-fashioned anger-glow. Or maybe disappointment, which is even worse.

Speaking of glowing, the hearth hob is practically lit up too, but hers is from a post-cleaning bliss. She must've gotten a hell of a power boost from cleaning up Lex's spill. Yet, she maintains her glare, as if she's put-out by having to clean.

Miur and Lex are standing in the kitchen again, a new tablecloth laid out on top of the table, not a stain or crumb anywhere in sight. No matter where I stand or what I say, Lex is pointedly ignoring me. It's the first time since finding her that I've actually felt invisible.

"Pinky," I call from across the kitchen. I'm trying to give her space as I lean against the wall, but really, all I want to do is stride over there and yank her out of her chair until she's flush against me and we can talk. But I can't, because she's blocked herself off from me again.

"Pinky," I repeat.

Nothing. Not so much as an eye twitch.

Lips pressing together, I straighten up, yanking my shoulder out from the wall in the process. "You were right in wanting to talk. I was a complete bastard back there, and I apologize for that," I tell her. "You can't avoid looking at me forever."

And she...yep. She avoids looking at me. Hopefully, she won't be on a mission to prove me wrong, because I can see her doing something like that.

I open my mouth to try to convince her to *not* do just that, but a sharp pang in my gut suddenly strangles the words right from my throat. I jolt forward, my back going rigid as the sensation overwhelms me.

Godsdammit.

A noise tries to cloy up my throat, but I clamp it down. There's an invisible line that wants to drag me away, pierced right through the middle of my body.

This can't happen.

I can't be pulled back now. Not when Lex is angry with me, not when there's still so much I want to say and do. I have to keep fighting it.

If I give in to this call to my deathplace, it could fuck me up permanently. I might not be able to come back from it, might not be able to find this perfectionist cupid of mine again. The thought of that hurts worse than this tugging demand.

I don't want to forget, and I don't want to be forgotten.

The pull intensifies, but instead of giving in, I center my gaze on Lex. I keep my focus wholly on her. I memorize the lines of her gorgeous face and adorable downturned mouth. Her pink hair pulled back tight, not even a strand out of place to betray that she was doing anything at all in the bathroom earlier. Red-feathered wings against her back like the curves of a heart, haloed behind her shoulders.

She really is exquisite. Far too vibrant, far too *alive* for the likes of me.

If I were a better ghost, I'd let myself be pulled away. I'd let her move on to live her life, without haunting her anymore.

But I'm not.

I will fight tooth and nail against the endless abyss to stay by her side.

When another seizing pull jerks at me, it goes through me from the top of my head to the bottom of my feet. My arms hang at my sides, and I try to curl my hands into fists, but I feel nothing. It's unnerving to not be able to tense up and physically brace myself. Instead, I have to do some sort of godsdamned breathing exercise. Which is ridiculous, considering I don't actually breathe.

After a few drawn-out moments, the pulling sensation fades enough that I can think straight again without feeling like I'm about to be yanked out of existence. I slump back against the wall, exhausted.

It takes me a few moments to realize that Lex is looking at me with a frown. I immediately try to straighten up and relax my face, but it's too late. I know she noticed the grimace that was there. I'll probably get asked a hundred questions about it too. The thought makes me smile.

As soon as my lips tip up, Lex looks away, and I deflate.

"Again, I'm so sorry about the mess," Lex tells her.

Miur sniffs, running a finger over her curly eyebrow. "See that you're more careful next time."

"As if you wouldn't set her up again just to get another cleaning boost," I say with a roll of my eyes.

Lex's eyes meet mine for a split second before she focuses on Miur again. It was not a *nice* look by any stretch of the word, but I still swell up with pride like I'm some sort of victor.

"Of course," she says to Miur with a quick nod before carefully twisting her fingers together. The nervous gesture of hers is unexplainably endearing.

"I suppose you'll be wanting to hear about the princess now."

Lex clears her throat, gaze flicking around with some uncertainty. "Actually, something has come up, and I'm afraid I won't be able to see your princess right now."

Miur was halfway to her chair but stops in her tracks when she hears Lex's words. "What do you mean you can't see her?" she demands. "You're Emelle. The cupid who helped her back at the palace. She said if you're ever here, that you're to be taken to her."

Lex winces a bit, and I realize it's because she hates disappointing anyone. She also doesn't like lying. "Yes, I realize that, but like I said, I'm going to have to come back another time."

There's an awkward silence that spreads between them where Miur watches her with displeasure, calculation turning in her gaze. Lex shifts where she stands, making her arrows and bow shift, her wings tightening against her back. Even I can feel the tension in the room, which is impressive since I can't feel anything else. But if this hob doesn't stop glaring at my cupid, I'm going to figure out how to haunt her dustbin and scare the shit out of her every time she goes to use it.

Lucky for her and her cleaning equipment, Miur finally nods, "Right. Well, I understand. Things do come up."

Lex visibly relaxes. "Yes, they do."

"I'm sure you'll understand my side as well," Miur says, nodding to herself. "The princess told us that she wanted to see the cupid if she ever showed her face here, and we are loyal to her."

"I admire your loyalty. Though I am curious—what happened during the rebellion?" Lex asks. "From what I understand, you were all against the elitist monarchy of the high fae. Soora had support from the 'lower fae' because of this stance, promising to help change things, but then she decided to flee instead of help at the end. Yet, you're still loyal to her."

My eyes widen slightly before my gaze fastens onto the hob to see how she'll take this line of questioning.

Unsurprisingly, anger flashes in Miur's eyes. "Princess Soora betrayed *nothing*," she snaps with vehemence. "And any fae who says otherwise is a dirty liar."

I suppose a *dirty liar* is a very terrible insult to a hearth hob. Perfectionist Lex doesn't seem to like it either, considering how she rears back.

Miur shakes her head. "Princess Soora is the one who gave fae like us a stepping stone for change. She advocated for us. She never liked that the high fae often looked down on every other fae kind with derision and scorn.

Prince Elphar backed her into a corner. The princess did what she thought was right, and every fae who speaks poorly of her now is disloyal scum," she practically spits, the blonde curls on her head bouncing with every jerky movement. "It's because of the princess that we no longer have a high fae sitting on the throne and that all other fae are being advocated for. She should be viewed as a hero. Not a traitor."

"I didn't mean to offend," Lex offers quietly.

Miur sniffs and whips out a cleaning rag, starting to wipe down the spotless kitchen counter. "I won't have anyone talk negatively about my princess."

"Understandable." Lex nods before taking a step away. "Well, anyway, I don't want to take up any more of your time."

Miur goes on like she didn't hear her. "Soora was good to all fae kind. Never treated them poorly just because someone was different. You should know that more than most," she says pointedly.

Lex looks confused for a moment before she tries to cover it up. "Oh, yes. Of course. Because I'm a cupid."

"Mm-hmm. Not many high fae in her position would've trusted someone like you, but she did. Even helped you get back your mates, from what I heard."

Even though I know Miur thinks Lex is Emelle, I still don't like hearing that she has mates. Irrational, yes, but the idea still irritates me.

"Soora was very helpful," Lex supplies before taking another step toward the door of the kitchen. "Well, I'd better be going. Thank you so much for the tea, and when I'm able to come and speak with the princess, I will come see you right away."

I get ready to follow her, more than ready to get the hell out of here so I can get Lex to talk to me again. Or just look at me. I'd settle for her threatening me, to be perfectly honest.

Miur stuffs her cleaning rag away in her brown cloak. "One moment," she says, holding up a finger.

Lex stops, adjusting the quiver's strap over her shoulder as she waits expectantly.

"I swear, if she tries to get you to make another mess..." My words trail off when Miur's eyes cut over to the window.

"Ah, right on time," she says.

Lex frowns. "What?"

I'm already moving, my body going right through the outer wall of the kitchen to see what she's looking at. When my head pops out far enough to get to the outside, I see a group of burly-looking hearth hobs coming right up to her doorstep.

I walk outside, my brows pulling together at the sight of the five males, something inside me growing gnarled with unease. Before I can get a good look at them all, the door is yanked open, and Miur lets them in. "She's right in the kitchen," she tells them.

Anger—dark and uninhibited—comes flaring to life inside of me. *What the fuck is happening?*

Following them, I demand, "What do you think you're doing?"

I receive no answer, of course.

The hobs barrel inside with me hot on their heels, and when I make it into the kitchen, Lex is wide-eyed. "What's going on?" she asks, her tone tinged with worry.

The fact that she's even a little bit apprehensive makes

me fucking crazy, but not as much as the fact that these males are cornering her. I shove right past them, not caring that one of their arms passes through me on my way to her.

I come up beside her, part of my body in front of hers. It would be effective if it weren't for the fact that I'm uselessly transparent and unseen by anyone else but her, yet I can't help but try to shield her anyway. For what it's worth, she seems to relax ever so slightly with my nearness.

Miur ignores Lex's question, stopping in front of the group she let in. "This is the cupid, Emelle, just like I said."

The one with red curly hair down to his shoulders scans his eyes over Lex. "You sure she's the cupid? I was expecting someone more...lovey looking."

I would think the offended look that crosses Lex's face was adorable if I weren't so pissed off.

A different hob cocks his head, scratching at his perfectly spiraled black beard. "No, that's her—it's gotta be. She's got stubbed ears and feathered wings. No one else looks like that."

The redhead shrugs. "If you say so."

"Lex," I growl out of the side of my mouth, because I don't like this. Not one fucking bit. "Turn and run out the door as fast as you can."

But she doesn't. Instead, my stickler-for-politeness cupid draws herself up and says, "It's rude to talk about people like they're not there."

"*Really?* That's what you're worried about right now?"

She shoots me a defensive look that says, *yes, really.* "Manners matter."

Oh, for the love of—

"What are you waiting for?" Miur snips impatiently. "Take her. I need to mop the floors."

Before I've fully processed her order, the hobs all move as one, instantly converging onto my cupid. Lex backs up, but when one of them reaches out to grab her, I see red. "Don't touch her!"

I take a step forward to shove the bastard, but my hand just goes right through him.

Godsdammit.

A frustrated growl wrenches out of me. Lex's exit is blocked, her back hitting the wall, face gone pale, and I fucking *lose it.*

A noise that's more animal than fae comes out of me, and I start mindlessly attacking, though fuck-all good it does. Every fist I throw goes right through the assholes, every snarled threat, unheard.

Useless. I'm a useless fucking ghost.

But Lex's yelp behind me has me feeling fury like I've never known before, and something in me seems to heat up into a molten rage.

My hand flies out at the nearest hob, and before I realize what I've done, my palm makes contact with the male's back. I send him flying across the room, where he lands in a terrific crash against the kitchen table. Glass and wood shatter to pieces, and Miur lets out a startled scream, while the rest of the room seems to freeze in place.

Heaving, I whirl around, fully expecting for the others to have my cupid in their clutches, but I grind to a surprised halt. The commotion has stopped, but not because of me. Not even because of the crashing table.

Nope, the rest of the males are all standing

completely still because of my pink-haired female. She's not cowering, and she's definitely not being held hostage. Instead, she has her bow nocked and her arrow aimed at the assholes like the fiercest cupid I could ever imagine.

I'm not going to lie, it's fucking sexy.

Lex flicks her eyes toward me, eyebrow slightly cocked. "Did you just shove that guy?"

Now she looks at me. Stubborn female.

The hobs in front of her who have their hands raised up look behind them nervously. Her question makes them just now realize that their last group member is groaning on the floor over a pile of table rubble.

"Dammit, Hankil, get up," the redhead hisses at him. "You're always tripping!"

"I didn't trip, Tiom!" Hankil snarls back as he tries and fails to roll onto his side, bits of table covering his stodgy form. "One of you clumsy asses pushed me."

"*Look at this mess!*" Miur cries shrilly, eyes as wide as the broken saucers on the floor.

At least three of the hobs all quickly call out at the same time, "I'll help clean it!"

"You will not," she snaps, and I think her curly hair puffs up a little like a territorial cat.

"You alright?" I ask Lex.

She gives a tiny, terse nod, body angled and arms held strong as she continues to aim her arrows.

"Now that we're all calmer, someone better tell me what you're trying to do with me, or else I'll start letting arrows fly," she threatens, eyes sweeping around the room.

No one says a word at first, and Lex narrows her eyes

and starts to pull back on the bowstring even more, making them all flinch.

"Wait a minute," Hankil pipes up, finger pointed as he finally gets to his feet. "That's just a cupid arrow—it's got a heart on the end of it."

The rest of them shift on their feet, studying her weapon more closely, as if they're considering trying to rush at her again. But Lex holds her ground and cocks a confident brow. "First of all, if you think love isn't more dangerous than a flesh wound, you're massively underestimating things. I could shoot you up with so much unrequited love that you'd be wallowing for *years*," she claims. "Secondly, I'm not in the Veil, which means these Love Arrows are *very* real right now."

"Yeah, sure."

She looks positively offended.

"You know, I don't appreciate the fact that you don't think Love Arrows are serious," she snaps. "You have to be a licensed cupid to even so much as handle one. And furthermore, they can be just as dangerous in the Veil. I once mis-shot a male when I was a new recruit, and he *never* recovered. Cried himself to sleep like a baby every night from the ache in his chest since his Match was already with someone else," she goes on, posture unyielding and tone firm. "Imagine what I can do to not only you, but this entire island. I can mess up so many love lives, tangle up so many heartstrings that it will take years to untangle them all."

Hankil audibly gulps while the black-bearded one leans over and whispers, "Can she really do that?"

"You bet your broom I can do that," she cuts in. "Trust me, you do *not* want to have a cupid on your bad side. I will make your love life so messy even you won't be able to clean it up."

Two of them back away a step. One of them looks a little green.

I don't even try to hide my smirk as I come up to stand beside her. "When you're all violent and proper like this, it really turns me on."

She clears her throat, trying to pretend she isn't affected by my words. Too bad her cheeks never lie.

"Now, what in the realm are you trying to do?" Lex demands.

"Sorry, Miss Cupid," the shortest of the bunch says, shoving his way to the front. He's tried to cut his hair short, the brown spirals looking like they're trying to sprout off his head in all different directions. "Miur here told us to come and to take you to the princess. Forcibly, if need be."

"Shut up, Fig," one of them hisses.

Anger shoots down my spine, and I idly wonder if I can punch one of the hobs this time or if it was a one-off.

Lex looks to Miur, where the female is picking up pieces of the broken table. "Why would you try to force me to go?"

Miur freezes in place but tries to play it off with a huff as she straightens up. "Well, the princess said if Emelle was ever to come here, we're to take her to meet up, so that's the end of it. We won't fail her," she says firmly. "The princess might trust you, but I don't. She needs you, so I'll make sure you go to her."

I can see Lex struggling with what to do and say. "I will go," she offers. "But I just...can't go right now."

"And why not?"

"It's complicated." Lex's eyes shift to me for a split second. "I'm…" She trails off before blowing out a conflicted breath. "I'm not Emelle," she admits with a wince, like she's bracing herself.

Instead of getting the shocked responses like she probably expects, Miur simply throws up her hands. "You hear this garbage?" she tells the others. "The cupid lies! *And* she threatened us!"

"No, I'm not lying, I'm telling the truth!" Lex says desperately. In a quick maneuver, she manages to press against her cupid mark like she's trying to summon the real Emelle. Before the hobs even realize she's dropped her arrow, she's got it back up and aimed perfectly again. "And I didn't threaten you until you tried to take me forcibly!"

Miur ignores her as she continues to implore the others. "She's trying to lie now because she has no intention of ever coming to see Princess Soora. Which means she's clearly not on our side. She's going to leave and tell other fae that we're hiding the princess!"

"I wouldn't do that!"

I can't help but snicker. "Yeah, the plan was to go on a murder spree. Not out her to the others."

"It's not a murder spree!" Lex hisses, pinning me with a glare.

"Who said anything about *murder*?" Miur chokes out, hand gripping her chest.

Lex's head whips back to face her, and she immediately shakes her head. "What? No one. There's nothing about murder. I didn't mean—"

"SHE'S PLANNING TO MURDER OUR PRINCESS!" Miur's scream is so loud that it nearly hurts *my* ears.

But her shriek makes the rest of the hobs leap into action. "Get her!"

The hobs rush at her, and Lex's arm jerks upright. She fires off the first arrow, making it hit the arm of the bearded hob closest to her. He staggers back with the force of it, clutching at where it landed, while bluish smoke pollutes the air.

"Lex! Go into the Veil!"

But it's too late.

I don't even get the words out, because two hobs have lifted their hands at the same time, and a blinding white light explodes from their palms, hitting Lex square in the chest. She doesn't even have time to scream as the force of their power lands on her, and then she's pitching forward, right onto the shoulder of the redheaded hob.

"What the *fuck* did you just do?" Fear and fury battle inside my chest, and when I try and fail to hit the male, I let out a bellow of rage. "*Lex!*"

All her arrows have spilled out onto the floor, quiver hanging uselessly around her shoulder.

The second hob who hit her with his magic goes up to her, not even realizing that he has a furious ghost watching his every move. "She's unconscious, Miur."

"Good," the female nods. "Take her now before she wakes. Fastest way—through the portal."

Oh, fuck no.

The snarl that tears from my throat is full of rage. I tear at them, a whirlwind of fury, but no matter how many hits I try to land, no matter how many fists I throw, I can't make contact. When flesh on flesh doesn't work, I go for kitchen chairs, the pottery, even the damn tablecloth so I can try to strangle the male holding my cupid. But nothing works. I can't fucking protect her.

I'm useless.

A useless fucking ghost who can't even keep his female from getting taken against her will. All I can do is watch as they carry Lex like a bag of oats out the front door and into the night.

"Be quick about it!" Miur shouts from her doorway.

The black-bearded one hesitates, looking forlornly at the mess in her kitchen. "I could stay to help tidy up..."

She practically shoves him out. "Go!" she shouts before slamming the door shut so she can scuttle off to clean.

I am going to haunt her ass so hard for this.

I rush through the wall and follow after the males, temper riling up a storm in my chest. The fact that she's slung over this male's shoulder, arms hanging down, head bobbing against his back, with his arm nearly touching her ass, makes me want to rip through the Veil and tear him limb from limb.

I get right up beside the redhead, trying to knock him off his ass, but every effort is futile. I can't fucking do *anything*. With a growl of frustration, I snarl in his face. "You move your arm up so much as an inch to touch her ass, and I will make it my afterlife's mission to figure out how to kill you and then make you be a ghost, just so I can enjoy watching you evaporate into fucking nothing."

The male looks around, frowning on the dark city street. "Anyone hear anything?"

True to hob fashion, the others are all walking behind him in a single file line. "No, everything's all clear."

"She's still out, right?" he checks.

"Tiom, you and Irrit hit her with enough power to put

someone out 'til spring cleaning day. Yes, she's out. What's the problem? Do you want me to carry her?" Hankil asks.

"I got her," Tiom snarls, tightening his hold and making me want to strangle him. "I'm the strongest out of you lot, anyway."

"No, you aren't!" the one at the back of the line argues, though he still doesn't step out of place, just sort of...leans sideways to shout ahead. "I'm the one the whole street calls when it's laundry day and they need me to drag their washing tubs out."

"That's just because you're fucking all of them, and they haven't figured it out yet!" someone else says.

Ignoring them, I check on my unconscious cupid. "Lex." Her eyes are shut, mouth hanging open slightly, and if she weren't upside down, she'd look like she was sleeping peacefully. "Wake up, Pinky. I need you to wake up so you can go into the Veil and get away from these assholes."

Of course, she doesn't wake up. Because when has she ever listened to me? Whatever power the hobs hit her with better not have hurt her. If she's hurt, I don't care what the fates think, I will make them my unfinished business and haunt them for the rest of their useless lives.

With every step, I keep trying to wake her up, but she continues to hang over Tiom's shoulder lifelessly. Then, we're suddenly coming upon a storefront, and no one even bothers to knock as they all file inside. As soon as I step in, I see a big, whirling cascade of bluish air converged in the middle of an empty room.

"Saw you coming down the street," a stout female says as she hops off a stool and straightens her brown cloak.

"Is the portal all set?" Tiom asks.

Portal?

"Yep," the female replies, motioning toward it, the orange curls around her head bouncing. "Go on through. It's ready now."

If I had a heart, it would be slamming against my chest. "Wait a fucking minute! No one is going through any damn portal," I growl, shoving my way toward it to block it.

Tiom turns around and says, "You go first, Irrit. The rest of you can go on home. We've got it."

The other three males nod and take their leave, filing out of the door. My momentary distraction at watching them makes me get caught off guard when Irrit abruptly walks right through me and disappears into the portal. I stagger back, jerking into the portal too, but I go right through it, ending up on the other side, instead of *into* it like he did.

Definitely not fucking good.

"Lex!" I shout, watching with frenzied eyes as Tiom starts to walk forward with her. "You need to wake up right the fuck now!"

She doesn't so much as twitch. This is happening way too fucking fast, and I watch, horrified, as Tiom takes his first step inside, the front of his shoe disappearing.

Time slows.

I have no idea where the fuck they're going. I have no way to follow them. If Lex disappears into that portal without me, I won't be able to make sure she's okay.

As if it can sense my weakness, that horrible tug comes back tenfold in my gut, punching a groan from my lips and jerking me back. Pure resentment makes me fight against it, a ferocious hate making me gnash my teeth in defiance.

I won't go.

My place is next to her, and I won't be yanked back like a fish on a line.

It wasn't the damn muck that let me stray from my deathplace, it was just *her*. Lex has been keeping me sane, keeping me feeling alive despite how fucking dead I am inside and out. Memories and past life be damned—all I want is to stay with her, and I won't let a fucking portal take her from me. I *won't*.

I watch in horror as Tiom's body starts to disappear through the portal, as if he's walking through a cascading waterfall and I can't see behind it. The tug nips at me harder, like I'm in some sort of torture device meant to stretch me in two, but it's nothing—*fucking nothing*—compared to watching Lex's body disappear inch by inch.

"Lex!" A curse tears from my throat, and my body goes taut, strain pummeling me, but I manage to propel forward and launch myself at her as a last-ditch effort.

I reach for her like it's a plea that's torn right from my forgotten soul.

When my fingers start to pass uelessly through her hand, the tug starts pulling me the other way, and I know I've lost it. Call it a ghost's intuition, but I knew from the first moment I saw her that I needed to stay with her at all costs.

"Lex!"

Tiom's back disappears, and then all that's left is Lex's pink hair and hands hanging down, and I know that's going to be swallowed up next, and she'll be going where I can't follow.

Fucking *useless*.

I close my eyes, unable to watch, but just as I start to give in to despair, I feel something. My hand—the one still reaching for hers—doesn't pass through. Instead, I suddenly feel her warm, solid fingers curl around mine.

In the next instant, time seems to return to its normal pace. I don't even get to open my eyes again before I'm yanked forward by Lex's death grip on my hand, and she drags me into the portal after her.

CHAPTER 27

LEX

I have a headache. And a chest...ache? The soles of my feet are oddly sore too, which perplexes me, because I usually wear the most comfortable flats I can find. Wearing sensible shoes is important.

I ebb in this perplexed state, eyes closed, flowing in my half-awake thoughts. My bodily pains, along with a dragging tiredness, make me not want to come back to full consciousness. Yet when strange bursts of memories come springing up, there's no stopping it.

I frown as I try to open my eyes and figure out what happened, but nausea slams into me like a freight train. Jolting, my body lurches to the side, and I barely manage to pivot far enough as my stomach heaves up its contents. It's *very* unladylike. There are some wet burping noises that accompany the spewing, and I just… This is not ideal. Not ideal at all. There's even spit.

Goodness.

I feel a hand come down to hold back my ponytail, and my cheeks flame with embarrassment that someone is observing this. There's nothing I can do about it though until my stomach decides to stop its rude awakening.

A hand with dark curly finger hair shoves in front of my face, holding out a handkerchief. I quickly take it and wipe my lips and then discreetly wipe my tongue as well, because yuck. There is a film layer on it that I do not want to think about.

Looking over, I see the male from Miur's house crouching in front of me. "Don't worry, that's perfectly normal," he tells me before he leaps back up and runs off. In the distance, I hear him calling, "Tiom! The cupid's awake!"

I groan from my pounding headache, and I squeeze my eyes shut, willing the dizziness to subside. I take slow, steadying breaths, but as my world stops tipping, my memories swirl just as sickeningly, and I remember everything all at once.

Miur's house. The fae attacking me with power, and me blacking out right after. They took me...

I try to jerk upright in my panic, but that move makes me yank against the grip that's still on my hair that I hadn't even noticed. I hiss out a breath, stopping immediately. "*Ouch!*"

The hand immediately releases me. "Fuck, sorry. You alright?"

Flinching, I turn to find Belren sitting at my side on the grassy ground with me, the other fae nowhere in sight. For a second, all I can do is stare at him, my eyes running over him in the darkness of the moonlight. Mussed white hair, silvery skin, curling horns, everything seems to be in place, right down to his outfit.

"You're here," I say, breathing out shaky relief.

"As if I'd be anywhere else but by your side, Pinky. Death couldn't keep me away," he says with a lopsided grin.

I melt a little. Butterflies flutter in my stomach, and my world seems to settle back on its axis as I let out a shaky breath. I was mad at him and utterly disappointed, but all of that has seemed to dissolve into thin air. I'm just glad nothing bad happened and that he's still here.

"What... How..." I shake my head, trying to clear it enough to come up with words that are more comprehensible, but I'm just too relieved.

In answer, Belren holds up his hand. His other hand... which I'm currently clutching onto for dear life. I didn't even notice.

I stare down at the way my fingers are gripping him so hard that my knuckles look strained. "What's...what's going on there?" I ask. I don't let go, though.

Belren's silvery eyes flick up to my face, a proud smile pulling at the corners of his eyes. "You grabbed me. Even unconscious, you grabbed me and pulled me through the portal with you."

A portal? I blink. Gods, that could've gone badly. "I...I did?"

He nods, turning serious. "I'm so fucking sorry about what I said before, Lex."

"It's okay. I know you are, and I am too."

Belren shakes his head as if he doesn't want me to let him off the hook that easily. "I've been trying to take the easy way out, to ignore everything that's going on. It feels like if I ignore it, the inevitable won't happen," he says with a dejected sigh, making a kernel of guilt for pushing him roll around in my stomach. "But I should tell you something."

I eye him curiously. "What?"

Belren shifts closer, thumb rubbing over the back of my hand that sends chills down my arms. "If I knew then what I know now, if I knew that leaping in front of you that day meant that I would die—that I would end up right here as a ghost, with you—then I would do it all over again. Gladly."

Tears fill my eyes, and I try to snag every single word out of his mouth and hold it inside of me.

I clear my throat, trying to get a hold of myself before I start blubbering like a baby. He already saw me vomit. I can only stand so much involuntary erupting. "Well. You should at least make a pros and cons list beforehand, if the situation arises. It's the responsible thing to do."

I'm rewarded with a beaming smile. It catches my breath and makes him seem almost alive. As if I could reach forward and feel the warmth of his skin and the beat of his heart.

"I don't need a list, Pinky. I'd rather haunt you in death than not be with you in life." He shrugs, like he didn't just rock my entire world. "Even before you grabbed hold of me, I knew you were mine. That just confirmed it."

My heart fills up with something until it feels like bursting, but my mouth won't work to say anything in return.

Belren gently lifts a hand and tucks a stray strand of hair behind my ear. "I hope you're good with me haunting you, Pinky, because I'm going to do it for as long as I can."

"I'm good with it," I blurt out so fast that it makes him chuckle.

"Good girl."

I'm probably staring at him with huge puppy dog eyes, but I don't care. My entire body is buzzing with something I've felt thousands of times—felt for *other* people and learned to nurture it for them. But I never, not in a million years, ever thought I'd feel it for myself. It wasn't meant for me, I was sure of that. Instead, it was simply my job to give it.

Yet here I am...fallen head over bow in love with a ghost.

It scares me to no end, to be honest. It feels irresponsible, even, like I'm not going to be as good of a cupid giving out love stories if I'm too caught up in my own. But maybe...maybe it's okay to let myself feel something for him.

"You doing alright over there?" Belren teases, and I realize I've been quiet for way too long. "Do you need your seven-foot think-radius? Because I have to tell you, you're going to have to let go of my hand in order to do that, and you don't seem to want to."

My cheeks flame and I look down at my fingers that are still wrapped around his like a constrictor snake. "Sorry," I mumble with a bit of embarrassment as I slowly release him. My fingers ache in protest at the movement, smarting at how firmly and how long I was holding him.

"Don't ever apologize, Pinky. If I had it my way, I'd never stop holding your hand."

Those butterflies in my stomach must fly all the way up to my throat, because I have to clear it in order to speak. "That would be very problematic when I need to shoot a Love Arrow," I point out.

He chuckles.

"Are you still puking?"

I startle at the fae's voice as two of the hearth hobs come ambling over, their silhouettes just shadows and their feet crunching in the grass. Belren made me forget all about the two of them, but now that they're walking up toward me, my anger comes surging up. I scramble to my feet, paying for the too-quick movement when my headache pounds with a vengeance. "*You*," I accuse. "You attacked me."

The brown-headed one scratches the back of his head with a guilty look on his face, but the redhead just lifts a shoulder. "Had to. Orders."

"Want me to try to shove them again?" Belren asks behind me, making my lips twitch.

I turn in a circle, my gaze bounces around at the empty landscape as I try to take stock of where we are. It's so dark out that it's hard to see anything at all, but I don't see any buildings around.

"Yeah, and like I said before, things get messy when you get hit with that much of our cleaning power. It's perfectly normal to puke up your guts," Tiom tells me.

I swing my eyes back to him with a glare. "I didn't *puke my guts up*. It was just a small retch," I argue, feeling embarrassed all over again. In fact...yep. There's my vomit in a little puddle right beside me in the grass.

Yuck.

I can't believe Belren and I just had a beautiful, touching moment next to *that*.

"I can clean it up!"

I jump as the other male hurries closer, pulling something that looks like a handheld mop from his cloak pocket with a glint in his eye.

Of course they carry mini-mops on their person.

I leap in front of him, barring his way. "Don't you dare go near my sick," I warn him. I can only take so much. Watching someone else get power from cleaning my vomit is a hard line.

"Yeah, Irrit. Don't touch the cupid's puke," Tiom gloats.

"You either," I scold, making the redhead frown.

They both grumble, but Irrit thankfully puts away his cleaning utensil, stowing it back in his brown cloak.

"Do you want me to take that?" Tiom asks, nodding toward the wadded up handkerchief in my hand. I forgot I was holding it, but I bunch it up harder in my hand.

"It's—no. No, I don't." I don't have any pockets—typical—so I shove it into my waistband instead.

The disappointment wafting off him just makes this whole thing even more uncomfortable.

Sighing, I take a moment to look around, though I'm still careful to not stray away. I don't trust these fae not to start cleaning behind my back. Belren must have the same thought, because I hear him say, "Eyes up, you bastard. Look at her face, not at her vomit."

Who said chivalry is dead? I mean, *he* is, but still.

"Where are we?" I ask, because something about this place seems familiar, but I can't put my finger on exactly what it is. I've been to so many islands in this realm it's hard to say, especially when it's so dark out.

"This is where the princess stays," Irrit tells me.

Uh oh.

I share a panicked look with Belren. "I have to go back. I can't be here."

"It's done," Tiom says, somewhat smugly. "We've already alerted the princess of your presence."

I'm ready to pop myself into the Veil and get the heck out of here, but when I ruffle my wings, I suddenly realize that a particular strap around my shoulders is missing, and I whirl around. "Where's my bow and quiver?" I demand.

Tiom waves his hands. "Oh, don't worry. We've got your cupid weapons here. We'll return them to you soon as you leave. D'you know, I was sure all your arrows fell out back at Miur's house, but it was full as a flask when you got here. That a cupid thing? Your weapons refill?"

They took them?

My eyebrows slam together. "They're *tools* not weapons, and of course they refill, we're not amateurs," I snap.

I drag a hand down my shoulder where the comforting weight of the strap usually rests. I don't like not having it there. I...I don't even remember a time when I didn't have them with me. This feels weird. Like I'm naked, and I can't help but start to fidget.

Belren points. "They stashed them over there, under that pile of branches."

Smiling, I give Tiom a victorious smile and then saunter over to where Belren directed. Tiom rushes over with me and tries to go for the bush, but I shoulder past him. I find my poor quiver buried under scratchy, over-grown boughs, and I yank it out, quickly strapping it around me and positioning it just right.

"That's better," I say with a sigh, looking over my shoulder at my feathered arrows. But then I frown.

Belren doesn't even need me to say anything, because he points to Tiom.

The fae is backing up sheepishly, but I hold my hand

out impatiently. He grumbles, and then his fingers dig beneath his cloak, and he pulls out the arrow he just tried to steal.

"Thank you," I say curtly before putting it back with a breath of contentment. The Veil would replace it, but it's the principle of the thing.

Irrit glances at Tiom and whispers rather loudly. "Is she allowed to do that?"

"Shut up, Irrit," he says, glaring at me, cheeks going as red as his hair. "We can't take you to the princess armed."

"Great," I chirp. "Then I guess I can't see her right now. I'll just have to come back another time." I turn toward Belren so we can get out of here, but I stop in my tracks when I see him.

His body has gone rigid, back ramrod straight. "What's wrong?"

"I just told you!" Tiom cries with exasperation. "We can't take you like this!"

I ignore him, watching Belren struggle through the pull that wants to take him away.

"How can I help? What do you want me to do?"

"It's like she's not even listening," Tiom complains behind me.

"Nothing," Belren gasps, hands going down to his abdomen. "It's not... Something is different."

"Different how?"

Instead of answering me, he reaches for my hand. I immediately give it, and his eyes close in relief when our fingers intertwine. He grips me firmly, like I'm the tether keeping him from floating away. "That's better. Feels like I'm being pulled in two different directions otherwise," he says hoarsely. "Don't let go."

I squeeze his hand. "I won't."

"Well, you'd better listen to the princess," Tiom snaps, clearly still thinking I'm talking to him. "Because here she comes."

Brows drawn together, I spin on my heel, watching as the dark air seems to ripple in front of us. It's like sheer curtains being pulled back, changing the landscape, until it morphs completely. What was nothing but an empty grass field is now a threadbare forest.

"What..."

"The princess just lifted the glamour she put over this spot," Tiom says, an edge of proud awe in his voice.

The hair on my arms rises at the charge of magic, so thick I can almost taste it. I squint at the sparse trees before my gaze zeroes in on a figure walking toward us, flanked by two guards.

Irrit and Tiom step around me and bow low. "Princess Soora."

Gaping, I watch as the shadowy figure stops in front of me, the pale moonlight illuminating her lavender skin. Her ears are pointed, eyes large, purple hair swept up in a fancy coif that matches her regal yet simple high-necked gown.

When I look back up at her face, I catch the tail end of a smile fading away, her large eyes narrowing on me. "You're not Emelle."

I cast a look at Tiom smugly so that he gets the full effect of an "I told you so" look. I'm quite good at them.

Red-faced and sputtering, he and Irrit straighten up. "Apologies, Princess. She's a cupid, and we thought..." His words trail off. "Are you sure this isn't her?"

Soora casts the males a gentle smile. "I'm sure, and it's

alright. Thank you for bringing her. She is indeed a cupid."

A pair of relieved sighs come out of the males. "We'll leave you to it then."

"Yes, thank you," Soora says.

"She has weapons we couldn't relieve her of!" Irrit calls, tattling on me.

I twist my head around. "They're *tools*!" Honestly, it's like no one understands the nuances of cupidity. When we hit you with Love, it's supposed to hurt a bit. That's how you know it's real.

Irrit and Tiom both disappear from sight, as they probably step outside the bounds of the princess's glamour.

My nerves jump to life at being left alone with the princess and her two guards. Belren is still stiff and shaking beside me, but his firm hold gives me comfort as the princess stares me down. My heart is beating so hard I feel it in my temples, and all I can think is, what if this triggers him? What if this really is his unfinished business?

Yet I can't risk going into the Veil, not now when he clearly needs me touching him. If holding my hand helps to ground him in some way, then I can't go incorporeal and risk losing him.

Soora continues to stare at me, expression giving nothing away.

Nothing about this current situation is ideal, but I can handle it. I have to.

"Oh!" Irrit calls, his disembodied voice startling me. "And she mentioned something about a murder spree! Might want to watch out for that!"

Of course. *Of course* he would say that right now, the jerk.

Belren would probably think it's hilarious if he weren't in his current state.

Soora's amethyst eyes narrow on me, and a bald-headed hearth hob guard steps forward. "Let's go," he says gruffly, tight black ringlets wobbling on his chin.

He grips my arm roughly and then starts pulling me into the creepy, meager forest. To be honest, I probably had the manhandling coming.

CHAPTER 28

I never expected to be led through a thinned-out forest by an ex-princess I once vowed to kill, yet here we are.

The walk is awkward, the guard gripping my arm the entire time, while with my other hand, I keep my grip onto Belren's ice-cold palm. He stumbles along, his expression distant and pained. I'm not even sure how aware he is right now.

After a few minutes, we reach a house in the middle of the scant trees, stuck between some rail-thin pines. Aside from the rather sad-looking forest, the structure itself is more like a palace than a house. What it lacks in length, it makes up for in its three-story height. The face of it is made of crude stone, but even in the dark, I can see that it's polished to perfection. The windows too are shiny and streak free, and there's an immaculate hedge garden that we pass by on the way to the front door.

The second guard opens it to let Soora sweep inside, while I'm dragged in right after, pulling Belren behind me. My brows lift as I take in the entryway. Aside from the pair of staircases on either side, the room commands attention solely for its color choice.

There's purple everywhere. Lavender, plum, mauve, eggplant, and every shade in between. There are also crystal vases filled with violet bouquets on every single flat surface we pass by.

I knew that the Wyndices' family colors were purple, and the sigil was a violet, but still, this interior decorating choice is very bold.

I glance at Belren to see if he's seeing this too, but the grimace on his face pulls at my stomach. "Are you okay?" I whisper.

He gives a short nod, but it doesn't convince either of us. He's struggling, looking like he's fighting an internal battle and not completely aware of the things going on around us. I squeeze his hand a little bit tighter.

I'm led into a sitting room—upholstery, rug, and curtains, all purple—and Soora turns toward the two guards. "You can leave us, thank you."

The one holding my arm doesn't let go. Instead, he starts to pull the strap of my quiver off my shoulder. "Hey!" I say, trying to bat him away.

"You can't have weapons," he growls at me.

"It's alright," Soora intervenes, making us both freeze. She casts a bored look at my bow. "I'm not worried."

"But Princess—"

Soora waves a dismissive hand at him. "I'm far more powerful than a few arrows, Werenz. Besides," she says, looking toward me, "you're not going to try anything, are you?"

I shake my head. "No."

The guard doesn't look convinced. "What was that about murder?" He glares, wayward curls from his eyelashes getting stuck in the ones from his eyebrows.

Soora doesn't intervene this time. Instead, she takes a seat on one of the plush purple chairs, crossing her ankles and holding her hands in her lap as she watches me regally.

"Well...it's...it's a funny story, really."

She perks up a single brow. "Hmm. Werenz doesn't really have a sense of humor."

I eye the guard warily. He just scowls back.

"You really need to fall in love," I tell him curtly.

He gives me an unimpressed look. "Excuse me?"

"It's true. I can feel the loneliness, you know. You'd be great at love when you find your Match. I could help you."

"Please refrain from trying to bribe my guard," Soora drawls.

I whip my head around. "It wasn't a bribe."

She doesn't look convinced, and now the guard seems even more hostile than before. When they just continue to stare at me, I finally let out a breath. "You're not going to believe me about the murder story."

"Tell me anyway. And start with why you are here and why you claimed to be Emelle."

She's very pushy. Probably because she used to be a princess.

"The Emelle thing was an accident. At first. But I've been looking for you, so I just went along with it."

"Why were you looking for me?"

This is the tricky part.

"Well...I actually was there the day your husband died."

Soora bristles, and for the first time, I see some real

emotion in the depths of her eyes. It's not mourning. It's anger. "He's not my husband," she snaps.

No love lost between those two, clearly.

"Prince Elphar," I amend. "He tried to attack Emelle, but he thought I was her, so his power was directed at me, and..." I steal a look at Belren, and my stomach dips when I see that he's finally looking at me, blinking the haze from his eyes. His shoulders are slumped, his entire posture looking like he's been kicked by a horse, but at least he seems to be aware again.

"You're the one that the Horned Hook leapt in front of."

My gaze pivots to Soora. "You know about that?"

"Of course I know about that," she replies shortly. "Why did he do it?" Soora casts a look over me. "Why you?"

I'm taken aback by the anger that's volleyed up into her voice. "Umm..." Words fail me, but then I feel Belren squeeze my hand.

"This is the princess?" he asks skeptically.

Relief floods me that he's feeling well enough to talk. I shoot him a look in my peripheral before I give a small nod. As inconspicuous as I tried to be with the movement, Soora's eyes narrow on me, her gaze traveling down to the hand holding Belren's. I didn't even think about how strange it probably looks.

"I don't know why he did it," I answer her.

"Liar," Belren says teasingly, though I can hear the strain of his voice—can practically feel the toll on him that it took to deny the pull. It worries me that it's getting this much worse. He was good at hiding it before, but it's obviously gotten to a point where he can't anymore. Sure, he didn't disappear when his muck was cleaned up, but maybe it just took a while for the strain to set in.

"Tell her the truth, Pinky," Belren says tiredly, running a thumb over the back of my hand. "Tell her it was because a ghost was meant to fall in love with a cupid."

My breath catches and my wings lift.

I can't help but look over at him, our eyes locking. For a moment, we're not here, in an overly purple room with a questionable ex-royal. Instead, it's just the two of us, the rest of the world faded away. Until that world shoulders its way back in.

"What are you looking at?" Soora asks, making me snap out of the moment.

"Nothing," I say quickly, jerking my gaze back to her.

She doesn't look convinced, eyes skating over to where I was looking. Trying to cover up my weird hand-holding posture, I walk forward to the chaise and sit down with Belren beside me, where I can rest our hands next to my leg so it's not so noticeable. I haven't missed the fact that the bald guard is still standing by the door, obviously not trusting me alone with her.

"So, you don't know why the Horned Hook jumped in front of you?" Soora asks again, suspicion thick in her tone.

Belren looks at me pointedly. "Not gonna say the cupid-ghost bit, hmm?" he asks. "Alright, then tell her it was because I thought you had a great ass and it would've been a shame to lose it."

My eyes nearly bug out of my head.

"He was just being nice?" I offer aloud instead, because there is exactly zero chance of me saying the word *ass* to a princess, ex or otherwise. Especially when said ass is mine.

Soora scoffs. "The Horned Hook didn't do things to be *nice*. He was a cunning thief and a master tracker. He wasn't altruistic by nature."

Belren cocks his head. "Sounds about right."

"Did you know him well?" I ask her, because I don't know all the details of their relationship other than the things Emelle relayed to me, which wasn't much.

"For a time, I knew him better than anybody."

That surprises me. Apparently, it surprises Belren too, because he sits forward, head cocked. "Shit. Did I fuck her?"

What? No. Soora was with his sister. The two of them couldn't have been together too... *Right?*

My stomach clenches, and my mind immediately conjures up an image of Belren with her. I don't like it. I squeeze his hand so hard that I make my fingernails dig into his skin. I only stop when he shoots me a narrowed look. It makes me feel marginally better.

"Were the two of you ever romantically involved?"

Soora's brows draw together, making a dainty line form between them. "Belren and me?" she asks incredulously before letting out a laugh that somehow manages to sound both musical and a little arrogant. "Of course not. I knew him well because of his sister, Benicia."

"Right, of course," I say, barely suppressing a sigh of relief.

As soon as Soora says the name, Belren's entire body straightens, and his hand becomes as stiff as a board. His lips move, and I hear him repeat the name under his breath. "Benicia."

I sneak a nervous glance at him.

"Benicia," he says again, brows furrowing in deep thought, hand coming up to his stomach absentmindedly. "She was missing."

He remembers?

I stiffen beside him, watching the faraway look that comes over his expression, the way his eyes grow troubled.

He shakes his head at himself. "I couldn't find her," he says, voice louder this time. "I could always find *anything*, but I couldn't find her. My own damn sister."

Dread comes in bursts, popping hot and cold through my veins. This isn't good. I've tried so hard not to push him, not to trigger anything, and—

"Benicia ran away. Because of *her*," Belren snaps, jabbing a finger toward the princess. "She broke my sister's heart when she married the prince. I remember. I remember that."

Uh oh.

"What's happening?" Soora cuts in, a confused irritation making her tone bristle as her eyes wander around me. I'm not doing a very good job of hiding Belren's presence.

"Tell me at once," she demands when I don't answer. It doesn't matter that she technically doesn't wear a crown anymore, her command is pure royalty.

"Well..."

At my hesitation, Soora's guard comes up behind me, his face stony. "Answer the princess at once."

The snappish bite to his tone is bristling enough, but when he reaches for my arm, the threatening move does not go over well. At all.

In a blink, Belren is on his feet with a growl, ready to attack. He yanks his hand out of mine before I can stop him, and by the time I jump to my feet, Belren's already turned and raised his hands up, doing a shoving motion in the air.

Somehow, even without touching him, Belren manages to make Werenz go flying back until his shoulder hits the wall. Belren bares his teeth like he's ready to rip him apart as I watch wide-eyed. *"Don't fucking touch her!"* he seethes.

"What the...?" The guard spins around in a craze, eyes wild. "What was that? How did you do that?"

"What just happened?" Soora demands as she gets to her feet.

Werenz points an accusatory finger at me. "She used some sort of power on me! She's telekinetic!"

Both he and Soora pin me in place with their stares, but I shake my head. "It wasn't me!"

Soora's eyes turn turbulent, and I feel the crackle of magic stain the air. "Something is going on, and I want to know what it is right *now*."

Wow. She can really be very scary when her voice drops an octave like that.

"It's Belren," I blurt out, looking from her to the guard. "He's the one who pushed you. He's protective."

Soora rears back, purple eyes flaring. *"Excuse me?"*

I nod warily. "I know it's hard to believe, but his ghost found me and, well, I think you might be his unfinished business."

She stares at me.

And stares some more.

The room becomes so quiet that my breath seems blaring.

"It's true," I go on. "We've been looking for you."

When she continues to say nothing, my hands wring together, my nerves getting the better of me. I'd really like to fly off and go shoot some people with Love to take the edge off, but considering the way the guard keeps eyeing my arrows, they're probably not the best thing to grab right now.

Finally, Soora breaks the silence. "Belren was telekinetic," she says quietly, almost to herself.

"Wow, I'm impressive," Belren jokes, but his voice is strained.

Then she asks, "Why would I be Belren's unfinished business?"

I shift on my feet. "Oh. Well, you know. Just for the whole betraying him and the entire rebellion thing."

Did that sound bad? I tried not to make it sound bad.

Her lips press together so tightly that the purple color drains right out of them. "I did what I had to do to save Benicia. He would've understood that eventually, once he'd had time to think."

Glancing over at Belren, I try to see if I can confirm that one way or another, but my question dies in my throat when I look at him.

His entire body has gone pale and lackluster. He's lost the luminescent edge to him, lost the substantialness he'd managed to claim. His brows are furrowed, but this time, it's not in thought, it's in pain.

I try to hurry over and grab hold of him again, but my hand goes right through him, and my stomach plummets. "Belren?"

A noise comes from him that seems to be pulled from the depths of his soul, and something flickers in his gaze that wasn't there before. "We're here."

Frowning, I ask, "Where?"

His sheer hand presses against the silhouette of his stomach. "The pull. It's different. It's...*here.*"

A sense of foreboding curls in my chest as I turn to Soora. "Where exactly are we?" I ask carefully.

Werenz gets his courage back and snarls, "That's not to be disclosed."

But Soora raises a hand. "It's alright," she tells him, still looking at me.

"We're here, aren't we?" I go on, looking between her and Belren. "We're at Belren's deathplace."

Ghost Island.

Maybe that's why he didn't disappear when he let go of my hand?

"How did you know that?" Soora asks, but she's not angry or suspicious like the guard. Instead, she looks...almost hopeful?

The way her gaze keeps skating around the room makes me think that she wants to believe me.

"This is a good thing, right?" I ask Belren. "We're back here, so the pull is better, right?"

But to my dismay, he shakes his head. "The pull is *stronger*. More intense," he grits out. If he weren't incorporeal, I have a feeling he'd be dripping in sweat and his face would be flushed from the strain.

"We need to get back to your exact deathplace," I say decisively, ready to march out of here and get him where he needs to go.

"No..." Belren replies, shaking his head absently.

335

"That's not it. There was always this draw, like I was supposed to stay there and find something, and that's stronger now."

My brows lower, and when I see him wincing, I try to grab his hand again to help anchor him here, but it still doesn't work. "I can't touch you..." I try once more, but nothing changes, and I don't think it's me blocking it this time. "I don't know what's happening," I say with growing alarm. "Do you think it's being here with the princess? What can I do to make this better?"

The way his form seems so faded is making my fear spike.

"Enough of this," Soora hisses suddenly, making me startle. "Belren is not a ghost. Stop your lies and playacting."

Wow. Okay. It's very rude to accuse someone of lying.

"I'm telling the truth," I snip back. "Something is wrong. We're on Ghost Island already, you're his unfinished business, and yet he's still in pain." A thought occurs to me, and I give Belren a nervous look. "Shoot. Do I really need to do the...you know." I drop my voice to a whisper. "Rhymes with *herder free?*"

Werenz's eyes widen. "Did you just openly admit to wanting to murder the princess right in front of me?"

I grimace. Right. Probably should've come up with a different code term.

The guard moves for me, sword drawn, at the same time that I take a defensive step in front of Belren. I'm not sure why, for obvious reasons, but it seems I have a protective streak as well.

"In my defense," I say, holding up my hands. "I mentioned the murdering in the heat of the moment when I found Belren's deathplace because I was upset. I was just as surprised as anyone when he actually showed up when I said it. But he seemed very keen, and I wanted to keep him around. Who am I to go against unfinished business if he really needs it?"

There. That sounds logical.

"Guards!" the guard snaps.

Seems redundant, but okay.

Two others burst into the room. "Contain her," Werenz growls as he moves in front of Soora. I think it's safe to assume he doesn't like me.

I swing my bow around and nock an arrow faster than they can draw swords, making the two skid to a halt.

"I'm sorry about this," I rush to say to Soora, since, you know, I'm pointing the arrow at her. Honestly though, she looks unbothered by the whole ordeal. Perhaps this isn't the first time someone has come into her home and threatened to murder her? Something to research later.

"I don't actually want to murder you. It was more of a to-do list thing I came up with so that I could get over Belren dying for me and scarring my existence."

"Lovely," Soora says dryly.

The guards look between us, as tense as bristling wolves waiting to bite. Soora keeps them in place with a hand gesture, and I feel sharp magic peppering the air as some sort of barrier shimmers around her.

"Her weapon is useless," Soora tells the guards impassively. "Leave us."

Werenz blanches. "But—"

"Leave us," she repeats, tone leaving zero room for argument. "We females are going to have a private chat."

The three of them stalk out of the room, obviously

unhappy with leaving their princess alone. As soon as the door shuts, I lower my bow and shove the arrow back into my quiver. "Again, sorry. I wasn't going to actually shoot at you." Unless Belren asked me to, then I'd have to try at least.

"I know," Soora replies coolly. I'm slightly offended that she doesn't seem to be the least bit threatened.

"I could've done it, though."

She looks me up and down. "No."

I wrinkle my nose and glance down at my sensible clothes and shoes. "I don't look like a murderess?"

"You're not a killer," Soora replies easily. "Though you seem to have very good aim."

My wings perk up at that. "Thank you. I actually came in first place for accuracy amongst all of cupidity."

"Very impressive."

I can't tell if she's actually impressed or if she's mocking me a bit.

It might be the latter.

"Don't worry," Belren murmurs behind me, voice hoarse. "She hasn't seen your full violent potential like I have. I know you have it in you."

"Are you okay?"

"Fine," he replies, but he doesn't sound or look it.

"You're not fine. Tell me what to do," I plead, hating this feeling of helplessness. "I think I can shoot an arrow at her if you really need me to. Possibly. I hope." Now that the situation is at hand, I'm feeling a bit squeamish about it.

I'm so focused on Belren that I don't even realize Soora has walked over until she's right next to me. "You're telling the truth, aren't you, cupid?"

"It's Lex. And if you're talking about Belren being a ghost, then yes, I am."

Soora eyes me for a long moment, her gaze assessing and measuring. Finally, she nods. "If Belren is truly here and he's a ghost, then his unfinished business wouldn't be with me."

"It wouldn't?"

She shakes her head, and for a second, I think her eyes land on Belren, as if she can sense where he is.

"No. Belren could find anything and anyone. But when his sister went missing, he couldn't track her down. It was the one time he failed, and he hated it. It ate away at him. When he finally saw her, it was too late, and then he died before he could find her again."

Beside me, Belren has gone stock-still, and my heart feels like it wants to pound out of my chest. "What are you saying?"

Soora's purple eyes latch onto me. "His unfinished business isn't with me. It's with finding his sister."

I suck in a breath, because I already know what she's going to say before she even utters a word.

"Benicia is here. We live on the island where he died."

CHAPTER 29

BELREN

The pull is incredible.

I thought it was strong before, and it was, but something is different. I felt the difference as soon as I was yanked here with Lex, but I thought it was because of the portal.

It's not the portal; that much is clear now.

The longer I've been here, it's become increasingly apparent that something has changed. I feel like time is running out.

At first, with Lex grounding me, I was able to keep it at bay, but now...

That all-encompassing *tug* is insistent. Without Lex's touch, I'm drifting. The invisible tide wants to drag me away, and for some reason, Lex can't touch me anymore. This time, I think it's because of me.

I don't want to admit the fact that I'm fading, but even I can see the way my body has gone translucent and drab.

Real fear simmers in me.

But then when my sister's name falls from the princess's

lips again, a jolt goes through me, like a bolt of lightning electrifying me from the inside out.

Benicia.

Then the rest of the princess's words filter through my mind, and my eyes go wide. "She's *here*?" I know Soora can't hear me, but Lex can, and with it, she can hear how hoarse my voice is, the struggle it is to speak.

Bits and pieces of my sister come swimming into my mind. I can't quite picture her face, but I can recall the fierce determination I had to find her. That, and the guilt for not being able to.

"Where is she?" I ask, but as soon as the question is out of my lips, another jolt goes through me, and preternatural realization suddenly slams into me. "Soora's glamour power," I whisper hoarsely. "It was hiding it."

Lex shoots me a worried look. "Hiding what?"

"I wasn't being pulled to my deathplace. I was being pulled to *her*, but Soora's magic was blocking me."

I stagger on my feet, like someone has wrapped a rope around my midsection and is pulling me forward.

"Belren!" Lex comes forward like she's going to try to catch me, but our bodies pass right through each other.

"It's alright," I assure her.

And it is.

Everything clicks into place, and something quiet and settling drapes over my spirit. Like I know exactly what I have to do. I'm walking forward before I even register the movement. Instead of fighting the pull, I'm letting it lead me. *This is what I have to do.*

The feeling I have adds another missing puzzle piece from my past life. This deeper intuition is something I used to get. I'd just know where to go, and I'd follow my gut when I tracked things down. Maybe it was some sort of sixth sense, but feeling it now makes me feel more like *me*.

I'm pulled forward by the invisible force, the soles of my shoes sinking through the floor as I go. I stop when I get to the thick purple curtains hanging from floor to ceiling.

I think I hear Lex say something behind me, but sound is nearly drowned out with a low-pitched hum that's droning in my ears. Like a long-forgotten song that I'm straining to hear.

I just need to get closer.

Without hesitation, I step into the curtains and go right through the wall. Once I'm inside the dark space, I realize it's not a wall at all, but a secret door. I stride forward, something like adrenaline and a nearly debilitating hope fueling my steps as I go.

Through the wall, there's a set of stairs that leads up, and up, and up. I'm not sure if I actually walk them or if I just float right up, but either way, I make it to another closed door at the very top.

I think I hear Lex calling my name below, but I can't turn back now. I can't stop. The tug is too insistent, the urge to find too strong.

I have to know...

Pushing my way in, I drift through the door, my eyes instantly taking in the scene. The room is circular, with beams all meeting at the same center point on the ceiling. Unlike the purple mash-up happening in the rest of the house, this room is clad in browns and creams. With a single sweep, I take in the fur rug and the plush bed before all awareness snags on the shadowed figure sitting on a window seat.

If I had breath to lose, it would've gotten stuck in my throat.

Even though she's sitting in the dark without any lanterns or candles lit, the moonlight coming in from the huge window she's sitting at allows me to see the silvery sheen of her skin and the darker horns curling back around her head. Her white hair is cut short, barely brushing against the tops of her ears. A pair of delicate wings that resemble a moth's are clasped together at her back, single eyes at the center of each one.

"Benicia."

Her name passes from my lips like a prayer to the fae gods of old. And the pull is just suddenly...*gone*.

I hadn't realized how constant the force was, just how strong, until this moment.

Soora was right.

The princess was never my unfinished business. I wasn't being pulled to my deathplace. I was being led *here*. To finally find my sister.

To do in death what I couldn't do in life.

She shouldn't hear me. Shouldn't know that I'm standing here like I'm the one seeing the ghost. She shouldn't, but when I call her name, my sister's spine suddenly goes stiff, and her head whips around.

Glowing gray eyes are wide as she looks wildly around the room. "Who's there?"

I'm stuck in shock for a second, my mind whirring as it tries to fill in all the blanks of everything I've forgotten about her, as it simultaneously realizes that she reacted to my voice.

I take a tentative step forward. "Benicia, can you hear me?"

She leaps to her feet this time, head snapping left and right. She might've heard me—or at least heard *something*—but she doesn't know where I am, considering her eyes keep jumping all over the room.

The door behind me opens, and Soora and Lex step inside. As soon as my cupid sees me, relief spreads over her expression.

"Soora..." At my sister's call, the princess immediately walks over, the two of them embracing.

"What's wrong?"

A deep frown line has appeared between Benicia's brows. "I thought I heard something." Then her eye snags on Lex, and she startles. "Who's that?"

"It's alright," Soora tells her. "This is Lex, and she's come to say hello."

Benicia doesn't let go of Soora, and she continues to eye Lex warily. I know I still have a lot of missing memories, but this vision of Benicia cowering and confused hits me hard, because this doesn't seem like her.

"Hello," Lex greets with a warm smile. I notice her glancing between the two of them, and then a soft sigh escapes her that I'm probably the only one who can hear since I'm standing so close. "You two...so much love," she says, almost dreamily. "I haven't felt that much love between two people in a long time."

Benicia doesn't seem to have heard Lex's words, but for the first time since we've gotten here, Soora's face softens until there's a barely-there smile.

The hot torch of anger I've been carrying gets smothered a bit because of it.

How can I hate her if she loves my sister that much?

"Are you okay?" Lex whispers beneath her breath. Her face is pinched with worry, her pretty lips pressed thin. But gods, is she beautiful.

I wish I could remember her more from before.

"I am now," I reply, and she must hear how the strain has left my voice, because her brows lift in surprise. "It was pulling me here all along."

Warring sentiments cross her face. She looks happy for me, and yet there's a sadness in the depths of her eyes that guts me.

"I'm glad you found her," she murmurs.

Benicia seems to get distracted and wanders back over to the window seat, where she tucks her legs beneath herself elegantly and gazes out at the moon.

A flash of vulnerable pain crosses Soora's face as she watches her. "Benicia has had some...difficulty. What the king and prince did to her, the mind control...it affected her. She doesn't like to leave this room. She forgets things sometimes, gets upset. But looking out the window soothes her, even when I can't."

A quick glance outside makes me realize that she's looking in the direction of my deathplace. Thick emotion clogs my throat.

"I couldn't let them kill her," Soora goes on, and I see a flash of a tear trail down her cheek before she quickly dashes it away. She sounds as if she's been waiting to say this to someone for years. Like it's been pent-up inside of her and she desperately needed to get it out, for someone to hear her.

Something like pity crosses Lex's face. "I understand."

As if she hates being so exposed and real, Soora takes

a breath and slams her internal barriers back up until she looks cool and collected again. "The entire realm can hate me. They can all wish me dead and call me a traitor. I don't care," she says with vehemence, cutting her gaze to Lex. "I made the mistake of sacrificing Benicia once, when I decided to go along with the plan to marry the prince to help the fae, and I broke her heart in the process. I couldn't sacrifice her again. So I chose *her* that day instead, and I'd do it all over again if I had to. Because she needs me, and I wasn't going to let her down again."

Well, fuck. I can't fault that.

"You did it for love," Lex says, giving a sad smile of understanding. "Love...changes things."

Soora nods tersely, but I see the minuscule tell of relief as her hands loosen slightly at her sides. "I don't know how Prince Elphar tracked Benicia down, but he did it because of me. He found my one weak point, and he exploited it." She turns to watch my sister, who's trailing a finger over the window. "I couldn't leave her at his mercy when it was my fault she was there in the first place."

All of those fae we've seen in the realm who spit at Soora's name and call her things worse than a traitor...I wonder what they'd say right now, if they could see her as we see her.

Because Lex is right. Love changes things.

"So," Soora starts, drawing herself up like she's raising an internal shield. "Do you still want to kill me?"

Lex shares a look with me. "No, I think I can pass on the whole premeditated murder thing. I'd much rather use my arrows for Love, though you don't seem to need my help on that front."

Soora glances affectionately at Benicia again. "No. I don't."

I move forward, stopping right next to my sister, watching as she continues to drag her finger against the glass, drawing lines through the condensation. As I observe her, a profound melancholy washes over me. "I'm sorry it took me so long to find you, Beni."

The nickname rolls off my tongue, forgotten until this very moment, but it feels inherently familiar.

My sister jerks away from the window, and then her head swings in my direction, her gray eyes locking onto me.

I rear back in surprise, and she mirrors the movement. "Belren?"

Shock slams into me, and it feels as if the ground is shaking, threatening to toss me off my feet, the movement roaring in my ears like an angry sea.

"What did you say?" Soora asks.

Benicia doesn't answer. She's too busy staring wide-eyed at me.

"You're here."

For a moment, I can't say anything at all. I'm afraid to even blink, worried that she'll lose this connection to me. Or worse, that I'll realize I was imagining it all.

But when she continues to stare at me, I finally come up with a response. "I'm here."

"Who's here, Benicia?" Soora asks carefully, coming to stand beside her.

Beni finally glances over at her, though she's quick to lock her eyes on me again, and then she gives me a smile that simultaneously breaks my heart and makes it soar.

"My brother. He finally found his way."

I'm not sure how much Soora really believed Lex before, but Benicia saying it, is a completely different story.

"Belren? He's really here?" she whispers, lavender skin going pale.

Beni smiles at me. "He's just there," she says with a nod. "I knew he'd find me eventually."

She's right. An unexplainable feeling inside me *knows* that she's right. I was always going to find her, because it was my life's mission. It just took death for me to be able to finally do it.

I give her a wry smile. "You were always the patient one," I say, somehow knowing it's true.

She laughs, but the joy from my sister's face slowly fades, and I can see every thought as it crosses her open face, right down to the sadness of her trembling lip. "You died."

My head tips. "I did."

"You weren't supposed to die, brother."

A lump forms in my throat, and I look back at Lex, who's still standing by the door, watching everything with a sorrowful look on her face. "Love changes things."

Lex sucks in a breath, tears collecting in her eyes. I might be dead, useless, incorporeal, but I know I love her.

Maybe I somehow knew I was going to.

I've always had a sixth sense when it came to finding things—to *taking* them. So perhaps in that split-second decision I made to jump in front of her, I was simply following my gut.

I knew I wanted to find her. To have her.

But it just wasn't in the fates for me to be able to keep her.

CHAPTER 30

LEX

*N*ever, since he first appeared to me on Ghost Island, has Belren ever looked this...ghostly.

His body is completely transparent, lacking every bit of the more substantial edge he'd had. His eyes no longer seem alight and vivid, his silvery skin now lusterless and drab.

Just since he came into this room, he's faded so much. It's almost hard to see him, his sheer body like a barely-there wisp of evaporating smoke.

It terrifies me.

"She's your unfinished business," I say, more to myself than to him, but he nods anyway.

Every time he glances at her, it's like he can't believe he finally found her. "I feel it," he tells me, passing a hand over his chest. "The pull is gone, and something just feels...settled."

It was never about the princess or revenge. His goal in life was always finding his sister, so of course it carried through in his death. It makes sense.

349

But then...why was he able to stick around with me?

Was it because I was a means to an end? Did the fates let him stay with me because they knew I would lead him to her?

I don't know how to feel about that.

I'm also trying really hard not to encroach on this moment with his sister, even though all I want to do is rush across the room to be closer to him. It's hard to hold myself back when I feel like he's slipping away, but I do it.

"I can almost see you...almost hear you perfectly," Benicia says reverently, finger coming up to trace the shape of his silhouette. "But it's like looking through a gauzy fabric and my ears stuffed with cotton."

"That's because I'm in the Veil," he tells her.

I have no idea how she's able to see him, but I'm so happy for them, because they deserve to have this moment together.

But as happy as I am...I hate it too.

Because this means that he's finishing his unfinished business, and I don't want him to fade away and disappear forever. I want him to stay, no matter how faded he may be.

"Can you see my brother?" Benicia asks Soora.

The princess shakes her head. "I can't."

An anxious look crosses Benicia's face. "But you believe me, don't you?"

"I do," Soora tells her, and I don't think it's just lip service to appease Benicia's delicate disposition. For whatever reason, she seems to be convinced.

As a cupid who is used to being in the Veil, unseen by any of the people I work my magic on, I can appreciate someone who believes in what they can't see.

Love and hauntings. Two of the most profound, invisible things. And sometimes, they happen at the same time, with the same person.

"What are you thinking?"

I blink, startled that I'd been so lost in my thoughts that I hadn't even noticed Belren come over. Hastily, I sniff and use the crook of my arm to wipe away the treacherous tears that fell. Hopefully, he'll just think it was happy tears for him finding his sister.

"I'm thinking that this is a lovely room."

Belren smiles. "What happened to that moral compass of not telling lies?"

Guilty.

Swallowing hard, I ask, "Is this it?"

A frown forms between his brows. "It must be. It feels like it is, although..."

"Although what?" I cling to his hesitation.

He studies me for a moment, like he's debating how forthcoming he wants to be. "Why aren't I disappearing?"

My hands wring anxiously in front of me. "Don't say that."

"It's true though, isn't it?" he persists. "If finding my sister was it, then I should go poof now...right?"

"I don't want you to," I say fiercely, hating that more tears are already springing up in my eyes.

Belren's expression softens to something heartbreaking. "I know, Pinky."

Suddenly, there's a loud bang from somewhere in the house, making us all jerk to attention, heads swinging toward the noise. "Princess Soora! There's someone here for you!"

The shout sounds like it's coming from downstairs,

from the sitting room we were in before Belren disappeared in the wall and Soora led me through her secret door.

At the commotion, Benicia cowers and practically leaps back onto her window seat, where she presses herself against the glass, looking wild-eyed and scared. Belren rushes to her.

"It's alright," Soora tries to soothe, but I'm not sure Benicia hears her.

"Princess!" the same voice calls, and then there's the sound of running up the stairs. Magic crackles in the air when Soora throws up a barrier.

I instinctively back away from the door. "What's going on?" I ask, my nerves jumping.

"I don't know—"

In the next instant, the door bursts open, and my eyes nearly bug out of my head when I see who topples inside.

"Emelle!"

Looking completely ruffled and pink-cheeked, my cupid boss struggles to fit her wings through the doorway as she shoves inside the room.

I barely have time to register her appearance before two more males are barging in right behind her, with about five guards hot on their heels, bottlenecking on the stairway.

The room suddenly feels very small.

"What is the meaning of this?" Soora demands, going full royal-tone again.

"Hi, Princess Soora," Emelle chirps after blowing pink hair out of her face and trying to elbow the two males behind her.

My eyes widen when I realize who it is.

All three Veil Majors are standing in this tiny room.

The head of all angels, Raziel, my own Madame Cupid as head of all of cupidity, and Jerkahf, head of all demon kind. Life, love, death. AKA kind of a big deal for them to all be standing here together.

I've seen them before, of course, but giving the proper amount of respect is never a bad thing. So I give a quick but respectable curtsy. I know it's respectable, because I've practiced in front of a mirror many times.

"Who are you and what are you doing in my house?" Soora demands, purple butterfly wings suddenly popping from her back. I suppose there's a lot of Big Wing Energy in the room right now, so they feel the need to compete with the demon's smoking wings and the angel's glowing ones.

My own even ruffle up a little.

"Hey," Emelle says, giving an awkward side wave. "Could you call your goons off?"

Soora's sharp eyes consider her for a moment before she finally glances over her shoulder to the guards. "You can go."

Werenz looks at her like she's insane. "But, Princess, I think..." He swallows nervously but forges on, dropping his voice lower as if it'll help the entities in front of him not hear. "This one said he was a *demon*," he says, pointing a crooked finger at Jerkahf.

The demon snorts, smoke tapering off the edges of his leathery wings.

"Yes, well, I suppose it wouldn't be smart to try to toss him out of the house then, would it?"

With a nod, the guards retreat, and Emelle kicks the

door closed behind her with her foot before turning and clapping her hands together. "Great, now it's just us."

Raziel crosses tanned arms in front of him, glowering at her. The shininess of his golden hair makes him a little less intimidating. Or it could be the toga.

"I cannot believe we let you talk us into going through a faerie portal," he seethes.

"Hey, they like to be called fae, not faeries," Emelle tells him. "And I didn't know you had a soft stomach and would get transport-sick."

Jerkahf laughs at the angel's expense. "I always knew angels were weaker than demons," he says, patting his stomach currently covered in a black leather jacket. "I have a much stronger disposition."

Raziel's eyes narrow on him, arms flexing a bit. Either he's purposely flexing them to seem more intimidating or they're jumping in agitation. It could be both options, really.

"It wasn't the portal that made me ill. Your wings smell like rotten eggs cracked over the pits of hell, and I'm sick of smelling them."

Jerkahf grins and lets his wing stretch, and Raziel swats it away on instinct before frowning down at his hand. "I need to wash."

Emelle rolls her eyes. "Gods, can you two just get along for *five minutes*?"

"No," they both answer at the same time.

"And anyway, you're the one who tricked us into coming here with you in the first place," Raziel points out.

Emelle looks incredibly proud of that fact. "It had to be done."

Raziel and Jerkahf both shake their heads but seem to

look around to study the room for the first time. Jerkahf's eyes land on me, and he shoots me a wicked smile. "Hello, little love dove. Aren't you a gorgeous slice of Librarian Lust?"

Why do people always say things like that? Is it the hair bun?

I clear my throat a little nervously at the amount of heat coming off him that I know has nothing to do with hell. "Hi there."

Belren is at my side in an instant. "I don't like him."

"Finally, someone I can relate to," Raziel mutters, and both Belren and I whip our heads in his direction.

"You can see him?" I ask in surprise.

Now Raziel looks affronted. "I'm an *angel*. Of course I can see him. He's a spirit."

Oh. Alright.

Soora interjects. "Let me break this up, because I'd love to know why you're here, in my house, and how you even found me, and what you want. You're upsetting Benicia."

I peel my attention away from the trio, finding Soora patting Benicia's back. The horned female is watching the angel with rapt attention, but she's no longer cowering, which I take as a good sign.

"I'm okay," Benicia murmurs, gaze never straying from Raziel. "Your wings are very nice."

The angel puffs up a bit, looking pleased.

"I'm sorry to barge in on you like this," Emelle interjects.

"I was wondering when you'd finally come and find me, though I must admit, your company is troubling," Soora replies, eyeing Jerkahf warily.

"We weren't looking for you, per se," Emelle admits somewhat sheepishly as she holds up her glowing head cupid mark. "Lex called me earlier, right when I was...in the middle of something. I came as soon as I could, following her call, and we rode a portal to get here. It was Raz who saw through your barrier magic."

"I've asked you repeatedly not to call me Raz," the angel complains.

Emelle pats him on the shoulder. "I know. You should really stop wasting your breath."

"You're my favorite Veil Major," Jerkahf tells her.

Emelle levels him with a look. "You threatened to set Cupidville alight with the fires of hell when I tricked you into coming here with me."

The demon shrugs. "I take it back."

Being in the presence of these three is a little bit like watching someone try to herd cats.

"Can we get back to the matter at hand?" Soora cuts in, looking more and more frustrated. "If you aren't here for me, then what are you doing here?"

"Right." Emelle looks to me. "I'm sorry it's taken me so long to come find you. Since I left you, I've been working night and day trying to come up with a solution to our umm...problem."

"It's okay," I tell her, because every moment I've had alone with Belren has been worth the wait.

"But I figured it out."

I go still at her words. "You...did? You can fix him?"

A beaming smile spreads across her face, and she even jumps a little, like she can't contain her excitement. "We can fix him!"

It feels like wind is suddenly rushing through my ears,

so loud I have to shake my head to clear it. I'm worried for a moment that I heard her wrong.

"You...you really can?"

Emelle walks forward and clasps my hands. "It took me and Sev and *a lot* of cupid interns round-the-clock researching, but we found the answer. A wayward spirit, AKA a ghost, can be sent back to processing in only one very specific situation: all three of the Veil Majors have to combine powers to send him there. He won't be a ghost anymore. He'll have a second chance."

My heart raps against my chest like an incessant knocking.

He won't be a ghost anymore.

When I'm sure that I'm not hearing this wrong, that I'm not simply hallucinating, a surge of ecstatic hope rises up and practically lifts me off my feet as I spin around. "Did you hear that?" I exclaim. "They can fix you! You won't be a ghost anymore. You won't fade away into nothing!"

Belren looks as shocked as I feel, eyes darting between Emelle and me.

To say crying comes quickly is an understatement. I already have happy tears falling down my cheeks before I even get the first sentence out.

I never truly comprehended the weight of the worry I was carrying until this moment, when it seems to buoy right off of me. I've been so afraid every single second since he found me, that he was going to disappear—that he would just disintegrate into nothing—or that his mind would fail him. But now, Emelle can reverse his status as a ghost. She can give him a *real* afterlife.

Forever.

"Is this true?" Belren asks, voice tentative.

Emelle can't see him, but Raziel moves forward with a quizzical look on his face. He stops right in front of Belren, ethereal eyes skating over him. "Curious."

"What's curious?" I ask.

Raziel continues to study him for a moment before he says, "Most ghosts have unfinished business. They're usually the ones who hold out the longest when it comes to not losing their minds. But I've never come across a spirit with *two* forms of it."

I blink in surprise. "What do you mean two?"

Raziel's gaze moves to Benicia. "Ahh. I see the tie here clearly. Another curiosity. Not many spirits actually *finish* their unfinished business. Well done," he tells Belren.

"But what's the second one?" Belren asks.

To my shock, the angel lifts his hand and waves it at me. "Her, of course. I can see the tie as clear as day. Though, this one hasn't been completed. It looks like it's her side that's blocking it from completion."

I rear back. "My side? What do you mean?"

For the first time, Raziel actually loses the arrogant expression on his face and gives me a look of sympathy. "It's quite common for the living to be unable to move on from the death of a loved one. But it's *uncommon* for them to actually *see* the loved one haunting them because of it."

His words filter in slowly, like hardened honey trying to drip from a spoon.

"Are you saying that *I'm* Belren's second unfinished business, but he can't finish it because I'm holding him back?"

Raziel nods. "That's exactly what I'm saying."

I don't know whether I should be horrified or pleased.

On one hand, I'm holding back a spirit from being able to move on. But since moving on is just disintegrating into nothingness, I am relieved as heck that I'm keeping him here.

But...I'm his unfinished business.

Me.

That's why he's been able to be with me all this time.

A fresh set of tears spring up like daisies, and Belren steps up into me. "Don't cry, Pinky," he says softly. "I hate seeing you upset."

"I'm—It's just...you cared enough about me that I'm your unfinished business," I weep. "How could I have mattered that much to you when you died?"

"How could you not?" he counters.

He loves me.

I don't need my cupid powers to tell me that, I can see it in his face. And I must love him, because I wouldn't be subconsciously keeping him here with me otherwise. I wouldn't get butterflies every time he looks at me, or have my heart break any time I think about losing him again.

"It had nothing to do with your muck in my quiver."

Across the room, the demon snorts.

"They can fix you," I whisper, relief streaming out of me. "You can stop being a ghost."

Belren smiles and looks over to Raziel, like he's ready to get started right this second.

I share the sentiment. "Let's do it," I say, spinning toward the trio. "How does this work?"

Emelle shares a look with the others and twists her hair around nervously. "Umm, Lex...there's something I need to tell you first."

"What?"

Her multi-colored eyes fill with troubled emotions. "There's one catch."

I hold my breath, willing for it to be okay.

"When we use our joined powers on him to send him back to be processed...it will wipe his memory, just like death does."

It will wipe his memory.

Wipe his memory.

His memory.

As in, every single moment we've shared since he found me. Every single scrap he's gathered since he's been with me.

I'm shaking my head before I even come up with a response. "But...I..."

"I know," Emelle says, touching my arm slightly. "I can tell."

"Everything?" I ask, voice cracking. "I know he'll forget his mortal life, but what about this?"

I hate the pitying expression that settles over her face. "I'm sorry."

The almost happy ending crashes around my ears, and I can't breathe. My eyes stare down at my shoes, my wings trembling against my back as I dig my fingernails into my palms.

I never considered that by restoring him physically, I'd lose him mentally. Emotionally.

How can I lose him all over again? How could the fates be so cruel?

"You said that she's my unfinished business," Belren intervenes. "So I could just...never finish things. I could stay with her and my sister, memories intact."

Raziel bobs his head left and right in thought. "Sure. For a time."

My stomach curdles.

"Why not?" Belren demands, anger on his faded face. "You said she was keeping me here."

"Spirits are not meant to stay forever. They will eventually fade, whether they still have unfinished business or not. In fact, most do fade, without ever fulfilling theirs."

"But that could be years from now. Decades even," he argues.

Raziel tips his head. "It could. But you're lucky that you've kept your mind as sharp thus far. Most spirits are not so fortunate. You might lose these precious memories anyway. Plus, if you fade too much more than you already have, it doesn't matter how many Veil entities you have at your disposal, pretty soon, we won't be able to reprocess you. So really, this is your only chance."

Only chance.

That phrase just repeats itself over and over again in my head.

This is his *only chance.*

How can I hold him back from that? It was my fault that day. I didn't stay in the Veil like he cautioned me to. I was too preoccupied with helping, and I never imagined anything bad would actually happen because, well, I'm a naive cupid. I thought about love, not death.

Not mourning.

I press a hand to my chest, as if I can feel the tie of unfinished business knotting us together. Every moment we've had with one another has been a gift. I asked for closure from the fates. Demanded it, even. And maybe this was their way of giving it to me.

They let me find him, have time with him. Time that I never had while he was alive. The fates let a cupid find out what love really means. What it *feels* like, and it's so much more powerful than I ever realized.

With wet-tipped lashes, I look up at Belren's handsome, pallid face. "You should do it," I whisper, the words falling out of me haltingly, stinging my throat on the way out and making my lips burn.

Belren looks at me like I've grown another pair of wings. "What?"

I nod, and it takes everything in me not to cry again. I have to be strong right now. I can't let him see me waver. Because I know, if I show the heartbreak on my face, that he'll do it—he'll give up this chance and choose to stay a ghost.

Shoring myself up, I try to appear straight-backed and confident. I even tuck my hands behind me so he won't notice my fingers twisting together. "Staying like this—constantly worried that it'll be the end...it's no way to be."

"No," Belren argues, head shaking with agitation. It's worse when he tries to run a hand down his face, only for his hand to go right through it. He lets out a frustrated growl that tears through my stomach. "This isn't what you really want."

My lip threatens to quiver, but I bite down hard on my tongue to make it stop. "This is what I want."

"But I'll *forget you*," he seethes. "Again."

Benicia's soft voice sounds out. "You can't stay a ghost, brother."

He stares at her, and then a humorless laugh crawls up his throat as he tips his head back to shake his head at the ceiling. "You too, Beni?" he asks jokingly, but I can see the hurt in his eyes.

She gets up, uncurling her legs to stand in front of him. She's at least a head shorter, but they look so much alike that it's endearing. "You found me," she says quietly. "You didn't give up on me, even in death. I can't let you give up on yourself."

"Beni—"

"It's okay, brother," she says, voice low and soothing, a sad smile curling her grayish lips. "We're going to be okay, because we'll know that *you're* okay."

She's right. So long as I know that Belren exists somewhere in the Veil, be it an angel or demon or one of the Veil minors, I will be okay.

I have to be.

Benicia gives him a smile and then backs away, clasping Soora's hand.

With an agonized expression, Belren shakes his head, "I can't do it."

"Yes, you can," I tell him.

"But what will you do?"

My throat wants to close up, but I force myself to reply. "I'll go back to work."

"There's a chance that I could *never* see you again. You get that, don't you? I could be shoved down into hell as a demon."

"You have much more angelic tendencies than demonic," Raziel cuts in.

Both Belren and Jerkahf seem insulted.

"I do not," Belren argues. "I was a thief all my mortal life."

Raziel shrugs. "Angels do not lie, spirit. I see what I see. Besides, you would be lucky to be under my rule."

"Oooh luck! Belren would be very good as a Lady Luck," Emelle pipes in. At Raziel's bewildered look, she says, "Oh, right. A Lord Luck. Whatever."

Shaking his head, Belren shifts his body left so that I turn with him, giving us a semblance of privacy as he searches my face. "This is ludicrous and we both know it. Tell me right now not to do it."

I swallow hard, trying to find the strength to convince him, but I can't, so I shake my head instead.

A flash of anger crosses his face. "Why are you doing this?"

I can hear it.

The heartbreak.

His heart may not beat, but it still *loves.*

That's apparent with the way he looks at his sister, and right now, with the way he's looking at me with a different sort of love.

Which is exactly what I need to solidify my motivation. "I'm doing this because I won't let you die for me again. No more sacrificing, Belren," I say, and I hate that my voice cracks, revealing the emotion beneath, but I keep going. "I need you to live. I need you to do this for yourself, and for us. Because we love you." When he goes still, I clear my throat so that there's absolutely zero chance he misunderstands. "Because *I* love you."

He hesitates, eyes swinging back and forth between mine like a pendulum. "You love me, Pinky?"

Don't cry.

"Yes," I breathe. "So please—*please* do this. And then I'll be able to breathe again. I'll know you're okay, wherever you are, that you'll always exist."

There isn't a clock in this room, but I swear, I can hear one. Every tick that goes by has my anxiety teetering from one edge to the other. I don't want him to do it, but I don't want him to *not* do it, either.

"Are you certain?"

Not at all.

My fingers twist so hard that I scrape off some of the skin as I count in my head, refusing to think. Because if I think, I'll blurt that I'm not sure at all, that I take it back, that I want him to stay.

But that's selfish. This isn't a real afterlife, and he deserves better. He already sacrificed himself for me once. I won't let him do it again. It's my turn to show him that he's worth a sacrifice too.

"Yes."

One...two...three...

His lips press into a thin line. "Trying to get rid of me already, Pinky?" he teases, but it lacks his usual flair.

Four...five...six...

"Are we doing this?" Jerkahf cuts in, dusting some ash off of his leathery wing. "I have things to do, people to torture."

Emelle wrinkles her nose. "That's aggressive," she mutters.

"Are you ready, spirit?" Raziel cuts in, looking at Belren.

Belren reaches up to try to cup my face, and I shudder, but when his fingers go through my cheek, my eyes burn. He curses under his breath, and then his forehead tips down toward mine, silhouette sending a cool brush of air against my scalp. "I'm glad I jumped in front of you that day, Lex," he whispers, and just like that, my own heart shatters. Crumbles into shards and then disintegrates into dust, becoming as intangible as him.

"So do this one last thing for me, Belren," I say, bottom lip trembling, voice choked.

Ghosts can't cry, but when he lifts his head again, the emotion is right there in his eyes.

Seven...eight...nine...

He glances at me and Benicia again, but when he sees the matching resolve on our faces, he nods to her and presses a hand to his heart. She sobs through a smile and mimics the movement, a tear rolling down her cheeks as Soora wraps an arm around her waist.

"Ready?" Raziel asks quietly, and Belren nods.

Breathe. Count. Don't think.

Emelle squeezes my arm as she, Jerkahf, and Raziel all come around to circle Belren. They clasp hands and start to speak in low tones, but I'm too busy staring at Belren to pay attention to what they're saying. Benicia appears at my side and slips her arm through mine, and I realize she's trembling just as much as I am.

Breathe. Count. Don't think.

A glow erupts from the trio surrounding Belren, and my eyes try to track the hazy lights of white and pink and black as it slips from their clasped palms and begins to surround my ghost.

My lips part, and it's right there on the tip of my tongue to yell for them to stop, to rush into the circle and try to plaster myself against him. But I force myself to keep my knees locked, heels dug into the floor. It's only Benicia's hold that keeps me from falling.

As the vaporous light wraps around more of him, I see his throat bob, his gray eyes locked on me. "I'll find you," he says, so fiercely that I want to believe him. "Did you hear me, Pinky? I'll find you."

A sob ruptures out of me, and I can't help it when my face scrunches up, my resolve cracking, because this *hurts*. This hurts so much that it surpasses anything physical, and I know I'll never recover. Benicia is the only one holding me up, because my knees have already buckled.

The light swishes up, swallowing his body, filling the room, and then it takes over his face, until I can't see his steady gray eyes anymore, and I squeeze my own shut tight. The light burns cold and sharp like a falling star, and then all at once, it swallows him completely and dies out.

When I open my eyes again, he's gone, and all the dusty fragments of my heart have gone with him.

CHAPTER 31

LEX

I did the right thing.

At least, that's what I tell myself over and over. Every minute. Every hour. Every day. Every week. I tell myself that again and again and again, every time my mind drifts to Belren. Which is often.

I wonder if Benicia does the same thing.

Before, when Belren died for me, I felt guilt and confusion. Now, I just feel hollow.

So, all in all, things aren't great.

My afterlife used to be so...*fulfilling*. When I said I loved my job, I meant it. I loved everything about it. Shooting Love Arrows got me giddy. I sighed with reverence every time I made a Match. I often couldn't wait to spread around Flirt Touches and watch the magic happen. I loved creating meaningful connections, I loved being a cupid. I loved *love*.

Now though? Now, I kind of hate it.

Not ideal for a cupid to hate love, but there it is.

I nock another Arrow onto my bowstring and pull it

back, watching the two fae in front of me. I let it fly, hitting my target perfectly, and a puff of red evaporates like mist. The male latches eyes with the person beside him on the bench, and just like that, love has begun.

Jerks.

My wings tingle a bit, and I feel the love soak in, but it's not gratifying like it used to be. Now, I'm too bitter to taste the sweet.

Walking away, I let my bow hang loosely in my hand, barely skirting around a couple of fae with goat legs as they go running by.

This spot is quite popular, no doubt for how picturesque it is. The island is small, but what it lacks in size, it makes up for in pretty romantic spots. Like the blooming meadow just behind me, and the tufts of trees that grow into natural archways, making little convenient spots for fae to hide beneath for passionate rendezvous. Fae of all kinds are around, many of them having a picnic by the crystalline lake, taking advantage of the sunshine.

If I were my old innocent, naive, blissful self, I would absolutely adore this place. But I can't find the adoration for it anymore, because it's been six weeks since Belren disappeared. Six weeks feels like a long time when you're grieving. It also reminds me of just how short it really is in the grand scheme of things, which just makes it worse, because for me, there's no end in sight.

Whether it's six weeks or six thousand weeks, I'll still miss him.

I did the right thing.

I'm sure I did, because he's somewhere, existing, without the fear of an expiration date. Yet still, when I lie awake at night in my corporeal form, or when I'm roaming the realm to give Love with a lackluster aim, all I want is him.

All I want is to be haunted again.

With a sigh, I stop in one of the shadowed archways and go corporeal, putting my bow and arrow away so I can just sit on the grass and enjoy the perfumed breeze in the air. I watch the fae around the island, half-heartedly trying to see if I can spot any other unmatched potentials, but just as I spot a group, my cupid mark glows pink.

Frowning, I look down at my number, my thumb rubbing over it. A second later, I hear a familiar and heavily accented voice coming up behind me. "So she *does* take breaks. Shocking, that."

My head jerks around, my brows shooting up in surprise when I see none other than Sev and Emelle walking up to me.

"What are you two doing here?" I ask, jumping to my feet.

Sev grins at me, raking his eyes up and down my form before he shoves his hands in the pockets of his bright orange pants. "Gotta say, I'm surprised to see you outta the librarian getup."

I self-consciously brush my hands down the formfitting pants and tunic I'm wearing. "I thought it would be good to have a new fae wardrobe, since I'm going to be staying in this realm for the near future."

Emelle winks, since she's wearing something similar. "You fit right in." She pulls me into a hug, squeezing me tight. "Sev tells me you've made four hundred Love Matches already this month. I don't want you to push yourself too much. After everything that happened..."

A lump forms in my throat, and I have to shove away

the emotions that I don't want to feel. It's easier to throw myself into my work again instead of thinking too much. I suppose I still haven't learned—I've reverted right back to old habits—and it all boils down to the fact that I don't know how to cope.

When we pull away, I give her what I hope is a reassuring smile. "I'm fine, truly. I'm happy to get back on track with all of my goals and cupidity standards. It...keeps me busy."

Wow. I'm really good at lying lately.

She nods like she was expecting that answer. "Still, I worry about you."

Sev tilts his head toward her. "She gets all weepy," he tells me. "I don't know how to deal with tears and shite."

Emelle rolls her eyes. "The last time I cried in front of him, he stripped off his shirt, shoved it in my face, and told me to cheer up because abs make everyone happy."

He shrugs and arches a black brow. "Did I lie?"

"Actually, no," she relents, looking back at me. "Do you think abs give off endorphins?"

I falter at that. "Oh. Well, um. I'd have to research it later."

"That's the spirit," Sev grins, clapping me on the back.

"Not that I'm not happy to see the two of you, but was there something you needed from me?" I ask.

Emelle nods and then gives me a guilty look. "Actually, yes."

Uh oh.

"What?" I ask warily.

She hesitates, and Sev cuts in. "She's got cupids for you to train. We got an influx of 'em."

I barely suppress a groan. "Recruits? I don't know..."

"Please," Emelle begs, grasping my hand. "You're the best cupid. And I'm not just saying that to flatter you. Sev looked it up back at Cupidville. You are *literally* the best-performing cupid to have ever cupided."

Well. That gives me a nice little boost.

Still...

"It takes meticulous attention and patience to train new cupids."

"I know," she agrees. "And you're the best person for the job."

My eyes narrow. "Are you doing this to distract me, or because the other trainers are all full?"

Emelle winces. "Both."

I let out a sigh and reach back to make sure my bun is still secure. "Alright, Madame Cupid. I'll handle the trainees."

"Thank you," she beams. "You can start today?"

That was quick.

"Of course," I tell her. She really has been the most understanding, relaxed, wonderful boss that cupidity has ever had. I haven't even been assisting like I should be, so I certainly can't complain. Maybe throwing myself into training will be a good thing. Aside from the distraction, it will mean I'm not alone, which is how I've been these past six weeks, since I've pretty much given up on the whole cupid partners thing. Apparently, I'm too aggressive at cupidity to be a good team player.

"Perfect. Thank you, Lex."

"It's my pleasure."

They continue to both stare at me, and I wait for them to say more. When they still don't, I wipe my face, checking to see if I have something on it. "Why are you looking at me like that?"

Emelle clears her throat. "Well. There's something else we wanted to ask you."

I look from her to Sev. "We?"

"This affects Sev just as much as it will affect me."

I'm intrigued. "Alright... What is it?"

"Well...I've been thinking," she begins, chewing on her bottom lip nervously. "See, the thing is, I'm here."

I wait for her to elaborate, but she doesn't. "Yes? You're here. Talking to me..."

Emelle shakes her head. "No, no. That's not what I mean. It's...well, I'm here *always*. I can't go into the Veil because of Ronak. And with my family, I can't, like, just go off onto Love rushes or Lust binges, you know? I'm here permanently."

"Okay..." I press. "I'm still not understanding what you're getting at."

Sev cuts in. "Boss lady here wants to take off the love chaps and pass 'em off, get it?"

I blink. "I'm sorry, *what*?"

Emelle takes a deep breath. "What I'm trying to say is, I think it's time for me to resign my place as Head of Cupidity."

My mouth instantly drops open. For a moment, I'm sure I heard her wrong. "*Resign*? But you can't! You've brought so much wonderful change to cupids everywhere!" I argue. "Cupid breaks, cupid partners, cupid parties... You've massively cut back on terminations, you've initiated wonderful training camps and installed trainers...the entire cupid world has changed so much because of you, and all of it has made our afterlives so much better and richer!"

I can't even imagine going back to how things were. I didn't know any other way then, but now that I do... Just the thought of all the cupids that will be affected by this change makes me nauseated.

At my list of examples, a proud smile fills Emelle's expression. "Yes, and I'm so glad I was able to do all of that. But let's face it, I'm just a figurehead," she says, shrugging a defeated shoulder. "I can't go to Cupidville. I can't even go into the Veil anymore. Heck, I even have all the Veil powers in me, like a bunch of puzzles mixed together, so I'm not wholly cupid anymore—I don't have the right pieces," she tells me. "I haven't shot a Love Arrow in months. I have no business being the boss. I've been lucky that I've had Sev to run things back in Cupidville, but it's not fair to him, and he wants to get back into the field."

I shoot a surprised look at Sev.

"What? I'm gettin' a bit bored. I mean, do you see this?" he asks, motioning down his body. "I'm not meant for administrative work, get it? And maybe I miss the bit o' Lust I used to blow out."

My head swims and my fingers tangle in anxious twists. "But...what if someone comes in and just...undoes all the changes you've implemented? That would be absolutely *horrible.* There could be a big cupid uprising. They love you as their boss. Someone else will mess everything up."

"They won't," she says with conviction.

"They might promise that in the beginning, but how can you know for sure?" I challenge.

"Because," Emelle states, "I'm giving the title to *you*."

Shock courses through me like waves crashing against my eardrums and beating against my heart. *"What?"*

"You're the best cupid ever, Lex. And not just because of all these crazy goals you've hit, but because of your heart," she tells me, rainbow eyes tearing up as she softly places a hand over the organ indicated. "You are the perfect cupid, because you love bestowing love on others, and you're dedicated to not only every Match, but every fellow cupid too."

"Emelle..." I shake my head, too much emotion flooding me, too many doubts swarming like wasps. "I can't possibly take over as Head of Cupidity."

"You can," she says firmly, dropping her hand. "And what's more is you deserve it, and cupidity deserves to have *you*. A true cupid at heart, leading by example."

A million doubts swarm in my head. "I can't," I whisper, denial thick on my tongue. "I'll mess up. Or the cupids won't accept me, or—"

"They'll fooking accept you, luv," Sev cuts in. "They're sick of me, to be honest. Too many orgies in the office."

Emelle casts him a look. "During break times though, right?"

He shoots me a conspiratorial wink. "Sure. Anyway, like I was saying, you'll be fine."

I blow out a heavy breath. "I don't know..."

"It's your decision," Emelle tells me. "But no one else will ever be as perfect for the job as you are."

Her faith in me makes my heart swell, and the prospect sounds...amazing. Shocking and terrifying, but also amazing. I never thought in a million years that I would ever be offered something like this. Yet here she is, handing it to me on a pink platter, because she thinks I'm the perfect cupid.

"I'm not as perfect as you think," I admit, feeling shame crawl up my neck and heat my cheeks. "Ever since, you know, I just...don't love *love* as much as I used to. For the first time, this"—I motion toward my bow and arrow—"feels like a job. So maybe I'm not the right fit after all. I would've been before, but now..."

Instead of looking worried, Emelle just nods. "I get what you're saying, but Lex, I don't think that's a bad thing. Because you see, you've been the perfect, peppy cupid who believed love is the answer to everything, and you've also experienced heartbreak firsthand. What better person to truly understand all the facets of love than you? Love isn't all sunshine and roses, and you understand that. You also know what it takes to be a great cupid, and you can inspire so many."

Well, when she puts it like that...

I swallow hard and then begin to pace inside our shadowed archway, putting a few feet between us so I can think. Mentally, I make up a pros and cons list of all the reasons why it would be good or bad for me to accept.

Emelle and Sev watch me quietly as I go back and forth, batting away wayward vines as I attempt to walk through my thoughts for this huge decision. Taking over all of cupidity, being in charge of every single cupid, being the one to make the decisions...

Can I do that?

I'm a perfectionist workaholic, sure. And I've probably researched more about cupids than anyone else, but does that mean I can actually lead?

"You're ready, Lex," Emelle says, as if she can tell the

direction my thoughts have headed. "I wouldn't offer this position to you if I didn't totally believe that. Plus, Sev and I will be here to support you every step of the way. Always."

I straighten the strap of my quiver and run a hand over my shirt before spinning on my heel and stopping in front of them. I look between the two of them, and I'm ready to tell her that I need a day, a week, a *year* to truly contemplate all the positives and negatives of this, but instead, what comes out is, "I'd need full training as an interim. At least ninety days. And you have to be okay with me popping in to ask you questions. I'll probably annoy you with how much I check in, but it's imperative that I—"

"Are you saying you'll take the job?" Emelle interjects, a smile starting to spread across her face.

I feel a little shell-shocked. "Yes, I suppose I am."

She lets out such a loud squeal that no doubt some fae probably heard it. Sev digs a finger in his ear like she broke his eardrum. "Fooking shite on a stick," he mumbles.

Once again, Emelle slams into me with a fierce hug. I never considered myself a hugger, but I'm starting to get used to hers. "You're going to be amazing, Lex. Much better than I ever was." I start to argue, but she pulls away and shakes her head. "No, really. You're what Cupidville needs."

Feeling a bit awkward at the proud way she's smiling at me, I clear my throat and pretend to straighten my sleeve. "Well, I'll certainly try my best," I promise. "So how does this work?"

"We figured that out already! We *researched* it," she says, wagging her brows proudly.

I can't help but smile.

"Anyway, it goes like this." Emelle takes hold of my arm with my cupid mark. "Ready?"

"*Now?*"

"No time like the present," she chirps.

I hesitate for a moment. "Alright, Madame Cupid."

Emelle tears up a little. "That'll be the last time you call me that."

Looking down at our arms, she runs a finger down her cupid mark, making her whole arm glow bright pink. "I, cupid one thousand fifty, name cupid sixty-nine my successor as Head of Cupidity." She presses her glowing marks against mine, and as soon as she does, I suck in a breath at the jolt that passes from her skin to mine.

Little pink lightning bolts erupt between us, like static electricity caught between blankets. It makes the hair on the back of my neck lift, and a warmth spreads up my arm and down my spine.

It's over in seconds, and when Emelle pulls her arm away, all she has now is her cupid number. But I stare at my arm, which now has a new mark—a heart with an arrow through it right below my number.

Adrenaline—or maybe newfound cupid power—seems to shoot through my veins.

I run a finger over the new mark, watching as it glows softly. Somehow, I inherently know how to call for her or Sev or any cupid I could possibly need, just as I know I could use the mark to bring me wherever I want to go.

"Wow."

"I know," Emelle says, dropping her hand. "Feels trippy, huh?"

That's one way to put it.

"I guess I should go to Cupidville?" I ask, still marveling at the mark. "Goodness, I have so much to do...I'll need to research all about past transitions and determine what methods were most successful. I'll also need to meet with the other Veil heads, as well as make sure cupid processing is running smoothly, oh, and I should probably throw a party? Though I'll need to come up with a theme..."

"Lex, breathe," Emelle tells me.

I take a huge breath. "Right. Thank you." My head is swimming with all the things I need to do now to make sure I can live up to Emelle's legacy. "I'm going to need an assistant."

Sev grins.

"Um. Maybe...maybe not you." I try to say it as politely as possible.

His grin gets wider. "See? You're already doing a right well job of it. Better judgment than this one," he says, elbowing Emelle.

"You did great too, Sev," she says, patting his arm. "Despite all the sexcapades during office hours."

"Thanks."

"And who knows, maybe you'll find the perfect assistant with your new trainees," Emelle points out.

Doubtful. Most new cupids are absolutely dreadful. Can't even properly drag a finger for some Flirt Touches. Their technique is usually way off.

Wait...

"You mean I still have to train some new cupids even though I'm going to be the boss?"

"Yep. No take-backsies. Why do you think I made you agree to that first?" she says with a smirk.

I let out a sigh. "Alright."

"Speaking of..."

Emelle looks to Sev, and he nods. "Right. Be back in a stiffie."

He disappears in a cloud of pink glitter.

"Went to go get your trainees," Emelle explains.

"Right. Okay. Umm..." I nervously run a hand over my scalp to make sure no hair is out of place. I don't have the best track record of working with other cupids, but I'm determined to be a good teacher and not the kind of teacher everyone hates. "How do I look?"

"You look perfect."

I blink at Emelle. Because the answer was somewhat expected.

The voice was not.

I'm frozen, staring at Emelle, wondering what just happened, but then I see her lips curve into a smile, and her teary eyes glance over my shoulder. "Your trainee is here."

My entire body erupts with goose bumps, and I slowly turn around, already shaking.

Because I know that voice.

Standing just a few feet away, the male before me has silver skin and gray molten eyes. He has gray horns curled around his head, and a pair of stark-red-feathered wings at his back. His loose hair that hangs at his shoulders was once white but now is the same pink as my own. But the best part?

He's as solid as the world around him, not a single inch of him sheer or muted.

"*Belren?*"

And it's that smirk. That curling, curving smirk that

makes me nearly faint as he strides over to me. I can't even breathe as he stops before me. Can't properly see with the way tears have flooded my eyes.

When he lifts a hand to grip my chin, a choked sob escapes me at the solid warmth of his touch just before he leans in and whispers against my cheek. "I told you I'd find you."

EPILOGUE

BELREN

*L*ex is in her element.

Here, inside the massive red-walled room, she looks confident, accomplished, *fulfilled*. Signature outfit perfectly in place, she's got on a knee-length skirt and button-up blouse, with her wings straight and proud at her back. Her hair is pulled back so tight not a single strand is out of place.

With a clipboard in hand, she walks behind the line of cupids she's training. They're all standing in their bow and arrow stances, strings pulled back as they aim toward their moving targets, bodies corporeal so they get a better feel for shooting. Today, the targets are shaped like centaurs and trolls. The trolls move surprisingly fast considering their size.

I made sure to take the very last spot all the way at the end of the room so I can watch her walk up and down, offering advice and making notes with her giant red-feathered pen. She makes note-taking look *good*.

With one shoulder leaning against the wall, I watch

her pick her way closer to me. She's so focused and professional in her role as trainer that she doesn't even notice the way some of these schmucks pine after her when she isn't looking.

Especially—

"Madame Cupid, could you help me with my pull again?"

My eyes narrow on the fucker. He's just three down from me, and I've got no clue what realm he was from when he died, because he's got tentacles for legs and holes where his ears would be. Definitely not fae or human. He also thinks he's got a shot with her, because he asks for her *assistance* like this at least once an hour.

"Of course, cupid eight sixteen," Lex says brightly, striding over to him.

"I'm having trouble with how far back I should pull," he tells her.

Lex nods and slips the clipboard between her wings to hold it before she stands behind eight sixteen. She places her hands over his and pulls back the string, all while efficiently and politely explaining some shit about tension and aim. Instead of actually trying to learn, he shoots me an arrogant look and interlocks their fingers.

The urge to maim him is strong. I'm sure he doesn't need all six tentacles to slop around.

Instead, my eyes flick to the bowstring, and with a single thought, I make it snap and hit the twit in the eye. He starts howling, clasped hands forgotten as he crouches and covers his eye. Lex doesn't miss a beat and picks two other students from the lineup to take him to the cupid nurse's room.

Sucker.

Finally, she's just one trainee away, murmuring soft praises to a very shy female with dark skin and vines of flowers growing from her scalp.

Then, Lex is standing in front of me, brow arched when she takes in my relaxed position as I lean against the bright red wall of Cupidville's target practice room.

"On your feet, cupid five hundred."

Lips curling, I straighten and get to my spot on the floor, black boots lining up on the heart marker.

"You know I prefer you to call me by the Roman numeral instead of the actual number," I tell her, shoving up my gray sleeve to display my cupid mark proudly.

Lex's eyes dart down to it and then back up to my face. "I think I'll stick with the number."

"Come on," I tease, pointing to the letter marked on my skin. "It's just a big D. You've seen it many, *many* times." Her eyes flare wide, and her cheeks go adorably pink. "Funny that a big D should fluster you when your own cupid number is *sixty-nine*."

"Sixty-nine is a perfectly respectable number."

"Oh, it's my favorite number for certain. I just wouldn't say it's *respectable*."

She shoots me a look. "Don't think you're getting away with that little stunt you pulled with cupid eight sixteen. I don't know how in the world you were able to keep your telekinetic powers, but you can't be a menace in my training sessions, or I'll put you in one of the other classes."

"Liar," I smirk. We both know she won't do it. I technically graduated from training weeks ago, but she likes my company just as much as I enjoy hers, so here I am. If anything, I think it's helping her come to terms with the fact that I'm not going to disappear on her again. Me dying and then fading into nothing left her a little jumpy. "You'd miss me far too much."

She doesn't deny it, but she doesn't like to be proven wrong either, so she clears her throat and gestures to the target across from me. "Enough chatter, cupid five hundred. Line up and make your shot."

"Of course, Madame Cupid," I murmur against her ear, and I relish the way a chill goes down her neck. I'm not sure if it's my breath against her skin or just the fact that she really likes being called Madame Cupid. Probably the latter, to be honest.

She circles around behind me as I grab an arrow and nock it, taking in my stance. "You need to spread your legs a bit more."

I snort. She makes it too easy.

When she sees my face, she reaches out and taps her finger on my nose. "Stop that."

"That's two nose bops in one day."

"They're effective," she replies, pulling down the hem of her blouse to straighten it. "Now, get into position and hit your target," she orders with pure authority riding her tone.

I love riling her up, but I love it even more when she puts me in my place. Like I said, she's in her element, and it's fucking sexy.

With a nod, I turn, pull back the string, and shoot. The arrow hits the heart of the centaur, right through the center.

Lex beams at me. "Very well done!"

"I do have a good teacher." I'm also cheating a bit with my powers, but that's beside the point.

Her head bobs with pride. "I told you all the extra practice after hours would pay off."

"Oh, I thoroughly enjoy every single thing we do *after hours*."

This time, she gets so flustered that she actually drops her eyes to my crotch. That's when I know I've really pulled her authoritative mind right down into the gutter. I think of it as a personal achievement. Ever since she's become Head of Cupidity, she's not easily ruffled—at least not in public. She's very professional in public.

But in private? My cupid is getting quite improper, which I also take as a personal achievement.

Lex tries to hide her blush and reaches behind her but then falters, giving me a look. "Belren."

I flash her a smirk and tap on my cupid mark.

She gives a quick peek around to make sure the other trainees are still practicing and not paying any attention to us. "Fine. *Big D*," she grits out.

A grin spreads across my face. "Yes?" I ask innocently.

She holds her hand out, trying to look stern, but I can see the amusement threatening to tilt up her lips. "Give it back."

With a thought, I bring her clipboard back down from where I'd sent it pinned to the ceiling. She catches it in her hands and scribbles something on it with a pointed look. "I'm marking you down for thievery."

"You do that, because later, I'll be stealing your pant—"

She spins around and claps her hand loudly against the clipboard. "Alright, good job, everyone, that's it for today! I'll summon you for our Practical Application of Flirt Touches tomorrow."

One by one, the newly-created cupids file out of the

room, with Lex and I bringing up the rear. I stay by her side as she meticulously checks over the room before heading to her office.

Inside, she has two cupid assistants waiting for her, and she spends the next hour or so going over things with them. It goes on and on. There's a lot of talk about sexual encounters, but it's not the good gossip kind, just the professional tally mark kind. She has the spark back full flame now, because I have never seen anyone love her job as much as this female. She gets *very* excited about tally marks.

I spend the time lying on my back on her plush rug across the room and pretending to doze, when really, I'm watching her profile as she talks animatedly with her assistants. She's too beautiful *not* to watch.

To think, I almost lost this chance. But I was meant to fall for her. Meant to *be* with her. And I wasn't going to let a little thing like a second death take her away from me.

So I fought. Clamped down on every memory and wrapped it around an iron-clad lock that even three Veil Major powers couldn't wipe away. It took me a while, but I fought against the tide, no matter how much the water wanted to wash away the grains of my memories. I stole them from the grip of the fates like the master thief I am, and then I found her all over again, just like I said I would.

When Lex finishes up, she dismisses her cupids, and then it's just the two of us again. She walks over to stand above me, looking down at where I'm lounging with my hands beneath my head, the heart-shaped rug beating beneath me in a comforting thrum.

"Ready to go?" I ask her.

Instead of answering, she does something very out of

character and lies down on the floor with me. She stares up at the swaths of pink clouds painted on the ceiling, and although she's silent, her mind is practically shouting.

"You're thinking awfully loud over there, Pinky. You want to talk about it?"

Lex nibbles on her lip, and a rare glimpse of vulnerability crosses her face. "Am I doing a good job?"

My brows nearly shoot up to my hairline. "Of course you're not doing a good job," I begin, and her face snaps over to look at me, eyes wide with surging panic. "You're doing a *great* job."

"Truly?"

"Truly." I prop myself up on one arm so I can look at her. "You've transitioned into your role flawlessly, just as everyone knew you would. The cupids love you. The trainee program has never been more successful, and you have this place so organized even the angels are jealous."

Lex smiles conspiratorially at that.

"You're the perfect Madame Cupid."

A little relieved breath passes between her lips. "Thank you. I needed to hear that."

My cupid likes to be praised, so I make a mental note to make sure I'm doing it more. "Don't doubt yourself. You're far too clever for that," I say, standing up before I quickly lean down and scoop her into my arms. The little squeal that comes out of her is downright adorable. Her arms wrap around my neck, wings hanging behind my forearm, and my entire chest feels like it could burst just from the way she looks at me. "Now let's get you home before you start spiraling."

"I don't spiral."

I give her a look. "Last week, you got so stuck in your

head with worry that you decided you need to color-code every single incident report from the last decade for the human realm, *and* just yesterday, you tried to get your assistants to change up the filing system again for the third time this week."

Her brow furrows. "I'm just not confident that alphabetically is the best way to organize."

My own lips twitch in response. "We'll go over the pros and cons of it after I get you some food, how about that?"

Her eyes light up at the pros and cons suggestion, but then she wavers. "We don't need to eat if we stay in the Veil, you know. Maybe I should stay here. Go over some more things before the next training session tomorrow. If I work all night, I could get a head start for the new trainees that will be coming in next week..." She trails off, looking increasingly worried.

I know from experience that if I leave her to her own devices, she will *never* stop working. Which is why I drop my voice an octave and look her in the eye until she focuses on me and not the endless to-do lists running through her mind. "What did I say about non-stop working, Madame Cupid?"

At the tone of my voice, her pupils dilate and a nervous dart of her tongue comes out to wet her bottom lip. "You said it was against the rules."

"That's right," I tell her with a nod. Over the past couple of months during her transition as Head of Cupidity, I've learned that she needs structure and for me to take the reins when she's feeling overwhelmed. Only when I take things out of her hands does she finally relax.

"And the rule states that you work your sexy ass off as

much as you want during office hours, but then you come home with me. Correct?"

She nods, somewhat dazedly, and I'm relieved that I've snapped her out of her worry so quickly. "Correct."

"Now, you wouldn't be trying to break that rule, would you?"

"No, certainly not."

I grin. "Good girl."

The pink blush that stains her cheeks nearly matches her hair.

In the next blink, she's transported us out of Cupidville and back into the fae realm. Time works differently in and out of the Veil, so it looks like it's nearly dawn when I stride across the grassy garden and duck into our domed house on the genfin island. It's just a stone's throw away from Emelle's house, since Lex wanted to be close so she could ask all sorts of cupid questions. Even though it's not my own home island, I have to admit, the place has grown on me. Though, that probably has to do with the female in my arms.

As soon as we're through the arched door, I set her down on the cushioned chair. Honestly, Soora's purple has nothing on this room, because Lex has *really* embraced the colors pink and red, so they've sort of taken over the house. Between her colors and my treasures that I hauled over here from my days as the Horned Hook, our place is...unique.

Of course, almost as soon as I set her down, Lex tries to jump right back up. "I'll get us something to eat."

Before she can so much as take a step, I've locked onto her shoes with my powers and dragged her in the other direction. "Hey!"

"You're not doing anything other than sitting down on the sofa and resting," I call to her as she careens through the sitting room.

"Stop telekineticking me!" she calls over her shoulder as my powers plop her down onto the sofa, making her bounce.

"Rest there for a minute, Madame Cupid. Then I'll feed you."

She grumbles something too low for me to hear, but slumps down onto the cushions, resting her head back as she gives an audible sigh after kicking her shoes off.

Whistling, I get to work in the kitchen, preparing something to eat. As quickly as I can, I have two bowls of soup and four different loaves of bread laid out on the table, because my cupid is a bread female, and I've noticed that the ratio of bread per meal greatly correlates with her food moans and overall happiness.

As she tucks in, I know I've done well when her shoulders shimmy and she's humming around every bite. I finish before her, so I relax, one arm over the back of my chair, wings hanging loosely at my sides as I watch her. Every time she does a little happy food dance, my lips twitch.

When she catches me looking, she blushes and wipes her mouth. "Why do you always watch me eat?"

I lift a shoulder. "You're adorable."

"The Head of Cupidity is not *adorable*."

"I disagree."

Her eyes narrow. "You know how I feel about disagreeing. I'd much rather go through a comprehensive discourse and pinpoint all the sides of the discussion before we both come to the correct conclusion."

"And the correct conclusion is..."

She blinks, like it should be obvious. "My side, of course."

I tip my head, barely suppressing a laugh, because she is completely serious. "Of course."

Lex studies me again. "You're making fun of me, aren't you?"

"Me?" I ask in mock innocence. "I would never."

With a less than impressed look, she gets to her feet and then walks around the table until she stands right in front of me. She leans down and then blows a puff of Lust right in my face, making me go rigid. *Every* part of me.

Straightening up, she smirks at me. "There. That will teach you to tease me."

She tries to walk away, but I'm on my feet and have her spinning right back before she can even blink. I lift her up on the table, her wings and thighs spread around my waist as I grip her ass and pull her against me. A gasp escapes her as I trap her there.

"Tsk tsk, Madame Cupid. I believe you just broke a rule about using Lust Breath responsibly. What would your trainees think?"

She squirms against me, which just makes me harder. The little minx knows it, too, because she rocks her hips with just the right movement so that I know she's chasing her own sort of pleasure. "I don't know what you mean," she replies primly, though the breathlessness of her tone gives her away.

With one hand, I reach up and deftly undo a row of buttons down her chest with slow precision. Her back arches as soon as I've freed her, her breasts larger than a

392

handful and perfectly held inside a lacy bra—pink, of course. No wonder I've grown so fond of the color.

"These fucking tits," I say on a groan as I pull the cups down, making her gasp as she spills out into my hands. "So gorgeous."

While I work her pretty pink nipples, I bring my other hand down to slip beneath the modest skirt that has ridden up very *immodestly*. As soon as I find what's there, I go still.

I blink past the shock, a wicked grin curling my lips as I drift them against her ear. "Oh, Pinky. You have been *very* naughty today, haven't you?"

"No," she quickly blurts, chest rising and falling rapidly.

I pinch her nipple, making her squirm. "Good girls wear panties," I tell her, and when I slip a finger against her slit, she moans and rocks against me harder. "So you were *definitely* naughty, walking around all day with the other cupids, holding that clipboard and ordering people around, looking all kinds of fucking sexy, while you had this pussy out the entire time."

She shudders, and I can see her pulse jumping in her neck. "Yes."

I don't need my cupid powers to know that she's dripping for me. Lex secretly loves to be praised...but she also loves to be caught being naughty.

"Hmm." I move my hand down from her chest so I can pull her skirt up even higher, revealing herself to me. I widen my stance, forcing her own legs to spread. In a surge of embarrassment, since my Pinky still gets shy, she tries to shove her skirt down, but I tap her inner thigh, making her pause. "Uh uh. You kept yourself bare for me all day, and now it's time to show me exactly what you've been wanting."

She swallows hard, a pretty blush spreading up her chest and neck as she looks up at me with so much trust that it nearly makes my knees buckle. Although, kneeling isn't such a bad idea.

I drop to my knees and yank her so far to the edge of the table that she yelps and nearly falls back, but my grip on her thighs grounds her. From between her legs, I lick a single swipe up her slit, making her gasp. "What's the rule, Pinky?"

"Grab your horns and don't let go," she immediately answers.

"Good girl. Now let me taste this naughty pussy."

My fingers spread her lips, and my tongue immediately rolls against her clit. She cries out, hands deftly gripping my horns, and I eat her out with even more vigor than she's ever eaten anything at this dining table.

Every lick and curl of my tongue makes her writhe, hands moving over my horns unconsciously as she focuses solely on her rising pleasure.

I plunge a finger into her dripping cunt, eliciting a garbled noise from her throat, and I grin before looking up at her. "Tell me why you didn't wear panties today, Pinky."

Her eyes flutter open, and she looks down at me almost in a daze. "Umm..."

"Go on," I urge. "I want to hear you say it. I want those naughty words I've been teaching you to come out of that perfect, polite mouth."

Her tongue darts out to lick her bottom lip. "I didn't wear panties because I wanted a secret."

That intrigues me.

I thrust my finger in and out of her, smirking when it makes her ass nearly jump off the table and her eyes roll back as my thumb presses down against her clit. "Explain."

When she doesn't, I thrust a second finger into her harder and reach up to twist her nipple, making her cry out in wanton pleasure. "Use your words."

"I-I wanted this secret," she rushes out. "Of what we do when we leave Cupidville. Of what you do to me when I'm not the proper Madame Cupid."

A thoughtful hum rises from my chest. "You wanted to be reminded that you're my secret naughty cupid, even when you have to be the boss, is that right?"

"Yes!" she pants, eyes closed tight as I start to curl my fingers inside of her and stroke against the spot that drives her wild.

"Does my naughty cupid need me to remind her that she's mine? That at any given moment, I can bend her over her own desk and fuck her from behind, messing up all her pretty organized files?"

A whine rips out of her. "Oh my goodness, I'm going to—"

I immediately remove my fingers and stand, making her eyes snap open with anger as her hands drop. "What are you doing? I wasn't finished!"

"Oh, I know," I tell her smoothly before I reach up and grip the pins in her hair, tossing them aside. Her long pink locks tumble down, and I spear my fingers through the strands, pulling with just the right amount of pressure to tilt her head back up. I fucking love doing this. "You'll finish with me buried deep inside of you, or you won't finish at all."

Her throat bobs, and the sight of her like this—flushed, pupils blown, skirt ridden all the way up to her waist to show off a glistening pussy with tits spilling out and her hair wrapped around my fist...it's goddamn perfection.

"You're the sexiest cupid that ever existed, do you know that?"

The anger leaves her eyes, and she traps a lip between her teeth.

"Now undo my pants and get my cock out. I want you laid out flat on this table, taking every inch of me."

She scrabbles for the ties, immediately loosening them so she can shove down my trousers. My cock springs out, and like she can't wait, her hand wraps around me, making my head tip back with a groan. "That's right. Feed it into your dripping wet cunt," I order.

"Goddess..." Every time I talk dirty to her, she blushes like mad, but there's no doubt that it makes her pulse race and her pussy even wetter. Like a good girl, she does exactly as she's told, and we both let out a groan when my tip breaches her.

"That's it," I croon. "Take me. Show me what you wanted all day when you had this pussy out, wanting to be filled."

"Gods, yes..." she chants, and my cupid wings flare.

Her breathless voice makes my control snap, and I punch my hips forward, entering her the rest of the way in one hard thrust.

"Fucking hell," I growl. "How do you feel better every time I fuck you?"

"I—like to always—be the—best," she pants out.

With my fingers still wrapped around her hair, I tilt her head up. "You're *perfect*."

I press my mouth against hers, tongue demanding her lips part for me. And they do with zero hesitation. I fuck her with my tongue just as I fuck her with my cock, and she takes it, every thrust from pussy to mouth, moaning and letting me swallow up her pleasure.

I want to drown in those sounds.

"I need to come, Belren..."

My hands drop to her hips, and I yank her harder into me, causing her back to arch and her wings to shoot out. The bowls knock down to the floor, but the sound of them breaking is drowned out by our bodies moving together.

"You can come, Pinky. Squeeze my cock like a good girl and make me come with you."

My fingers delve back to her clit, and I circle it relentlessly, pace quick and pressure hard as I rub her to pleasure, my pace evening out as I slam into her harder and harder.

"Oh...my...*goodness*."

She comes with a gasp, pussy clamping down on me so tightly, arms coming up to grip my shirt like a lifeline.

Her release sets off my own, and with one hand digging into her ass, I fuck her hard and fast, prolonging the waves of her pleasure until I empty myself inside of her.

We're left panting together, my hands around her waist, hers still tangled in my shirt, foreheads together as we lift back up from the delicious plummet.

"That was..."

"Dirty? Fast? Rough?" I offer.

She laughs, and I swear to fuck, my heart swells at the sound. "I was going to say A plus."

With a chuckle, I place a kiss on her head and step back, tucking myself back in my pants before I get a clean rag and start to clean her up. She always gets embarrassed at this part, but I like to take care of my female. When I'm finished, I scoop her up in my arms, and she lets out a little noise of surprise before pinning her arms around my neck.

"Where are we going?" she giggles, but she already knows.

I make it into the bedroom, which is, you guessed it, pink and red. All over.

Laying her down on the bed, I take a moment to strip her down, and then I simply admire her as the sun starts brightening up the room. I shake my head. "Look at you, all spread out and sexy. I can't let you leave this room for two days. At least."

She sits up on her elbows with a shake of her head. "Sorry, no. We're going to make Love Matches tomorrow after the training session, remember? It's going to take *hours.*"

Her eyes are practically glittering with giddiness. She gets really excited about making Love Matches.

I groan. "Why? Some of those fuckers out there probably don't deserve it," I say, putting a knee down on the bed so I can lean over her and trail my fingers across her curves. "Besides, I'd much rather be here, ravishing you."

She pouts. "But I thought you wanted to make Love Matches? They're a fundamental part of being a cupid. Seeing people fall in love is the *best.* I for one can't wait for you to experience it, and you haven't done it yet in the real realm."

"I already have firsthand. There's nothing better than that," I tell her.

She sucks in a breath. "Don't distract me with romance."

I smirk. "Why not, is it working?"

"Yes," she says glumly. "But remember when I supported you doing your favorite thing?"

"You mean thieving?"

She tilts her head in thought. "Well, that. Plus you and Emelle's mates going to track down that fae? The one you all hated who worked with the prince?"

"Oh, right. Chaucel." I grin fondly at the memory of us hunting him down and ending him. "That was a good day."

"Exactly!" Lex says. "I supported you for the thieving and the murder spree."

"Well, you *did* set the precedent for murder sprees, Pinky."

She sighs. "Anyways, the point is, it's time to make some Love Matches together, It's going to be so fun!"

Her enthusiasm is contagious.

"I've even made a target raffle so we can be surprised about which realm we visit, and I'm going to have our bows *polished* in the morning," she adds, clapping her hands together.

See? Excited.

"Alright, you convinced me. But I get to ravish you for hours after we're done."

A smile creeps across her face. "I can agree to those terms, on one condition."

I lie over her, nipping down her neck. "And what's that, Pinky?"

Her eyes dart over to the bedside table where my old Horned Hook mask lies. "You wear your mask during… you know."

I laugh, lifting up to look down at her. "You've got yourself a deal." I trail my lips down her neck to her collarbone, and I'm about to make my way to her breasts again when there's a ridiculously loud knock at the door.

Lifting my head, I shout, "Go away!"

"That's not polite, what if it's Benicia?"

I shake my head. "We just saw her when she and Soora had us over for dinner three days ago, and my sister knows better than to drop in on us unannounced. We both know who's at the door."

She grins, pushing me off before rushing into the closet where she pulls on a dress that goes all the way down to her toes.

She tosses pants at me on her way out. "Come on."

I pull them up and follow her down the corridor as she runs her fingers through her hair to try to brush away the *just fucked* look. Personally, I think it looks nice.

When she gets to the door, she tosses open the lock, but before she can open it, I engage it again with my powers. She glares at me over her shoulder. "*Belren.*"

A little sigh escapes me. "Fine."

The lock snaps back, and as soon as it does, we have a whole damn covey crammed into my house.

Ronak, Okot, Sylred, Evert, all surrounding Emelle, while their gaggle of kids instantly shriek and start running through the house.

The eldest one, Amorette, looks at me with a disgruntled

expression, eyes skating up and down my form like she finds me lacking. "You haunted me," she says with accusation, her tone unimpressed. She likes to bring this up every time she comes over. "My mom didn't believe me, you know."

"Yes, as I've said, I'm sorry about that." I try to smile, but her deadpan expression makes me falter.

Her eyes narrow. "I liked you better as a ghost."

She says that every time too.

"Sorry to disappoint you."

She rolls her eyes and bounces away, dismissing me to catch up with her siblings.

I swear, I appeared to her *one* time when I was a ghost, and she's never let me live it down. The fact that she prefers me dead is probably concerning. As are the many, *many* weapons she knows how to wield.

Not to mention that she can apparently see Veil entities, but I digress.

"We brought cinnamon rolls!" Emelle says brightly, carrying in a tray of them.

"That was so nice of you." Lex leads her into the kitchen, where I hear her hastily excusing the mess of broken bowls on the floor.

Knowing she's probably blushing, I give a smirk before looking back at the males who've shoved themselves into our living room. "Why do I feel like every time those two get together, they're planning something?"

Ronak shrugs, while Okot tries to comically fit himself into the armchair that is much too small for him.

"That's because they usually are," Sylred pipes in unhelpfully.

I can hear the females laughing in the other room. They *really* like being neighbors.

I settle down on the chair, ready for another few hours of shooting the shit with Emelle's covey while she and my cupid talk shop and reminisce about love.

Evert walks over to the curtains, his fingers pinching the fabric as he looks around the room. "I know I say this every time...but there's just so much fucking *pink*."

"Yep," I say with a grin.

It's everywhere, but I wouldn't have it any other way.

Pink hair, red wings.

These colors are my anchor, my lifeline. The root to the memories I was somehow able to keep.

And that cupid in the next room, whispering about her cupid goals? She's *mine*.

I stole her heart.

But the best part?

She stole mine right back.

The End

ACKNOWLEDGMENTS

Acknowledgements definitely feels fitting here, because I want to acknowledge every single reader who has been waiting for this book. It took me a lot longer than I anticipated to write and release it, and I appreciate the loyalty I've had over the years for this series and these characters. It was so nice to return to this world and see some friendly faces, because I hadn't realized just how much I'd missed them! I hope you leave with all the warm and fuzzies, and that you love Belren and Lex as much as I do.

Whether you read the other Cupidity books years ago, or just came upon them recently, thank you so much for taking a chance on the series. Signs of Cupidity was my first published book, and it changed my life.

Of course, I couldn't continue to write if it weren't for the love and support from my family and friends.

No, really.

I'm an anxious, full-of-doubts, not so hot mess most days. If it weren't for my family and friends, I wouldn't be able to do this. So thank you all for being in my life and helping me cross these finish lines one marathon at a time. I couldn't do this without you.

And everyone in the social media book world who has read, reviewed, and shared this series, thank you. You all are a wonderful part of the book community and I am eternally grateful for your support.

XOXO —RK

Want more of Raven Kennedy?

Check out the phenomenal and addictive Plated Prisoner Series.

A fantasy retelling of the notorious King Midas myth, with a dark and magical twist . . .

And the final epic chapter in the series . . .

GOLD coming December 2023

WHICH BOOK WILL YOU READ NEXT?

He just wanted a decent book to read ...

Not too much to ask, is it? It was in 1935 when Allen Lane, Managing Director of Bodley Head Publishers, stood on a platform at Exeter railway station looking for something good to read on his journey back to London. His choice was limited to popular magazines and poor-quality paperbacks – the same choice faced every day by the vast majority of readers, few of whom could afford hardbacks. Lane's disappointment and subsequent anger at the range of books generally available led him to found a company – and change the world.

'We believed in the existence in this country of a vast reading public for intelligent books at a low price, and staked everything on it'
Sir Allen Lane, 1902–1970, founder of Penguin Books

The quality paperback had arrived – and not just in bookshops. Lane was adamant that his Penguins should appear in chain stores and tobacconists, and should cost no more than a packet of cigarettes.

Reading habits (and cigarette prices) have changed since 1935, but Penguin still believes in publishing the best books for everybody to enjoy. We still believe that good design costs no more than bad design, and we still believe that quality books published passionately and responsibly make the world a better place.

So wherever you see the little bird – whether it's on a piece of prize-winning literary fiction or a celebrity autobiography, political tour de force or historical masterpiece, a serial-killer thriller, reference book, world classic or a piece of pure escapism – you can bet that it represents the very best that the genre has to offer.

Whatever you like to read – trust Penguin.